ALL THAT FALL

ALL THAT FALL

KRIS CALVIN

W🌐RLDWIDE

TORONTO • NEW YORK • LONDON
AMSTERDAM • PARIS • SYDNEY • HAMBURG
STOCKHOLM • ATHENS • TOKYO • MILAN
MADRID • WARSAW • BUDAPEST • AUCKLAND

Recycling programs
for this product may
not exist in your area.

WORLDWIDE™

ISBN-13: 978-1-335-45442-3

All That Fall

First published in 2021 by Crooked Lane Books, an imprint of
The Quick Brown Fox & Company LLC.
This edition published in 2022.

For questions and comments about the quality of this book,
please contact us at CustomerService@Harlequin.com.

Harlequin Enterprises ULC
22 Adelaide St. West, 41st Floor
Toronto, Ontario M5H 4E3, Canada
www.ReaderService.com

Printed in U.S.A.

ALL THAT FALL

For Kathy

PART ONE

THURSDAY NIGHT

ONE

The River

JANIE KIEU FELT exposed in the driver's seat of the borrowed red Corolla.

She'd parked at the front of the lot to have a clear view of a public walkway that ran parallel to the meanderings of the Sacramento River, a broad swath of water down a gentle incline some forty feet below. Behind her, "Welcome to the River Top" flashed in blue neon at thirty-second intervals above the motel's glassed-in lobby as though asserting, despite all evidence to the contrary, that the arrival of paying guests was imminent.

She lowered the driver's side window. A listless breeze carried with it the scent of dank soil.

Her phone pinged.

Where are you?

Janie typed her reply.

Picking up Samson.

The lie came easily, it was close enough to the truth.

There was a low rumble of traffic from behind the motel, but the walkway in front of her was deserted, eleven pm on a weeknight apparently having passed some unwritten cutoff time for Sacramento's active community of dog walkers, joggers, and cyclists. Or maybe they just didn't make it this far south, where the charming 1930s bungalows of midtown gave way to dimly lit, nondescript apartment complexes and sad little houses in disrepair.

She slipped her phone into a large black backpack on the passenger seat next to her, on top of its other contents. Neat, thin, bundled stacks of mostly twenties, a few fifty- and hundred-dollar bills among them, were just as she'd packed them that morning. After zipping the bag closed, she opened the Corolla's door a crack to confirm that the overhead light remained disabled.

Each thing being as it should reassured her.

While Janie's plan was not complicated, she was acutely aware that any number of things could go wrong. She felt something brush against her cheek, and reached up to find a wayward strand of her waist-length dark hair had escaped the black baseball-style cap she wore. She tucked it back in place and waited.

It didn't take long.

Samson approached from the direction of town. His walk was unmistakable, the way he favored, ever so slightly, his left foot where he'd broken it when he was eight in a failed attempt to climb a tree much too tall for him in the park. Janie slipped down in the driver's seat, only her eyes and the top of the dark cap visible above the window line.

She held her breath, but her brother didn't look her way.

She fought the urge to call out to him, to end this cloak-and-dagger stuff and find out exactly what was going on. He'd been acting strangely for weeks.

When she'd discovered the money stashed under his

bed, it had been the last straw. No way could he have saved it working part-time at the bike shop. Still, she'd known better than to ask him about the cash. If pressed, he would have responded with a nearly believable story of a found lottery ticket or a reward from a wealthy man he'd pushed out of the path of a speeding car.

It wasn't that her brother was a liar. Not exactly. Or at least Janie found the term too harsh for her only sibling. But he was an incorrigible teller of tall tales and had been for as long as she could remember.

When he was five, he hadn't wandered to the river where he was forbidden to play, pirates had dragged him to their ship and made him walk the plank. And at seven, he'd protested he was unavoidably late for dinner (again) because he'd had to vanquish, in hand-to-paw combat, a roaring lion from their backyard.

She eyed the backpack. It made her uncomfortable to have the money with her, but she couldn't leave it unattended in their apartment, not in that part of town. There were times she wished she could live in her head, like Samson did.

She watched as he turned and started down the slope. There was a tight circle of eucalyptus trees at the bottom along the river bank. He slipped inside.

She knew how it looked. What anyone else would have seen. Large, unexplained sums of money, all in cash, a clandestine meeting in the dark, and a teenage boy raised by a sister scarcely older than he was. Anyone who watched crime shows on TV or read the news would have concluded that something illegal was going on, a drug deal or the exchange of stolen goods.

It was obvious. It checked all the boxes.

The problem for Janie was that the obvious didn't fit the Samson she knew, not even close. She couldn't picture him with the kind of people who did desperate things. In the rare instances her brother had failed to meet expectations at school or at home, it had never been due to ill intent, but rather to folly, missteps mired in an innocence Samson hadn't outgrown, a rich imagination he seemed unable to reign in. Janie was the one who bent the rules to make their lives work, the one who could have made crime pay, if she'd wanted to.

A crisp staccato crack carried through the still night air. In the beat it took Janie to realize it was a gunshot, in quick succession there were two more. She gasped, a sharp, involuntary intake of breath.

Though she'd imagined a lot of things might happen if she followed her brother to the river, none had involved gunfire. She felt a surge of adrenaline as she reached for the backpack to retrieve her phone, but when she thought of the stacks of money inside she stopped. She replayed, as best she could, what she'd heard.

There'd been no shout, no screams, no evidence of the consequences a bullet in close quarters should yield. Perhaps it was a truck backfiring on the road, some trick of acoustics making it seem as though the sound had come from the river's edge. But as the silence persisted, it felt ominous rather than reassuring. Janie considered, for the first time, what it might mean if her brother had taken the money from people who didn't want to give it up.

She'd attended a mandatory assembly on self-defense in high school, something about breaking holds and seeking vulnerable spots. But she couldn't recall anything specific, and at one hundred and ten pounds she doubted she could execute any of the moves with enough force to ward off an attacker.

She opened the glove box of the borrowed Corolla.

Beneath loose papers she found a hairbrush and a travel size can of hairspray. She briefly assessed the small silver canister's possibilities as a defensive weapon. It didn't inspire confidence.

She reached for the backpack again, this time following through on extracting her phone, although not to make a call. She checked her messages. There was nothing from Samson, neither reassuring as she'd hoped, nor desperate as she'd feared.

She used the phone's light to look under the seats and on the floor in the back, finding only loose change and a flattened to-go coffee cup. Reluctantly, she returned to the hairspray.

Pressing down on the cap produced a burst of dense, sticky droplets with a harsh, chemical smell. If she was able to score a direct hit in the gunman's eyes, it could be briefly incapacitating. Giving her time to…

Time to what? Wrestle away his weapon?

It was a bad plan. Janie knew that, even as she palmed the can and got out, pausing only to lock the door behind her.

It seemed a far worse one when a man emerged from the trees in the spot where Samson had gone in.

Janie froze.

But as the stranger made his way up the hill, the panic in her brain took a more functional route, ordering her body to drop to a crouch. Kneeling awkwardly, one hand on the ground for balance, the other holding the hairspray at the ready, she watched, transfixed, as the man drew closer.

About ten feet from the walkway, he stopped.

Abruptly, he shook his head hard, twice to the right, an odd motion. It could have been an involuntary tic, but Janie wondered if it was an expression of the man's dismay, even disgust, at whatever he'd just seen or done. As though he might roll back the events of the night if he could only shake his head "no" hard enough.

She lost interest in interpreting the stranger's body language when he stepped into range of the light from the motel, and the gun in his hand shone bright in a flash of blue neon.

She threw herself flat, a jolt passing up her spine as one elbow, then a knee, hit the hard surface of the parking lot. Squeezing her eyes shut, she braced for the moment when the man would loom over her and deliver a final, well-placed bullet. But though she waited for what seemed like forever, nothing happened. She raised her head an inch.

The man suddenly broke into a jog and crossed into the motel lot. A moment later, an engine roared to life, followed by the crunch of wheels on gravel. The sound diminished in the direction of the main road until a distant hum of passing traffic was once again all she could hear.

Samson's safety reemerged foremost in Janie's mind. Ignoring a burning pain in her knee where it had hit the asphalt, she took off at a run, skidding down the dusty slope toward the river.

Inside the circle of trees, the air was humid and thick with the hum of countless unknown insects. Intertwining branches overhead encased the small space in utter darkness. She breathed rapidly, shallowly, as she stood otherwise absolutely still. Willing her eyes to adjust, she could make out a second gap in the trees, this one on the river side. As she puzzled through what it might mean if Samson had slipped away, she scanned the area.

Janie's heart rose to her throat when she saw that she was not alone.

On the far side of the grove, a body sprawled, motionless, barely distinguishable from the earth on which it lay.

FRIDAY MORNING

TWO

Matchbook Lane

EMMA LAWSON WATCHED the tiny bubbles multiply, crowding against one another. The modern electric kettle made of sleek Italian glass had been a gift from her colleagues upon her recent promotion. At age thirty-two, she was now the youngest government ethics investigator California's Hayden Commission had ever had. As she selected a mug, she heard the heavy deadbolt on her front door turn. Three people knew where the key was hidden, under the last step. Any one of them would be a welcome visitor, even at this early hour.

"Emma, love, have you forgotten? I'm right screwed if we don't get to the mechanics before they open. I haven't an appointment."

Kate Doyle's Irish lilt echoed down the hall from the entryway.

In addition to being neighbors and best friends, the two women were also newly minted business partners. Five months ago, having completed the last course for her advanced early childhood education degree, Kate had taken over the lease on a rundown preschool near the capitol building. Her vision had been to create a state-of-the-art educational experience for Sacramento's youngest residents. Emma, confident anything Kate did would be done well, had contributed significant funds from her savings to the remodel and modernization of the site. She hadn't intended her involvement to extend beyond being a silent investor, but Kate had asked her to accept the title of "codirector," arguing that Emma's highly visible role at the independent ethics commission would cause legislators and high-level bureaucrats to trust the school with their offspring, jump-starting enrollment.

After consulting with commission lawyers to be sure it would not present a conflict of interest, Emma had agreed, though she'd made clear she'd be a director in name only. She couldn't possibly be active in the school's management, given the demands of her new position at work. It had pained her to take even one day off today to help Kate prepare for the one hundred and twenty pint-sized Rainbow Alley Preschool and Childcare Center enrollees who would arrive bright and early Monday on the new center's doorstep.

Kate pushed through the swinging door from Emma's living room into the kitchen. Though small by modern standards, it was a good size for its mid-century heritage. The kettle, condensation forming on its sides, sat atop a vintage, chrome-legged dinette table that together with matching red and chrome chairs occupied most of the floor space.

At just over five feet tall, Kate was slim and fit with spiky, short brown hair. Dressed in her usual all black—a plain black cotton top and a black denim skirt that ended just above her knees—the only color she wore was in the small, sparkling gems in varied hues that occupied the multiple piercings in her ears. Despite being only a year younger than Emma and the single mother of a teen, if not for the sprinkle of soft lines around her eyes and mouth, she could have passed for a college undergrad.

"I suppose we have time, if we're quick about it," she said, handing Emma a stack of mail. "The one on top looks important. Keeping up your skills, that's the way to go." There was a playful glint in her eyes.

Emma read the return address. It was from Shoot the Lights Out, a gun shop and indoor firing range. She'd briefly dated a Marine who had taken her there when the movie they'd planned to see had sold out. The range had been crowded and loud, and unlike the Varsity Theater, it didn't serve hot buttered popcorn. It was only because she'd been the worst shooter in the place, even among first-timers, that Emma had returned week after week, long after the Marine was gone. She'd persevered until she'd become slightly less terrible and could (sometimes) hit the target, though she hadn't shot a gun since and had no intention of doing so ever again.

Whatever the Shoot the Lights Out people were selling now, Emma didn't want any.

She and Kate had just sat down at the dinette table when Kate's phone buzzed. The image of a toddler with fine features, dark, curly hair, and a quiet, thoughtful air appeared on the screen above an incoming text message. Kate's son, Luke, would be sixteen in two days, and the curls were gone. Kate had reported to Emma in grave tones that he'd shaved his head, something about a dare related to his upcoming birthday.

"He set his alarm, hoping we could practice driving this morning," Kate said as she poured milk into her cup, then added tea. "Not that he appreciates my instruction. I think he's gone desperate. His driver's license exam is next week."

"You could take mine," Emma offered.

She and Kate occasionally borrowed each other's

cars, though Luke hadn't yet driven Emma's beloved 1967 Mustang.

She supposed it was inevitable. It seemed unlikely to her that a teen of any era could resist the chance to pilot the sleek, black-topped, white-bodied, convertible.

"Right, good," Kate said, though she didn't meet Emma's eyes. "Perhaps you could have a go at supervising his behind-the-wheel training."

Emma readily agreed.

As her friendship with Kate had grown over the years, so, too, had her relationship with Luke. She'd enjoy the time with him. Plus, lately, mother and son seemed to be getting on one another's last nerve, which seemed a poor recipe for safety on the road.

Having finished her tea, she stood to take her empty cup to the sink.

Kate seemed only then to notice Emma was in the faded T-shirt and sweatpants she'd slept in.

"You're not planning on wearing that to the center, are you?"

Kate had put everything into this new venture and would leave nothing to chance to guarantee its success, including what impression Emma might make on one of the parents if they happened to drop by unannounced today. It was a fair point. Still, at times like these, Emma understood why Luke bristled at the steady stream of guidance his mother seemed unable to restrain herself from offering.

"I'll change now," she said.

But as she turned to leave the kitchen, she hesitated.

There would likely be no better time to tell Kate what had happened last night. Not that it was a big deal. Not at all. But Kate might wrongly suspect there was more to it if she didn't say something right away.

Emma focused on keeping her voice even.

"I ran into Tommy last night."

Kate set her cup down. She looked squarely at Emma. "And?"

"And nothing, really," Emma said.

It was a poor bluff.

She could feel her cheeks redden as she recalled the moment she'd noticed him across the room, his eyes on her. She'd found it hard to swallow, a raw heat still hovering between them. But on seeing Tommy again, she'd also been reminded of the reason for their breakup, of the secrets he couldn't or wouldn't share.

THREE

The Overpass

DETECTIVE TOMMY NOONAN sat curbside on a tree-lined street in midtown Sacramento, his state-issued Taurus idling roughly. He focused on his breathing. When he'd been dating Emma, she'd talked him into attending a yoga class and that had been his takeaway.

A soft yellow light illuminated the porch of the modest ranch-style home where Officer Carlos Sifuentes was saying goodbye to the toddler in his husband's arms. Two men married to one another didn't offend Tommy. After what he'd lost, he experienced only envy. He checked the time. The junior officer could make a sentence into a paragraph on any topic, even in conversation with a two-year-old. The boy was smiling, all the encouragement Carlos would need.

Tommy closed his eyes and pictured the yoga studio, warm and bright, Emma on the mat beside his. He recalled the flex in her thighs as she rose to stand, the curve of her arms as she formed a pose, each move bearing the promise of her stretched beneath him, her body slick with pleasure, her auburn hair tangled in his hands. He reached back for the feeling of invincibility he'd experienced whenever she was near, as though he could step into a red-hot fire without pain. It was no use. The call he'd received from headquarters an hour earlier intruded, crowding out the images.

Dispatch had described the body facedown on the bank of the Sacramento River as a young Asian male, fatally shot before dawn. Tommy wondered if they had an ID yet, and if they did whether he'd made any mistakes that might cause them to connect the victim back to him.

Easing his foot down on the accelerator, he revved the engine once. It seemed more polite than laying on the horn, and less likely to wake the neighbors. Carlos kissed his son on the forehead and jumped from the low front stoop to the gravel path below. He broke into a jog and was already talking as he opened the passenger door.

Tommy's partner was on maternity leave, so he'd been riding with Carlos for nearly a month. He found the junior officer's Salvadoran accent soothing.

"It might be robbery," Carlos said, "or a drug deal gone wrong."

Tommy didn't respond. No telling what he might let slip.

As they approached the overpass on Crestview Drive, the Taurus was laboring. It was a persistent problem, he would need to have it looked at.

"Funny, how the neighborhoods change so quickly," Carlos said. "This can't be more than two miles from my house."

Tommy followed Carlos's eyes to a row of rundown apartments.

He recognized the building, though he'd been there only once. The Crestview Arms was a no-frills 1970s design like the others on the street, but the mustard-yellow exterior made it easy to spot. He recalled the boy's bedroom, it's bunker-like feel in the shadow of the thick concrete supports of the overpass. The frequent rumble and roar of passing diesel trucks had made their whispered conversation difficult.

He was absorbed in his thoughts when he realized Carlos's monologue about the scourge of drugs and gangs in this community had become something else.

"There, see her?" Carlos said, his tone urgent. "Slow down."

A young woman stood on the wrong side of a worn chain-link fence that barred access to a narrow concrete ledge bordering the overpass, twenty feet above the freeway. Her head was bowed, her back to them. Her dark hair fell in a single thick braid, nearly reaching her waist.

Tommy braked gently to a stop on the opposite side of the road. He didn't want to spook her.

She removed her sweater, then pulled her T-shirt off over her head, revealing a plain beige bra. The narrow waistline of her black jeans was encircled by a hot pink belt, a shock of color.

If she was preparing for a swim, Tommy knew this was the wrong place for it. The river was three miles south. There was solid concrete in all directions two stories below her. Fifteen feet to her left, a bent gate hung crookedly from one hinge, wide open, as though mocking a nearby sign: "No Entry, City Workers Only."

Tommy was calculating whether he could make it to the gap along the ledge to where the woman stood before she jumped, if that's what she had in mind, when Carlos burst from the passenger seat and took off at a dead run directly toward her.

She turned her head, but Carlos was already there and had grabbed her belt through the chain-link fence. She strained against his hold, screaming. The fence bowed toward the edge, threatening to give way and take the woman and Carlos with it. She kicked, wailed and writhed, the seam of her leather belt tearing into Carlos's palms.

Tommy, just past forty, was of average height but bull-like in stature, with a broad back and neck. Though he'd put on a few pounds in recent years, he was still more muscle than fat. When he reached the spot where Carlos stood, he found his hands too large to fit through the diamond-shaped openings in the fence.

He put his arms around Carlos's waist and leaned back, his weight helping to pull the fence upright. There was something darkly comic about it, he thought, the woman on one side, he and Carlos on the other.

A tug-of-war, except it was anything but a game.

He heard sirens and doors slamming, the crackle of two-way radios. One black-and-white had stopped on the overpass behind him, and two formed an impromptu roadblock on the freeway below. Someone must've seen them and called it in.

Two officers approached. One helped steady the fence. The other tried to reach through to grab the woman's wrist, but couldn't get a purchase on it. Tommy jogged toward the gate and made his way onto the ledge. He didn't like it, it was a long way down. He kept one hand lightly on the chain-link for balance.

Carlos maintained his grip on the woman's belt, beads of sweat forming on his forehead. He made eye contact with Tommy. Tommy shook his head hard, twice, to the right. It was a motion his typically silent father had employed when he wanted to make clear his answer was "no," and one Tommy unconsciously emulated in times of stress.

The woman stopped struggling. She stared at him with a wide-eyed intensity. It wasn't fear, Tommy had seen that often enough as a homicide cop. It was recognition, as though she suddenly realized she knew him, that she'd seen him before.

Tommy tried to place her. Now, only a few feet away, it was evident she was very young, likely still in her teens. His daughter's age. A former arrest? A friend of a friend? Nothing fit.

He took the last few steps, pulled the young woman close and held her tightly in his arms. Not out of sympathy, though he felt that, but to keep her from the edge. He nodded at Carlos to release his hold on her belt.

Untethered at last, she made no move to free herself from Tommy's awkward embrace.

Instead, she leaned into him.

"It was you by the river last night," she hissed with a venom he could not have imagined she might possess. "You killed my Samson. It was you."

Then in a single motion, before he could react, she tensed and jerked and threw them both off balance, over the precipice and into the endless void.

The Blue House

TWENTY-FIVE MILES NORTH, Dylan Johnson pulled his Jeep to a stop in front of a modest, box-like house painted a color his mother used to call cornflower blue. Walnut trees heavy with bounty, the harvest only weeks away, stood deathly still in the orchards that flanked the house. The last of the breezes that had rustled their leaves in spring were long gone.

He knocked on the cream-colored front door. A minute passed. He knocked again. No response. Sweat formed on the back of his neck, dampening the collar of his sports coat. The man inside was expecting him.

Dylan tried the door. Finding it unlocked, he eased it open.

He stood on the threshold of a single room, large and bright, with a shining oak floor and clean white walls. Opposite him, midnight blue drapes were drawn half-way across a sliding glass door. A broad vista stretched for a good mile before sloping downward, out of sight. Other than tall, dense hedges lining either side of the property, the space was bare of vegetation, an expanse of dirt broken only by two outbuildings, one large, one small, each painted the same cornflower blue as the house.

Gregg Corbel was seated in an executive-style desk chair behind a table of polished blond wood. Thick jet-black hair flowed from a widow's peak high on his forehead to his shoulders. His complexion, a smooth, toneless white, was like milk drained of the cream. He held a bright yellow pencil sharpened to a fine point, which he used to make check marks on a spreadsheet laid out before him, dense with numbers. Only when he'd reached the bottom of the page did he look up, the thin line of his mouth unsmiling as he placed the pencil atop a small notepad and, without comment, slid both across the table toward Dylan.

Dylan was conscious of the soft tapping sound his new hiking boots made on the uncarpeted floor as he crossed the room. He lifted the pencil and neatly printed a name on the pad.

Upon reading it, Corbel's voice was calm, but his dark eyes glistened, as though feverish.

"Are you sure?"

Dylan was sure. It had been easy enough to use his access as an elected official, albeit a minor one, to trace the license plate to get the policeman's name. Even so, he hesitated before confirming. He recalled the three men he'd glimpsed on the back patio the last time he'd been summoned to the blue house, one with a gun in his hand. He hadn't asked why they were there. He hadn't really wanted to know. The man's business required large cash transactions, so he'd decided to believe the firepower on site was all about security. Besides, everything was legal on Dylan's end. He'd checked it all out because it had to be, what with the scrutiny he would be facing soon.

Still, the intensity with which Corbel now studied Dylan's face made it clear his two am phone call hadn't been about fixing a parking ticket, and any question about a policeman put things in a new light.

Something about it suddenly felt very wrong.

Dylan spoke softly, acting on the same impulse that sometimes caused him to carry an umbrella on a cloudless day, as though exposing his concern would ensure it could not come true.

"No one has to die," he said.

Gregg Corbel shrugged, a slight lifting of one shoulder. "Someone always dies."

Corbel's tone was conversational. They might have been discussing the weather. But Dylan hadn't been referring to the natural deaths—God, he hoped they were natural—at the heart of the man's business, and he was sure Corbel knew it. Those were all right. It was murder that had never been part of the plan.

Fifteen minutes later, Dylan had driven less than a mile on the narrow country road that would return him to Sacramento when he pulled onto the shoulder, turned off the Jeep's engine and with it the air-conditioning. He closed his eyes and rested his head back on the seat. As the minutes passed, he welcomed the gradual sensation of warming he felt, letting it permeate the muscles of his neck and arms. There'd been something crypt-like about the chill, the sterility, and the silence inside the blue house.

Word for word, he reviewed the last thing Corbel had said to him.

You've fulfilled your contract. We won't need to meet again.

Dylan allowed himself a cautious smile. He would finally be able to focus on the goal that had brought him to the man in the first place.

Sitting upright, he removed a wallet-sized photo from the inner breast pocket of his jacket. The print was sharp and the colors clear. Emma Lawson's dark auburn hair, parted in the middle, fell thick and straight in a styl-ish cut that ended several inches above her shoulders. It shimmered in the light. Her chin was lifted, her long neck arched. Her eyes, emerald green with flecks of gold, appeared intent upon something in the distance.

FOUR

The Overpass

SHORTLY AFTER EMMA left her house, the newest appointee to the nine-member Hayden Commission, Diane Warhol, phoned to say she would like to stop by Emma's office to meet her in person if it "was convenient," though Emma's convenience didn't really enter into it.

Despite being appointed by the governor, the Hayden Commissioners were not mere political figureheads. They had to approve every request from their investigators to look into the activities of a government agency or a specific state employee. It was crucial for Emma's career success and her job satisfaction that she have a good working relationship with all nine, and Commissioner Warhol was the only one she'd not yet met.

Fortunately, Warhol didn't want to get together until five, giving Emma plenty of time to make a significant dent in Kate's Rainbow Alley to-do list, including essential tasks like buying more red fingerpaint.

As she navigated the streets of midtown Sacramento, Emma was grateful Kate had questioned her fashion choice that morning. Absent that, she would still be in the clothes she'd slept in instead of her work ready sage-green linen suit. She lowered the Mustang's convertible top, hoping for a breeze, and made good time until the freeway approach at Crestview Drive, where she found herself in a line of cars that wasn't going anywhere.

She tuned the old-school AM radio to the local news to see if she could get a traffic update. The anchor's chirpy delivery was at odds with the copy he read.

"The body of an Asian male in his late teens was discovered early today, shot and killed by the Sacramento River. Mrs. Carp, visiting from Goldonna, Louisiana was walking her dog when she made the gruesome pre-dawn find."

Eloise Carp spoke with a distinct, down-home, Southern twang.

"Moxie's usually a good girl on the leash, but this morning she kept pulling me toward a stand of trees. I thought there might be a squirrel up one of 'em, but when we got to the edge I saw a man lying there. No mistake about it. He was dead. Moxie was barking to beat the band, and he didn't move a speck."

At least it isn't the work of the Gambler, Emma thought.

Three months earlier, a succession of execution-style killings of young people as they went about their daily lives had terrorized and fascinated Sacramento residents. Seemingly carried out on a theme, playing cards had been tossed onto each lifeless body where it lay. The cards varied and might have been chosen at random, except that the total face value was always twenty-three. A talking head on a cable news show had made much of the fact that in the game of blackjack a player who drew more than twenty-one was out. Or in this case, dead. He'd dubbed the murderer "the Gambler," and the nickname, like the images of the innocent young faces of the victims, had gone viral.

Even after the real meaning of the cards was uncovered, the name stuck to Samuel Miller, arrested and charged with the crimes and now a resident of the high-security wing of the Sacramento County Jail, where he awaited trial. Emma knew more about the string of killings than she cared to since Kate followed the story zealously, as she did all violence in the area.

When Luke had first entered his teen years, Emma noticed her friend's already hands-on approach to parenting ratcheted up a notch. When asked about it, Kate had told her, "Even a lad who is the dog's bollocks can go a bit barmy when his hormones kick in." Emma hadn't needed a translation.

From what little Kate had shared about Luke's father, Emma understood he'd been a thuggish type, disappearing after Kate fell pregnant at fifteen. So perhaps it wasn't surprising that tattoos, gang affiliation, and a future prison term topped Kate's list of fears for her only child.

But Emma didn't think Kate had reason to worry. Though not a parent herself, it seemed to her that Luke's testing of limits, even at times being untruthful, was normal adolescent stuff. Besides, how could he have time to find trouble? He played in a band, worked hard at school, and had a job at the local bike shop. It was true he'd been picked up once by the police with another kid from work, but that had been a case of being in the wrong place at the wrong time. Tommy had been at the station that night and had sworn there was nothing to it. Still, she'd kept an eye on him, especially since last fall, when just before Thanksgiving Kate had asked her to review an addendum to her will that would make Emma Luke's legal guardian in the event something happened to Kate.

Although she'd made the request in her usual, no-nonsense tone—"Really, love, there's no one else"—Kate's fingers had trembled as she'd smoothed the page on her desk.

She needn't have been concerned.

Emma signed the document and had it notarized that same day. It would have been unthinkable to her to leave her closest friend without backup and Luke alone in the world.

Trapped at a standstill for nearly ten minutes, the decades-old Mustang protested, emitting a sound closer to a death rattle than the hum of a smoothly idling engine. Emma reached for her khaki satchel on the floor of the passenger side. Frayed on the edges, it had served as her purse, briefcase, and backpack since college.

Retrieving her phone, a search for "Crestview traffic" yielded several links.

"Deadly Leap off Crestview"
"Death before Dawn"
"Veteran Officer Dies in Line of Duty"
She clicked on the last one.

"A veteran homicide detective gave his life this morning in the rescue of a young woman who was attempting suicide. According to an eyewitness, when the woman threw herself from the Crestview overpass, the officer was pulled off with her, his body breaking her fall. A Sutter Hospital spokesperson describes the woman's condition as critical."

Although Emma figured there were a dozen or more homicide detectives in the Sacramento area, she assumed only a few would qualify as veteran. She directed the phone to search the web for the keywords "Tommy Noonan."

Multiple links came up, nearly all several years old, related to the death of Tommy's wife, which had been front-page news at the time. The only recent piece was a local blog entry that featured the charity event where Emma had seen Tommy the night before. He was highlighted for having commanded the top prize in an auction of dates with "bachelors and bachelorettes" to support the Sacramento police department's youth activities.

Emma recalled how uncomfortable Tommy had appeared when it was his turn in the spotlight, his hands thrust deep in his pants pockets, head down, studying his unfamiliar dress shoes. It was the first time she'd seen him wearing anything other than his worn desert boots.

"Next, this virile, dashing man in blue. You'll hope he brings out the cuffs!" The emcee's pitch had resulted in laughter, followed by one woman after another calling out her bid.

Emma could have testified to Tommy being virile, absolutely. But not to the handcuffs. He'd never needed help to hold her captive once he touched her.

She'd first met Tommy in the spring, when she was picking up Luke at a citywide jazz camp. Another teen, carrying a large instrument case that had appeared to outweigh her, had exited the auditorium with Luke. As Emma approached the pair, a man walked toward them from the other side. Stocky and broad, with unruly, curly brown hair, Tommy Noonan had moved with the authority of someone with places to be.

At the sight of him, the girl had quickened her pace, smiling.

"Dad, I can't believe you're on time."

"Lily, my love, if only—"

"I know, if only you could fly, you would have been here yesterday."

With still no forward progress in the line of cars, Emma refreshed her phone. More articles, some with stock photos of the freeway, but nothing new on the officer who had died that morning. Maneuvering the Mustang onto the shoulder, she got out and walked toward the towering overpass, visible beyond a curve in the road.

Rounding the turn, she scanned the scene. There were two police cars parked to block any traffic. Past the black and whites a circle of pavement was set off by cones. The asphalt within it was a deeper color than the rest. The sky was clear. The difference might have been the product of a shadow cast by the early morning sun.

As she got closer, Emma knew it wasn't. It was blood, a lot of it, the horrifying residue left by two people plummeting from the ledge far above onto the unforgiving concrete. Her stomach rose and lurched as though she were cresting the steepest hill of a thrill ride.

One she desperately didn't want to be on.

She thought again of the day she'd met Tommy, of the words she'd heard him say so many times since.

If only I could fly.

FIVE

The River

SACRAMENTO'S NEW HEAD of Major Crimes, Alibi Morning Sun, had done little fieldwork since his promotion. But when he'd received the news of the on-duty death of Detective Tommy Noonan, his first partner in homicide nearly a decade ago, the walls of his well-appointed office with its expansive view of downtown and the white-domed capitol building in the distance had felt oppressive.

Alibi swung his Camry into the lot of the River Top Motel and parked at the front, near the spot where a tourist had called in the predawn shooting. The 911 recording was dominated by the woman's attempts to quiet her yapping dog, but she'd gotten her message across.

Stepping out of the car, he removed his suit jacket and tossed it onto the back seat. At nine am, it was already too hot for anything but rolled-up shirtsleeves. Although unable to see the body from where he stood, the path to it couldn't have been clearer. Yellow crime scene tape stretched the fifty feet from the top of the embankment to the river, cordoning off an area on either side of a thick grove of eucalyptus trees.

Despite the heat, it felt good to stretch his legs. Tall and lanky, Alibi had never been able to get truly comfortable driving the Camry.

A beat cop greeted him just above the waterline. Her manner was professional, arms clasped behind her back, head up, parade-rest fashion.

Former military, Alibi thought.

"Is the ME here?" he asked, referring to the medical examiner.

"No, sir."

"How about Dr. Oliver?"

"Yes, sir. She arrived ten minutes ago."

Dr. Jacqueline Oliver, known to colleagues and friends as "Jackie O," was in the eighth month of a two-year, federally funded position to assist Sacramento in reducing the area's increasing gang violence. To Alibi's mind, she'd already proven her worth, having given the department the break it needed in a series of murders initially thought to be the work of a lone serial killer with a twisted relationship to games of chance. Ms. Oliver had suggested the playing cards with a total value of twenty-three left behind on each victim might have a more sinister meaning than the link to blackjack dominating the media. She'd explained that since "W" was the twenty-third letter in the alphabet, some gangs used the number twenty-three to represent white power.

Once that angle had been opened up, the focus of the investigation shifted to the fact that the victims—a recently graduated computer programmer in her first job, a minimum-wage baker's assistant, and an artist/stay-at-home father of a two-month-old—were all young people of color, first-or second-generation immigrants. Soon, multiple triggermen with gang connections were identified, and their orders to kill tracked back to Samuel Miller, founder of a tight-knit, Sacramento-area white supremacist organization with the members-only code name "Hallowed 23."

Since then, Alibi sought Jackie O's input on all homicides where gang involvement was a possibility, including this one.

Inside the grove, the air was thick with the smell of damp earth and the honey-pine scent of the eucalyptus. The canopy formed by their branches overhead blocked the light of the rising summer sun, creating an atmosphere of dusk-like gloom. The young man's body lay facedown, one arm thrown wide, the other bent awkwardly beneath him.

He looked so out of place in the natural setting that for a moment Alibi indulged the sensation that he bore witness to the result of a supernatural phenomenon, the roots of the trees rising above ground to fell the intruder, their branches wielding the blows that had killed him. But the three bullet holes in the victim told a more mundane story. One of willful, man-made homicide.

At the far edge of the clearing a crime tech sporting a heavy mustache squatted, rifling through his kit. Next to him stood Jackie O. It was easy to see how she'd gotten her nickname. Twenty-six years old, tall, with dark eyes and dark hair in soft waves, she could've doubled for a young Jackie Kennedy. Years after the assassination of her husband, the widowed Kennedy wed billionaire Aristotle Onassis, taking his name, which had led to the former First Lady forever being known as "Jackie O."

Not that Alibi would judge anyone for having an unusual name, though he did wonder whether Jackie O had resisted hers before giving in to the inevitable. He'd never had a choice about his. When he was fifteen, he'd overheard his aunt telling his uncle that he'd been christened Alibi because the timing of his birth cleared his father of a murder rap.

The tech found what he was looking for, a shiny silver computer tablet. Everyone in the department had been issued one. Alibi's sat unopened in the box in his office. He preferred a pocket-size paper notebook with a dark blue cover, of the type he'd carried for years.

The tech approached Alibi and turned the screen so they both could see the computer-generated image of a body in the same position as the one on the ground, a red "X" marking each place a bullet had entered. One on the upper thigh, one on the lower back, and one at the base of the neck. It didn't take a genius to figure out which had killed him.

"Shot at close range, two to three feet," the tech said. "The ME's the expert, but I don't see any signs the body was moved after death."

"ID?" Alibi asked.

"Nope. No wallet, no phone. I've e-mailed you the initial report, photos attached. Okay if I go to the van? The rest of the team is already up there. It'll give you room to work—it's a little tight in here."

Alibi nodded.

As the tech turned to go, he gave Jackie O a blatant head-to-toe assessment. The gold wedding band she wore didn't appear to give him pause.

Irrespective of her marital status, Alibi didn't like it. He resolved to have a word with the guy's supervisor to make it clear sexist actions, including ogling, would not be tolerated under his leadership. That standard applied, even if it was difficult to look elsewhere than at the beautiful young gang expert, given that the only other choice was a recently deceased corpse.

SIX

The River

"BASED ON the color of his shirt, he might have been a member of the Red Vua," Jackie O said. She added, annoyance evident in her voice, "We won't know until we have an ID whether he's in our database."

Alibi didn't have to ask what was bothering her. One of the first things Jackie O had done when she started with the department was an analysis of Sacramento County's regional gang member database, linked to the California Department of Justice's statewide system. A cross-agency task force had identified eleven factors as significant indicators of gang affiliation or membership. If a suspect met any two, they were slapped with a gang designation, potentially enhancing sentencing if a relevant conviction occurred. The eleven criteria had never been made public, the argument being that if they were, gang members could game the system, finding ways to avoid being properly tagged.

The database was mined aggressively if a Sacramento-area crime was assumed to be gang-related, a virtual one-stop shop for bad guys. But in Jackie O's opinion, having done her doctoral dissertation on the social determinants of gang membership, the low threshold of only two of eleven criteria meant nonviolent individuals clogged the pool of suspects, impeding the department's ability to track those actually responsible for serious and violent gang crimes.

After checking over her shoulder to be sure she remained within the zones the tech had marked as acceptable, Jackie O took a few steps back, stopping roughly three feet from the fallen boy. She appeared to Alibi to be imagining the crime as it might have occurred, viewing the scene from the killer's perspective. Though the air in the grove was stifling, he didn't rush her. She'd shown a natural aptitude for the investigative aspects of homicide, and she wasn't squeamish, not even in this contained and arguably claustrophobic space, a few feet from a dead man. He could picture her with a future in law enforcement, despite the academic path she'd laid out for herself.

"The shooter's first goal was only to stop the victim," she said, indicating the entry wounds on the boy's back and thigh. "Neither of these was aimed to kill."

"Or he was a terrible shot," Alibi said.

She looked at the body again, reassessing.

He encouraged her to keep going. "What about motive?"

Her eyes came to rest on a gap between the trees that offered a glimpse of the dusty incline leading up to the motel lot.

"Robbery," she said. "The boy was walking on the path above. The shooter forced him down here at gunpoint. When the kid wouldn't give up his valuables and tried to run, the thief, maybe high on something, panicked and shot him in the back, twice. He finished him off, standing over him because—"

She stopped short and frowned.

Alibi could see she was struggling with how a simple theft might have become a murder, execution style.

"He didn't want the victim alive to identify him," she concluded.

Alibi shrugged. "Why not rob him on the spot, up on the path? Take his phone so he couldn't call for help, then make a run for it. Why go to the trouble to move the victim down here?"

"So no one could witness it?"

"Middle of the night or very early morning, that path was likely deserted," he responded.

Jackie O hesitated. "A drug deal gone wrong?"

Alibi knew their challenge wasn't going to be a lack of any plausible explanation for the violence that had taken the boy's life. It was that there would be too many.

"Let's finish this discussion in the car," he said. "With the air-conditioning on." He felt beads of sweat forming on his forehead and at the base of his neck. He'd worn his thick black hair long since he was a kid, nearly to his shoulders, despite it not being practical for Sacramento summers. "We can wait there until the coroner arrives."

As they moved single file toward the designated exit, Jackie O said, "At least there are no playing cards."

Alibi thought about that, and about what they knew so far.

A young person of color
Killed in a secluded setting
An inexperienced shooter
The death of the victim intentional, possibly even necessary

He stopped walking and turned slowly in a circle. Urging himself to miss nothing, he noticed a second gap between the trees, narrower and harder to see, opposite the one that led up the hill.

"Was the ground photographed through there, all the way to the river?"

Jackie O followed his gaze. "I think so. I can check."

Alibi turned his attention back to the teen. His head and shoulders had landed on a tree root when he'd fallen, leaving a narrow space between his upper body and the ground from his chest to his waist.

Alibi took a step closer and knelt, his hair grazing the damp earth as he leaned in to get a better view. When he stood, his expression was grim.

"What is it?" Jackie O asked.

He stepped back so she could see for herself.

She withdrew a penlight from one of the many pockets of her khaki vest and focused the bright beam beneath the boy. Then, standing with more grace and ease than Alibi had done, she gave her assessment.

"Ten of clubs, ten of hearts. I can't see the front of the third card, but it's a safe bet it's a three. Total value twenty-three, and same royal blue backs." She held up a hand, as though to stop him from coming to the obvious conclusion. "The similarities end there. These cards are shiny, no evidence of wear. They're new, manufactured by a modern company."

Alibi let what she'd said sink in.

Named by one of the shooters as the mastermind behind the killings, Samuel Miller had seemed an unlikely suspect for the Gambler's killing spree. Having graduated from college in accounting, he'd made a success of his father's struggling dry-cleaning business. He'd even been featured in the local paper. *"Second Generation Sacramento Business Man Cleans Up."*

Significant progress had been made in the case only when Jackie O had determined that the cards at the murder scenes were old. Very old. Vintage originals produced in Nazi Germany. Miller's arrest followed when an electronic trail to the purchase of the unusual cards had been unearthed on his hard drive.

"Few people know exactly what the Gambler's cards looked like, where they were from," Jackie O said.

Alibi nodded. The DA had been able to keep their unusual provenance from the press and public as part of the ongoing investigation.

"So this is a copycat killer," she said. "Or the murderer is trying to persuade us that the Hallowed 23 gang initiations have started up again to cover for some other reason to kill this kid. Either way, they didn't know the details to get the cards right, only what they'd seen on the news."

Alibi recalled the tremendous relief he'd felt when the execution-style killings that had terrorized the Sacramento immigrant community were believed to have come to an end. But faced with what they'd just found, he had to acknowledge another possibility.

"Just because Miller's on the inside doesn't mean he couldn't have ordered this hit," he said. "He may even have reasoned that changing the type of cards would weaken any link back to him."

He saw the question in Jackie O's eyes.

Did he really believe Samuel Miller had started killing again?

As he was giving this consideration, she blurted out, "I almost forgot. There's something else you need to see." She extended the penlight to him. "A tattoo on the victim's chest on the far side where his shirt is torn. Some kind of warrior. It's in the shadows but visible with the light."

Alibi repeated the process of kneeling to get a clear view beneath the body, then slid back and rose to his feet.

"It's Samson," he said.

Jackie O's finely arched brows went up, apparently surprised by the speed with which he'd come to his conclusion.

"You can see the supports, the columns, cracking," Alibi said. "When Delilah cut Samson's hair she stole his strength, but when it returned he pulled down the temple. Killing everyone inside." He frowned. "It's a vengeful and violent image."

Jackie O pulled a tablet just like the tech's from a large pocket in her vest, moved back to the youth's side and took several photos.

When Alibi viewed them, brightened by the flash and enlarged by the zoom, he thought he might have seen that tattoo before. "Let's run it through the gang database." Anticipating her objections, he added, "If it's there, the match will be much faster than waiting for fingerprints."

Headquarters

AN HOUR LATER, back at headquarters or what passed for it these days, Alibi directed his assistant, Nishad, to hold anything but urgent calls.

The sprawling complex of buildings housing Sacramento's police and fire departments had been bursting at the seams for years. Fortunately, funding had finally been secured to expand, but construction required relocating some personnel for at least a year while the massive renovation was under way. Alibi's unit, having drawn the short straw, was temporarily stationed in a concrete-and-glass, fifteen-story high-rise, which the state had been able to lease for a song from a bankrupt venture capitalist.

The new accommodations were less convenient than being with everyone else, and the location downtown meant more traffic to contend with. But for Alibi, in addition to the penthouse-level view, another perk of having been assigned the former office suite of a vice president of a hedge fund was the full private bath outfitted for a top executive, complete with a shower that offered a pulsating massage stream. He rarely used it but had decided the pungent odor of sweat and river water emanating from him after his visit to the crime scene provided, literally, strong justification.

Having adjusted the water to a pleasantly cool temperature, he stripped and stepped into the large, white-tiled shower stall, resolving to let the jets that mimicked a cascading waterfall rinse the morning away. But as he closed his eyes to fully experience the moment, he was struck by a vivid memory of Tommy from several months ago, as real as though his former partner was standing there, impatiently waiting for him to get cleaned up so they could meet their dates.

They'd argued good-naturedly over the restaurant choice, Tommy insisting a hole-in-the-wall that served authentic Hawaiian food was just the thing. *Easy for him to say*, Alibi had thought at the time. Tommy's girlfriend, Emma, though evidently Type A about her work, had seemed flexible in most other things. But Alibi had invited a woman he'd recently met at the public library. Knowing little about her other than that they both were vintage mystery fans, he'd reasoned a more traditional option, like pasta or a main dish salad, seemed a safer bet.

In exchange for agreeing to push the meal back half

an hour to allow Alibi time to change, Tommy had won out, though they'd still arrived at Delicious Island Fare ahead of the women. Taking the edge off their hunger with an appetizer of curried shrimp and grilled pineapple (which Alibi was pleased to find lived up to the restaurant's name) they'd discussed one of Tommy's new cases. Tommy had been certain the victim's ex-husband had battered her to death, but Alibi had thought it worth checking out the woman's sister, who might have had a financial motive. With a grin, Tommy had responded as he always did when he thought Alibi was making things too complicated.

"If you hear hoofbeats, don't look for zebras. You might miss the horses galloping by."

As the memory faded, Alibi toweled off, and after donning a clean set of clothes that he kept in the posh walk-in closet, his thoughts returned to Samuel Miller. If convicted of current charges, Miller was already facing life in prison. If he was found to have ordered yet another hit from inside, the time he served would be much harder. He might never get out of solitary. Alibi concluded the man simply had too much to lose. The answer to the morning's riverside shooting would surely be the simpler one, that the killer of the boy had tried to throw them off the scent by mimicking the Gambler's signature cards.

Alibi resolved he would not go looking for zebras. Just a quick trip to the jail, nothing more than due diligence to be sure Miller's security was as tight as promised.

SEVEN

Matchbook Lane

LUKE HAD SET his alarm because he wanted to practice driving, but his mom had taken the car into the mechanics and getting out of bed to bike to the fancy preschool she was opening on Monday had no appeal. He threw an arm across his eyes to block the morning sunlight streaming through the gap between his window shade and sill. He didn't mind entertaining little kids while their parents took a tour. But sign-ups were over, so he figured today he'd be doing last-minute tasks like sorting blocks, sweeping up dust the construction crew had missed, and any other boring work his mother could come up with.

Two weeks ago, she'd made him quit his job at Marty's Wheels, the local bike store where he'd worked the register and assisted with simple repairs. She'd said it was his responsibility to help out in their new family business. He hadn't bought that as the reason. She didn't like the atmosphere in the shop or the friends he'd made, most of whom were older than he was. Sure, some of the employees partied hard, and their ideas about immigrants, guns and the Second Amendment didn't fit with his mother's. But it was no big deal.

It was ridiculous, she acted like they were murderers or child molesters or something.

Samson, closest to Luke's age, was really cool. He

played electric bass and Luke had brought his saxophone so they could jam a few times when their shifts were over. There was that night he and Samson had been picked up by the cops, but the world wasn't the same as when his mom was growing up. Besides, Luke wasn't a kid anymore and he didn't intend to be a bystander.

He reached for his laptop, charging on the nightstand. Propping the computer on his knees, he waited for it to power up. A hand-me-down from his mom, it took its time. When the screen finally came to life, a small dictionary icon flashed in the lower corner. Luke clicked on it. Bold black letters against a bright green background announced the "SAT Prep Word of the Day" was "bombastic." A timer ticked down from thirty, the number of seconds Luke had in which to offer his definition. After a moment's thought, he typed "warlike, angry." The computer responded with an unpleasant electronic tone and countered with "high-sounding, inflated, pretentious."

Luke shook his head. He must've been thinking of "belligerent." If he'd matched at least one of the words in the correct definition, he would've gotten credit. He held out little hope that when Emma logged onto the game, she would confuse the two words as he had done. They'd been playing for over three months and she still had a perfect score.

He would have liked to close the gap between them, but he appreciated that she didn't pretend she didn't know a word, or tell him she'd take him for ice cream or something equally childish if he improved his performance. When he'd stopped calling her "Aunt Emma" she hadn't said a thing about it.

She could accept that he'd grown up. He wondered if his mom ever would.

He clicked to move to the summer jazz band home page. In a photo of their last performance he could just make out Lily next to him in the back row in the horn section. He tried to message her, but the screen froze.

He closed the laptop hard and pushed it aside. With a crappy computer and no phone, sometimes he felt like he lived in the Dark Ages.

He was certain his mom wouldn't have been able to go a day without her "mobile" as she called it, where she kept her calendar and the many lists she made, and where she was able to check gossip sites for her favorite Hollywood celebrities' latest fitness regimens. Yet when his phone, his only reliable internet access, permanently died three weeks ago, she'd told him he'd have to wait for his birthday for a replacement.

He couldn't see why she didn't understand his need for connecting online was at least as great as hers. Weren't there studies in all that stuff she read that proved teenagers become dangerously depressed if they can't log on?

Locating one black Converse high top under the edge of his bed and the other beneath his desk, he'd just finished lacing them up when he heard an insistent, deep barking from his backyard.

He jogged through the living room into the kitchen, and had the back door halfway open when Crash charged inside. Nose to the floor, the big dog inspected every inch of linoleum to be sure no scraps had been overlooked in the cleanup from last night's dinner.

His mom never missed a spot, but for Crash, hope sprang eternal.

Luke grinned, once again amazed he had a dog.

When he'd witnessed the prevalence of American dog ownership, he'd begged for a puppy. Not a fan of dirt, dust, or anything that might clog the vacuum, his mom had responded that the primary reason houses were constructed with exterior walls was to keep animals and their shedding coats away from areas of human habitation.

At the time, Luke had been the target of bullies at his new school for his Irish accent, his small stature and, as far as he could tell for nothing at all. On one especially bad day, the ninety-pound Rottweiler—German Shepherd mix had shown up across the street on Emma's doorstep.

When Luke met the big dog, he'd buried his face in his fur and wrapped his arms around his massive neck. When he'd looked up, his mom had had the intense look she got when she was feeling something she'd rather not say. A few hours later, she'd brokered a shared ownership agreement with Emma, and the newly christened Crash, who Luke had named for "Crash Bandicoot" of video game fame, was allowed to stay, splitting his time between the two houses.

Luke opened a kitchen cabinet and grabbed a couple of dog treats along with a granola bar for himself. Crash swallowed the treats whole, gone before Luke had his breakfast bar unwrapped. The dog's heavy tail thumped loudly on the floor, his gaze locked on Luke's meal.

"No, boy, this isn't for you."

Luke ate the bar quickly to remove any temptation, then knelt to let Crash lick his face. He lowered his chin so the dog could explore the scratchy stubble on top of his nearly bare scalp. Lily had used her dad's electric razor. The result hadn't been as smooth as she'd wanted, but Luke thought the slight dark shadow she'd left looked good. He definitely appeared older. Not that anything could close the two-year gap between his age and Lily's. She would start college in a week and had already moved into her dorm, while he would still be stuck at Thompson High.

Lily often felt to Luke like the sister he'd never had. But at times he'd lose the thread of what she was saying, aware only that her lips were moving. Something about her mouth barely open, then closing and opening again in the innocent act of forming words would make him catch his breath.

He'd kissed only one girl in his life. Or more accurately, been kissed by her. He was pretty sure now that it had been a pity kiss. He'd been the shortest kid, skinny too, at the start of high school. But in the last year he'd shot up more than half a foot. He'd started doing push-ups and pull-ups and filled out some. Girls treated him differently, even a few of the popular ones, but he didn't trust it.

He'd just finished a glass of milk and set it in the sink when Crash bolted, racing to the living room. When Luke caught up and reached the front window, he saw the cause of Crash's concern. A sky-blue Jeep was idling at the curb across the street. Luke didn't recognize the man in shadow behind the wheel, but before he could consider why he might be parked with his engine running in front of Emma's house, the driver took off. Crash let out a commanding "that's right, buster, you better keep driving" bark.

Luke figured it was time for him to leave, too. He hurried to his room to grab his laptop with the intention of putting it in his backpack, then decided it wasn't worth lugging around. There'd be a computer he could use at the daycare center. He considered also leaving his bike helmet behind since his mom had purchased the dorkiest style. She'd said it was the safest, but he couldn't get over feeling she did it because it made him look like he was still twelve. He wavered, then picked it up.

He'd worked at a bike shop, he knew the statistics. No sense dying just to prove a point.

EIGHT

The Jail

CARLOS LOOKED TERRIBLE. His eyes were puffy, and the cheerful, near-kinetic energy that typically ran through him was absent. It appeared as though just staying upright was a chore. Not surprising, given that he'd witnessed the death of a fellow officer only a few hours earlier. And not just any officer. Carlos had looked up to Tommy. In the short time they'd ridden together, they'd formed a strong bond.

Alibi had suggested he take the rest of the day off, but Carlos insisted he preferred to work. Still, the junior officer's unsteady hand as he produced identification for the guard at the entry station gave Alibi second thoughts about having brought him along for this particular interview.

In his ten years on the force, Alibi had concluded that most homicides resulted from the many things that could go wrong in an otherwise ordinary life, from desperate financial straits to perceived betrayal in crimes of passion and obsession. But there was one category of killings that seemed to exist on another plane altogether: the murder of an individual for the sole purpose of sending the brutal and terrifying message that "their kind" was disposable and dispensable, crimes like orchestrating executions of the innocent, for which Samuel Miller stood accused. Evil felt tangibly present in those acts and in the subcultures of hatred that enabled them, straining the capacity for empathy of even the most compassionate on Alibi's team.

He wondered now whether asking Carlos to confront that reality today, to sit across from Samuel Miller while Tommy Noonan's body lay cold and shrouded in the morgue, had been appropriate. But he didn't have time to reassess. As soon as they'd cleared security, he and Carlos were shown directly to Warden Trainor's office.

Neil Trainor greeted them at his open door with a broad smile. Tall with cropped reddish-blond hair, he wore a brown suit and a tie in a pattern of colorful flowers on a purple background. Though not much older than forty, the crinkles around the warden's eyes and mouth suggested the smile he'd given them was a common occurrence that had left its mark. He showed them into his office, offering them seats on a tweedy sofa flanked by matching armchairs. He remained standing, leaning back comfortably against his desk, his arms crossed.

"I understand you're here regarding Samuel Miller. What can I do for you?"

Trainor had been hired two years ago to take over after a second prisoner's death in the Sacramento jail had caused the former warden to be let go. Though both incidents were ultimately ruled accidents, postmortem investigations had shown that each resulted from what at best could be termed incompetence at the hands of guards, and at worst a willful disregard for the humanity of the inmates in their charge.

"The Trainor Way," as it had come to be known, combined near ubiquitous Big Brother monitoring, cameras everywhere, with better training of staff and increased support for those incarcerated, including counseling and education. At his last post, intra-gang, individual, and guard-on-inmate violence had all dropped precipitously during his tenure. Sacramento was eager to replicate those results.

"A murder late last night has elements that resemble those for which Miller was arrested," Alibi said. "Shooting of a young person of color, playing cards left with the body."

He watched Neil Trainor closely for his reaction. While highly unlikely, one way information could have passed from a high-security inmate to someone outside would have been via the warden.

Trainor's eyes met Alibi's. He seemed at ease when he responded.

"Since Mr. Miller has been charged with ordering murders rather than committing them himself, a strict monitoring protocol of all his communications inside and outside the jail is in place. Of course, his conversations with his lawyer are privileged, but beyond that his orchestrating a killing from inside would present significant challenges to him. Although, as you and I both know, it wouldn't be impossible."

Carlos was following the warden's comments closely. He looked to Alibi, who nodded, giving silent permission for him to ask his own questions.

"I was thinking," Carlos began, "Miller doesn't have a large network to turn to. At its height his gang had no more than a dozen members, mostly guys he'd known since college, and as far as our unit can tell it appears to have been disbanded since his arrest. So it's really unclear who he could have gotten to kill for him again. But say Miller did have someone loyal to him, someone still willing to murder on his orders, wouldn't a guard have been the most likely conduit? A guard who shared Miller's white supremacy beliefs?"

Trainor moved to his desk and logged into his computer as he spoke.

"When hiring, we reject applicants with histories that are incompatible with the responsibilities our personnel have for a diverse population. But it's not a perfect system. There are privacy rights that mean we can't know our employees' complete political or personal views on issues like race and immigration." After a quick navigation of the screen and a few clicks of the mouse he looked up. "I've ordered a copy for you of the schedule of Miller's staffing from the day he arrived. We've permitted only a tight cohort of experienced senior guards to have access to him. He's been accompanied in all aspects of his stay here, including meals and time in the yard."

Trainor's phone buzzed and a red light flashed. After lifting the handset and listening for a moment, he hung up and bestowed another broad smile on Alibi and Carlos.

"Miller's attorney, Leo Clarkson, came to the jail today to meet with a different client. But he received your request through his office and has spoken with Miller. You won't have to wait, they're willing to see you now."

SEATED ACROSS FROM Samuel Miller in the small windowless interview room, Alibi was reminded of the old adage that appearances can be misleading. With sandy brown hair, thinning on top, at thirty-two years of age Miller was clean-cut and relaxed in manner. Dressed in a short-sleeved, gray, prison-issued shirt, he didn't seem to have availed himself of the jail's weight-training equipment. His arms and chest were no more pumped than a deskbound clerk's. In fact, since Alibi had agreed to his attorney's request that Miller be permitted to participate in the interview unmanacled, there really was nothing about the accused that called out, "I'm a stone-cold xenophobe who believes in the inherent superiority of the white race" or "I ordered multiple execution killings of innocent young people."

Following the obligatory introductions for the record, Alibi began his questioning.

"We are investigating the death of a young man late last night by the Sacramento River. Were you aware of this incident?"

Miller's relaxed posture remained unchanged.

"No."

"Have you had any unmonitored communications with anyone outside the jail other than your attorney, written, verbal, or electronic?"

"No."

True to form, Miller seemed to give no more weight to the exchange than if Alibi had been conducting a door-to-door survey on preferences in laundry detergent. In Alibi's review of the case files, he'd learned Miller was not generally an expressive guy. Whether a strategy or a core personality trait, it had worked for him. The restraint he'd shown in not shouting his bigoted beliefs in person or in online forums meant that prior to this arrest he'd escaped the notice of the FBI. But Alibi wasn't quite ready to give up. He had a strategy he'd used successfully with other inmates to get them talking that he hoped might induce Miller to offer more than one-word answers.

"I plan to ask the administration to search your cell to ensure there is no evidence of outside contact." He turned to Carlos. "If I don't remember to ask the warden before we leave, would you put in a call to him when we get back to headquarters that I'd like that done this afternoon?"

Uncertainty flashed in Carlos's eyes. Alibi knew he must be wondering why he'd given Miller advance notice of a search, highly valuable information for any prisoner, since it provided time to "clean up" his cell. Nothing as exciting as filling in a half-built escape tunnel under the bed, but disposing of drugs or a small, handmade weapon would be typical. He would explain to Carlos later that he was proffering the unexpected gift in the hope that Miller might view it as a sign of goodwill and be more cooperative.

Miller looked at the ceiling, then at his attorney, before leaning forward, his gaze finally settling on Alibi.

When he spoke, it was not to comment on the search.

"I might have heard something about that incident last night."

Alibi could see this was a surprise to Leo Clarkson. Color flushed the attorney's face. He didn't look pleased that his client seemed headed down a path unknown to him. But he'd barely opened his mouth to advise Miller when the inmate gave him a stark look of warning, his eyes lit with an unspoken rebuke.

The sound of heavy boots clomped up the hallway, followed by a brief murmured exchange among the guards. When Miller spoke next, his relaxed and clean-cut pose was gone. His tone was commanding and carried authority.

"If I share the information, I want to be compensated."

Alibi felt tension building in his arms and hands. With difficulty, he masked his desire to physically wipe off the look of arrogance and superiority that had suddenly infused the accused killer's face. He spoke calmly.

"I can convey to the district attorney's office your willingness to be cooperative in this matter, should you choose to do so."

Miller said nothing.

At that moment, Alibi felt the nickname the Gambler was exactly right, as the man across from him appeared to be considering the strength of his hand and what cards to play next.

NINE

Rainbow Alley

RAINBOW ALLEY PRESCHOOL had been closed for business for over a year and the building that housed it allowed to fall into disrepair long before that. The many hues of the rainbow above the entrance had faded until all were some version of gray.

Emma had tried to convince Kate since the sign needed to be replaced they might as well start fresh and choose a new name, but Kate wouldn't hear of it. She'd said Rainbow Alley made her think of Harry Potter's world, of Diagon Alley lined with tiny shops stocked with wands, butter beer, and snowy white owls.

Emma usually parked in a spot in the back. But after her encounter with the body-sized bloodstains below the overpass, she didn't trust her legs to carry her across the school's large lot. Fortunately, there were no tours scheduled on this last weekday before the center opened, so she pulled the Mustang into the yellow drop-off zone without concern that she'd inconvenience prospective students and their families.

She'd texted Tommy. She hadn't known what to say. If he was fine—*he had to be fine*—there was a closure conversation out there he'd repeatedly insisted he wanted. Sending a message asking if he was alive seemed a poor substitute. She'd settled for "Call me." She'd also texted Kate, who'd responded she would take a ride service from the mechanics to Rainbow Alley. It wasn't far. She should have arrived by now.

Emma pushed open one of the double glass doors and stepped into the air-conditioned entryway. Past brightly colored cubbies where children would soon store their belongings, she could see Kate, head down, absorbed in something on her phone. Emma would have bet her remaining savings after investing in Rainbow Alley that it was a virtual to-do list of some sort. She took a few quick steps into the room to break the spell and Kate looked up.

"That must have been some traffic jam to take you so long. Not an accident, was it?" Kate asked her.

"No," Emma said without elaboration.

She didn't want to think about, let alone talk about, what had happened at the overpass until she'd heard Tommy's voice, until she'd confirmed he was okay.

"I'll check the enrollment lists," she offered, aiming for a cheery tone as she turned to head up the hall to Kate's new office, past classrooms on the left and the staff break room and bathrooms on the right.

Rainbow Alley's location across the street from the capitol building was a strong draw, but it had been Emma's connections with elected officials from her four years at the Hayden Commission that had generated a steady flow of sign-ups. And after word had gotten out that Governor Lange had enrolled his three-year-old granddaughter, interest had been so great there was a waiting list of twelve anxious parents still hoping they might get a space for their little one. It wasn't that Paul Lange was a popular politician. But in Sacramento, informal access to any top decision maker was gold. If Kate and Emma hadn't drawn the line, lobbyists, junior senators, and assembly members would've taken all the spots for their kids or, absent children of their own, would have signed up a neighbor's offspring to shuttle back and forth during drop-off and pick-up times when a high-level legislative deal might be cut.

Emma set her satchel on the bright blue table that served as Kate's work space and moved to the back wall of the office where a fire-engine red metal filing cabinet stood next to a canary-yellow refrigerator, all in keeping with Rainbow Alley's colorful theme. She unlocked the top drawer and removed the laptop she and Kate used exclusively for their business.

Seating herself at the table, she powered it up and was greeted by the SAT Word of the Day, a program she'd synched on all her devices: "bombastic." She typed "pompous, inflated" and was rewarded with a gold star and a trumpet playing, an indication the artificial intelligence judge residing in the inner workings of the machine had deemed her definition accurate.

She was pleased to keep her streak alive, although her main satisfaction in the game was the daily connection it gave her with Luke. She also thought the SAT game was a good way to remind him college applications were only a year away. She guessed he was like all teens in his fixation on the present, on his music and his social life, though he was the only adolescent with whom she had close contact, so she couldn't be sure. Of course, there was Tommy's daughter, Lily, but Emma hadn't gotten to know her well before she and Tommy had called it quits.

She was in the process of drafting an e-mail to deliver the bad news to the families hoping for a last-minute spot that none had opened up when her phone rang.

No caller ID.

A sense of relief spread through her.

Finally, Tommy. He must be using a secure department line.

But when she pressed the green icon to accept, an unfamiliar male voice asked, "Law, is that you?"

Emma frowned. No one called her "Law" anymore, a nickname she'd shed long ago.

"This is Emma Lawson."

"Dylan Johnson here. I'm glad I have the right number."

If it were possible for Emma's mind to do a backflip, then a somersault, she was certain that's what would have happened when Dylan Johnson identified himself. They'd gone to high school together, and though they hadn't spoken since, his was a name she would never forget.

"Emma, are you there?"

She struggled for a point of reference, for a path into the wholly unexpected conversation. She thought she'd heard Dylan had moved to Los Angeles, or maybe it was San Diego.

"Where are you?" she asked.

"Sacramento. For a few days anyway. I saw your name on an advertisement in the *Sacramento Bee* this morning. You're codirector of a preschool? That's terrific."

He sounded confident, warm, and enthusiastic, a far cry from his demeanor the last time they'd spoken, over a decade ago. But Emma found she was having trouble holding up her end of the exchange. Certainly, her emotional resources had been depleted waiting to hear from Tommy, but a telephone call from Dylan Johnson would have presented a challenge at any time.

"The article said you're also a state investigator.

Looking into good government practices at agencies and in the legislature," Dylan said. "That's impressive."

Emma didn't respond. Fortunately, he seemed happy to keep talking.

"I have to confess this isn't just a friendly hello. I'm a city councilman up in Border Lake. I'm enjoying elected office and am considering throwing my hat into the ring for the state senate seat. I was hoping you might fill me in on the ins and outs of the California legislature, how I can stay on the right side of all those ethics rules. Any chance you could get together for coffee later today? It won't take long, I promise."

Here, at last, was something that made sense to Emma, since most of what happened in California's capital was one person asking another for a favor. Still, she hesitated. There was so much to do to prepare for the school's opening. She'd promised Kate that would be her top priority. Plus, there was her five o'clock appointment with Commissioner Warhol, and she wanted to get to the pool for her daily lap swim.

But after a beat, Emma said yes. She owed Dylan Johnson at least that. If not much more.

TEN

The Jail

ALIBI PACED SEVERAL feet in each direction in the hallway outside the interview room. He was not at all happy that Leo Clarkson had put a stop to Samuel Miller's ad hoc negotiations regarding information Miller might have about Samson's murder. But there was nothing to be done. Miller and Clarkson had to be left alone, with the recording equipment turned off.

Carlos ended a brief phone conversation he'd been having at the far end of the hall.

Tommy's daughter, Lily Noonan, had been informed of her father's death that morning by two officers trained in such matters. Carlos had requested permission to make a follow-up call to her.

"Did you reach Lily?" Alibi asked.

"Yes." Carlos said, his voice low and subdued. "I asked if I could pick up handwritten notes or physical files Tommy might have at his apartment related to ongoing cases. She agreed to meet me there when we're done here. She said he doesn't… I mean, he didn't have a home office so I doubt there's much. But I thought it might be a good way to see her in person, to check on how she's doing."

Alibi's first thought was Carlos should have arranged the visit through the appropriate channels. Then he recalled Tommy's death, though tragic, had been an accident. There would be no case file, no investigating officer, no one with whom Carlos should have cleared it.

"Rachel Cogdill completed our joint training with social services for interactions with minors," Alibi said. "See if she's available to go with you."

"She's eighteen," Carlos said.

Alibi gave him a questioning look.

Officer Rachel Cogdill was a young cop, but she couldn't possibly be only eighteen. Then he realized Carlos was referring to Lily. He gave him a small smile.

"Though Lily is technically an adult, I imagine you'd benefit from having someone trained in working with youth along with you."

Carlos nodded, then pressed his fingertips against his eyes as though to forestall tears. Alibi glanced at the closed interview door and wondered again whether it had been a good idea to bring Carlos along.

He didn't know Carlos's specific family history, only that he had relatives in El Salvador. He thought it likely he was a first- or second-generation immigrant.

Which meant Samuel Miller could as easily have targeted Carlos as he had the three young people he'd ordered killed.

"Listen—" he began.

But as he was about to suggest to Carlos that he return to headquarters, to tell him he could handle this on his own, his phone buzzed.

It was a text from Jackie O.

Victim is Samson Kieu.
Age 18. In gang database tagged
with white supremacist affiliation.

Alibi read the message twice. That couldn't be right. Then he recalled Jackie O saying some white supremacist groups welcomed U.S.-born Christian Asians into their fold, provided they shared the group's anti-immigrant views. But what exactly did she mean by this kid being tagged with that designation? *Who had Samson hung out with and what had he done?* He was about to send her a request for clarification when the door to the interview room opened.

He pocketed his phone. He and Carlos went back inside.

When they'd restarted the recording equipment, Leo Clarkson spoke first. The attorney's mastery of "legalese" was on full display.

"My client overheard a conversation, which upon reflection he believes may relate to the death by the river you referenced earlier today. He would like to be helpful. Mr. Miller is interested in an accommodation to his stay here while he awaits trial and he would ask that his cooperation in this matter be taken into consideration relative to that request."

Alibi didn't comment that Miller should not have been in a position to overhear anything in the jail since he was not supposed to take meals or exercise with other inmates. If true, somehow Miller was getting around those restrictions. But Alibi wanted to hear the information, so he chose to stay quiet about that. For now.

When Miller spoke again it was deadpan, without expression.

"I'd like a fish."

Alibi was uncertain whether he was being played.

"You'd like an accommodation in your diet? You'd like to be served fish once? Once a week?"

"No." Miller said.

They were back to single-word answers.

Fortunately, Leo Clarkson filled in the gap.

"Mr. Miller, as you know, is kept in isolation. He understands it is impossible to permit him to have a dog or other more interactive companion, but he would appreciate a fish. He had fish as pets as a kid and knows how to care for them."

Alibi half-expected Samuel Miller and Leo Clarkson to burst out laughing, that they were testing how gullible he was. Then he remembered a program where inmates were permitted pet birds, and he thought he'd heard of a condemned man on death row somewhere who'd been allowed to keep a cat. An independent film was receiving awards and decent-sized audiences—he couldn't think of the name—featuring prisoners training wild horses. He was pretty sure all those initiatives had demonstrated lower recidivism rates and less violence among those who participated.

Maybe for an innovative warden like Trainor, a fish for Miller wouldn't be out of the question.

"I don't know what's possible," Alibi said, "but I'm willing to convey Mr. Miller's request with a positive recommendation if the information he shares is of value."

Samuel Miller studied Alibi for a beat. Then apparently having made his decision, he said, "The word is the victim last night was one of yours."

Eighteen-year-old cops, inmates who want a fish, now a victim that is "one of mine"?

Alibi looked to Leo Clarkson for help.

The attorney's tone made clear that this, at least, was no joke.

"Mr. Miller was told by a credible source that the victim killed by the river last night was a police informant."

ELEVEN

BACK AT HIS office, Alibi pressed one hand flat on top of the closed folder on his desk, as though by doing so he might prevent its contents from escaping, a flurry of paperwork flying around the room accosting him about the face and head in a cartoon-like frenzy. In the other, he held a chilled bottle of ginger kombucha, a drink to which Jackie O had recently introduced him.

After a sizable swig, he put the bottle down and opened Quan Noonan's file. He was only momentarily surprised when the papers inside lay perfectly still.

On top was a standard form filled with the basic facts of the case, followed by the investigating officers' notes, mostly computer printouts, a few handwritten. He and Tommy had gone through those a hundred times, or at least it had felt like it. He knew most of it by heart. But as he turned over the last page of those routine documents, he realized he should have prepared himself for what came next. Though he supposed there wasn't any way he could have, no matter how many times he'd seen it before: an eight-by-ten photo of Quan, lying on her back across the threshold of the open door to the Noonans' kitchen.

The loose, dark shift she wore hid her early pregnancy, and muted the bloodstain that had spread outward from the fatal chest wound she'd received. Impossible to hide, however, was her mangled right arm where a bullet had gone clean through, shattering the bone and rendering the limb nearly unrecognizable. A cloth grocery bag lay nearby, half-empty, the fresh artisan pasta, ripe tomatoes, and garlic she'd planned to use to make dinner that night scattered across the tile floor.

Alibi rose and walked to the large picture window behind his desk. The view of the capitol dome in the distance set against the robin's-egg blue sky was breathtaking. But he didn't see it. His mind had turned inward to memories of a dark-haired and vibrant Quan, very much alive, kissing her daughter, Lily, on the top of her head, then pushing Tommy away with a smile when he'd encircled her in a bear hug as she stood at the stove, trying to cook.

He thought about the reasons he could not let Quan rest today.

When the deaths of Samson Kieu and then Tommy had occurred one after the other, Alibi had done his best to ignore his almost knee-jerk reaction that he should make sure what looked like coincidence was, in fact, only that. People died every day in his line of work. Surely, Tommy's fatal fall only hours after Samson's murder was happenstance, nothing more. But then Samuel Miller had asserted Samson had been a police informant, and a subsequent search revealed the teen's name wasn't on the internal list as required, per department policy.

It might have been sloppy casework, Miller could have been lying, or his source could have been wrong. But another possibility was that Samson Kieu had been paid off the books by an officer for a personal, unsanctioned investigation.

Alibi returned to his desk and opened a second

folder. Tommy's personnel file. Again, on top were standard forms, this time a letter of hire, annual reviews, and paperwork regarding health care and other benefits. Behind that were several paper-clipped sets of documents.

When Quan was murdered, Tommy had refused to accept the department's conclusion that it was a random home invasion burglary, albeit one that had gone badly wrong. And when her killing was relegated to the cold case files, he'd appealed that decision, repeatedly, his requests devolving from polite to angry and, finally, to desperate.

The first set of clipped papers contained those appeals, handwritten. Alibi felt a deep ache at the sight of his friend's familiar scrawl. His looping cursive had often been unintelligible to anyone but its author. But writing about his wife's death, Tommy had taken care to be sure his meaning was clear.

Alibi reread the appeal letters thoughtfully. In them, Tommy returned to two points again and again, each time with increasing urgency.

First, he challenged the department's theory that the thousand dollars' worth of heroin found plainly visible on his kitchen counter had been left behind in an amateur heist by hopped-up kids seeking jewelry or cash or a TV they might sell, who had panicked and forgotten the drugs when Quan walked in on them. Tommy asserted this was patently absurd and that the only reasonable explanation was his wife's killer had intended to plant the heroin on him, a police officer, in his home. Even more vehemently, Tommy had insisted Quan's death had not been accidental. In the months prior, he'd received mailed threats, ugly and racist in nature, with photos of the two of them together. He believed if his wife had been white, she would still be alive.

Alibi recalled how much the investigating officers had wanted to solve the murder of the pregnant spouse of a fellow officer. But they'd had nothing to go on. No weapon, no witnesses, no usable forensic evidence. Still, there'd been no convincing Tommy that enough was being done. Alibi braced himself as he turned to the next set of papers, to the story of his friend and partner's slide into violence and darkness.

Fueled by rage and grief when the department had remained unmoved by his appeals, Tommy had conducted his own unofficial interrogations, in the process brutally beating two Aryan Nation gang members, nearly killing one before it was determined they'd had nothing to do with Quan's death. There were photos here too, one man's face a bloody pulp, his nose flattened, his jaw busted, his eyes tiny slits looking out through a misshapen rearrangement of his bones. The other man would end up in a body cast, his face perhaps the only part of him left untouched and unbroken.

Loose in the back of the file was the evidence of Tommy's hard climb up and out of his obsession. The months of mandatory counseling and anger management classes that had prepared him to return to active duty were documented. There was also a copy of an official warning cautioning Tommy not to further investigate his wife's closed case. To do so, it was made clear, would result in his immediate and permanent removal from the force.

Alibi closed Tommy's folder and set it atop Quan's.

He thought again about Samuel Miller's statement regarding Samson Kieu.

He's one of yours, a police informant.

He wondered what information Samson might have had access to that would have been of value to a cop. The kid had worked at a locus of white supremacists. Would that have been enough for anyone but Tommy to pay him to report on their activities? And if it had been Tommy taking Samson on, would he have done it as a long shot, a last Hail Mary pass four years after Quan's unsolved killing?

What worried Alibi most was if Tommy had gotten close to identifying his wife's killer after so many frustrating years, had he pushed too hard? So hard that it had cost his young informant, Samson Kieu, his life?

TWELVE

The Capitol

EMMA WAS HAVING trouble clearing her head after the surprising emergence of Dylan Johnson from her past. She was pretty sure sharing with Kate what had happened so many years ago would help, but when she'd tried to have the conversation at Rainbow Alley there'd been too many distractions from Kate's to-do list. So they'd agreed to meet in the basement cafeteria in California's capitol building before Emma headed to the pool.

Having purchased a bottled water, she selected a table in the back of the largely unoccupied room. She uncapped her water and took a long sip.

Looking around, it seemed to her as though the space had been designed to dampen the passion and fury generated by hard-fought legislative battles occurring overhead on the Senate floor. Its brick walls absorbed sound, and the lighting was not so much soft as dim. Mismatched colonial-style chairs circled scarred wooden tables. The only nod to modernity was the chrome and glass food prep area, complete with grill, a refrigerated section, and a decent salad bar.

When Kate arrived she crossed the room briskly, not stopping for a drink or food and sat down across from Emma. She wasted no time in getting to the point.

"Is this about Tommy? What happened last night?"

The bloodstains below the overpass flashed through Emma's mind. She pushed them away. That wasn't why she'd asked Kate to come.

"No. It's someone else."

Kate frowned. She didn't trust Emma's judgment about men, which Emma had to admit was for good reason.

She made an effort to clear things up.

"It's not about a man." She backtracked. "No. It is." She tried again. "It's not about a man now, it's about…"

She stopped. She'd never told anyone what had happened with Dylan.

"You're not making sense, love," Kate said gently.

Emma pulled her shoulders back and sat up straight, unconsciously adopting the posture she used when testifying in front of a legislative committee on behalf of the commission.

"It happened back in high school. My friends and I were at our usual lunch table, talking over one another, when this boy, Dylan Johnson, approached us." She hesitated. "Approached me."

The memory was captured like a screenshot in Emma's mind. Dylan had been a sophomore, two years behind her. Pale and slight, no more than five feet tall, he'd stood stock-still, his arms at his sides. Without waiting for a pause in the girls' socializing he'd spoken, his eyes fixed on Emma.

"He asked me to prom." Emma's next words tumbled out. "Without a greeting. In front of everyone, he said, 'Will you go to prom with me?' I don't remember him being loud, but he must have been to get our attention."

She willed herself to slow down. Maybe if she could make Kate understand, it would lessen her sense of responsibility for what had come after.

"I don't think we'd ever spoken. We certainly weren't friends. We didn't run in the same circles. I mean, Dylan wasn't in any circles. He wasn't a jock, for sure, but he also wasn't a geek or part of what we called the indies, the art and drama crowd. He was just a weird kid, maybe fourteen or fifteen years old when I was seventeen."

Someone called across the cafeteria to a colleague. Emma took a long drink from her water bottle, then continued.

"One of the girls laughed, kind of under her breath. Another followed. Soon it was the whole table laughing." She hesitated. "I joined in."

Reliving it this way, sharing it, suddenly felt to Emma like a bad idea. It must have shown in her face. Kate reached her hand across the table to take hers. Emma shook her head.

She didn't want to be comforted—not yet.

"I didn't answer him. I was cruel. We all were. But I was especially cruel because he had asked me."

She remembered how Dylan had flushed bright red, then turned and walked stiffly away as though on autopilot, without another word.

That night in bed, surrounded by artifacts of the innocence of her childhood, her dollhouse on the floor in a corner, her stuffed animals on the shelves, Emma had been unable to sleep, tormented by her fear that the way she'd behaved at lunchtime meant she was a bad person. But after a brief period of soul-searching at age seventeen, she'd decided it didn't. Because it had been Dylan Johnson's fault.

She hadn't asked to be put in that position. It wouldn't have happened if he hadn't started it. If he'd left her alone. If he hadn't been so horribly odd.

The next day and every day thereafter of her senior year, she'd avoided him. When that was impossible, when he'd passed close by in the hall, she'd put her head down, never offering so much as an acknowledgment that he existed.

In the years that followed, she'd tried to convince herself it had been a small thing. But she'd known all along that for Dylan, it had been anything but small.

"I would've thought you would've said yes," Kate said. "It would've been like you to adopt a stray boy, to bring him in out of the cold. After all, that's how Crash found a home."

Though Emma could see Kate was trying to lighten the mood, she felt as though she'd been stung. Kate's choice of words and the image they brought forth of Dylan shivering and alone like a lost, whipped dog, huddled without a home, made her feel she'd humiliated him all over again by sharing the story.

Kate must have realized her error. When she spoke next, it was softly and with such caring in her eyes that Emma wished she could believe she deserved it.

"So you hurt the lad—why think of it now? We all do foolish things when we're young. You're just doing too much, with your new position at work, the pressure I've put on you with the school. I'll manage things today. Take the afternoon off. You'll feel better tomorrow."

"It's not that," Emma said. "He called, he's shown up. Out of the blue. Dylan's here in Sacramento. I've agreed to meet him later for tea."

"You did, did you?" A smile spread across Kate's face. "You might have been a hard young woman once, Emma Lawson, but you've outgrown it. You planned to skive off today just to spare a bloke you haven't seen in years from a spot of pain, assuming he would even experience it that way."

Emma thought about that.

Perhaps she was being "a bit daft" (as Kate would put it) worrying about ancient history. Dylan had seemed confident, even happy, on the phone. He was a local elected official and was considering a run for the state senate. What had happened over a decade ago couldn't possibly matter to him anymore.

THIRTEEN

The Capitol

WHEN KATE DASHED out to an appointment at the City Planning Department, Emma stayed behind to pick up a prepackaged salad to eat after her swim. She was next in line to pay when she noticed Lieutenant Governor Aminah Ali-Rosenberg seated at a table just inside the archway marking the entrance to the cafeteria. As always, everything about California's second-highest executive, from her classic fitted black pantsuit to her jewel-tone turquoise hijab, struck Emma as elegant.

When she'd completed her purchase, Emma walked over to say hello.

Aminah greeted her warmly. "It's so nice to see you. Are you able to join me?" She had a bowl of soup and a cup of tea in front of her.

"Of course," Emma said, as she set down her bag and pulled out a chair. "For a few minutes."

She didn't really have time, but she missed seeing Aminah. The two women had hit it off when they'd worked together on a task force to improve early trauma screening for underserved children.

"How are things with your new venture? The preschool." Aminah asked.

Emma's first thought was the media blitz Kate had undertaken for Rainbow Alley's opening had certainly had the desired effect. Both Dylan and Aminah knew of Emma's involvement in the school. Then she caught herself as her eyes moved to the lieutenant governor's softly rounded stomach. There had been rumors she was newly pregnant.

"I understand from Governor Lange his granddaughter has enrolled there," Aminah added.

So, not pregnant, Emma thought. Or at least her question about Rainbow Alley didn't necessarily signal a pending birth.

As she was about to explain her less than hands-on role at Rainbow Alley, to be sure Aminah didn't think she was giving up her work at the commission, Senator Ted Hutchins, leader of California's Republican caucus, approached their table.

In his late seventies, he was tall and trim, with a full head of salt-and-pepper hair.

"I was hoping I might run into you," he said, addressing Aminah before turning to Emma. "Emma, it's nice to see you."

She was reminded that working in the capitol building could feel like attending a large urban high school, with its cliques and power hierarchies, where everyone knew everyone else or at least knew of them.

She liked Ted Hutchins. Though he was sometimes out of step with newer colleagues in his approach and his beliefs, he was still a highly effective leader. She'd worked closely with him on her first commission investigation. A state contractor whose role it was to assist victims of human trafficking had been suspected of profiting from confidential knowledge about vulnerable teens, committing the very crimes he'd been hired to prevent. As chair of the Senate Oversight Committee, Ted Hutchins had backed Emma up in her request to have access to the sensitive personnel records that had broken the case and stopped the abuse.

As the senator took a step closer to the table, Emma could sense a legislative deal in the air.

"I need to be going," she said, collecting her bag.

"Not on my account, please," Hutchins said. "This will only take a minute." He turned to Aminah. "I'm concerned about the addiction treatment bill I introduced. The governor doesn't appear to be inclined to sign it." He lowered his voice. "It seems foolhardy on his part, under the circumstances, but I haven't been able to make progress with him or his staff. Any chance you might have a word with him?"

"My legislative coordinator took a close look at that bill," Aminah said, matching his confidential tone. "He thinks the tax you've proposed on opioid manufacturers to fund treatment on demand for individuals could help California make real progress in addressing the opioid addiction and overdose crisis. Are your numbers solid?"

Hutchins visibly relaxed. "Absolutely. That's why the Chamber of Commerce has come on board as a cosponsor. Savings in emergency room costs alone will lower the burden on taxpayers, including small businesses, and make it a win for everyone. Can I count on your support?"

Aminah smiled. "Yes, if the numbers work. But you do know I don't have a vote."

"True," Ted Hutchins said, "but with your large social media following, you've got something even better. The attention of the press and the public. That should matter to the governor, especially now."

After the senator walked away, Emma picked up her bag. She had to leave if she wanted to fit in her mile swim before Kate sent a team of tracker dogs to hunt her down and bring her back to Rainbow Alley.

She and Aminah said their goodbyes. They promised to meet for tea and a longer chat soon.

THE GLARE OF Sacramento's midday sun and the accompanying heat had both exceeded bearable levels. Still, despite Emma's desire to get to her air-conditioned car, she stopped at the bottom of the Capitol steps to make sure she hadn't missed a text from Tommy.

She had two new messages, but both were from Kate. The first asked when she would be back at Rainbow Alley. The second, sent minutes after the first, said there were documents from the planning department that needed her signature, immediately. The brief communications were easily recognizable as Kate's trademark "get-it-done" style.

Emma picked up her pace.

When she reached the intersection and waited for the light to change, a man across the street waved a hand in greeting.

The sun was in her eyes, so she couldn't make out his features. He was tall, dressed all in black. Not a suit, it looked like a T-shirt and jeans so it was unlikely he was a lobbyist or legislator, though it could be a Friday "business-casual" look. She glanced over her shoulder and seeing no one, decided his brief motion was meant for her.

When the walk sign came on he stayed put. She stepped off the curb, and as she closed the distance between them she could see what her mistake had been. The man who had waved at her from across the street wasn't a man. Not quite. Not yet. It was Kate's son, Luke. The long, soft, curls that had reached his shoulders were gone. Shaving them off had altered his appearance dramatically.

She could see in an instant why he'd done it. It wasn't only that he appeared older, though she assumed he liked that. The few days growth on his scalp, not yet the length of a buzz cut, more like a dark shadow, gave him an edgy vibe. And while his gray-green eyes had always been striking, they now commanded attention.

When she reached him, he smiled tentatively as he raised one hand self-consciously to his head.

"I like it," she said. "Big change, but it suits you."

She knew Kate would've preferred she not encourage Luke in what she considered extremes in his appearance, but Emma saw no harm in it. His smile broadened, and she could see echoes of the nine-year-old boy she'd met six years ago. He extended to her a file folder he was holding.

"Mum told me these papers need to be signed. She sent me to the cafeteria to find you."

"Do you have a pen?" she asked.

He shook his head. She rummaged through her satchel, removing her phone so she could see to the bottom of the large bag.

Luke gestured to it. "Can I borrow that?"

She handed her phone to him, and after some effort successfully located a pen.

Luke checked her phone's screen. After a moment, he looked up and asked if she had an app for instant messaging that Emma had never heard of.

"No. But you can send a text," she said, feeling old.

She reviewed the papers he'd given her while he turned his back and texted.

When both were done, they began the short walk to return to Rainbow Alley.

Emma wanted to ask about Lily Noonan, whether Luke had spoken with her today, to confirm that Tommy was all right. But she resisted since her primary rule for being an adult friend of a teen was to engage in conversation about the teen's private life only at the teen's initiation. Instead, they discussed the latest SAT words from the game and made plans to practice driving tomorrow, whether in Kate's Range Rover if back from the mechanics, or in Emma's Mustang, at which point they'd reached her car.

"Please let your mom know I'm going to the pool, and I'll be back soon. An hour and a half, no more. I'll see you then."

"I'll tell her. But I'm not staying that long. I've got band practice."

As she opened her car door, she reflected that on their brief walk over Luke had held up his end of a conversation that had likely bored him. Not bad for someone only fifteen. *Make that almost sixteen,* she reminded herself. Once in the car, she left her door open, turned the air-conditioning on high and let it run. The Mustang's black convertible top and black leather interior, contrasting with the bright white body of the car, had seemed a good idea when she'd purchased it over a decade ago in San Francisco. But Sacramento summers were on average thirty degrees warmer. It felt like a sauna inside.

As she waited for the air-conditioning to perform its magic, an idea occurred to her. She still had Ted Hutchins's number in her contacts from when he'd helped her line up committee votes on the commission's human trafficking case.

His receptionist answered on the first ring.

"Senator Hutchins's office. May I help you?"

"This is Emma Lawson. I just spoke with Ted." She used the powerful senator's first name to signal to his staff that she knew him well. "Is he available? I have something time sensitive I'd like to discuss with him."

"Hold, please."

A long two minutes passed. Emma was grateful the interior of the car had finally cooled off. She closed the driver's door.

"Emma? What is it?" The senator's voice was clear and strong.

"I've a friend in town," Emma said. "He's on city council in Border Lake. He's contemplating a run for the vacant Senate seat up there, in the special election. Any chance you could meet with him for a few minutes, give him an insider perspective?"

No response.

"It's a personal favor," she said. "I completely understand if it doesn't work."

"Of course," the senator finally said.

Emma concluded Hutchins felt more comfortable with a personal request from her than if she'd been laying groundwork for another political favor on behalf of the commission.

"Is your friend available in the next hour? I've had a committee hearing cancelled."

Classic Sacramento choice, Emma thought. *Now or never.*

"I can check. Should I let your receptionist know if he'll be there shortly? His name is Dylan Johnson."

When they'd ended the call, Emma texted Dylan immediately at the number he'd given her, advising him that a senator she knew would be happy to meet with him now to answer his questions about launching a campaign but that, otherwise, she wasn't sure when the senator might find time.

That accomplished, she was determined to get to the pool without further delay.

She was stopped at a light at a busy intersection when her phone rang.

No caller ID. She allowed herself to again hope it might be Tommy, though she knew it was more likely Dylan following up on the narrow window he had in which to see Senator Hutchins.

Her car was too old to have a built-in, hands-free system, so she hit "Speaker" and set it on the seat next to her.

"Emma Lawson here."

"Emma, it's Alibi."

Emma's stomach dropped. She felt a sudden desire to hang up.

She'd always liked Alibi, it wasn't that. When she and Tommy had been dating, the three had socialized often. But she hadn't spoken to him since the breakup, and she couldn't think of a single good reason for his call now. At least none that didn't involve the bloodstains on the asphalt that morning.

"Are you where you can talk?" he asked.

It was hard to hear him over the blast of the air-conditioning, so Emma rolled down her window and turned off the fan.

"I have bad news," he said.

Emma's breath caught in her chest. She closed her eyes tightly, as though that might fend off his words, perhaps deflect them into some alternate universe.

"You may have seen reports of an officer who rescued a woman on the Crestview overpass this morning." He paused. "Tommy was able to save her, but he gave his life in the line of duty." Another pause. "You're not listed in department records to generate an official notification. But I didn't want you to find out some other way."

She looked up and saw the light had changed to green, but it had no meaning to her. Just green. Not red. She moved slowly, tentatively, as though in a trance, and managed to open the door and get out.

Alibi's voice seemed to float through the open window of the Mustang.

"Emma, are you there?"

She kept a hand on the body of the car for support, but it was no use. Her legs trembled, then shook, and she had to lower herself to her knees. The asphalt felt rough and warm through her thin cotton skirt. She was numbly aware cars moved close by, but it was as though the volume had been muted, that she'd fallen onto the set of a silent film.

As her tears spilled onto the ground where they mixed with dust and dirt and traces of oil, she heard only her own voice, calling out one word, over and over.

Tommy.

FOURTEEN

The Capitol

DYLAN WAS SURPRISED to find that the senior senator's reception area was smaller than his own in Border Lake's City Hall. In four steps he'd crossed the floor and reached the reception desk. He was ten minutes early, but he hadn't wanted to be even a minute late.

"I've an appointment with Senator Hutchins at noon."

A young man behind the desk peered at his computer screen. "Are you certain it's for today?"

"Yes. It was just arranged," Dylan said.

The phone on the desk rang, and the young man picked it up. Dylan could hear a loud voice sounding irate on the other end. The receptionist nodded vigorously, as though the caller could see that, then began rifling through a stack of papers. After a moment, he hung up and hurried down a hall behind him, toward the back of the office suite. When he didn't promptly return, Dylan felt awkward standing at his desk, so he moved to an undersized chair tucked against the wall next to the door where he'd come in.

He resolved to use the time before he was called to see the senator to review how best to achieve his goal for that conversation. But his mind wandered to the question of why Emma had arranged this meeting for him.

Though he'd kept up with her life in ways he wasn't proud of, going as far as hiring a private detective, it had been worth it as he'd been able to confirm that brains, power, and outsized accomplishments were still the characteristics that attracted Emma Lawson most to a man.

He'd witnessed it in high school when she'd dated the class president. Then he'd learned from the investigator that in college she'd been involved with a Nobel Prize—winning scientist, and recently had dated a former Marine and war hero.

In short, the men Emma Lawson had been with, whether rich or poor, short or tall, younger or older than she was, were all top tier at something.

Dylan was pleased his plans were falling into place, such that he was well on his way to joining them.

He wondered whether Emma had been able to tell by his voice over the phone that he was a changed man. Had she used her precious contact with the senator on his behalf because she wanted to see him succeed? Because she believed now that he could? In the end, he decided, it didn't matter. Even if it had been only a simple kindness on Emma's part, he would make the most of it.

His thoughts were interrupted by the receptionist.

"Mr. Johnson? The senator is running late. It will be about ten more minutes."

Dylan thanked the young man and this time firmly put Emma out of his mind, though that was never easy. Seated in California's capitol building, about to have a meeting with one of the state's most powerful legislators, he reviewed how he'd ended up here.

When he'd first sought a seat on the Border Lake City Council, Dylan had lost, badly. The winner, Carmela Ruse, was heir to a biotech fortune, and her smiling face had seemed to be everywhere, on mailers, in cable TV ads and on two of the three billboards in town.

But when she'd grown bored and resigned, Dylan had beaten other challengers to fill her seat in a landslide. Critical to his victory had been his newfound ability to fill his campaign coffers so successfully that he had money left over to seed his senate run. The sudden windfall had been the result of a real estate deal, an unexpected one.

Dylan's widowed mother owned a modest home in the sunset district of San Francisco, purchased decades ago for next to nothing, worth close to two million dollars now. Though it was a significant asset, she had a bad heart, and he would never have put her through the stressful process of borrowing against her home from a bank.

He was an only child, he loved her dearly, and she came first.

But when he'd learned of a man named Gregg Corbel who made private loans to people just like him, those with anticipation of future wealth due to elderly ailing relatives, Dylan had leapt at it.

With next to no paperwork, in exchange for giving Corbel the future rights to the property, he'd received $1.2 million cash in hand and a legal agreement that his mother could remain in the house until her death, whenever that might occur.

All had gone smoothly, at least until this morning when a policeman whose name Dylan had given Corbel had suddenly turned up dead. But after digging into every news report he could find, Dylan was satisfied the officer's death had been a freak accident.

He realized his thoughts had again drifted away from reviewing what he would speak to Senator Hutchins about when the receptionist announced it was time to go in.

The phone on the young man's desk rang again, so he motioned Dylan to proceed on his own down the short hall.

Dylan passed several small offices before reaching a heavy, dark wood door at the end just as it opened and an attractive young woman emerged from inside, carrying a toddler in her arms. Behind her, Ted Hutchins was bending to pick up a plastic orange excavator off the plush rug. When he looked up to see Dylan, he called to him to come in, offering him a seat in one of two matching red armchairs.

The senator's private office was grand in scale, especially when compared to the modest reception area. The richly paneled space was home to a large desk and a conference table. One wall was lined with bookshelves, and on another there were so many plaques, framed proclamations, and certificates of recognition that it looked as though the senator might have to decline any future honors.

"That was my daughter and grandson," Hutchins told Dylan with a smile. "They're frequent visitors." Apparently, that was it for small talk. "I understand you're considering a run for the District 4 senate seat."

"Yes," Dylan said. "I'm a city council member up north, in Border Lake. My background is in California history, I've a doctorate in that field. I'd like to move our state forward by learning from the lessons of the past."

It was a canned campaign line. He knew Hutchins would recognize it as such, but he appreciated that the senator nodded politely and appeared interested.

The two men spent several minutes discussing Dylan's community involvement in Border Lake, including his emphasis on youth activities and mental health services.

Then Hutchins turned the conversation to money. "It's expensive to run for state office. Compared to what it costs to compete for a local seat, your cash needs will be on the order of five times greater."

"That won't be a problem," Dylan said.

Hutchins frowned slightly.

Dylan suspected he'd answered too quickly. "It will be challenging, of course, but I have a bit of a nest egg put away, and I'm prepared to put in the time raising funds."

That seemed to satisfy the senator, who nodded.

The receptionist appeared at the door, holding a file.

"Excuse me," Hutchins said to Dylan as he accepted the file, then opened it to review its contents.

While he did, Dylan took in the many framed photos on the desk and around the room. Several were of the woman and boy he'd passed in the hall. The senator closed the folder, and his gaze followed Dylan's to the photos.

"Do you have children?"

"No. But it won't be long," Dylan responded, smiling. He had no doubt it would happen.

He pictured Emma, her belly round and firm, her pale skin glowing, her hand in his as they lovingly awaited the birth of their first child.

FIFTEEN

The Blue House

GREGG CORBEL ENTERED one last number, then turned back a page to compare.

No question, the bike shop had become a liability.

It wasn't only the growing amounts of the loans, a highly inaccurate term for funds that would never be paid back. Blood money or blackmail would have been closer to the truth, but there wasn't a column for either on the profit and loss sheet. Still, he and Marty had reached an agreement, and for years they both had stuck to it.

Gregg paid Marty hush money, and in return Marty stayed quiet. At least Marty had, until last night when in a fit of anger he'd called Gregg a murderer loudly enough for a stranger to overhear.

It had been an outrageous breach of their terms.

Fortunately, the immediate problem of the eavesdropper had been dealt with and the police were none the wiser, though Gregg might be forced to take additional steps in the future.

He thought of what Dylan Johnson had said to him that morning.

"No one has to die."

He wished that were true. But Gregg had learned the hard way that like everything else, death was a numbers game. The average person lost 3.75 loved ones in a lifetime, a grandparent or two, a parent, even a child.

Or a woman who could never be replaced.

He closed the ledger and ran his fingers across the words "Gregg Corbel Properties" embossed in gold on the cover. He'd added the second "g" to his name after Giselle had died to keep her with him, so he wouldn't forget. A baseless fear, he knew now. It had been wishful thinking that a selective amnesia, erasing his pain, might have been possible. Though he took solace in the fact that he'd been able to absolve himself of guilt since he'd lost exactly what he'd taken.

His tab to the universe had been paid.

As he pushed his chair back from the table and stood, he wondered how many could say the same.

He entered the kitchen, a long and narrow room. Everything was laid out in a line on the wall facing the door: a white-tiled counter with oak cabinets above and below, flanked by stainless steel appliances.

As he retrieved three fine china plates from the upper cabinet nearest the sink, he reflected with satisfaction that despite the wrinkle caused by Marty, the bottom line of his business had never been better.

Although flipping houses was nothing new, he'd discovered a twist that had proven exceedingly profitable.

By advancing funds to the heirs of terminally ill homeowners, he'd been able to pay much less than the market value for properties. Adult offspring in difficult circumstances welcomed the cash, while he was made comfortable financially and didn't want for more. Though some might view his business as preying on the vulnerable, shorting individuals on their assets when real estate prices were not the first thing on their minds, he was satisfied the deals were fair to all concerned.

He selected a heavy crystal shot glass and two small crystal bowls and placed one in the middle of each of the plates on the counter below. Then he passed through a door to his right into a former breakfast nook remodeled for his private use. It held a small table and two chairs, a sleek leather sofa that converted to a bed, and floor-to-ceiling cabinets painted the same white as the walls.

What he'd come for was in the last cabinet at the end.

A bottle of the finest quality scotch, a vial of potent pain pills, and a sealed translucent bag with a dozen carefully hand-rolled joints. There was also a white lacquered tray, on which he carried the items the few steps back into the kitchen.

He'd just finished judiciously pouring scotch into the shot glass, shaking two pills into one of the bowls and setting a joint gently in the center of the remaining bowl when there was a knock on the door from the main room.

He didn't immediately respond, not wanting to pull his attention away from the tableau he'd created, each item of the highest quality, each dose carefully considered, the placement symmetrical.

When he felt ready, he called out, "Come in."

A handsome man, well over six feet with even features and cropped, bleached white hair opened the door. He did not enter until Gregg motioned him forward.

He handed Gregg a thin file.

"Thank you, Barry," Gregg said. "Is the back room ready for them?"

Barry nodded.

"Good. One more thing. Please make clear to everyone there are to be no communications once the operations start."

When no further instructions were forthcoming, Barry left as soundlessly as he'd arrived.

Gregg set the file on the end of the counter and opened it. It contained two pieces of paper.

First, a close-up of a woman wearing a hijab in a modern style. She was, Gregg thought, inarguably attractive, with intelligent eyes and smooth dark skin, the color of a starless night. But her celebrity derived not from her appearance, but from her power. Aminah Ali-Rosenberg was the first Muslim-American woman to hold the position of Lieutenant Governor in any state-house in the country, which in California meant she was a heartbeat away from being governor of the fifth-largest economy in the world.

Gregg turned to the second item, a schematic of the preschool. A cursory look told him it was as he'd expected. Classrooms and offices, with a large parking lot in the back. It was located a single busy street away from the capitol building with its extensive security on-site, but that shouldn't pose a problem, not if things went as planned. Satisfied, he closed the folder and returned his attention to the three plates.

Lifting the shot glass, he inhaled the rich, smoky scent of the perfectly aged scotch. Then, careful not to prematurely spill a drop, he tipped the glass slowly over the sink so that a gentle flow carried the amber liquid down the drain. Next, he extracted the pills from the crystal bowl, and placed them on the palm of his other hand. The opioids had no scent so he used his fingers to experience them as fully as possible, rolling them over and pressing them into his skin, before tenderly pushing them inside the disposal, past the rubber guards. Finally, he picked up the joint, which, like the alcohol, had its own rich odor. He breathed it in deeply before adding it to the mix, turning on the faucet and then flipping the switch.

As the expensive disposal softly whirred, Gregg tuned into the power he felt, born of self-control and self-denial. He pictured the sensation as a clean white light, centered at his heart, emanating outward through his veins into every cell, every atom, every microscopic element of his being. Taking a deep breath, he closed his eyes and accepted his daily renewal. He continued to breathe consciously, in and out, in and out, fighting the urge to go faster, in a measured rhythm that brought him close to bliss.

But there was again a knock on the door, this time loud and uneven. The interruption caused a spike of anger that threatened Gregg's calm.

He took a long, slow breath. He knew who it was. Who it had to be.

"Come in."

A short, wiry man with flat dark hair, thin lips, and narrow eyes opened the door. He was a collection of spurts, tics, starts, and stops. The large handgun he held in one hand seemed to cause his body to tilt slightly to one side, as he nervously shifted from foot to foot. His free hand fluttered on and off against the side pocket to his jeans, as though checking to be certain something was there.

"What is it, Lee?" Gregg asked.

"The van's ready." Lee's voice was as scratchy and uneven as his movements. "Walter's picking up Kelly now, then he'll come here for me. We'll be there on time, no problem."

He continued to wave his gun as he spoke, whether for emphasis or as an outlet for energy, Gregg couldn't tell.

"I want you to take care of something important for me," Gregg said.

Lee's tics increased. He was bouncing with excited anticipation.

"Walter and Kelly will handle the business at the school. Send Barry in. After he and I speak, he'll brief you on your new responsibilities."

Lee frowned. He looked as though he had a question on his lips but knew better than to ask. Gregg appreciated how hard fought that restraint was for Lee. He wasn't a bad man. Loyal as they come. Just look at what he'd delivered without being asked. Not perfectly, but Gregg of all people knew even grievous mistakes, if deriving from pure motives, deserved to be forgiven.

When Lee had gone, he returned to the file and studied Lieutenant Governor Aminah Ali-Rosenberg's face.

Within mere hours, he would initiate a process to even the odds for the innocent. A modest reordering of the universe, but one with ripple effects that would affect the lives of hundreds of thousands.

He corrected himself.

Of millions, if future generations are taken into account.

Extreme? Perhaps others would see it that way.

But for Gregg, it was a well-reasoned and warranted play.

He'd run the numbers.

PART TWO

PART TWO

FRIDAY AFTERNOON

SIXTEEN

The Pool

EMMA PULLED ON her navy racing suit, then stored her khaki bag in a locker, her work clothes folded neatly on top.

The women's dressing room at Midtown Fitness was small and dated, with a shared shower space behind a flowered vinyl curtain, two bathroom stalls, a single large sink, and a bank of lockers painted a distressing salmon color.

As she stood in front of the oversized mirror, she found the process of tucking her hair beneath her swimming cap to be unusually difficult. Her fingers felt clumsy. Still, moving through her pre-swim routine seemed to hold at bay the grief that had threatened to overwhelm her when she'd exited the Mustang in a daze, leaving its door wide open.

She didn't know how long she'd stayed on her knees, shielded by her car as downtown Sacramento drivers whooshed by while she struggled to make sense of the call from Alibi, of his news that it was Tommy who had fallen to his death, that it was Tommy's blood she'd seen beneath the overpass that morning. She had friends who in similar circumstances became sick to their stomachs, others that experienced searing, migraine-like headaches, but Emma's legs always buckled when her heart was under siege.

When she reached the gated pool area, all the lanes were full. Fortunately, within minutes a man had completed his swim. Emma moved to the edge of the pool, took a deep breath and dove in. The water felt glorious. She focused on her stroke, and her mind began to clear. She looked forward to the near-meditative state she achieved during her mile-long workouts, the product of years of practice.

As a child, with each extension of her arms and kick of her legs, she'd imagined she was a superhero who needed neither wings nor airplane to fly. But today when she made the turn into her sixth lap, a chorus of recollections demanded her attention, slowing her skyward trajectory.

She should have known. She could ignore most things, but not loss and grief. Those were her kryptonite. Though the memories flooding her now were not, as she might have expected, of Tommy.

They were of her father, Atticus. An exceedingly rare occurrence these days. Emma had been only ten and her sister, Jasmine, six, when they'd discovered their mother lying on the kitchen floor, the pain of a massive heart attack evident in her eyes. Three days later in intensive care Margaret Lawson was gone.

Emma and Jasmine's mother had been a registered nurse, their father a self-employed artist. Whether it had been their respective roles or their temperaments, Margaret Lawson was the one who had yelled in exasperation and enforced time-outs, while Atticus had been the nurturer and teacher. He'd fussed over Emma's scraped knees and patiently helped Jasmine with her homework.

At least he had, until he'd left them, too.

In the days following their mother's death, neither of the girls had been able to sleep much. Emma had dragged Jasmine's twin bed, with its bright blue and red sheets in a rocket ship motif, into her room. Sometimes they played whispered word games, like twenty questions, long past midnight. On one such night, Atticus had appeared, carrying a large sketchbook.

"How about a story?" he'd asked, turning on the bedside lamp, seating himself on the end of Emma's bed and opening the book so she and Jasmine could see inside.

Rendered in charcoal in shades of black and gray in Atticus's broad and flowing style, a man and a woman held hands as they walked toward a tall, bare-branched tree in the distance.

When Atticus turned the page, the woman cradled a newborn, while the man was barely visible, a shadowy figure standing beneath the broad branches of the faraway tree.

In the next image, the man held a young child on his lap in the foreground and the woman was beneath the tree, a new baby in her arms.

Pointing to the woman and the baby, Jasmine had asked, "Is that Mama and me?"

Atticus had nodded.

On the next page, tiny flowers blossomed amid heavy foliage, weighing down the tree's once bare branches. The faces of the family were upturned, gazing in wonder at the new life springtime had brought. Emma remembered thinking then that their father had created a place where they could always be together. Where their mother would never truly be gone. But that sketch hadn't been the end of the story.

When Atticus had turned the page one last time, the two children, older now, were alone. Holding hands, they walked away, their postures mirroring that of the man and woman in the first sketch.

"Daddy, where are you?" Jasmine had asked. "Where's mommy?"

Atticus hadn't answered. His smile had been small and sad as he'd closed the book and handed it to Emma. A silence had cloaked the room. Even Jasmine, who typically had a question about everything, had stilled.

The next morning, Atticus was gone, and their Grandma Lawson, though ill-suited for the role, had arrived to shepherd them through what remained of their childhood.

A muffled announcement over the gym's loud-speaker jolted Emma back to the present.

It had been so long ago.

It was hard for her to believe more than two decades had passed since she and Jasmine had entered the ranks of fatherless daughters. And even harder to fully grasp that Lily, Tommy's daughter, had joined that unenviable club today.

Perhaps that was why her memories of Atticus had suddenly surfaced. Of course, there were important differences. He might still be alive, no body-sized bloodstains had marked his demise. But which was worse for those left behind, she wondered, the finality of Tommy's death or her own father's status unknown, after twenty years unresolved? Because if Atticus Lawson still walked the earth, unlike Tommy, his abandonment of his children, of her and of Jasmine, had been willful. Emma pushed herself into a sprint.

Her lungs burned as she held her breath, refusing to turn her head for air, not wanting to slow her momentum, hoping she might escape the pain of her grief and the shadow of sadness in the world, at least for a little while, if only she moved fast enough.

SEVENTEEN

Rainbow Alley

FOR TWO YEARS, Kate had been the assistant director of a large, state-funded childcare facility, gaining the experience she needed to open a center of her own. Still, she'd been surprised by the volume and complexity of regulatory approvals required to reinstate Rainbow Alley's private license. She was in the process of labeling a folder for the final forms she'd pick up at the city planning department, bearing official signatures, when the soaring voice of Judy Garland singing "Somewhere Over The Rainbow" filled her new office. It was the ringtone she'd chosen to indicate Rainbow Alley's direct line had been forwarded to her mobile. She switched the phone to speaker so she could continue organizing papers while she took the call.

"Rainbow Alley, how can I help you?" she asked.

"This is Cassandra Lange. I'd like to speak with Emma Lawson."

Kate experienced a moment of fan girl excitement.

Anyone who followed California's gossip pages knew that name. Cassandra Lange was the governor's daughter and mother to his only grandchild, three-year-old Vivian.

A journalist, an adventurer, an accomplished rock climber and skydiver, Cassandra had been open with the public about all aspects of her life, including her bisexuality. She'd been linked romantically to several high-profile men and women, and there was ongoing speculation about who the father (or sperm donor) of her child might be.

Her voice was younger and less formal than Kate would've imagined.

She took the phone off speaker, put it to her ear and gave the call her full attention.

"This is Kate Doyle, codirector of Rainbow Alley. Emma is unavailable. Perhaps I can help. I understand your daughter, Vivian, will be joining us on Monday."

"I'm calling to confirm the security walk-through scheduled with Emma for one o'clock today." Cassandra sounded a bit put out that the person to whom she expected to speak was not there. "It was set several weeks ago."

Not a small oversight on Emma's part, Kate thought with frustration, before reminding herself Emma had a full-time assistant at the commission and wasn't accustomed to tracking these kinds of things on her own.

"Unfortunately, Emma had an unavoidable, last-minute conflict," she told Cassandra. "I can show you and Vivian around the center and answer any questions you might have."

The line went quiet. Kate took the phone from her ear to check the screen to confirm the call was still engaged. Finally, Cassandra spoke again.

"Emma was at my father's office a few weeks ago, something to do with her work. He was delayed, and she was kind enough to entertain Vivian while I resolved an issue with capitol security. Vivian is a cautious child, but she really took to Emma. It's one of the reasons I selected this school." After a beat, she sounded less annoyed. "But if it can't be helped, it's fine. Shelby Moore, Vivian's nanny, will be there with her at one."

It took Kate a moment to realize Cassandra was indicating she would not personally come on the tour. "I might have questions for you about the security arrangements as we do the walk-through. Will Shelby know the best way to reach you?"

"No, I'm leaving now, and I'll be off-grid through the weekend."

Kate thought if she were under the microscope the way Cassandra was, she'd want to get completely away now and then too. A local spa package would do, though she figured Cassandra was likely headed out on a wilderness trip, and if the stories were true she'd be accompanied by her latest as yet unnamed lover. Even more reason to want complete privacy.

"Shelby is highly qualified," Cassandra continued. "She acts not only as Vivian's nanny but also as her bodyguard. You've no doubt heard some of the things we've been through."

Kate had seen news reports of death threats to the governor's granddaughter, including something about a SWAT team being called once to Cassandra's home. She couldn't recall the details, she thought it had been at least a year ago. But it made sense security would always be a concern for family members of those in powerful political posts.

Kate was adding Vivian and Shelby to the schedule when she heard recognizable footsteps in the hall. A moment later Luke appeared in the office doorway. He dropped into the chair farthest from her, then yawned broadly, not bothering to cover his mouth, though Kate had told him countless times the behavior was rude. She reminded herself it wasn't worth arguing over every little thing.

She kept her voice upbeat, hoping to pull him with her, willing or not, into a brighter mood.

"We have an unexpected tour today, an important one. The governor's granddaughter is on her way. It would be lovely if you would entertain her while I settle the details."

When she'd asked Luke, ordered him really, to quit the bike store and work at Rainbow Alley she'd been surprised he'd shown both an interest and aptitude for spending time with prospective enrollees while their mums and dads visited the center. The smiles he'd bestowed on her freely when he was little, the kindness he'd shown toward his own childhood pals, had returned to him when he sat cross-legged on the floor helping a three-year-old build a castle with Legos or reading Goodnight Moon to a sleepy two-year-old.

She thought of Cassandra's adventurous spirit and wondered what her daughter would be like.

"We had the sandbox filled yesterday. There's a tarp to keep the neighborhood cats away. Would you fold that up and put it in the shed, and take a tricycle out? Perhaps Vivian will want to ride."

Luke rose slowly and rolled his shoulders, making no move toward the door. He seemed stuck in slow motion these days when with her, unable to move freely or with any haste. Yet Kate knew he could effortlessly summon the energy for band practice or even for schoolwork. It was only those things she asked him to do that he routinely resisted, as though it were an unbreakable policy he'd adopted.

Still, she tried once more to be positive.

"When parents and nannies tour, you always keep the wee ones happy. Thank you."

She thought she caught a glimpse of acknowledgment of the compliment in Luke's face.

Not quite a smile, but perhaps his expression had softened a bit.

No matter.

Cranky and surly or not, her heart warmed at the sight of him.

She'd give anything and everything for her boy, and she hoped he knew that.

EIGHTEEN

Headquarters

IT HAD BEEN six hours since Mrs. Eloise Carp, visiting from the small town of Goldonna, Louisiana, had discovered Samson Kieu's body. Having briefed his full team downstairs, Alibi wanted this quiet (and hopefully uninterrupted) time with Jackie O and Carlos to consider theories of the case.

He stood next to a large whiteboard that hung on the wall, an uncapped black marker in his hand. Jackie O and Carlos were seated in high-back leather desk chairs at the spacious conference table. Each had their department-issued computer tablet and a mug of coffee Alibi had freshly brewed in front of them,

Before getting down to work, he asked Carlos, "How did it go with Lily? Did Rachel connect her to services?"

"She didn't appear interested." With a small smile, Carlos added, "Apparently, she's inherited Tommy's stubbornness."

Alibi nodded. He turned to Jackie O. "Have you found out anything more about our riverside victim?"

She read from her tablet's screen.

"Samson Kieu. Age eighteen. Home address Crestview Arms, 16 Crestview Drive, Apartment 4B. He was a senior at South Sacramento High School."

Alibi printed neatly in the center of the whiteboard

in block letters "SAMSON KIEU" with the word "VICTIM" underneath.

"Gang involvement?" he asked, referencing the text Jackie O sent him when he and Carlos were at the jail.

"Samson is in our gang database. He met the minimum to qualify, two of the eleven criteria." She briefly rolled her eyes, expressing her lack of faith in the department's gang designation system.

Alibi thought it made her look even younger than her twenty-six years.

"Two months ago he and a friend were picked up late at night three blocks from Wildfield Synagogue, where swastikas had been hastily spray-painted on the outside. The boys were running. It looked to the officer who took the call as though they were fleeing the scene."

Alibi recalled the incident, though he didn't think anyone had been charged or even arrested.

Jackie O again referenced her screen, apparently refreshing her memory on the details, then looked up.

"Samson had streaks of paint on the hem of his T-shirt and a bit on his hands. He said they happened to be passing by, saw the debasement of the wall and returned with paper towels dampened with cleaning fluid from a nearby gas station. He reported they thought they might be able to rub off the symbols since the paint was fresh, but when they heard sirens they figured they wouldn't be believed and took off."

"But they were believed?" Carlos asked.

"Neither had priors," Jackie O said. "And yes, their story must have been convincing, though the Wildfield Synagogue is at least half a mile from any other buildings. It didn't seem the kind of place someone would randomly stroll past." She once again checked her notes. "The boys were cautioned and let go. But the officer who picked them up thought there was enough to start a file, flagging possible gang association and activity. As for the second criteria, Samson was wearing a red T-shirt the night he was shot. I thought at the time he might be a member of the Red Vua, a Vietnamese gang."

Since Carlos hadn't been at the crime scene, Alibi knew she'd stated this for Carlos's benefit.

"But when his body was moved, we were able to see the front of the shirt. It was imprinted with a white and black logo for Marty's Wheels, a bike shop on Eighteenth Street. Turns out red shirts worn with black bike shorts are the workplace uniform. Several of the staff have a history of some level of involvement with white supremacist activities. Employment there, at the discretion of the case officer, can generate a gang tag for the database."

Alibi printed "GANG?" underneath Samson's name, then asked Carlos, "How about the questions we put to the warden? Anything promising there?"

Carlos looked at the board, frowning.

"The kid's Vietnamese, right? I mean his heritage? Last name Kieu."

Jackie nodded.

"But you're saying the second criteria that put him in the database was his known affiliation with white supremacists at the shop where he worked?" He sounded skeptical. "Isn't that more likely a coincidence? How could he have been part of a neo-Nazi group? I mean, Samson Kieu wasn't white. Isn't that a requirement?"

Jackie O repeated what she'd told Alibi earlier. "Some white supremacist groups admit Asians if they're U.S. born and Christian. Samson was both. His mother came here from Vietnam when she was young and didn't have proper paperwork to be in the country. But Samson was a citizen, born right here in Sacramento at Sutter Memorial."

Alibi glanced at the time. He doubted they'd have much longer without being interrupted.

"Carlos, anything in what Warden Trainor sent over to support the possibility Samuel Miller ordered the hit from the inside? We need to account for those playing cards found on Samson's body, imperfect matches or not."

"There could be." Carlos said. "The rotation of guards assigned to Miller was strictly limited, each a long-standing employee making good money who regularly passed routine drug testing. Seems unlikely one of them could have been bribed to communicate an order from Miller to the outside. But Miller went to the medical ward this morning before we spoke with him, for assessment of persistent headaches. Though one of his usual guards was with him, it seems worth tracking down who else might've been there, patient or staff. I've requested the login sheet and the video feed for the time Miller was there. Could be one of them was the source of Miller's claim Samson was a police informant."

"Good work," Alibi said.

He added "POLICE INFORMANT?" under Samson's name.

When he turned back, Jackie O was absorbed in her tablet.

"Jackie, do you have something?"

"I've accessed Marty Lightzer's file. He's the owner of the bike shop." She tapped the touchscreen in front of her. "He has a record and brief time inside for drug dealing. But here's the interesting part. He was identified as a founding member of Hallowed 23, Samuel Miller's organization." She scrolled down the page. "Although probation reports show Lightzer severed ties with the gang before starting up his shop two years ago."

Alibi wrote "MARTY LIGHTZER" on the board, and underneath that, "EMPLOYER", then drew a line from Lightzer to Samson. Next, he wrote "THE GAMBLER/MILLER" above Lightzer's name with a line between the two and labeled it "HALLOWED 23."

"I'd like the two of you to talk to Marty Lightzer," Alibi said. "See if you can determine whether he's really out of the gang life, and identify anything else criminal he might be into. Also, find out when he hired Samson and what kind of relationship they had."

"Okay if I take care of something downstairs first?" Jackie O asked. "It's on another case."

He nodded. "But I want you two to get to Lightzer as soon as you're done. His work relationship with the victim combined with his links to Hallowed 23 make him a person of interest in Samson's death."

While Carlos caught up on e-mail, Alibi sat down at the table and copied what was on the whiteboard into his notebook. He'd just finished when Jackie O returned. Her cheeks were flushed. Her eyes lit up as she shared her news.

"They've identified Samson's next of kin. His parents are dead. It's his sister. Here, look."

She handed Alibi a department press release titled "Detective Tommy Noonan Dies a Hero's Death." It was stamped "Embargoed until Notification of Next of Kin."

Alibi read the first few lines, then threw Jackie a questioning look.

"Read it through," she said.

He saw it, near the end. He read aloud for Carlos's benefit.

"The woman saved by Detective Noonan's heroic actions today has been identified as Janie Kieu, nineteen, a resident of South Sacramento." He could feel his heart speed up. "We've got a connection now between the two deaths. The sister of our riverside victim is the woman who Tommy gave his life to save." He paused before asking, "Is it coincidence?"

"Yes." Carlos answered without hesitation. "Tommy's death was an accident. We happened upon that girl, we didn't know she would be there. I was the first to see her and called Tommy's attention to her. Tommy didn't say anything when we stopped, he didn't recognize her. I don't see where there could have been any prior relationship between them." His voice rose as he spoke.

"Okay." Alibi said, more calmly than he felt. He hoped Carlos would follow his lead and see they needed to keep emotion out of it. "But if Tommy didn't know Janie Kieu, where does that leave us?"

They all stared at the whiteboard.

"Let's back up," Alibi said. "What caused Janie Kieu to try to kill herself today?"

Carlos again responded quickly. "Her brother's death."

Alibi shook his head. "Couldn't have been. Janie wouldn't have known Samson was dead when she jumped. Her suicide attempt happened at roughly the same time his body was first discovered. It hadn't been on the news. We didn't even know yet."

Jackie spoke next. "If her grief didn't cause her to want to end her life, maybe whatever trouble her brother was in, whatever motivated his murder, also involved her." She looked grim. "The siblings could have been into something criminal. With no way out."

Alibi pursed his lips, considering what she'd just said.

"Even so, even if Janie Kieu was into something illegal up to her eyeballs, if she believed her brother was alive would she have taken her own life and left him alone in the world? Without living parents or grandparents?" He thought of Lily, knowing Tommy would never have willingly left her behind. "Do we know how long the brother and sister were on their own? Did she raise him?"

Neither Jackie O nor Carlos had an answer, though Jackie O appeared to make a note on her tablet to follow up on those questions.

Alibi stood and crossed to the window behind his desk. It had become the place in his temporary office where he did his best thinking.

When he turned back to face his team, he said, "Carlos, maybe you had it right."

Carlos looked uncertain. "When?"

"When you said Janie Kieu jumped because she knew her brother was dead."

Jackie O said, "I thought the timeline shows she couldn't have known."

"There is one way around that," Alibi said. "If she was present at the killing. The truth is, we don't have any idea where Janie Kieu was last night or early this morning. Before she went to the overpass."

Jackie O's tablet buzzed. She consulted her screen. "It's more from downstairs. Samson's sister is out of surgery. Not in good shape, and her prognosis is uncertain. But she's conscious."

Alibi jammed the cap on the marker and threw it on

the table, pulled his suit coat off the back of his chair and headed for the door.

"You two get to the bike shop, talk to Marty Light-zer. I'm going to the hospital."

NINETEEN

The Hospital

UPON ARRIVING AT the hospital, Alibi was briefed by Dr. Raelene Walker, the physician in charge of Janie Kieu's case. She was accompanied by a man who identified himself by title only, as the chief public affairs officer for the hospital.

The doctor's tone was serious when she said that Janie had suffered numerous broken bones and a severe concussion. But the good news, the public affairs officer chimed in, was the girl's head was cushioned by Tommy Noonan's broad chest when she fell, so she hadn't fractured her skull. He added, almost as an afterthought, that the heroic officer's back had broken instantly when he hit the ground first.

Alibi felt a spasm of sympathetic pain travel up his spine.

Dr. Walker exchanged cell numbers with Alibi, cautioning him not to notify Janie of her brother's death until she'd advised him the teen's condition had improved sufficiently to weather the shock. Assuming it did. That was fine with Alibi since his first order of business was to determine whether such notification was necessary or whether Janie already knew of Samson's death because she'd been at the scene when he was shot.

The door to Janie Kieu's room was open. A gray

gloom pervaded the small space, broken only by the glow from a silent TV. A nurse seated against the wall to Alibi's right rose and approached him when he entered. He showed her his badge. After carefully examining it, she introduced herself as Nurse Meredith.

She addressed him softly, but with authority. Alibi noticed a Jamaican lilt to her voice.

"You can't be alone with the patient. Hospital policy. I'll be staying." Gesturing toward a chair on the far side of the bed she added, "You can wait there for her to wake. I don't know when that will be."

As he crossed the room, Alibi was struck by how helpless the young woman looked. Though the records said she was nineteen she appeared far younger, and he doubted she weighed more than a hundred pounds.

He seated himself as directed and glanced back at the nurse. She sat up straight, watchful.

Next to him, Janie's thin chest rose and fell. He pulled his notebook from his jacket pocket and was reviewing the web of names and relationships he'd copied from the whiteboard when Janie opened her eyes. She blinked heavily, as though to clear her vision or perhaps to be certain she wasn't imagining him there.

"Hello, Janie," he said, softly. "I'm Chief Detective Alibi Morning Sun."

"Strange name," she said. Her voice was low, her speech slightly slurred.

"Yes, Alibi isn't typical…" he began.

"No. Morning Sun, thassa strange name."

He couldn't read the label on her IV bag from where he sat. *Morphine or something like it,* he thought. "I'm pretty sure my father made it up," he said. Not something he typically shared, but he couldn't see the harm of it here.

"My brother does that."

"Your brother chooses new names?" he asked.

"He makes things up." She managed a weak smile. It seemed a pleasant thought for her.

Alibi chose his next words carefully. "That's why I'm here, Janie. To talk to you about Samson."

She looked past him toward the door to the hall, as though her brother might walk through it at the mention of his name.

That could indicate she's unaware her brother is gone, Alibi thought.

But didn't he still talk to Tommy after his death?

Perhaps it was not Samson's physical presence that Janie felt in the doorway, but something more ethereal.

"When did you last see him?" he asked.

Janie eyed the window, he guessed to gauge the light, the time of day. But the shade was down and tightly closed.

"Walk me through what you do remember," he said. "Perhaps we can figure it out together."

She tried to sit up but had barely lifted her head off the pillow when she groaned and lay back down. The sooner he could get her through this, the sooner she could rest, he thought. He kept his tone conversational.

"Do you know where you were the last time you and your brother were together?"

Janie's eyelids fluttered open and closed. Alibi sensed her drifting away. He eased off the direct questions that might tell him whether she'd been present at her brother's death, and moved to something she might be better able to recall than memories potentially colored by trauma.

"Samson may have been helping a police officer. Did he ever talk to you about that?"

She frowned.

"Did he seem to be keeping secrets? Perhaps more than the typical teen?"

Suddenly, Janie bit down on her lip, hard, and let out a small cry of pain. Drops of blood colored her chin, then ran onto her blue gown. Alibi grabbed a handful of tissues from a box on a table next to the bed. He extended them to her, then realized she couldn't move either of her arms.

"Okay?" he asked, holding up the tissues and gesturing toward her chin.

Janie stared directly into his eyes. He saw anger there. It was unsettling. Then she gave him a tiny nod. He gently blotted her lip before sensing Nurse Meredith at his side. The nurse took the bloodstained tissues from him and substituted fresh ones, periodically checking until she seemed satisfied the bleeding had stopped.

"We'll take a break," the nurse said to Janie. "The officer can come back later."

The teen's voice was weak, but her expression was fierce as she croaked, "No."

Nurse Meredith looked from Janie to Alibi and back again.

"Alright. I'll get Dr. Walker," she said. "She'll determine what's best."

She left the room, leaving the door open. Alibi could see her say something to another nurse who had a clear view into Janie's room from a computer station across the hall.

He didn't know what passed between them, but he was fairly certain "what was best" when Dr. Walker arrived wasn't going to include his continuing the interview.

"Would it be all right if I ask a few more questions?" Alibi asked Janie.

She nodded, though she was even paler now.

"Did you ever see Samson talking with someone much older than he is? A private conversation?" Much too broad, he realized, he didn't have time for subtlety. "A policeman? Did you ever see Samson meet with a policeman?

"No." But her brow furrowed. Her next words came slowly. "Maybe. Once… Samson said the guy was a policeman." She closed her eyes. "Collecting for charity."

Alibi forced himself to keep his tone even, to hide his excitement. "When was this?

Janie grimaced. "Two months ago, maybe three…" Each word seemed an effort.

"Could you describe him?" Alibi asked gently.

"No."

"Do you remember anything about what he looked like?"

"No. He was down the hall. Leaving. I only saw his back from a distance." She stopped, her exhaustion clear.

"Was he tall?" Alibi asked.

"No, but…" Then frowning as though in concentration, she gingerly made a fist with her left hand. She looked down at it and then up at Alibi, as though wanting him to see something there.

He thought about what it could mean. "Strong?" he asked.

She tilted her head a fraction.

Maybe, he thought. "Broad? Not tall, but big?"

She appeared relieved that he'd understood and relaxed her hand. He knew he was leading her, but this wasn't a courtroom. "How about his hair? Light?"

She said nothing.

"Or like mine, black?" he asked.

In barely a whisper, Janie said, "Not black. Brown." And for a moment, she looked more alert. She seemed to be reviewing the memory. Then she spoke tentatively, a single word, slurred, hard to understand.

Alibi thought he'd heard her correctly.

"Messy?" he asked. "The policeman's hair was messy?"

She nodded and he found himself nodding back, as though to cement that small detail. He needed just a minute more. She might be able to help him take the next step. To define what Samson and Tommy's relationship might have been.

"Sometimes police officers pay for information. Did your brother have unexpected spending money?"

The last of Janie's color drained. She went ghostly white. Her eyes opened wide. Before Alibi had time to process it, she'd seized up, shaking all over. He could hear her teeth chattering. Alarms sounded on the monitor. Several people in hospital scrubs rushed into the room. Alibi jumped up and backed away as they swarmed Janie's bed.

Her violent movements stopped almost as abruptly as they'd started.

Someone barked an order and one of the staff members ran back out.

Alibi thought he could see Janie's chest moving. He stepped to the side to view the monitor. A line rose and fell erratically, up and down.

She's breathing. That's a heartbeat.

But beyond that...

Alibi wanted to ask what was happening. Whether she would be okay. But he knew he had no right.

Head down, he went out into the hallway to wait.

TWENTY

The Bike Shop

THE BIKE SHOP occupied three times the square footage of any of the other businesses in the small strip mall: a frozen yogurt shop, a German deli, and a discount women's clothing store. Though "Reliable Tires" was still visible in faded blue lettering above the entrance, "Marty's Wheels" had been brightly painted in red on one of the heavy glass doors. The sound of an old-fashioned bicycle bell greeted Jackie O and Carlos when they entered the large, air-conditioned shop.

There were rows and rows of bikes to their left, from sleek silver racing models to colorful red and blue children's tricycles. To their right were helmets, locks, shiny red and black bike racks, and other accessories, as well as form-fitting racing apparel of the type Jackie O, though an avid cyclist, had long ago vowed she would never wear.

Down a wide center aisle behind a counter-height display case, a young man in a Marty's Wheels shirt identical to the one in which Samson Kieu had been shot and killed was helping a heavy-set woman with a selection of designer titanium sunglasses.

An older man, also in the store uniform, left his post restocking helmets and approached Jackie O and Carlos. He was fit and muscular, with neatly combed, short brown hair streaked with gray.

"Welcome to Marty's Wheels," he said, smiling. "Can I help you?"

"Is Mr. Lightzer in?" Carlos asked.

"Marty's in the back. I'm Ron, the manager. Are you looking for a new bike or picking up one that's been repaired?"

"We have a private matter to discuss with Mr. Lightzer."

When Jackie O had first accompanied plainclothes inspectors in the field, she'd been surprised that they didn't always immediately identify themselves. She'd since learned the practice was in place not only to respect the privacy of the person they'd come to interview but also to reduce the likelihood that, if forewarned, an unwilling witness or suspect might sneak out the back.

No matter. Ron didn't seem to require an explanation.

He took them around the side of the front counter into a long, wide hallway, painted a bright white. They passed two bathrooms on the left before encountering a wall display on the right filled with individual eight-by-ten photographs of people wearing Marty's Wheels shirts. Each was standing next to a bike, from shiny new racers like those for sale on the shop floor to an older model with peeling green paint. Above the photos a small printed sign read "Marty's Team."

Ron held a door open at the end of the hall. "Through here," he offered.

Carlos hurried to catch up, but Jackie O said, "I'm going to stop in the bathroom."

She made a show of pushing against the bathroom door, but didn't go inside. Once they were gone she moved to the photo display of staff members. It was a homogeneous group. Though her work in sociology had made her a believer that gender was a continuum, not always easily externally typed, based on appearance one Marty's team member was a woman. The rest looked to be male and all were white, except for one Asian teen. *Samson.* She withdrew her tablet from her vest and set it to camera. When she was certain she'd captured everyone, she tucked the tablet away and went through the door where Carlos and Ron had gone.

She found herself in a large open bay with a concrete floor. Three side-by-side, massive roll-up metal doors, each big enough for a car or truck to drive through, were open to reveal a paved alley bordered by a vacant field. Clearly, this was where tires had been installed and rotated, and alignments performed when the space had housed Reliable Tires.

All around her, men were working on bicycles in various states of assembly. Despite huge fans running on high around the room, it was much hotter here than on the sales floor. Several of the employees had half moons of sweat visible under the arms of their Marty's Bikes shirts. She guessed there was no point in air-conditioning the back of the shop, not with the wide open doors, through which she saw people passing to use the alleyway to test new and repaired bikes.

There was an office to her left, glassed-in on two sides with large windows facing the repair bay and the back alley. There were blinds, but none were drawn.

The sole occupant, also in a Marty's Wheels shirt, was on the telephone, pacing the floor. Though she couldn't make out what he was saying above the chatter among the repair staff and the sounds of automatic screwdrivers and hydraulic air pumps, there was no mistaking who he was. The mugshot of Marty Lightzer in the department's file was out of date, but the man in the office was the spitting image of the photos of him featured in his ads, including one on a new billboard that had just gone up by the nearest freeway exit from the I-5 into town.

In his mid-thirties, Lightzer had a natural-looking outdoor tan, thick blond hair, and straight white teeth. Like the shop's manager, he was fit, though much smaller in stature, no more than five foot five. Jackie O thought he was a good-looking man. To her mind, his modest height humanized him, preventing him from looking like a Ken doll built to order for a Barbie, right out of the box.

Carlos was chatting amiably with Ron on the opposite side of the floor. Not wanting to interrupt what might be a fruitful conversation, Jackie O followed a small boy and his father taking what appeared to be the child's first two-wheeler, complete with training wheels, out into the alley, where she assumed the boy was going to try it on for size. The father seemed to be experiencing even more excitement and joy at the milestone event than his son.

Restless despite the heat, and not wanting to be in the boy's unsteady path as he tried to pilot the bike, she walked to the corner of the building, where she was surprised to find without the background noise of the shop she could hear Marty on the phone more clearly than inside. Then she saw that the office windows that faced the alley were screened, but open.

"No, I told you, no delivery on weekends... Only four of those... No, man, beach cruisers aren't selling like they used to... You're not listening..."

She found nothing out of the ordinary in Marty's conversation, unless beach cruisers was code for street-cut heroin, which Jackie O highly doubted. The only thing that interested her was the edge in his voice. Lightzer sounded like a guy with a temper that wasn't far from the surface.

Carlos appeared around one of the open doors to the repair floor and waved her inside.

When she was next to him, Jackie O asked quietly, "Anything good from Ron?"

Carlos shook his head no as they approached the office door, which unlike the windows on either side was solid wood. He knocked.

"What is it?" Marty called from inside.

Carlos opened the door and introduced himself as an officer and Jackie O as a consultant with the Sacramento Police Department. He gave no more information than that.

Marty stood behind his desk, his phone in hand.

"What's this about?" he asked.

Jackie thought Lightzer was making an effort to sound casual, but his eyes darted back and forth between them.

"We'd like to speak with you about one of your employees," Carlos said. "Samson Kieu."

"I haven't seen him today," Lightzer said curtly, his hand poised to punch a new number into his phone.

"Do you mind if we sit down?" Carlos asked, gesturing to two folding chairs in front of Marty's desk.

Marty seemed to think for a beat, then shrugged. "Knock yourself out." He seated himself in a rolling chair behind his desk.

"Okay if I make a few notes?" Carlos asked, extracting his tablet from his messenger bag.

The mention of a record of the conversation seemed to rattle Marty. He picked up a pencil, tapped it a few times on the desk, put it down, picked it up and tapped it again, as though he couldn't commit to the rhythm.

Jackie O recognized a nervousness she'd seen in ex-cons when officers showed up, even those who'd done nothing criminal since they'd been released.

"When did Samson start working here?" Carlos asked.

"Ron will have that in our personnel records. I'll get him."

He was moving to stand when Carlos said, "An approximate date is fine. Which month?"

"Ron will know," Marty said, this time making it to his feet. "I wouldn't want to guess."

Jackie O thought it likely Lightzer hoped Ron being present might take the focus off him. But Carlos had moved on.

"Is Samson a good employee?"

Marty sat back down, apparently accepting that going to get Ron was not an option. He appeared to give Carlos's question consideration, or perhaps he was buying time.

"Samson is sometimes forgetful. You know the type—a daydreamer. He mixes up orders now and then. But the customers like him."

There was a burst of loud laughter from the repair floor. Carlos looked out the interior window at the activity, which hadn't slowed, one bike after another getting new life.

"How many do you have, six, maybe ten employees?" Carlos asked. "When did you open?"

"More than a dozen," Marty said, and for the first time he smiled. It looked like Carlos had finally hit on a topic he was comfortable with. "Two years in business. I received a Chamber of Commerce award this year for community service."

"That's great." Then, without missing a beat, Carlos said, "You have a history with the white supremacist gang that Samuel Miller started."

It had been a statement, not a question, but Marty shook his head no. Though he was not, as Jackie O had first thought, denying his past involvement with the gang.

"Hallowed 23 were white nationalists, not white supremacists," Lightzer said firmly, his expression smug, as though Carlos had failed a basic math question like two plus two equals four. Then, possibly realizing he might have taken some kind of bait, he changed tack, using a consciously measured tone. "That's behind me. Old news. I was a kid."

"When was the last time you spoke with him?" Carlos asked.

"To Miller? Like I said, that's all behind me. I've got nothing to do with the violence he got into. It's been years. Literally years, man."

"Years since you've communicated with him in any way?"

Though Carlos's voice remained even, as though to convey this was all routine, Marty clearly didn't like his answer being challenged.

"You must think I'm crazy. That I'd throw all this away," he barked, opening his arms wide as though to encompass the kingdom that was Marty's Wheels.

"Years?" Carlos repeated. "Do you have an estimate?"

Lightzer took a breath. He appeared to try to settle himself down. "Look, I met Miller in college. I don't know, seven, maybe eight years ago. We were accounting majors. We lived together." For a moment he looked horrified at what he'd just said. "No, not like that. Not just him and me. There was another guy too. We were just friends, okay? I left as soon as he started all that white power crap."

Ignoring the homophobic comment, Carlos asked, "Who was the other guy?"

"Just some guy," Marty said, looking away.

But not before Jackie O saw what she thought was fear cross his face.

She noticed Carlos made a note on his tablet.

"And when did you last see Samson?" Carlos asked.

"I think yesterday." Then, after a beat, "Yes, yesterday. He had a late shift. He was the last one here."

"Did he leave before you did?" Carlos asked.

Marty seemed to consider before answering.

"Yes, I saw him out in the alley, on his bike. He took off."

"Where did you go when you left?"

"I went home," Marty said. "Why?"

Carlos let the moment extend. But Marty said nothing more. Then Carlos said in a matter-of-fact tone, "Samson Kieu was shot and killed last night."

"What do you mean?" Marty asked.

Carlos said nothing.

Marty looked out the window toward the alleyway. He seemed to be seeing something there other than a boy trying out a bike. His mouth was set. He looked solemn, even grim.

When he turned back to face them, anger seemed to overtake him.

He spit out, "I've got to go." But as he pushed back the chair and stood, he seemed to think better of leaving. Before he took a step, he asked Carlos, "Murdered? You're sure?"

Carlos nodded.

Marty lay his hands flat on the desk and leaned toward them, his knuckles white as he pressed hard against the surface of the desk. "When? Exactly when?" A drop of sweat dripped from his golden boy hair onto his forehead.

He looked to Jackie O like a firecracker about to go off.

Then he let out a long exhale, as though he'd been holding his breath.

His arms were trembling when they fell to his sides.

"Leave," he said quietly. "Now."

That sounded like a good idea to her. Whatever was going on, she didn't have to be asked twice. Neither, it appeared, did Carlos.

"No problem," Carlos said, standing slowly, raising his palms in a placating manner.

He motioned with his chin for Jackie O to stand, too, and to move behind him. He remained facing Marty, his palms up, until she'd opened the door to the office and stepped outside.

TWENTY-ONE

Headquarters

THE MIDDAY SUN had dipped sufficiently in the sky to be at exactly the right angle to blind Alibi as he sat at his desk. He rose and hit the switch to close the shade electronically, one of the many modern conveniences of his temporary office. Then he crossed to the bar where he selected a few Belgian chocolates from the stash of snacks left behind in the hedge fund executive's hasty exit.

Though he didn't typically have a sweet tooth, he unwrapped and popped one into his mouth right away. Chocolate had worked for Harry Potter after the Dementors showed up, and Alibi figured he needed all the help he could get to cope with his growing conviction that Tommy's obsession with finding Quan's killer had played a role in the events leading to Samson Kieu's murder.

He returned to his desk and typed a message to his assistant, Nishad, requesting three hard copies of the updated forensics report from the riverside crime scene. He'd just hit "Send" when Jackie O and Carlos came through his open office door.

"That was an interesting interview," Carlos said, pulling his tablet from his messenger bag and setting it on the conference table.

He looked better than he had that morning. The color

in his face had returned, as had his energy. Still, having witnessed Tommy's death would likely hit him hard again at day's end. Alibi was glad Carlos had his husband and son to go home to.

Alibi ate a second chocolate, then suggested to Jackie O and Carlos if they wanted something to eat or drink they should get it now.

Carlos returned to the table with a kombucha for Jackie O, a sparkling water for himself, and a large bag of honey-roasted cashews to share.

"How did it go at the hospital?" he asked Alibi as he poured cashews into his hand.

"We'll get to that," Alibi said.

Dr. Walker had explained seizures of the type he'd witnessed in Janie could occur post-surgery, particularly given the extent of the young woman's injuries. She'd also reminded him the teen's prognosis had never been good. Still, he worried the stress of his questioning had caused the episode. He wasn't keen to relive it by sharing it now.

"What made the interview with Marty Lightzer interesting?" he asked, moving to stand at the whiteboard.

Though Carlos had been the lead on the interview, he had a mouth full of cashews so Jackie O began their report.

"Lightzer was clearly not happy to see us, but he kept it together when Carlos stuck to general questions about Samson, like how long the teen had worked there and whether he was a good employee. But when Carlos stated Samson had been shot and killed, Lightzer freaked out." She opened the bottle of kombucha as she spoke. It fizzed loudly and threatened to overflow, so she quickly took a sip before continuing. "Marty might have lost it because he was afraid that as an ex-con he'd be falsely accused or because he was guilty and hadn't expected to be caught. But honestly, it didn't seem like either of those. He appeared genuinely shocked and really upset that Samson had been killed. More than I would have expected for a random part-time employee." She took another sip from her drink. "Whatever it was, for a guy who has no record of violence, Marty Lightzer was pretty scary."

"I agree," Carlos said. "Still, we were able to get some concrete answers from him. He told us that at the time of Samson's murder he was home with his wife."

Jackie O smiled. "You were amazing," she told Carlos. "You stayed calm, even as you pushed."

Alibi wrote below Marty Lightzer's name on the board "ALIBI: WIFE?" Then he asked, "Anything on Lightzer's relationship with Samuel Miller?"

"He claims not to have had contact with him for years," Carlos said. "He also said he didn't hold with Miller's white power beliefs and that's why he cut off their friendship."

Jackie O said, "I don't buy it."

"Why not?" Alibi asked.

"Lightzer corrected Carlos's use of the term white supremacist. He told him members of Miller's Hallowed 23 gang were white nationalists."

"Yeah, that was weird." Carlos said.

"It's a branding thing," Jackie O said. "Those inside that circle of hate argue that 'white supremacist' is someone who thinks the white race is superior to other races, while 'white nationalist' is a person who believes only that everyone would be happier if they had their own nation-states, divided by race. It's an extension of the old 'separate but equal' vision pushed by racists during the civil rights era. Plus, based on the display of photos in his shop," she continued, "Marty's employees are all white males, except for one African American female and Samson. It's unlikely that happened by chance in a city as diverse as Sacramento. Seems Lightzer wanted a lily-white, testosterone-heavy team, with a few exceptions to keep enforcement of equal employment laws at bay."

Alibi capped the marker and joined them at the table. "So Marty Lightzer has a quick trigger temper, persistent white power beliefs, and a weak alibi for the time of Samson's death, his wife. Good work, both of you. But how about motive? Any thoughts on why he might have committed this morning's riverside murder, if in fact he did?"

Carlos and Jackie both gazed at their screens. He guessed they were reviewing the Marty Lightzer interview notes Carlos had taken.

Jackie O looked up first. "I'm not sure this is relevant."

"Everything is relevant until we decide it's not," Alibi said.

She nodded, though she still seemed hesitant. "I stepped out into the alley behind the bike shop for a few minutes. Marty's office has windows on that side. He had them open. He has a loud voice. He's not a quiet guy."

She paused. It was clear to Alibi that whatever she was about to say, it was not something she would volunteer unless he urged her to continue. "The reason we do this with only the three of us," he said gently, "is to put everything on the table, far-fetched or not, before we engage anyone else in running it down."

"Okay." She took a deep breath. "Suppose Samson was out in the alley and overheard Marty say something that revealed Lightzer was involved in criminal activities again? Maybe more drug dealing. With his record, if caught, Marty would definitely go back to prison, perhaps for a long time."

Carlos nodded. "That might be something Lightzer would kill to keep quiet."

Encouraged, Jackie O continued. "I was also thinking, what if Samson tried to blackmail Marty with the information? That would provide even more of a reason for Lightzer to want to get rid of him."

"We'll want to see Marty's phone records for yesterday," Alibi said, as he stood and returned to the board. "For the time he overlapped with Samson at work when the teen might have overheard something."

He wrote "BLACKMAIL?", with an arrow from Samson's name to Marty's.

Nishad knocked on the open office door. Alibi motioned him in and accepted a thin stack of folders with a thank-you.

"These contain the updated forensics report from the scene this morning," he said, handing one each to Carlos and Jackie O. "I've reviewed it. Most of it we already knew or had guessed. Time of death, between ten pm last night and two am this morning. Cause of death, a shot to the base of the neck, execution-style. Weapon was a standard 9mm." After a pause, he added. "Like many of us carry here." He sat down again. "There is also important new information. Turn to the second-to-last page, and let me know your impressions."

Jackie O's eyes moved calmly from line to line, her expression studious. She might have been reading a paper for school. But in under a minute, Carlos had abruptly pushed his chair back and stood, dropping the file folder as though it were red-hot.

"What is it?" Jackie O asked him.

Carlos stared at the folder. Then he looked at Alibi, a challenge in his eyes. "It doesn't mean—" he began.

"Carlos, let's bring Jackie up to speed," Alibi said calmly. "Then we can talk about what we've got."

He waited for Carlos to realize they weren't going to continue until he'd composed himself.

Carlos retook his seat.

"As you can see in the report," Alibi said, "it wasn't possible to isolate footprints on the motel side of the grove. Too many people veer off the main path during the course of a day to walk down to the river or to let their dogs do their business, as our witness, Mrs. Carp, did. But the riverside entrance to the grove, which is largely untraveled, yielded two distinct sets of fresh footprints, preserved in the damp earth." He opened to the page in the report. "One set is a man's size-nine running shoe. Forensics hasn't yet confirmed the make. The other is a size-thirteen Clarks desert boot. Those prints leave no doubt regarding the brand."

Carlos's face had taken on a gray pallor.

Jackie O noticed and looked to Alibi for an explanation.

"Tommy wore Clarks desert boots," Alibi said, responding to her unstated question. "I don't know the exact size, but his feet were much larger than average. He was ribbed about it, as guys will do. A thirteen sounds about right." He addressed Carlos. "All this does is put Tommy at the scene, if it's verified." He hesitated before adding, "But we will want to have Tommy's weapon tested to see whether it was recently fired."

"It won't have been," Carlos said sharply. "Tommy wouldn't gun down an unarmed kid. He wouldn't."

Alibi put up a hand. "You know we have to follow

all evidence where it leads. But I agree. I don't believe Tommy killed Samson Kieu. I have information from my interview with Janie Kieu that I think may explain Tommy's presence at the scene."

He had their full attention.

"Janie Kieu told me a police officer matching Tommy's general description came to the apartment she shares with Samson a few months ago. She also reacted strongly to my question regarding whether Samson recently had unexpected amounts of spending money." With effort, Alibi shut out the image of Janie shaking violently on the hospital bed, a team of doctors and nurses surrounding her. "We all know Tommy was convinced his wife, Quan, was murdered by white supremacists. If we could find out Marty Lightzer has a history in that world, so could Tommy." When he added Tommy's name to the whiteboard, he saw Carlos grimace, but he kept going. "Let's say Tommy looked for someone employed at the bike shop to help him out, off books, to share any information they could uncover about Quan's murder." He paused. "It would have been a long shot, but that's all Tommy would have had four years after the fact."

He drew a dotted line between Tommy and Samson and under it wrote "INFORMANT?"

Carlos nodded and jumped in. "Tommy and Samson must have been planning to meet last night so Samson could share what he'd learned. Someone at the store didn't want that exchange to take place. Maybe Marty Lightzer, maybe someone else. They followed Samson to the river, got there before Tommy did, and killed Samson."

Some version of that was what Alibi had also concluded. But he was happy to have let Carlos get there on his own, since he looked considerably less ill now that there was an explanation for Tommy being at the scene other than that he was the murderer. Still, he didn't want Carlos to get too far ahead of the evidence. "Some of the links are weak," he cautioned. "We don't know how Tommy first connected with Samson, what it is that would have led him to choose him."

Jackie O frowned. "If Tommy found Samson's body after he'd been killed, why wouldn't he have called it in?"

Fully engaged now, Carlos fielded that one.

"Tommy was prohibited from doing any investigation into his wife's murder. He would have been dismissed from the force if he'd been found out. If the meeting had been set for noon in a less secluded spot, Tommy might have claimed he came across Samson's body by accident. But discovering it in a secluded grove at two in the morning, without saying he was there to meet Samson as his informant would have been really difficult for Tommy to explain."

Both Jackie O and Carlos paused to use their tablets to take photos of the information on the whiteboard.

Then Jackie O asked, "What happens now?"

"First, we check Marty Lightzer's shoe size." Alibi said. "Odds are the owner of that size nine set of footprints is our killer."

"I wear a size nine," Carlos said. "I can go back to the bike shop and eyeball whether his shoes look similar in size to mine."

As they powered down their tablets and prepared to leave, a ping from Alibi's phone signaled he'd received a new text. When he read the message, he felt his insides turn cold. But aware his team was still packing up, he used every ounce of willpower he possessed not to visibly react.

AFTER CARLOS AND Jackie O had left, Alibi asked Nishad to hold his calls. He made a cup of hot tea, took it to his desk, logged in and opened Carlos's notes from the Marty Lightzer interview. He needed to engage his brain in a new activity, something—anything—to tamp down the hum in his head, buzzing and growing larger by the second, taking shape into thoughts he could not yet face. But after reading Carlos's interview notes once through, he had the distinct feeling he'd missed something important. He wasn't up to the task. He would have to go back to it later.

He reached for his phone where he'd left it, face-down, and flipped it over. At the motion, it came to life and the most recent text message again filled the screen.

Janie Kieu didn't make it.
Her heart stopped. Given her injuries, there
could be any number of reasons for that.
It was a natural death.
Raelene Walker, MD

Alibi wondered whether the doctor had stated it that way because he worked in homicide and might otherwise think there'd been foul play. Or if it was to make clear it hadn't been suicide, or at least not a new suicide attempt, but rather a result of complications from Janie's leap from the overpass that morning.

If either or both had been Dr. Walker's concerns, her effort had been wasted.

Because Alibi hadn't thought of homicide or suicide.

Instead, he'd wondered only one thing, the thing that had caused a dull pain in his gut and a one-note hum, now a symphony, in his ears.

Was it my fault?

Many times, Alibi had played a role in someone's death. He'd ordered the action that had led to a tense standoff, and a trigger had been pulled. A car chase had ended in a fatal crash. Hell, he'd even killed someone once.

But it had never felt like this.

Suppose he hadn't interviewed Janie Kieu today? Would she be alive to see tomorrow if he'd put her needs before his drive to solve the case?

He closed his eyes for what seemed to him to be a long time.

When he opened them, the chairs around the conference table across the room appeared occupied by translucent figures coming in and out of focus.

On the far side, facing him, sat Janie, her long hair in a single braid, her eyes shining, her head turned toward the boy next to her. It was unmistakably Samson, his shirt still torn, the tattoo of his namesake visible, but the smile he gave his sister left no doubt the pain of the bullets did not touch him here. One chair over sat Tommy, his broad frame filling the space, his back straight, no sign of his spine having shattered on impact from his fall. He gazed to his left at Quan, dressed in pure white, so different from the black, bloodstained dress in which she'd died.

In the chairs on the near side of the table, three more figures shimmered with the light. Their backs were to him, but Alibi knew instantly who they were. Their silhouettes, the cut of their hair, were fully recognizable from their viral travels through cyberspace at the time of their deaths: a baker's assistant, a stay-at-home father of an infant, and a young computer technician. The victims of Samuel Miller, aka the Gambler.

Alibi was struck that he felt no sadness in the presence of the room's ethereal guests. He was comforted by them, even as they began to fade.

Then he noticed the seat at the table's head had remained vacant, and he felt a chill. But he didn't flee from the now distressing fantasy. He'd learned to trust his subconscious, the way it could weave together threads his conscious mind failed to see. He focused all of his mind's energy on the question the ghostly scene raised. Did the empty chair mean there was another death yet to come?

Suddenly, he realized what it was in Carlos's notes from the interview with Marty Lightzer that might matter, that he'd failed to grasp earlier. He returned to the document and hastily scrolled through until he saw it. When Marty Lightzer lived with Samuel Miller in college, they'd had a third roommate. Carlos had made a note that Lightzer seemed fearful when he let slip that the third man existed, and he'd avoided sharing the man's name.

Alibi wondered, *Could that be important? For Samson's case, for Quan's, or for both?*

What exactly had made Marty Lightzer so afraid of disclosing the third roommate's name during a police interview?

TWENTY-TWO

Rainbow Alley

THE DOUBLE DOORS of Rainbow Alley beneath the faded sign marking the entrance opened onto a wide walkway leading to a fenced play area on one side and a newly landscaped patio with benches and small tables on the other. A smooth stucco wall, three and a half feet high, ran the length of the building, creating a solid barrier between the area the kids could access and the parking lot. The only exit was a single self-closing wooden gate opposite the school doors, with a heavy latch on top, inaccessible to pint-sized persons with little fingers. A walk-in storage shed at the far end of the building past the play area was similarly childproofed.

Luke went inside the shed and selected a shiny yellow tricycle. After wheeling it to the play area to have it ready for the governor's granddaughter, he returned for a blue scooter for himself. In his short time helping out with student tours, he'd learned many of the kids had more fun if someone shared in whatever activity they were doing, even if that someone was a grown-up.

Which was what he was, despite his mom stubbornly refusing to see it.

Last year, in Mr. Williams' class on the history of civilization, Luke had been amazed to learn that in the olden days "when the world was young" (as Mr. Williams liked to put it), by his sixteenth birthday

Luke could have been a warrior, even a leader, while his mom, at the ripe old age of thirty-one would have been off somewhere with the other elders, maybe giving advice now and then, but definitely staying out of his way.

Not deciding where I can work, who I can hang out with, when I have to be home. Sometimes living in the twenty-first century really sucked.

As he struggled with removing the large tarp covering the sandbox filled with pristine white sand, not yet played in by any child, he wished he'd worn something other than his black T-shirt and jeans. He wondered if the temperature had topped a hundred degrees yet. It sure felt like it.

He'd gone back inside the shed and was busy folding the tarp to store it when he heard someone call his name. He stepped out to see Lily, one slender arm raised to draw his attention, standing in the shadow of the row of stately oaks that separated Rainbow Alley's parking lot from the lot for the office building next door. He grinned and started toward her, but had taken only a few steps when he paused to look over his shoulder.

Luke's mom wouldn't like him continuing to hang out with a college girl, not now that the summer jazz program was over and he was returning to high school. He could already hear her droning on about the benefits of socializing with kids his own age, warning against the dangers of drugs and easy sex that carried with it disease, and who knows what else college kids got up to. The fact that Lily was a policeman's daughter should have helped, but Luke knew his mom wouldn't give anyone a pass. She probably would have locked him in a tower like Rapunzel until he was twenty-one, if she could have gotten away with it.

The coast was clear so he broke into a jog, aiming for the cover of the trees. But when he stepped into the welcome shade, his concerns about his mother immediately disappeared. Something was terribly wrong. Lily's eyes were puffy and rimmed in red.

She searched his face.

Her lips trembled.

"You haven't heard, have you? It's on the news. Because they've notified next of kin." Her voice broke. "Notified me."

Luke felt a pain in his chest. *If Lily is the next of kin, that can only mean...*

She seemed to guess what he was thinking.

"My dad," she said.

Silent tears ran down her cheeks. She made no effort to wipe them away. She stood stiffly, almost defiantly, as she watched him for his response.

Luke realized he might be the first person Lily had told about what had happened. Her mom was gone, she didn't have siblings, and she never spoke of other close friends. He desperately wanted to comfort her, but his mind was a blank. He couldn't think what to say, and a hug was out of the question. Her body seemed to radiate an invisible force field, a barrier he had neither the tools nor the strength to breach. For the first time in a long time, he wished his mom was there. He thought about running to get her, when Lily spoke again.

"Growing up, I overheard my dad and mom talk about the people he'd arrested, some really bad people. I knew they must hate him for it. And I knew about the gun my dad kept locked at home... I thought he'd...and then..." She swallowed hard. "It ends with an accident."

An accident? A car crash? Did his gun go off by mistake?

But watching Lily, Luke knew the details didn't matter. Though he hadn't known his own father, his mother had always been there. Lily's mom had been murdered when she was fourteen, and now her dad was gone too.

As he thought about the enormity of it, Lily stepped toward him and didn't stop until she'd put her arms around him. Nearly a foot shorter than he was, she pressed her cheek against his chest. He could feel the dampness of her tears through his T-shirt. It was a beat before she released him.

She turned and jogged toward her bike, locked to a rack in front of the office building.

He watched her leave.

He thought about what had just happened, about the sense he'd had that he might be able to protect Lily, to keep her safe, if only he could keep her in his arms. Or maybe, if he was honest, that she might be able to protect him. Though from what, he wasn't sure.

Luke was still thinking about that when he heard the rumble of a car's engine close by.

TWENTY-THREE

Rainbow Alley

LUKE STAYED WHERE he was, standing in the tree line that separated the two parking lots, leaning against the broad trunk of one of the towering oaks. He wanted, he felt he needed, a moment more with the swirling thoughts of loss and death and love and friendship Lily had left him with.

The engine noise he'd heard had been a large black SUV pulling into Rainbow Alley, driven by a woman he did not recognize. As he watched idly, his thoughts still with Lily, the driver began to execute a tight U-turn. That got his attention. Any miscalculation and she would jump the curb and hit the stucco wall. He'd practiced parallel parking but was still concerned that would be what he'd mess up on his license exam next week.

When the driver got out, walked around the front of the vehicle and appeared on the passenger side, he knew one thing for sure. It wasn't the governor's daughter, Cassandra Lange, who they were expecting for a tour with her kid. Everyone knew what she looked like. Her fan site had almost as many followers on Instagram as Kim Kardashian's.

Cassandra was tanned and athletic in appearance with shoulder-length, dark, wavy hair. The driver of the SUV was pale with short red hair. She wore a white sundress, flat navy sneakers that tied, and a denim jacket, which Luke thought must be uncomfortable in this heat.

As he was processing who she might be and what she was doing at Rainbow Alley, a white van pulled into the school lot. It also made a U-turn, though nowhere near as smoothly as the SUV had, stopping abruptly at an angle along the tree line ten feet from where Luke stood. On its back door was a bright checkerboard logo with "Pierre's Painting" written in a swirling black font.

The woman in the sundress looked up. Luke couldn't see the cab of the van, but within seconds a man had come into view, crossing the lot toward her. He wore a black T-shirt and black jeans, the same bad fashion choice for an August Sacramento day Luke had made, though he also had on a black baseball cap, pulled low, and mirrored sunglasses. He carried a clipboard.

The man smiled at the woman, said something Luke couldn't hear, and waved the clipboard as though it held something the woman had to sign.

But she raised a hand in what clearly was a direction to him to stop. She looked dead serious.

Then everything happened quickly, though to Luke it felt as though he was experiencing it in slow motion.

The woman pulled a large handgun from under her jacket and with both hands aimed it at Clipboard Man, this time sharply barking her order for him to stop. He dropped the clipboard with a clatter and held his palms up in an "I surrender" gesture when the back door to the van opened. A second man, dressed the same as the first, same black hat and mirrored glasses, jumped out holding his own gun, which he pointed at the woman.

The volley of shots that followed was thunderous.

Without thinking, Luke covered his ears as the man from the back of the van fell backward while blood blossomed on the front of the woman's sundress. As she hit the ground she kept her gun up, her arm extended. There was another crack, and Clipboard Man fell to his knees.

The lot was suddenly silent, its occupants all motionless.

Luke's mouth was agape, his heart pounding so hard he thought his chest would split in two.

He found that all he was capable of doing was counting the bodies, looking at each one in turn, in the order they'd fallen.

One, Back of the Van Man
Two, Sundress Woman
Three, Clipboard Man

It couldn't be. He couldn't have just seen three people die in a shootout. But as he was wondering whether they were all, in fact, dead, his mother appeared through the back door of the school. Maybe she'd heard the sound or she could just be looking for him, checking on his work. Regardless, since everyone else was flat on the ground, Luke was sure she couldn't see them over the wall from where she stood.

He was about to call out to her when, to his horror, Clipboard Man pushed himself to standing. He was staggering, left, then right, and looked likely to fall again at any moment. But the only thing that mattered to Luke was, unstable or not, Clipboard Man now held a gun in his hand.

"Mom," Luke yelled as he broke into a run, out of the trees toward her.

He was too late.

Clipboard Man squeezed the trigger. Luke's mother

went down without a sound. She was there and then she wasn't, hidden, on the opposite side of the wall.

That seemed to have been all Clipboard Man had in him.

He collapsed again, first to his hands and knees, then onto his side, groaning.

Luke didn't look back as he sprinted to his mother, giving the man a wide berth, then vaulting the wall with one hand and kneeling next to her. There was blood running from her scalp over her face on the left side of her head, more blood pulsing from her neck, like another wound, but he'd only heard one shot.

Both her eyes were closed. She didn't move.

"Mom." He picked up her hand. "Mom, I'm here."

His heart leapt as he felt her respond, the smallest movement of her fingers, as though she'd made an effort to squeeze his hand but lacked the strength to do it. He looked wildly around. No purse, no pockets in her skirt. Her phone must be inside. He wanted nothing more than to stay with her, but he forced himself to release her hand.

"I'll be right back," he choked out. "I'll get help." But he'd just managed to stand when he heard the gravelly command.

"Don't move."

What the hell?

It was Clipboard Man, once again apparently having risen from the dead while Luke had been focused solely on his mother.

Luke could see only the man's upper half, above the wall, leaning against the SUV, his gun wavering up and down as he tried to keep it trained on Luke, his strength, his vision, or both failing him.

"It's my mom," Luke said in what he knew must

sound like a child's voice, desperate, pleading, "I've got to get her help."

Clipboard Man, leaning heavily against the SUV for support, used both hands to steady his gun.

It felt to Luke as though he was targeting his eyes.

His breath coming in spurts, ragged, Clipboard Man said, "Move slowly, over the wall." When Luke didn't move, he added, " If you don't come here right now, if she's not dead already, I will kill her."

Luke's legs felt like jelly, but his mind was clear. He shuffled the few steps toward the wall, every inch he moved away from his mother an agony. He accomplished it by keeping his thoughts narrowed to a single goal. Once he climbed back into the lot, he would tackle the man, hit him with his gun, kick him, slug him, whatever was necessary, then call 911 and get his mother help. He had to stay alive long enough to make that call. That was all that mattered.

Steeling himself, he put both hands on the wall and boosted himself over, planning that as his feet hit the pavement he would burst into a run at Clipboard Man to take him by surprise. The man wouldn't expect him to resist.

Luke was wrong about that.

"Don't think about it," Clipboard Man said, edging himself along the back of the SUV until he could transfer his weight to the wall and point his gun over it, aiming it at Kate on the ground. His tone softer, he said, "If you help me, your mother has a chance." He cleared his throat and coughed. "Inside, on the driver's side, find the latch for the back of the SUV. Open it."

Luke tried to calm himself enough to consider whether he had any other play. He noticed exhaust coming from the tailpipe of the vehicle. Sundress Woman had left it running. But he couldn't jump in and drive it away or Clipboard Man would shoot his mother.

"Now," the man said, shifting the gun to point it at Luke.

Luke didn't see that he had any other choice. But as he walked along the side of the SUV toward the front door, he was caught up short by what he saw.

In the backseat was a child in a car seat, a large headset over her ears, looking down at a computer tablet where a video was playing. She was smiling—she even giggled for a moment, completely oblivious to her surroundings. Between the air-conditioning fan and her headphones, Luke realized she hadn't heard a thing.

Luke turned to the man. "There's a child in the car."

Clipboard Man was unfazed. If anything, he sounded more determined. "Open the back. Hurry up."

That was when Luke put it together. Regardless of who had driven her, the little girl in the SUV had to be the governor's granddaughter, and Clipboard Man hadn't seemed surprised because whatever this was, it was all about her.

PART THREE

TWENTY-FOUR

On the Road

CLIPBOARD MAN DIRECTED Luke to lift Sundress Woman's body into the back of the SUV.

He set her down as gently as he could on her side in the cargo space, then pulled the hem of her dress to her knees, as though comfort and modesty might still matter to her. No sooner had he accomplished that, than Clipboard Man ordered him to get into the vehicle.

Luke protested he couldn't leave his mother.

"Do you think she's safer if I stay here with her?" the man asked.

When Luke moved toward the front passenger door to comply, Clipboard Man said, "No. You drive."

So now Luke was trying to figure out how to get the automatic gearshift on the center console from park into drive.

Not that he had any intention of taking Clipboard Man wherever it was he wanted them to go, because when the man had gotten into the SUV and pulled the passenger door shut after him, his shirt had risen an inch to reveal a gaping hole leaking blood from his abdomen just above his jeans.

That's when Luke had formulated his plan.

He would move slowly, drive slowly, buy time until Clipboard Man bled so much he either passed out or died. But for now, he figured he'd stalled as long as he could. He didn't want to anger the man while he still had some strength left, not with the gun resting on his thigh.

A small, clear voice came from the back seat.

"Where's Shelby?"

It wasn't that Luke had forgotten about the girl. But she'd been so quiet, and what with Clipboard Man pointing the gun at him and then at his mother, Luke's attention had been elsewhere.

Clipboard Man mouthed "you" so Luke turned in his seat to respond.

Against her chest, the girl hugged a small blue bunny with floppy ears, a frayed blue-and-white-checked ribbon around its neck. Luke hadn't noticed the stuffed toy when he'd first seen her, though he realized now he hadn't noticed a lot of things. The child's hair was short, glossy, and black with bangs. She wore a sleeveless white top with a pleated red skirt, white socks, and shiny black shoes that buckled on the sides. Her nails were painted a pale pink, and in each of her earlobes was a single miniature pearl.

"Shelby is talking to your teacher," Luke said as calmly as he could, though his heart tore at the thought of the body in the back of the car, the dead woman who now had a name.

The girl frowned.

"Who are you?"

After a beat he answered, "I'm the school driver."

She seemed to think about that.

"Where are we going?" she asked.

"To pick up another child for school," Luke said.

"Who is he?" she asked, pointing at Clipboard Man.

Luke said, "He knows how to get to the other child's home."

He hoped his lies added up to a believable story, because he didn't know how the man might react if the girl started crying or protesting.

He didn't think it would be good.

Clipboard Man made a rolling motion with the gun, indicating Luke should move things along, so Luke returned his gaze to the front. He put his hands on the wheel at "ten and two," just like he'd learned in driver's education, though his palms had never been this slippery with sweat.

He did his best to concentrate on driving the unfamiliar vehicle, following each direction as Clipboard Man called it out. But an image of his mother, blood thick in her hair, was superimposed on everything he saw. He experienced a sudden impulse to plow the SUV into a solid barrier, a wall or a building, anything that would kill the man next to him, the man who had shot her.

But he kept driving.

There was, of course, the girl.

And in that last moment, before Clipboard Man had caught him, had captured him, had forced him to drive, Luke's mother had squeezed his hand. She was alive and she would need him. He would take care of her.

But first, he had to survive this.

Up ahead, he saw the entrance to several freeways. He was glad he'd practiced on the highway with the driving instructor, though he still felt his heart speed up. He was nervous about how fast they'd be traveling, and he didn't like the idea of leaving downtown, of being farther away from his mom.

"Take the 113 North." Clipboard Man said, his voice low, his breathing labored. "Exit at Linville."

It was some small relief that they weren't headed to an unknown destination. Luke knew the small town,

and he could get there all right. Emma had a friend in
Linville with a kid Luke's age. She'd taken him every
month or so to visit since he first moved to the States.
They'd pack a picnic lunch or go to the Linville Creek
Café for lemonade and pie. He remembered it as being
about thirty minutes from Sacramento, though it sometimes took much longer if traffic was bad.

He merged onto the freeway, bringing the SUV grad-
ually up to speed.

Clipboard Man shifted in his seat, one hand pressed
flat against his stomach. Luke could see blood seeping
around it, through his fingers. He tried to think ahead.

He considered whether once they'd exited the freeway and had come to an intersection or a stop sign, he
could manage an escape. Maybe get his seat belt un-
done, roll out of the car when it wasn't moving, open
the back door and get the girl out. But when he looked
to his right, as though considering changing lanes, he
saw the man's eyes were still watchful, his finger resting near the trigger of his gun.

He'd never be able to get the little girl unbuckled
from her car seat before the man started shooting.

Luke wasn't sure how much longer he could take this.

All of it. Any of it. The bodies, the blood, and a child
whose only hope was him.

He worked on summoning a positive thought. Gunfire in downtown Sacramento wasn't commonplace.
Someone must have reported it, which meant his mom
should be at the hospital by now. And the girl's absence
couldn't possibly go unnoticed for long. She was the
governor's granddaughter. Once someone realized she
was missing, every resource in the state would be mo-
bilized to find her. *Doctors at his mom's side. SWAT*

teams on their way. Luke tried hard to hold on to those images, but doubt crept in. It had been over so quickly.

Back of the Van Man had shot Shelby. Shelby had shot that man and Clipboard Man. Clipboard Man had shot his mom. *Had it taken more than a minute?* With downtown traffic noise and that big rally across the street, maybe no one had noticed.

Then he thought of Emma. She'd gone to swim laps at the pool and said she'd be back at Rainbow Alley in an hour and a half. It must have been almost that long already. When she got to the school, everything would be all right. She would get his mom to the hospital and she would find a way to save him and the little girl.

Luke focused his energy into sending Emma a telepathic message. Into telling her to hurry. He didn't care if that was crazy. This whole thing was crazy.

Crazy was all he had right now.

TWENTY-FIVE

The Blue House

THE SOARING TONES of the violins and flutes of Vivaldi's *La Stravaganza* drifted toward Gregg through the open doorway at the end of the hall. He stepped forward until he could glimpse Barry, shirtless, his pale muscled back flexing, executing rapid-fire push-ups in perfect form on the thickly carpeted floor.

Gregg was glad he'd made Barry his second-in-command. Studies had shown self-discipline has a greater influence on success than intelligence, and Barry made self-discipline a way of life.

But even though he was sure Barry would have gotten everything ready, Gregg wanted to see for himself. He turned back up the hall and entered the first room on his left.

Inside, a twin bed was neatly made. A student-style desk sat beneath the single window. He crossed to it and opened the drapes. He noted the alarm sensors in place along the aluminum slider's closure. Nothing fancy, the do-it-yourself kind, he hadn't wanted a record with a security company for this house. But Barry had put them in, which meant they'd been thoroughly tested and would do the job.

The view outside was pleasant, a dense line of evergreen hedges under a brilliant summer sky.

He passed through the shared bathroom, a tiny, all-white space, into a mirror image room on the other side. It was set up as a den with a sofa, a folding card table, and a couple of chairs. Gregg had thought his men would come here in their downtime, but they kept to the large master in the back, where Barry was now. That had worked out well because Gregg liked the small room's uninhabited character. It gave him the feeling of being insulated from the masses that moved through the world without a plan, who foolishly heralded spontaneity as a virtue.

For a time after Giselle's death, Gregg had been one of them. Back then, he'd let social norms dictate his behavior, and his greatest fear had been of being alone. It had seemed a punishment to have no one to hold, no one's voice to break the silence but his own.

That had all changed when he'd chosen a life of abstinence, not only foregoing mind-altering substances, but also turning his back on the judgment of others.

Placing two fingers on the inside of his wrist, he checked his pulse.

Ninety-five. Elevated. That was fine, since it was a product of anticipation, not worry.

He'd have twenty-four hours with the girl.

Plenty of time.

Cassandra Lange was out of reach by phone or e-mail, counting on her reliable nanny to take good care of her daughter until Sunday night, which the reliable nanny would do, although in far different circumstances than the girl's mother had in mind. And with Cassandra unconcerned, no one would sound the alarm.

No one would even know Vivian Lange was missing so long as Walter and Kelly followed the plan at the school. Quick and clean, in and out. Gregg was pleased he'd made the last-minute adjustment in Lee's duties.

No telling what might have happened if he'd been there, waving his gun around. True, Lee's new role was important, acting as an added layer of security for the lieutenant governor at the Muslim Americans for Justice Rally. But it wasn't rocket science.

The unexpected sound of multiple beeps from the home's alarm system, indicating it had been disengaged, jolted Gregg from his thoughts.

They shouldn't be here yet.

He hastily considered his options. The only way to his private room off the kitchen, where he was supposed to be, out of sight when they arrived, was to go back into the open hallway.

The nanny would be blindfolded. But what if the girl saw him?

He'd researched the credibility of eyewitness testimony from very young children and had felt confident enough that it could be dismissed by a good attorney that he'd let his staff be seen by the girl. But he wasn't willing to extend that risk to himself.

Tense, he moved silently to close and lock both doors to the den, when he heard Lee's excited voice call out.

"Barry, where are you?"

Gregg threw open the hallway door, forcing Lee back a step.

He couldn't believe it.

"Lee, what on earth are you doing here?"

TWENTY-SIX

The Blue House

GREGG ASKED THE question because he wanted an answer. But the words coming out of Lee's mouth in response as he twitched and bounced were anything but helpful.

"I went to the rally like Barry told me to and she came, the lieutenant governor, Alabama-Roseberger, right?" He paused, clearly uncertain about the name, then swallowed hard and kept going. "I was ready, no problem. There were a lot of people, really a lot of people, but I figured out the best place to stand. I would have seen any shooter. I could have stopped him in his tracks. There's no way he would have gotten her. I was ready."

It felt to Gregg like a long windup by a minor league pitcher before the ball slips from his grasp and rolls down the mound, never reaching the batter's box. Fortunately, Barry appeared from the room at the end of the hall.

"Please take over with Lee," Gregg said to him. "I think a debrief would be helpful."

"No," Lee said, shaking his head and stepping back away from Barry, looking like a ten-year-old who had just been called to the woodshed for a whooping.

Barry spoke calmly. "Let's go to the front room, Lee, so we can hear when they arrive."

Then he turned the corner from the hall into the main room without looking back. Lee hesitated, but after a beat shuffled after him. Gregg passed them both and went into the kitchen, where he could smell the results of Barry's morning baking.

Cheddar and jalapeño muffins were covered on a plate on the table under the front window. He selected one and returned to stand by the open door to the main room. He always learned something from Barry's debriefs.

Barry had seated himself in one of the two armchairs while Lee paced in ever-widening circles in front of him.

Without commenting on his apparent need to be in motion and without telling him to sit down, Barry asked, "Do you remember the three components of the debrief?"

Lee nodded, though his eyes darted around the room as though he was hoping he wouldn't have to take a quiz.

"Good," Barry said. "One, what was the mission's objective?

Lee smiled. He appeared confident, like he knew this one. "To protect the lieutenant governor against all threats, taking down any shooter without hesitation if necessary."

Barry nodded at the memorized response, then asked, "Two, did you achieve the mission objective?"

As Lee started to open his mouth, Barry added, "A one-word answer, please."

Lee began another circle, his head down, before coming to an unstable stop and saying, "Yes?"

Gregg smiled to himself. It was one word, but it

hadn't been an answer. It was another question. He was interested to see how Barry would handle it.

"'Yes,' meaning you accomplished your mission?" Barry asked. "Or do you have some uncertainty about that?"

Lee looked relieved he would have a chance to explain.

"Yes. Not to the uncertainty part. No. Not that. But yes. Because she didn't get hurt. And she couldn't get hurt because her security had decided the threat was too big for her to stay outside for her speech. They worked out for her to do her part from inside the building in a secure space. They put up a big screen outside. So my mission was accomplished because she was protected. Completely protected. There wasn't any way for anyone to harm her."

Lee took a deep breath and looked at Barry.

Barry, his expression unchanged, gave no indication whether that had been an acceptable answer or not. He moved on.

"Three, what would you do differently on that operation, if you could?"

Lee screwed up his face in apparent concentration and walked in another, larger circle. Then he shrugged. "Nothing?"

Barry said, "Perhaps if given a similar assignment, you might stay throughout the rally. To the end. In case something changed that required your presence."

Lee looked confused. "But—"

"There are circumstances under which you might have been needed." Barry had cut in calmly, his voice still even. "For example, the audiovisual equipment might have failed, and they could have moved the target back outside. Or the target might have decided she didn't like being inside and insisted on going out where she was at risk."

Lee dropped his eyes, patted his front pocket, and took another walk in a circle, then another.

Gregg turned away. As he crossed the kitchen toward his office he reflected that the end of a debrief was always the most important. When, hopefully, a difficult balance had been achieved. Because chastened staff would strive to do better, but men who felt demeaned could present a grave internal danger to leadership and to the mission.

Barry will handle it, Gregg thought. *He always does.*

He smiled when he heard Barry say, "Would you like a muffin, Lee? I made some fresh."

GREGG SAT DOWN, intending to review this month's costs. They seemed a little high. But when his eyes fell on the gold-embossed second "G" in his name on the ledger's cover, honoring his wife, Giselle, he stopped. He thought about the debrief he'd just witnessed, and given the importance of the operation underway today, he wondered if it might be time for him to finally formally debrief the shooting four years ago.

After a moment, with some trepidation (he felt a little like Lee, there would be no gold star for him at the end of this), he mentally walked through the steps.

One, what was your mission?

That was easy to answer. The mission had been to smear the reputation of Thomas Noonan, a white police officer who had married a brown woman and who had flaunted her as though she were his equal.

Two, did you accomplish your mission?

The first answer that crossed Gregg's mind was not an answer at all. Just like Lee, he wanted to say, "Yes?"

He sat with that feeling for a moment, forcing himself to exercise self-discipline in order to assess the outcome of his mission accurately. After careful thought, he felt the right response was an unequivocal "yes". They accomplished their mission. In fact, they'd done so beyond their wildest dreams. They'd never expected the drug charges to stick, but Samuel had been right that just the investigation, without a conviction, would end Noonan's chances for promotion.

It was the next step in the debrief that Gregg, like Lee before him, dreaded.

Three, what would you do differently on that operation, if you could?

Gregg had suffered great pain and remorse after the shooting at Officer Noonan's apartment four years ago. He had changed his behavior fundamentally as a result, and then had put the horror of what happened away. He didn't think about it. He supposed he didn't allow himself to. But now faced with the purpose of a debrief, to not permit errors of judgment to hide, to assess them honestly without emotion so no gains made could be lost to subconscious and dormant weakness, Gregg dredged up the memories and answered question three as unflinchingly as he could.

If he had the chance to do it over, he would have been sober, of clean mind and body, every day, but especially on that day four years ago.

Completely sober, instead of clumsy and dopey from the opioids, angry from the alcohol, and paranoid from extraordinary amounts of weed so that when the kitchen door had opened he'd whirled and "seen" (hallucinated, really) Officer Thomas Noonan, gun drawn.

And doped up, drunk, and high, thinking he was under attack, Gregg had fired. It wasn't until he stood by her fallen body that he'd realized he'd killed a woman, a pregnant woman, Tommy Noonan's wife. Had Marty not hustled him out of there, sobbing, barely able to walk, he would've lain down beside Quan Noonan, and without a second thought shot himself in the head.

He opened the ledger and took a long, deep, cleansing breath.

Debrief complete. Lessons learned and changes made. The operation today was planned and undertaken with a clear head. It would be marked by no such errors. There would be no unnecessary and accidental loss of life.

He didn't realize he was crying until his tears fell onto the neatly penciled numbers on the page, blurring them beyond recognition.

There was a sharp knock on the door.

Gregg cleared his throat and raised his voice to be heard.

"Are they here? Are we ready?"

TWENTY-SEVEN

Rainbow Alley

IT DIDN'T MATTER how many times Emma had driven past California's capitol building, she was always affected by it. Despite having witnessed firsthand the partisan battles for power and the outright stupidity sometimes on display in its halls, the white-domed symbol of democracy never failed to lift her up, to give her some measure of hope for the future.

As she signaled to turn into the Rainbow Alley lot, she saw a white van parked along the tree line. She was relieved. It must be the painters because they were the only work crew scheduled for today.

There'd always been the possibility they wouldn't show, and she felt it important that the sign be bright and welcoming for the kids on their first day, now only a weekend away. Of course, there might be other things they hadn't thought of, but she reassured herself that with Kate's lists and her own approach of tackling whatever seemed most immediate, they'd have everything ready in time.

As she parked in the drop-off area along the curb, she saw the back door to the van was open. With no one at work yet on the sign, she figured they'd just arrived and were unloading. Slinging her satchel over one shoulder, she crossed the lot to greet them.

She stopped short at the sight of a pair of black trainers sticking out on the pavement just past the open van door. She took a few more steps and saw they belonged to a man who lay on his back. His arms were thrown wide, his face shattered and unrecognizable beneath a mass of blood. He wore a black T-shirt and black jeans, his head was shaved, and for a horrible split second, Emma thought it was Luke.

But the guy's shoes were wrong. Luke never wore standard trainers, only Converse.

Numb, her next thought was *why would someone shoot the painter?* Then it occurred to her a far more pressing question was *where is the shooter now?*

She scanned the line of trees, the play area, and the patio. She saw no one. There was a large handgun on the ground several feet from the body. She instinctively stepped back from it.

Her call to 911 immediately connected.

"There's been a shooting," she said. She gave the address. The operator, having taken it down along with Emma's assessment that the painter was definitely dead, asked if there was anyone else there.

Emma gasped. Luke had said he was going to band practice, but Kate could be inside.

She eyed the gun on the ground. She'd never win in a shoot-out, but if the attacker was in the building and Kate was at risk, if she had a weapon she might be able to bluff. To stall until the police arrived. She had to try.

She told the operator she would leave the line open, and over his protests set the phone down and retrieved the gun. It was sticky with the fallen man's blood. Her stomach roiled as she wiped it on her skirt. But clasping it firmly, she moved to the gate, pushed it open, and nearly stepped on Kate.

She sank to her knees. She felt as though she'd been struck.

Kate lay perfectly still, blood matted on the side of her head, a deep red stripe down her face, the rest ghostly white. Trembling, Emma leaned down and placed her cheek next to Kate's mouth.

She felt a faint movement of air. *A breath*. Still, Emma couldn't stop shaking.

Then she became aware of the weight of the gun she'd let fall in her lap. She put her hand on it. She felt a bit better. She had a weapon to protect them if the shooter came back, and she'd called 911. They must be on their way.

Still, she felt a desperate need to do more.

She hadn't been raised with prayer, and wasn't in the habit of it. But she concentrated on laying her thoughts bare, on asking that Kate be allowed to live. She took Kate's hand and urged her to hold on so that she might go home to Luke.

To her boy, who needed her.

If this were a movie, Emma thought, *Kate would open her eyes now.*

She would smile through her pain, maybe even say something funny.

Kate did none of that.

So Emma kept up her prayers and her pleas, over and over.

A mantra, a rhythm, CPR for the soul.

Let her live. Please, let her live.

She was so engrossed in her self-appointed task that

she didn't hear the sirens, and she didn't notice Alibi when he knelt beside her.

She wasn't aware he was there until he put his hand lightly on her arm and said, "Emma, let go. You need to let go."

TWENTY-EIGHT

The Hospital

THEY'D GIVEN EMMA something for the shock, told her
to lie down, and she realized now she must have fallen
asleep. Afternoon sunlight streamed through the sparkling clean pane of an unfamiliar window. The view
held nothing but clear sky in all directions, a blanket
of blue.

When she sat up, Alibi was leaning against the door-
frame to the hall.

He took a step into the room.

"Where's Kate?" she asked.

"She's…" He hesitated. "You've been given a seda-
tive, nothing strong, but—"

"She's what? Kate's what? She's alive? She's…"
Emma was unable to finish.

Alibi approached the bed. He put his hand gently
on her arm. She recalled him making the same gesture
when she'd been kneeling next to Kate on the ground.

Kate, bleeding from the head.

She pulled away.

He stepped back. "She was alive when they brought
her in," he said. "I don't know more than that."

Emma took a deep, shuddering breath. Alive was
good. Alive was a relief.

But it wasn't enough.

"Please, find someone who does know," she said.

A YOUNG WOMAN with curly red hair wearing a white coat over a lavender dress shirt and black pants was walking his way, her head down, reviewing a chart.

"Excuse me," Alibi said. "I'm Detective Morning Sun."

She raised her head.

"Are you here to see Dr. Walker? I'm so sorry about—"

She was one of the team who'd rushed into Janie Kieu's room.

"No. Thank you," he said, cutting her off. He didn't want to think about Janie. Not now.

"The woman in the room behind me needs an update on the condition of a patient who was just brought in. A gunshot victim. Kate Doyle."

"I'll call downstairs," she said. "Was the injury serious?"

"She was shot in the head at close range."

The young woman winced.

Alibi looked at her badge. Yasuko Fukuda, MD. He wondered how many gunshot wounds she'd treated or seen. She didn't look like she could have been doing this long. Still, too many, he was sure.

"I'll make the call," she said.

Dr. Fukuda walked back the way she'd come. Her pace had quickened, the chart in her hands forgotten.

Alibi took his phone from his pocket and was about to call Jackie O to check on the lead he'd given her when he noticed a small sign on the wall directly across from him.

A phone in a circle with a red line through it.

Looking both ways, he saw identical signs posted every ten feet or so. Though he figured the prohibition might not be enforced inside patients' rooms, the things

he needed to say couldn't be said in front of Emma.
As he was deciding which way to go to locate a public
space in which he could make the call, perhaps a lounge
or balcony, two men emerged from the elevator at the
end of the hall.

One wore a white coat and wire-rimmed glasses. His
dark hair was generously streaked with silver. Next to
him, a younger man had thick, short brown hair and a
tidy mustache. His suit and tie were conservative in cut
and color, and his shoes looked recently shined, motionless on the footrest of his wheelchair.

When they reached Alibi, the younger man asked,
"Detective Morning Sun?"

Alibi nodded.

Dr. Fukuda had done well. It looked like he would
get information about Kate's condition in person.

"I'm Jason Field, the hospital's community liaison.
This is Dr. Eric Ball, Chief of Neurosurgery." Field
pulled a computer tablet from a bag on the side of his
chair. "We understand you're interested in an update
on Kate Doyle's condition to provide to a woman who
is here. Of course, we're able to share information with
you since Ms. Doyle came in as a result of a criminal
action. We will do all we can to help with your investigation. But we have restrictions on sharing patient
information beyond law enforcement and other designated individuals."

"Emma Lawson is a witness," Alibi said. "She was
with Ms. Doyle at the scene when I arrived there." He
added, "Kate Doyle is her best friend."

Field referred to his tablet.

"Emma Lawson? Spelled L-A-W-S-O-N?" he asked.

Alibi nodded.

"Then there's no problem. Ms. Lawson is listed as

Ms. Doyle's next of kin. She controls her health directive. We would have had to call her anyway."

When they entered Emma's room she was coming out of the small bathroom at the foot of the bed. She'd made an attempt to remove the bloodstains from her jacket and skirt. They were damp with water and less pronounced, but still visible on the light green fabric of her suit.

The cop in Alibi felt an automatic concern at evidence lost.

Since he'd discovered Emma holding Kate's hand as she bled, at least some of the blood was almost certainly Kate's. But Emma had had a gun in her lap when he found her, one that had recently been fired. And the crime team had reported they'd found spots of blood away from both where Kate was lying and the location of the body of the unidentified young man, presumed to be a painter. It would be less than due diligence if he didn't make certain Emma's clothing hadn't been marked with blood from the shooter, who it now appeared had been injured. He'd have to see if the hospital staff could get her something else to wear home.

Emma moved to stand next to him, a bit unsteady on her feet. Her eyes didn't leave the doctor.

"Ms. Lawson, I'm Dr. Eric Ball. Ms. Doyle is comfortable. She's not in any pain."

Alibi felt Emma slide her hand into his, though she didn't look at him. Her jaw was firmly set.

He assumed she must be thinking what he was thinking.

That if "no pain" was the good news the doctor chose to lead with, the bad news could be anything awful they might imagine.

"We don't know much yet," Dr. Ball said, as though

reading their thoughts. "The bullet entered here." He touched above his left eye. "Then traveled on the outside of her skull, here, before moving down this trajectory into her shoulder." His fingertips carefully traced the path.

Emma squeezed Alibi's hand so tightly that it hurt. "Does that mean—?"

"We don't know the extent of her injury," Dr. Ball said before Emma could complete her question. "We could see on the scan that the force of the bullet caused small fragments of a thin bone in her skull to break off."

Without warning, Emma collapsed to her knees.

Without a sound.

Alibi was pulled down with her, she was still holding his hand. The doctor took a hurried step toward them. Field wheeled his chair backward toward the bed and pressed a red button.

"I'm all right," Emma said. "I'm all right," She waved off the doctor with her hand.

Alibi helped her up, an arm around her waist. She leaned into him as he guided her to a chair by the bed.

"I didn't faint," she said firmly, looking at the doctor. "I have weak knees, that's all. I need to hear anything else you can tell me."

Alibi recognized in Emma a state familiar to him, what he thought of as his "analytical mode," where it seemed only new information might offer a way out of whatever nightmare was taking place.

Dr. Ball asked, "Weak knees? Does that happen often?"

Emma looked annoyed. "If you insist, we can do my neurological workup another time. Right now, I have to know Kate's condition in order to exercise my responsibilities as her health care proxy."

The doctor gave a small, frustrated smile.

Alibi thought he probably recognized a stubborn patient when he saw one.

"Ms. Doyle is heavily sedated while we wait for the swelling in her brain to subside. This is normal procedure. We want to make sure everything is as we need it to be before we make a decision about any surgeries." The doctor paused, his tone softened. "At this time, we don't expect the injury to be life-threatening, although there is always the possibility of infection or other problems. But it could be life-altering in some way. Besides any possible difficulties with the brain, there may be nerve damage to her face, as well as hearing issues."

Emma took a quick sharp breath, but she didn't move.

Her back straight, she said nothing.

Jason Field consulted the computer tablet he'd taken from his bag. "Ms. Lawson, I'd like to confirm some things with you. Since Ms. Doyle has given you decision-making power over her health care, it will be important that we have your current information so that when you leave the hospital, we can get in touch with you quickly."

"Leave?" Emma sounded alarmed. "I'm not leaving. If you need this room, I can wait downstairs."

"No, that's not necessary," Field said. "We understand from the detective that there are special circumstances. We can keep the room for your use for as long as it's needed."

Emma gave Alibi a warm look and a grateful smile. He felt a sharp stab of guilt. She seemed to think he'd arranged the room for her as a favor. The truth was, he couldn't let her go. Not until he'd been able to question her about why the school at which she was a codirector might have been targeted for violence.

TWENTY-NINE

On the Road

LUKE KEPT TO the middle lane, away from cars merging onto the freeway on his right and from those most in a hurry in the fast lane to his left. When he glanced in his rearview mirror, he saw the girl had gone back to watching something on her tablet, though she no longer smiled or giggled. She kept her bunny clutched tightly in one arm.

He wished he knew what Clipboard Man's plans were for her.

Is this a kidnapping for ransom, all about the money, where once that's received she'll be returned unharmed?

Luke realized he didn't want to consider the other possibilities.

A large green sign indicated two miles to the Linville Exit. He remembered Emma having said it was only six miles from one side of Linville to the other. If their destination was inside the town limits, it wouldn't be long before they were there.

Clipboard Man made a sound that approximated a small laugh, though it was shot clean through with pain.

Then he said, "I guess that wasn't a good idea."

Luke didn't know exactly what the man was referring to, but he wholeheartedly agreed that none of this had been a good idea.

He exited as directed onto Linville's main thorough-
fare, an uncrowded two-lane road. In minutes, they had
reached the heart of the small town's shopping district.
A few clothing stores, a pharmacy, a hardware store,
and at the far end, the Linville Creek Café. At the memory of the afternoons he'd spent there with Emma, he
made an effort to remain hopeful that help was on its
way, that she would make that happen. But he really
couldn't see how, and he experienced a new wave of
sadness and fear. Then he saw a stop sign up ahead and
a beat-up Toyota coming from the opposite direction.

He thought of how he might signal the driver, to let
them know he and a child were being kidnapped at
gunpoint, without making Clipboard Man aware. But
as he braked, the driver of the Toyota turned his head to
speak to someone in the passenger seat and rolled right
through the two-way stop, oblivious to the fact Luke's
SUV was even there.

Deflated, Luke glanced at the odometer as they left
the shops behind. For several miles he saw nothing but
rows of nut trees, walnuts on one side, almonds on the
other. The SUV's air-conditioning whirred to keep the
heat at bay.

When Clipboard Man spoke again, his tone was urgent.

He sounded agitated.

"Make sure Deb gets my share. Do you hear me,
Kelly? Don't let them keep it."

Luke wondered if he'd heard him correctly.

Then Clipboard Man was back to giving directions.
"Turn right, up there."

Luke didn't see anywhere to turn, just more trees.

"Kelly, turn. Now."

Luke nearly missed the unmarked road. He had to

spin the wheel hard to avoid ending up in a ditch, but he barely noticed. His mind was racing. Clipboard Man thought he was somebody named Kelly. It must be a sign of hysteria or delusion, Luke wasn't sure there was a difference. But whatever the reason for it, he guessed it was probably for the best since being Luke seemed a good way to get himself killed.

Meanwhile, driving was becoming increasingly challenging. He found it impossible to avoid the many potholes on the narrow, poorly paved road that seemed to be taking them into the heart of an orchard, unending rows of trees on either side. He saw no buildings until they passed a weathered brown ranch house, and then again nothing until the asphalt gave way to gravel, and around a curve a small blue home came into view.

Clipboard Man mumbled something so low that at first Luke couldn't understand.

He repeated it, a little louder. "Stop. Park."

Luke was doing his best to parallel park on the dirt shoulder across from the blue house without hitting a tree when Clipboard Man, possibly feeling he'd done what he had to do since he'd gotten them here, seemed to give up. He let out a sob, and his head fell back. His eyes rolled up, then closed.

Luke gripped the wheel hard.

Had he just seen another man die? This one close up?

It doesn't matter, he told himself, swallowing hard. *Whether Clipboard Man only passed out or is finally dead, this is it.*

This was the plan.

All he had to do now was drive away.

He quickly checked on the girl. She had both arms around her bunny, her head down, and was speaking to it in rapid, low tones. But when she saw Luke turn, she asked, "Where are we?"

"It's gonna be okay," he told her.

She whispered something else to the bunny. Then, her deep brown eyes steady on his, she asked Luke, "Are you a good guy or a bad guy?"

Luke thought that was a fair question. He'd just opened his mouth to respond when he heard a loud grinding noise. He looked up to see the door to the garage attached to the blue house opening. Two men appeared from inside, approaching the SUV at a fast clip. One was tall, with a shock of short, bleached white hair. The other, small, nervous, and dark, held a large handgun by his side.

THIRTY

The Blue House

THOUGH FOR YEARS Luke had played video games in which massive gun fights were common, until today he'd not appreciated how a single gun changed everything in real life. His options had just narrowed to one: doing what these men told him to do.

The white-haired man gestured toward the open garage. "Move it inside."

The smaller man watched Luke closely, the gun bouncing up and down against his leg.

Luke had never driven a car into a garage before. Looking at it, he thought there should be enough space to accommodate the big SUV next to the small gray car and in front of the red bicycle rack leaning against the far wall, but he wasn't sure. Talk about pressure. He figured after this, his license test would be a piece of cake, assuming he returned alive to take it.

Fortunately, he maneuvered the SUV inside without incident. He'd just put the car in park when the small man pulled open Luke's door and barked, "Give me the keys."

Luke let out a small gasp when he realized the man appeared familiar to him. He tried to cover the sound by turning it into a cough. He was relieved when he didn't see any recognition in the man's face when he looked back at him.

"Lee, get over here. I need help with Walter," the white-haired man called from the passenger's side.

The name "Lee" didn't ring a bell for Luke. But he felt certain he'd seen him before.

The two men managed to get Clipboard Man, who Luke now understood was named Walter, out of the car and upright, though his head fell forward and his feet dragged as they maneuvered him, unconscious, around the SUV, where White-Haired Man entered a code onto a keypad next to a narrow white door, resulting in multiple loud beeps.

He looked back at Luke and said, "Get the girl," before he and the man he'd called Lee hoisted Walter through the door and disappeared to the right.

There was no part of Luke that wanted to follow them into the house. He put his head down on the steering wheel and considered whether doing nothing might be best, at least for a little while. But he concluded that was probably a good way to get shot, and he knew if his mom were here, she'd tell him, "There's no way out but through." Highly annoying when she used it to get him to do his homework or clean the kitchen, but probably appropriate now. He wiped his sweaty palms on his jeans, exited the SUV, and opened the door to the backseat.

Up close, the girl looked so small. For a moment, he forgot his own fear.

Her eyes were alert and watchful, but whatever she was thinking, she kept it to herself.

At Rainbow Alley, he'd learned to give a kid a choice whenever he could, especially when they didn't like that their mom or dad had gone off on the tour and left them with him.

He decided to try that here.

"I'm going to help you out of your car seat. Is that okay?" he asked her.

When he unclicked the buckle, she leaned away from him but did not protest.

"Do you want to walk into the house? Or do you want me to carry you?"

She shook her head no. It seemed she was refusing both options. That was a tough position to argue against, but Luke knew he had to do what he'd been told, and quickly. He worried if he didn't, the men might return, wonder why and ask him questions. He didn't know what those questions might be, but he was pretty sure he wouldn't know any of the answers.

"We have to go inside now," he told her.

So much for choices. In this situation the direct approach was apparently best since this time she responded without hesitation, if indignantly.

"I can do it. I'm not a baby."

She climbed down to the floor of the car and picked up a small purple backpack that had slid part way under the seat. She unzipped it, packed her headset and tablet inside, and then in a practiced motion slipped the straps over her shoulders.

After a beat, she wordlessly extended both her arms toward Luke, the floppy bunny held in one of her hands by its ear.

Luke inhaled deeply. *I can do this,* he thought.

Then he lifted her up, and with the governor's granddaughter in his arms walked out of the garage and into the blue house.

THIRTY-ONE

The Blue House

THE DOOR FROM the garage opened onto a large room that was minimally furnished as though the occupants had just moved in. Everything looked modern and new.

Luke heard muffled voices coming from a hallway to his right.

"Check the kitchen," the white-haired man said.

Within seconds the small man charged out of the first door down the hall. He skidded to a stop less than a foot away from Luke. Though the rest of his body stilled, his eyes moved slowly over the girl, resting first on her bare arms, then on her legs. His expression alarmed Luke.

It seemed calculating, even greedy. Luke could tell the girl felt it too. She pressed her face to his chest, as though hiding from the other man.

He seemed less familiar to Luke now. In any case, he was sure he hadn't seen him at Rainbow Alley or anywhere with children nearby. He would have remembered that look.

The white-haired man popped his head out of the room.

"Lee, hurry it up." Then, to Luke, "Last door on your right. Stay with her."

As Luke passed the room the men were in, he saw Clipboard Man, who the other men had referred to as "Walter," laid out on the couch. The last door on the right opened onto a small bedroom, like a dorm room, with a twin bed and a student-style desk and chair beneath a window with closed drapes. Once they were in the small room, an open door to Luke's right revealed a bathroom that must be shared, since there was a matching door that exited the bathroom into the room the men were in. The bathroom also had a direct door to the hall, the closed door he'd just passed.

For a little house, Luke thought, *it has an awful lot of doors.*

The girl pointed to the bathroom. Luke helped her slide her backpack off and set it on the bed before carrying her into the white-tiled space. He was glad to see the three bathroom doors all had locks. They were the flimsy button kind, but it was something. He locked the door to the room the men were in and the one to the hall before setting the girl down on her feet. He wondered if she would need help, but she looked old enough to take care of things on her own.

"Don't go in here," he said, gesturing to what he now thought of as Walter's room, "Or through here," he said, pointing to the door to the hall. Then, after stepping back into the room they'd been assigned, he kept one hand on that doorknob and said, "Leave this unlocked in case you need me, okay?"

But as soon as he'd closed the door behind him, he heard her lock it from her side. He experienced a moment of panic that she might go out the door from the bathroom into the hall or even into Walter's room. But as he worried and waited and finally was about to knock, he heard the button pop.

"I can't reach the faucet," she said, holding her hands out to him.

When he'd turned on the water and given her a hand

towel, he realized it might help her to trust him if he had a name, although it would be an odd kind of trust since he couldn't be truthful.

"I'm Kelly," he said. "What's your name?"

She reached for the bunny on the counter next to the sink.

"This is BeeBee."

"Nice to meet you, BeeBee."

"I'm Vivian." She held up three small fingers. "I'm three."

Luke realized he could make good use of a bathroom now too.

"I'd like to use the bathroom," he told her. "I'll just be a minute."

She quickly turned away, ran toward the bed, and began to hoist herself up onto it. Luke glanced at the bedroom door to the hallway and saw it didn't have a lock.

"I have a better idea than you and BeeBee waiting all the way over on the bed," he said. "I want you to stand here, next to the bathroom door. When I go in, I won't lock it."

"I'm not coming in," Vivian said, making a disgusted face, "I don't want to see you go potty."

"Of course not," Luke said, "But if you had an emergency, like if one of the men came in, you could call to me to be sure I was ready and then walk in here. It would be faster than coming down from the bed."

Vivian looked at the hallway door and frowned. Luke could tell she didn't like either option, walking into the bathroom when he was using it or staying in the small bedroom alone, since the Creep (a name Luke found more appropriate than "Lee") might come back. Finally, she put both her hands over her eyes so she couldn't see,

BeeBee's ear still grasped in one, and said, "I can do this, to be sure I won't see you go potty."

"Yes, you can do that," Luke said.

And for the first time since this nightmare had started, he felt like smiling. But since she looked quite serious, he kept it to himself.

As he closed the door to the bathroom, he heard Vivian's voice.

"It's okay, BeeBee. That's Kelly. He's a good guy."

THIRTY-TWO

The Blue House

LUKE HAD JUST finished washing his hands when he heard a knock.

It wasn't Vivian. It had come from Walter's room.

He shook the water from his hands and opened the door. It was the tall man with the white hair. Over his shoulder, Luke could see Walter still lying on the sofa, eyes closed.

White-Haired Man spoke calmly, quietly.

"Kelly, I'm Barry. I'm pleased to finally meet you, despite the circumstances. Walter's said good things about you. Now, tell me, what happened?"

Luke stepped to the towel bar to dry his hands, taking longer than he needed as he tried to keep the men's names straight and to think of what to say.

Which lie will be safest?

"I know you're upset," Barry said. "Your cousin's"—he paused—"in a bad way. But the Chief needs to know what happened."

My cousin? The Chief?

Before Luke had time to consider what it might mean that, evidently, he and Walter were related and, more importantly, there was some unknown person in charge, Barry spoke again.

"It's being reported a security guard was shot and

killed at the preschool and a woman was injured and taken to the hospital. What happened?"

Luke covered his face with both hands so his overwhelming relief that his mother was alive, that she'd been taken to the hospital, wouldn't show.

Barry seemed to interpret Luke's actions as meaning something else. "Look, I get it. You were just the driver, and there wasn't supposed to be any violence."

Luke dropped his hands, his mouth fell open, and he stared at the man.

No violence? Man, did Walter and Kelly screw up.

"We didn't know there was a guard," Barry continued, apparently processing Luke's look of surprise, even shock, as appropriate given all that had happened. "I understand his death might have been unavoidable, collateral damage. But that doesn't change the orders, that Walter and you were supposed to bring the girl and the nanny here alive. But I take it that's the nanny in the back of the SUV?"

The white-haired man didn't sound angry, but he was firm as he asked the question for the third time.

"What happened?"

Luke could lie, he was fully capable of it. He'd done it enough with his mother this past year. He told himself to use the same tricks, to tell the truth where he could, say as little as possible when he couldn't, and to let Barry fill in the blanks.

"The nanny had a gun," Luke began. Then he took a detour away from the truth. "She shot first. At Walter. He shot back. He killed her and the security guard."

In reality, Kelly had started the gunfight, leaping from the back of the van, his weapon drawn, exchanging gunfire with the nanny, during which he'd been shot dead on the spot. And the last thing that happened, not the first, was the ninja nanny managing to wound Walter before she died.

He'd had to leave out Kelly's role, well, because *he* was now Kelly.

Barry seemed to think it over, then nodded.

"Who was the other woman?" he asked. "The one who was injured?"

"I don't know," Luke said.

"Did she see you? Or Walter? Were you wearing the caps and glasses?"

Luke realized Barry was concerned his mother might be able to identify them. But his own focus shifted to whether she was all right. He couldn't help it.

"Is she conscious? What do the doctors say? Will she be okay?" Then he thought to put it in the context of Barry's question. "Able to speak, I mean?"

"We don't know," Barry said. "We've got to be ready for anything."

He left without saying anything more.

Luke felt awful. Though there had been good news, there was too much uncertainty. His mom had been taken to the hospital—that was great, but he didn't know anything else about her. He thought he might throw up. He paused by the toilet, then realized he hadn't heard a peep out of Vivian. She was only three. She might have left the room. He rushed to their door and threw it open.

"I'm not ready," Vivian yelled as she covered her eyes with both hands, BeeBee held by the ear, like she'd practiced before he'd gone in.

"It's okay," Luke said. "I'm done. I'm all dressed."

She cautiously removed her hands from her eyes. Luke saw not only alarm in them but exhaustion too, the look of a child who had been pushed way past nap time, who couldn't handle more stimulation without melting down.

He thought of the children who had visited the school.

"Did you bring something for BeeBee to snack on?" he asked. "Do you think he's hungry?"

Vivian perked up a bit. She looked at BeeBee.

"He would like a snack," she said.

She marched past Luke to the bed, climbed up and adjusted the pillow so she could sit against it with BeeBee next to her. Then she looked at Luke expectantly. But when he unzipped the backpack and reached inside, getting Vivian and BeeBee their snack was suddenly the furthest thing from Luke's mind.

The screen on her tablet had come to life at his touch. The battery icon was more than half green, and next to it were two bars showing internet access. He hurriedly checked out the options on the home screen. Two kid movies, a kid audiobook, a game, and—*bingo*—the image of a gear, which in his experience meant settings. But when he tapped it, his hopes fell.

Beneath the words "Parental Controls" was a blank line labeled "Password."

Of course, that made sense. A young child wouldn't be permitted to roam about online. She'd only be able to access what had already been downloaded, first approved by Shelby or someone else as kid-friendly.

"That's mine," Vivian said, annoyed, reaching out both hands for the tablet.

"I know," Luke said. "It's cool. I want to check one thing real quick, and I'll give it back to you. Do you know the password?"

She scowled at him. "That's for grown-ups." Then she added, "Only Mommy and Shelby."

Luke smiled as he handed her the tablet, determined to hide his disappointment.

Besides, he realized there might be something else in the bag that would help. A cell phone would be great.

Though it seemed unlikely the average three-year-old would have a phone of her own, Vivian was the governor's granddaughter. Maybe they'd thought ahead to a situation like this, one where her nanny might be dead, her mother who-knows-where, and the only guy she could count on had a busted phone.

Okay, not exactly like this, but something bad.

He emptied the bag under Vivian's watchful eye. There was a storybook about bunnies and a coloring book with horses on the cover. Two reusable snack containers, one filled with pieces of broccoli and cauliflower, another with dark brown bread slices slathered with jam. He handed those to Vivian, who struggled to pop the airtight tops so he paused to assist her. There was a small water bottle, full to the top, with a sippy cup-type opening, which he set next to her. At the bottom of the bag was a soft cloth in pale lavender, trimmed in satin on the edges like a blanket, not much bigger than a hand towel.

That was it. No phone. He put the items back. Then he noticed two small outside pockets. All they held was a child-sized toothbrush and toothpaste in one, and a box of crayons in the other.

He sat back and thought of the men who were holding them.

Barry.

The Creep.

Walter.

The Chief.

At least two of them, Barry and The Creep, had guns,

and Luke wasn't sure what had happened to Walter's weapon.

He needed a plan.

If his mother were here, she would be considering strategies, testing ideas, moving through every obstacle until she found a way to check off each item on her to-do list and achieve her objective. And while Emma didn't make lists, she thought about things fast and acted. She'd be in motion in one direction and then another until she hit on something that would help. Still, his mom and his aunt weren't quite the inspiration he was looking for. In science class, he'd learned that picturing fictional heroes fighting cancer cells helped kids to heal faster, even to live longer.

That's what I need, Luke thought.

He liked the old Jason Bourne movies, and he'd played hours of the Spiderman video games. A rebel secret agent and a teen superhero would be great to have around right now. Those guys would know what to do.

Then he noticed that Vivian was lying down, her head on the pillow, her short cap of dark hair framing her face, her eyes closed, BeeBee tucked under one arm. He took the square of blanket from the bag and laid it over her.

He suddenly felt tired too. He wanted nothing more than to close his eyes, to let go of all this until he was rested, until he could think more clearly. But with a half smile he told himself Jason Bourne and Spiderman would definitely not pause for a nap. So he pulled himself together, rose and checked the desk drawers. Empty. The small plastic wastebasket. Also empty. He knelt and looked below the bed. Nothing. He pulled the drapes aside. The window was big, chest high, a slider. It looked out the side of the house onto a wall of thick hedges. It had possibilities. Then he noticed small, white, button-size circles on the window's seam. He thought about the keypad he'd seen when they came inside. Luke had never had an alarm system, but Barry had used a code. Luke was pretty sure if he opened the window without first entering the right numbers on the pad, all hell would break loose.

Ultimately, the conclusion he arrived at was simple.

He wasn't bionic or a superhero. He wouldn't be able to get Vivian to safety on his own. He needed to get word to people who could rescue them. The police. Or Emma. Or even Lily would figure something out. But he had no phone, no computer, and there were no neighbors close enough to signal through the window. If he yelled, his cover as Kelly would be blown.

Then it came to him. A long shot, but it just might work. He reached for Vivian's backpack.

THIRTY-THREE

Headquarters

THERE'D BEEN NO update on Kate's condition. The doctors thought it would be a while, and Alibi didn't think Emma would be able to handle a witness interview until then. So he'd returned to his office and was contemplating the names and relationships on the whiteboard when Jackie O arrived.

She'd been at Rainbow Alley making sure no evidence was missed that might suggest a gang connection to Kate Doyle's shooting, and no doubt had a preliminary assessment on that to share. But Alibi was more interested in whether she'd made any progress on the lead he'd asked her to pursue from Carlos's notes on the Marty Lightzer interview. He'd given it to her because he figured like cops, academics had their networks.

"Any luck getting the name of the man who lived with Samuel Miller and Marty Lightzer in college?"

"Not yet. But I found someone willing to look into it, an old friend who works in admissions at Miller and Lightzer's alma mater."

"Good. It's a start," Alibi said.

Jackie O said, "It's really hot out there. Is it all right if I get a drink?"

Alibi smiled. "Would you bring me an iced tea?"

Returning to the table with two chilled bottles, Jackie O asked, "Do you think Marty's unwillingness to provide the third roommate's name had something to do with Samson's murder? Couldn't there be any number of reasons Marty didn't want to share it?"

"Sure. There could be," Alibi said.

He didn't elaborate. He was not about to explain that he'd had a vision of ghosts and an empty chair at the conference table, which because of the timing had led him to feel at a purely emotional level that the roommate's name and Samson's death might be related. He changed the subject.

"How about the shooting at Rainbow Alley? Anything jump out at you?"

She powered up her tablet. "Kate Doyle is an immigrant. Her wallet contained a green card issued six years ago."

Alibi had met Kate when he'd gone with Tommy to Emma's house, back in the spring. Charming Irish accent, animated, funny, and she'd looked far too young to have a teenage son.

"No playing cards though, right?" he asked.

There hadn't been any that he could see when he'd knelt with Emma beside Kate, but what with the unexpected discovery of cards beneath Samson's body, he wanted to be sure none had been left elsewhere at this scene, perhaps even tucked in Kate's purse.

"Right. None," Jackie O said.

Alibi backed up a few feet from the whiteboard, his phone in hand, and took several photos of the notes on Samson Kieu's case that now filled its surface. When he finished, he noticed a smile in Jackie O's eyes, a hint of it on her lips.

"You actually can teach an old dog new tricks," he said.

In his mid-forties, it pained Alibi to refer to himself

as old, but he knew that was probably how Jackie O and Carlos viewed him.

Having saved the information, he wiped the board clean, picked up a marker and created column headings across the top, underlining each one:

<u>SAMSON</u>   <u>TOMMY</u>   <u>KATE</u>

"We've got three victims of violence over a twelve-hour period. Samson was shot and killed around midnight last night. Tommy fell to his death at seven this morning. Kate was shot in an apparent murder attempt at roughly noon today." He thought about how he wanted to structure the discussion. "Let's identify the most important things we know about the crimes against each of them. Prioritize. No more than three facts or aspects of each case."

Jackie O looked thoughtful but said nothing.

"What comes to mind first for you?" Alibi asked. "What seems most meaningful for our investigations?" When she still didn't answer, he said, "Let's start with Samson."

With that prompt, Jackie O responded quickly, apparently not needing to weigh her choices.

"First, based on the tip from Samuel Miller in jail and on your interview with Janie, Samson was almost certainly an informant, hired by Tommy."

Alibi made notes on the board as she spoke.

"Second, Samson had connections to white supremacists through his job at Marty's bike shop. He wasn't necessarily a believer, but he had contact and access. Third, though this is the least certain, he could have overheard one or more of Marty's conversations from the alleyway, and that knowledge might be what got him killed. Tommy's presence at the scene suggests they might have been planning an information exchange." She hesitated. "Those are all related? Do they count as one?"

Alibi didn't want Jackie O's academic training, the careful way she typically built each argument in a linear fashion as though she might have to teach it in a college course, to block more free-wheeling brainstorming.

"We don't care if the elements overlap," he said. "We just want to have in front of us what seems most important about what we know."

"Okay," she said, gaining enthusiasm, "maybe add that Samson's sister tried to kill herself the morning after he was killed? I'm not sure how that fits, but it seems important. Oh, and also the modern-day playing cards found with his body. We want to know whether those mean anything."

"Great," Alibi said, still writing, though he was up to five points under Samson's name. He moved on. "How about Tommy?"

Jackie O thought longer about that. "I guess, first, that we think he was still obsessed with finding out who killed his wife and that he believed it was a white supremacist who did it." She paused. "Or are those two? And also, that his death was an accident."

"Those are good," Alibi said, still writing.

When he turned around, he saw Carlos standing in the office doorway, examining the board.

"Come in," Alibi said. "Good timing." He explained the exercise. "We're recording the most important things we know so far about each of the cases on the board, aiming for three points under each one." He looked at what he'd written thus far. "Make that three to five."

"I've got two to put under Samson." Carlos said, joining Jackie O at the table. "Marty's story for the time of Samson's murder checked out. His wife stopped by the bike shop to pick up a deposit for the bank. Evidently, she helps with things like that. Obviously, I didn't want to do the questioning there, but Marty brought her over to me and she swore up and down that he'd been with her all last night. She said a neighbor stopped by, and gave me his name. She was pretty convincing. Though there was a weird moment after that. When I stepped away to respond to a text, I saw them arguing as they looked in my direction. She seemed to want Marty to speak with me right then, even gave him a light push physically at one point toward me. I'd like to know what that was about. But the main thing that happened was I checked out his shoes, compared to mine. Lightzer wears at least a ten, maybe an eleven. He may not be a tall guy, but he's got good size feet, they won't match either of the prints by the river."

Alibi did his best to condense Carlos's extended monologue about Lightzer into concise notes on the board.

Meanwhile, Carlos had a question about Kate.

"Why is the preschool director up there? Seems her only relationship to Samson and Tommy's deaths is timing, that she was shot on the same day. Which reminds me, Nishad gave me this when I passed his desk." He took a folder out of his messenger bag. "It's the preliminary crime scene report from the school. He says you'll have it electronically, but he thought you'd want to see the printed copy, including the photos."

Alibi handed Jackie the marker. "Please fill in what you think might be important about Kate Doyle." He sat at the table and opened the folder while Jackie wrote "IMMIGRANT" beneath Kate's name.

"Carlos, we found out Kate Doyle is here on a green card," she told him.

"You think it was an anti-immigrant crime?" Carlos asked.

But Jackie O wasn't listening. Something had caught her attention in the open folder in front of Alibi. She set the marker down, picked up her tablet and briskly navigated its contents.

When she saw Alibi had turned to the next page of the report she told him to go back. He did as she asked, returning to a wide-frame shot of the back of the school. Jackie O set her tablet down next to the open file.

On her screen was the image of a young man with shoulder-length dark curls wearing a red Marty's Bikes shirt and standing next to an older bicycle with peeling green paint.

Carlos came around to where he could also view the two screens. "That's the same bike," he said, pointing to one leaning against a shiny silver storage shed at the far end of the photo in Alibi's file.

Alibi asked Jackie, "Where did you take this?"

"It's from a wall display of employee photos at Marty's."

"The kid in that photo works at Marty's bike shop?" Alibi asked.

"Looks like it," Jackie O said.

"I've met him. That's Luke Doyle," Alibi said softly. "Kate Doyle's son."

He found he needed a moment. He got up and filled a pitcher with filtered water from the bar tap and grabbed three glasses. When he was seated again at the conference table, he asked, "How likely is it that Luke and Samson knew each other since they both worked at the bike shop? Carlos, I think I saw it in your notes. How many employees does Marty have?"

"Around a dozen," Carlos said.

Carlos looked to Jackie O for verification, but she was deep into something on her tablet, tapping and scrolling.

"So they might have worked different shifts with little overlap?" Alibi asked.

"Maybe," Carlos said. "But they must have been among the youngest on the staff, both still in high school. They might have gravitated toward each other for that reason."

Jackie O looked up. "They knew each other," she said. "I thought that name, Luke Doyle rang a bell. He was the other boy picked up with Samson the night the swastikas were painted on Wildwood Synagogue."

Alibi took a long sip of his water before retrieving the marker and returning to the board.

He wrote "LUKE DOYLE" at the bottom with one line to Samson and another to Kate.

"There's more," Jackie O said. "The adult who signed Luke out of the department the night the boys were brought in was Tommy Noonan."

THIRTY-FOUR

The Hospital

DR. BALL hadn't been specific about when he might be able to make a decision regarding surgery for Kate. Emma figured at a minimum it would be several hours before she had any news, and the problem was, she wasn't good at waiting. In fact, "not waiting" was her signature move.

When she'd been nine and Jasmine only five, near-miss kitchen fires and food prep injuries had resulted in their being forbidden to cook unsupervised. But on their mother's birthday, while Jasmine was still bossily listing the risks and benefits of breaking the rule and baking their mother a surprise cake, Emma had already cracked the eggs into a bowl.

At the thought of her sister, Emma realized if today's shooting made the national news, all it would take was a reference to "a childcare center across from the capitol," and Jasmine would know it had taken place at Rainbow Alley.

She reached for the corded landline the hospital provided next to the bed when she noticed her satchel leaning against a pillow on a chair beneath the window. Alibi must have picked it up at the scene or had one of his officers bring it here for her. She went to it and retrieved her phone. The volume was off. There were two missed calls from Jasmine, who picked up on the first ring.

"Emma, thank goodness. Are you okay?"

"Yes," Emma said, though she doubted she sounded that way.

"I was so worried. I heard there was a shooting at a Sacramento preschool. It's all over online. There's no official detail, but some of the reports say a woman was injured. I thought…" Her voice broke.

"I'm fine," Emma said.

She hesitated.

Kate had been her "plus one," accompanying her to Iowa for the christening of Jasmine's daughter six months ago, and Jasmine knew how much Kate meant to her.

She pictured her younger sister now, twenty-eight years old, pregnant with her second child, a worrier in the best of circumstances, and decided to repeat only the doctor's initial vague words.

"Kate was injured. I'm at the hospital with her. She's resting. She's not in any pain." She decided a change of subject was in order. "Where's Nadia? Is it nap time?"

She hadn't heard her niece's usual fussiness or cries in the background. She wasn't an easy baby.

"Reggie has taken Nadia and Fox for a walk," Jasmine said.

Fox was Jasmine and Reggie's latest addition to their growing family, a sweet and loyal mini-Bernese Mountain dog and poodle mix the size of a large house cat.

Emma reflected, not for the first time, that Jasmine had responded to their lack of extended family—no parents, no other siblings—by filling her home as quickly as she could, first Reggie, next Nadia, then Fox, and soon baby number two, as yet unnamed.

While she'd done the opposite, hadn't invited anyone in because she didn't trust anyone to stay.

Not until Kate, she thought.

"Is there anything I can do?" Jasmine asked. "Have food delivered to the hospital? It must be past lunchtime out there. Have you eaten?" Jasmine couldn't compete with Kate in the list-making department, but she definitely thought further ahead than Emma. "Could I call people for you? Your work or friends? I can let them know you're okay."

As Emma was considering how to answer, how to convey without upsetting Jasmine that the only thing that mattered to her right now was Kate's condition, that she had no space in her mind or her heart to think of anything or anyone else, she remembered Luke.

Luke.

As soon as Kate was settled here, safe, with the doctors, she should have gone to him, to tell him what had happened to his mom, to reassure him, to help him through this.

But instead, her singular focus had been her own need to know Kate would be all right.

In order to get through this time, she'd blocked everything and everyone else out.

Even Luke.

She was the worst guardian in the history of the world. She felt cold all over.

Not that she'd have the gig long term, because Kate *would* get better. But for now she was like the vice-president when the president was under anesthesia for a double root canal. She was supposed to step up and take responsibility until Kate was back on the job.

Jasmine began, "Emma, are you—"

"I don't need anything, Sis. I'll call you if I do." Emma was moving, phone in hand, to retrieve her satchel. "I've got to go. Love you. Kiss Nadia for me."

THIRTY-FIVE

Matchbook Lane

EMMA THANKED THE ride service driver and hurried to Kate's front door, using her key to open the lock as she called out Luke's name.

The duplex was small. It didn't take her long to do a quick circuit of the two bedrooms and single bath, the living room, and kitchen. He wasn't there. She tried to think how she might reach him. Two days short of his birthday, he'd yet to receive the coveted new iPhone Kate had told her about, already wrapped and topped with a loving card.

Was that really only hours ago, this same morning?

It didn't seem possible that in the short time since then Tommy had died, Kate had been shot, and she was now the designated responsible adult in Luke's life, his location unknown.

She returned to Luke's room. His bed was unmade. The faded quilt Kate had found for him at an estate sale years ago, each square depicting a musical instrument, was bunched up where he'd pushed it to the end of the bed. On the walls, posters of bands Emma didn't recognize coexisted with one of Mohammed Ali and another of Warriors basketball star Steph Curry. The floor was littered with schoolbooks and random articles of clothing. Luke's saxophone stood in its case in a corner.

She'd turned to leave when she noticed his laptop

open on a low nightstand beyond the bed, covered in stickers that made it fade into the general chaos and clutter.

Emma didn't want to violate the careful boundaries of privacy she'd observed with Luke. But after a beat, she decided the circumstances definitely warranted it. She sat on the edge of the bed, picked up the laptop, and scanned the home screen to see if she could find an open program that might have recent messages indicating where Luke had gone.

He didn't appear to be active on social media, or at least not on any of the applications she was familiar with. She was able to locate his e-mail, but not surprisingly it required a password.

She accessed her own e-mail, and after a moment's thought, typed a brief message and hit "Send."

Luke,

I need to speak with you urgently.
Please find a way to call me.
Everything will be okay.
Emma

She knew she'd been vague, even cryptic, but she wanted to tell him about what had happened to his mother in person or at least over the phone, if she could.

When she opened the front door of the duplex to leave, she was greeted by frantic barking from across the street. Crash's large head appeared in her living room window, then disappeared as he raced out of sight to the front door, then appeared again at the window, ratcheting the volume up a notch in case she hadn't gotten the message.

Having retrieved her key from under the step and opened her door, Crash's entire body wriggled as he struggled to maintain his "I'm a Good Boy!" sit, his large tail thumping loudly on the oak floor. She knelt to give him a reassuring scratch behind the ears. He pushed his head against her chest, making clear all was forgiven now that she was home. He trailed her into the kitchen, where she gave him two treats, then a third and another scratch before suddenly feeling overcome with exhaustion.

She wondered if what they'd given her at the hospital for the shock hadn't worn off yet, or if it was the shock itself that was making her tired. In any case, there seemed nothing more she could do now but wait for a response from Luke or news from the hospital about Kate.

Dispirited, she sat down heavily at the kitchen table.

But within a minute, she'd gotten back to her feet. Tired or not, she had to be in motion. In her experience, that was the only way progress was ever made, even if she wasn't sure in which direction to go.

After filling the kettle for tea, she headed down the hall to her bedroom. Crash padded softly behind her, calmer now that the kettle was on, a sure signal she wasn't leaving anytime soon.

Though Emma's room was technically the master bedroom, with its own bathroom, its 1960s vintage meant it was smaller than most guest bedrooms in modern houses. She'd furnished it with items true to the era, including a mid-century bed frame and matching makeup table, both with clean lines in pale blond wood.

She slipped off her flats, then took off her suit jacket. But when she moved to drop it into the hamper, she found she couldn't. Her attempt to wash out the blood had failed.

Kate's blood, she thought.

The stains were still visible, not red or brown, but like a pale gray shadow on the green linen fabric. She laid the jacket out carefully on the bed and resolved not to have it cleaned until her best friend was home. She'd just finished undressing, stepping out of her skirt, then her panties, and had turned on the shower when Crash bolted out of the bedroom. In seconds, she could hear his bark over the flow of the water, insistent, sounding the alarm.

She pulled on the terrycloth robe she kept on the back of the bathroom door and went to see what the fuss was about.

When it occurred to her it could be Luke, she hurried up the hall.

Crash was at his post at the living room window. The source of his concern was a sky-blue jeep that had pulled up directly in front of her house. As Emma watched, a man unfolded from the driver's side.

In one sense, he'd changed little over the years. His light brown hair was still parted on the side, cut above his ears, and his unremarkable features remained boyish. But Dylan Johnson had been small and childlike in appearance in high school, and he was now close to six feet tall and solid-looking. It was as though someone had taken the Dylan she'd known and blown him up like a balloon in the Macy's Thanksgiving Day Parade to the size of a full-grown man.

Dylan saw her through the window and waved, smiling, as he approached her front door.

When she opened it, Crash pushed past her to sniff out the newcomer, standard procedure to determine whether he was friend or foe.

"Law," he said, "it's great to see you."

She found herself unable to say anything in response. Her mind returned to the trio of urgent concerns currently dominating her existence: Tommy's death, Kate's shooting, her need to find Luke. *And now I have to add to it Dylan Johnson, man-sized, at my front door?*

Unsteady on her feet, she swayed. She felt Dylan's arm around her shoulder. He helped her to the sofa, then took a few respectful steps back. Crash growled at him, as though having come to the conclusion that Dylan's appearance was the cause of her distress.

Dylan addressed the dog directly. "It's okay. Good dog."

Crash seemed to take that under advisement. He stopped growling but was still alert and tense.

Dylan turned back to Emma.

"I went to the preschool to meet you. I couldn't get in, there were police cars blocking the street. What happened? Is everything all right?"

THIRTY-SIX

The Blue House

THE SIMPLE, cartoon-like image of a prancing pony, one front hoof poised in the air, a perfectly round sun overhead, was just right for a three-year-old to be able to stay between the lines. But Luke had chosen this particular page in Vivian's coloring book for another reason altogether. It had offered lots of open space.

He put down the fat blue crayon, the only color he'd used, and considered his work. Most of what he'd written was crossed out. He reread what was left and decided it was the best he could do, then repeated it silently to himself until he'd committed it to memory.

As he went to close the book, he stopped. Though he doubted Vivian would miss one picture of a pony at play out of twenty similar scenes, he was pretty sure she'd be upset if she saw he hadn't even tried to "make something pretty." So he carefully tore out the page, balled it up and tossed it into the small plastic wastebasket beneath the desk.

She hadn't been asleep long. One of her small hands clutched BeeBee and the other the handkerchief-sized blanket with the satin trim. He wished he didn't have to disturb her, but he couldn't risk her waking to find him gone. She might leave the room in search of him. The memory of the Creep's expression as he'd eyed

Vivian made Luke's skin crawl. He sat down next to her and spoke gently.

"Vivian? Vivian, it's Lu—" He stopped himself. "It's Kelly. I need to talk to you."

Her eyelids lifted sleepily as her lips curved into a sweet smile. But when she saw it was him, she stiffened. Her smile disappeared and she pulled BeeBee closer to her.

Luke realized she must have expected to see her mother or Shelby at her bedside, the start of a normal day. A day of love and play and tears and small disappointments, not one spent in a strange room in a house filled with unknown, scary men.

"I'm sorry to wake you," he told her, "but I have to check on the man who was hurt. I need you to stay here while I do that."

Vivian frowned. "Where is he? When are you coming back?" She looked fully awake now. She held her bunny tightly to her.

"He's just through there, remember?" Luke said, gesturing to the open bathroom. "See that closed door, on the other side? I'm going to leave that ajar." Then realizing she might not know what that meant, he said, "I'll leave that door open a little bit. In case you need anything."

Vivian whispered something to BeeBee.

"Tell BeeBee if either of you hear someone nearby, I want you to call out to me. Loudly. Call out 'Kelly' and I'll come right back."

Luke wished he could shove the desk in front of the door that led from their room into the hall. Not that it would stop anyone from entering, but at least he would hear them protest when they met resistance. But blocking the door was something Kelly, a member of the kidnapping team, would never do. He hoped if someone did come and Vivian called him, it would look like he'd just been in the bathroom.

"I'll be right back," he said again, turning to go. He wanted to get this over with.

But she looked so small, so alone, and so clearly worried that he paused and retrieved the picture book of bunnies from her backpack and handed it to her.

"Why don't you read this to BeeBee?"

A movie on the tablet would be a better distraction. It would make it easier for her to wait patiently for him, but her headphones had proven to be exceptionally good at blocking out all exterior sounds, and he needed her to be able to hear the men if they came so she could warn him.

"You may have to read it a few times before I get back. Does BeeBee like that book?

She nodded, her expression grave. She seemed to understand something serious was happening and that Luke's leaving was not negotiable. Positioning BeeBee on her lap so he could see the book, she dutifully began to tell him the story of ten silly bunnies hop, hop, hopping to town.

Luke hurried through the bathroom and slowly eased the door to Walter's room open.

He wanted to make sure he wasn't walking in on more than he could handle. He was relieved to see the door to the hall from Walter's room was shut.

Walter still lay on the sofa, motionless, his eyes closed. Luke could hear his breathing, raspy and labored. A thin brown blanket was pulled up to his chest, his head was propped on a pillow. A dim floor lamp in the corner was on, so Luke pulled the door to the bathroom nearly closed behind him. He wouldn't need the extra light.

He jostled the coffee table as he squeezed past to reach Walter, knocking over a small brown bottle of pills. It made a rattling noise, but Walter didn't stir. Luke set the bottle back upright. Fortunately, a heavy glass next to it, half full with water, hadn't spilled.

Luke's hand shook as he gingerly pulled the blanket down. Below the edge of Walter's T-shirt, he could see a bit of the bandage Barry had put over his wound. It was clean and white. Perhaps Walter had stopped bleeding, or maybe he had no more blood to give. He lowered the blanket another few inches, exposing the pockets of Walter's jeans. As he patted one gently, Walter groaned. Luke jumped, barely able to stifle a yell, but Walter's eyes didn't open as he turned his head to the side and quieted again. Luke waited a moment and then checked Walter's other front pocket.

Success.

He slid the phone out, covered Walter with the blanket again, and backed away. He powered it up, then quickly pressed the side button to make sure the ringer was off and the volume was down. The words "Input Password" appeared above a display of nine digits from which to choose. Luke had thought there might be something like that. But above it was an option he had not expected. A red "Emergency" icon that didn't require a password.

Luke felt hope, then excitement surge in his chest. His finger hovered over it, about to tap, when he heard heavy footsteps in the hall. He froze and held his breath. Whoever it was moved past without stopping, the sound fading away at the juncture with the main room. There had been no pause at Vivian's door or at Walter's. Luke exhaled. But the reminder that the men were there, so close by, made him consider the horrifying thought that if he was caught calling 911 it could land him with a bullet in his head in the back of the SUV with Shelby.

Even if he said nothing and hung up, the operator might call back.

So he decided to stick with the plan he'd made when he'd recalled that Walter's phone was an older model, like the one he'd had before it recently gave up the ghost. He pressed the "Home" button and the phrase "Input Password" was replaced by the question "Print ID?" Returning to Walter's side, Luke bent and carefully pressed Walter's limp right thumb to the button. The screen promptly cleared and provided a menu of choices.

Luke selected the text message icon and inputted a number he knew by heart.

His head down, he was so intent on typing the words he'd written in crayon and memorized that he didn't hear the door to the hall open.

"What are you doing?"

The Creep's voice was hard and cold. His right eye twitched as he stared at Luke, waiting for an answer.

Luke knew if he appeared nervous or defensive, it would only make things worse. He put on the surly look he gave his mother when she interrupted him doing something he wasn't supposed to.

"Sending a text. What's it to you?"

He returned to typing, as though it was his right, but the Creep stepped forward and grabbed the phone from his hand.

"You're new," he said, "and you're only here because you're Walter's cousin. He vouched for you, and look where that got him."

He has a point, Luke thought. It was Kelly who had ramped the whole thing up when he jumped out of the back of the van with his gun. Kelly who had started the events into motion that had resulted in Walter being shot. But that wasn't Luke's concern right now.

The Creep looked at the phone's screen, then scrolled up, apparently checking what else had been written recently. Luke felt his stomach drop.

"This isn't your phone," the Creep said. "These earlier texts are to me." He peered at the screen again. "From Walter." He turned to Walter, lying on the couch, as though for confirmation. But Walter, thankfully, was either asleep or unconscious, so couldn't help him out.

The Creep snapped at Luke.

"What are you doing with Walter's phone?"

He sounded like he was about to lose it, and Luke did not want to see what that looked like.

"Walter told me to message Deb," Luke said firmly. He let his genuine frustration and anger come through.

Luke didn't know whether Deb was Walter's wife, girlfriend, or sister, but hopefully he wouldn't get questioned about that, or maybe the Creep didn't know either. He extended his hand toward the phone, but the Creep ignored him as he appeared to reread, carefully, the text Luke had just typed. His lips moved on some of the words. It was slow going.

Then Luke heard a whoosh. The Creep had sent the text. So Luke didn't care that when he looked up, the man's expression was something between a thin smile and a sneer. But he did care when a moment later the Creep tucked Walter's phone into the front pocket of his jacket.

"We should give that back to Walter," Luke said, willing his voice to remain calm.

The Creep bounced from foot to foot. His head swiveled from Luke to the unconscious Walter and back again.

"Nah," he finally said. "If he needs it, he'll know where to find me."

THIRTY-SEVEN

Matchbook Lane

"WHAT HAPPENED? Is everything okay?"

Dylan was speaking, his lips were moving, but his words seemed to be coming from far away. Emma pressed her palm against her chest to feel her heart beating, to reassure herself it was still functioning, and felt the soft fabric of her robe.

She'd forgotten she hadn't dressed yet when she'd rushed to her front door, thinking it might be Luke. She quickly pulled the front of her robe closed, hoping nothing had been visible that shouldn't have been, when she heard a muffled ping.

It repeated twice more before she recognized it as her phone inside her bag, which she'd left in the kitchen. She jumped up, Crash trailing her. She was vaguely aware that Dylan was coming too.

Her first thought was that it was news about Kate. No, the doctor would call, not text. It could be Luke. Perhaps he'd borrowed a phone. Then it occurred to her it might be Alibi. She'd left the hospital so suddenly she hadn't let him know, even after he'd gone to the trouble of having a private room held for her.

When she got to the phone, she had six new messages. She scrolled quickly through them. Two were Rainbow Alley parents with questions and two were

press inquiries, asking her to comment on the shooting.
She expected there would be many more of those soon.
It would take little digging for a journalist to identify
her as co-owner of the school.

Her heart sank when she read the next text. It was
from her assistant at work, Hailey.

Emma had completely forgotten about her five pm
appointment with the new commissioner. She checked
the time: 4:22 pm. She looked down at her bathrobe.

If I race to change, if traffic is with me.

But then she nearly laughed out loud as she caught
herself.

*What am I doing? Kate is lying in the hospital, Luke
is God knows where, and Dylan Johnson is standing
in my kitchen.*

Missing a work meeting was the least of her worries.
She typed a response to Hailey, asking her to let Commissioner Warhol know she'd had an emergency, and
could they reschedule? That Emma could fly to LA for
an in-person meeting with the commissioner any day
next week that would suit her. Finally, she skimmed the
last text in her inbox. It was a wrong number, a message
meant for someone named Deb about concert tickets.

She sat down at the kitchen table, wishing she could
will into being one of the messages she'd hoped for, a
positive update about Kate, or Luke letting her know
where he was. Idly, she read through the last text, the
wrong number, then sat bolt upright. Her hand flew to
her mouth.

"What's wrong?" Dylan asked, taking the chair next
to her. Crash pushed between them, pressing his body
against Emma's thigh, forcing Dylan to slide his chair
over.

Emma read it again.

Deb,

You at Beryl's house?
I got Death by Violetall Rejoinder tix for us!!
Don't tell Antiphon.
Serious don't. Concert is total surprise HAHA.
Would be like LCC × 5, right on!
A 10 plus one if they open with Ubiety of Gendar

"What does it mean?" Dylan asked.

When she heard his voice she realized he must have leaned over and read the text. Some other time it would have bothered her that he'd invaded her privacy that way, but she had other, more pressing things on her mind.

"Is Deb the one who was injured that they mentioned on the news?" he asked.

"No. That's Kate. It's Kate who is injured."

Emma wished Dylan weren't there. She had to focus. "Lots of these words are from a game Luke and I play," she muttered, mostly to herself. "It can't be a coincidence."

She looked carefully at the return number at the top of the screen. It wasn't from anyone in her contacts. If it had been, the name would have shown with the number. She scratched Crash behind his ear and tried to think it through.

"He doesn't have a phone," she said slowly.

"Who?" Dylan asked.

She heard the impatience in Dylan's voice, or maybe it was concern at not knowing what was going on. She told herself not to take this out on him. Not again.

"This message is definitely from Luke," she said.

"He's a teenager. He's family. I can't explain it all now. But this is beyond odd. I need to find him and make sure he's okay."

"Text him back," Dylan said reasonably.

Emma began typing.

Luke, what's going on?
I need to talk to you.
It's urgent.

But as she was about to hit "Send," she thought about the specific words Luke had chosen in his text and what they meant.

She hurriedly deleted the response she'd started.

"He doesn't want me to reply," she said to Dylan, then looked to Crash, as though the dog she shared with Luke might better understand, before she returned to speaking largely to herself. "He's warning me off. 'Death by rejoinder' means 'death by reply,' and "don't tell Antiphon, serious" means 'don't reply, don't react.' It's all telling me the same thing. Don't text back."

At first, she couldn't see a reasonable explanation for Luke having written to her in code. Then, all at once, it seemed obvious.

He must have borrowed another kid's phone, someone he didn't want to know that he was contacting an adult. Maybe they'd been drinking or smoking weed, and Luke needed a ride. But where was he? How was she supposed to pick him up without that information?

She retrieved a small pad of paper and pen from a drawer next to the refrigerator, returned to the table, and ignoring Dylan's quizzical look, copied the text in its entirety, adding in parentheses simpler words that conveyed the meaning of the SAT practice words that Luke had used.

Deb,

You at Beryl's (BLUE-GREEN) house?
I got Death by Violetall (OPPOSITE) Rejoinder (RESPOND) tix for us!! Don't tell Antiphon (RESPONSE IN A CHANT).
Serious don't. Concert is total surprise HAHA.
Would be like LCC (LINVILLE CREEK CAFE) x 5, right on! (?).
A 10 plus one(?) if they open with Ubiety (POSITION/STATE OF EXISTENCE) of Gendar (GENDER MISSPELLED?)

Dylan slid his chair closer so he could read what she'd written. Crash didn't growl this time, but he did give Dylan his undivided attention.

"LCC was an SAT word?" Dylan asked.

"No. It's an abbreviation locals use for a place Luke and I have been going to for years."

As Emma said it, the most important part of the message became clear to her.

"He's telling me he's there." She hesitated. "At least, I think so. I wish I knew what the numbers 'five times' and 'ten plus one' meant."

She stood. She didn't have time to figure it all out. It didn't appear Luke had heard about Kate yet. Maybe she would be able to break the news to him in person, then bring him back with her to the hospital. She called over her shoulder to Dylan as she hurried down the hall toward her bedroom. "I've got to get dressed. I've got to go."

Crash dashed ahead of her, not wanting to be shut out if she got there first. He'd already begun his nose-down circuit of the room when she caught up and closed the door.

She dropped her robe on the floor and hastily selected a light blue T-shirt and a pair of faded jeans, both of which she'd had since college. Comfort clothes, like comfort food. She pulled them on, then slipped into lightweight, mini-crew socks and a pair of well-worn, off-white sneakers.

She was back in the kitchen in under five minutes.

"I'm sorry it didn't work out today," she said to Dylan. "Tea, I mean."

"No problem," he said. "We'll do it another time."

"You go ahead," she said, as she held Crash by the collar so Dylan could leave unimpeded.

But rather than starting for the door, Dylan stepped toward her and gave her a chaste hug, arms only, a gap between their bodies. "It will be okay," he said.

Emma nodded, though she was still having trouble processing this fully grown and socially appropriate Dylan.

Once he was gone, she checked Crash's water bowl to be sure he had enough, then knelt and spoke to him, eye to eye. "I know you want to come but I need you to stay here. Luke might get back and I don't want him to be alone today." She gave the big dog one last scratch. "Bark if he shows up across the street, and he'll come and get you."

She put her phone in her bag and had made it as far as the living room before turning back. For a moment, she appreciated why Kate made lists for everything. She returned to the kitchen, picked up the pen and wrote above the translation she'd done of the SAT words:

Luke,

I've gone to LCC to find you.
If we miss each other there,
message me as soon as you see this.
Love,
Aunt Emma

She read it over and hesitated when she saw she'd
reverted to "Aunt Emma" in her sign-off. It had been
at least a year since Luke had called her that. She knew
he'd dropped it because it signaled they had evolved
into being two adults on equal footing. But she didn't
have time to redo it now. She grabbed her bag, with effort looking away from Crash's woeful "stay with me"
brown eyes, and headed out.

DYLAN SAT IN his Jeep at the curb, letting the air-conditioning run on high, watching Emma's front door. It
was taking longer than he'd expected. He'd thought she
would be right out, but when she finally did step onto
her front landing her reaction was predictable.

She stared at her short driveway, at the place where
her car should have been, as he knew she would. He'd
seen her black and white Mustang in the school lot, behind the yellow crime-scene tape when he'd driven by.

She hadn't noticed him yet. She reached into her
bag, he assumed to retrieve her phone, to call a friend
or a ride service. He couldn't let that happen. He lightly
tapped the horn of the Jeep, one short beep, then rolled
down his window.

"Is something wrong?" he called to her.

She looked up.

He couldn't read her expression. A long moment passed. Then she hurried down the steps toward him.

"I don't know what your plans are," she said, "but I've got to get out to Linville to pick up Luke. Is there any chance you could drive me? I'm not sure how long it will take, I don't know exactly—"

He stopped her. His tone was supportive but decisive.

"Of course. Get in."

He held his breath as she hesitated, not letting it out until she'd gone to the passenger side and opened the door.

THIRTY-EIGHT

Headquarters

ALIBI TOLD JACKIE O and Carlos to take a break, asking them to return in twenty minutes. He wanted to check his messages to make sure he hadn't missed anything urgent on other cases.

After he'd quickly responded to those that couldn't wait, he phoned Emma for an update on Kate and to see when she might be available for an interview.

No answer. He figured she must be in one of those no cell zones at the hospital. He stood and crossed to the whiteboard.

Scanning its contents, it occurred to him that Emma had links to everyone up there except Samson.

He'd just picked up the marker and printed "EMMA LAWSON" next to "LUKE DOYLE" when Jackie O and Carlos returned.

Once they were settled at the conference table he explained his reasoning, gesturing with the marker as he reviewed the additions to the board.

"Upon finding Kate Doyle at Rainbow Alley, Emma Lawson phoned 911. Emma was holding the shooter's weapon when I arrived. She'll need to be interviewed about what she saw, and any impressions she had. We'll also want to know whether the site itself is significant, whether the motive for Kate's shooting might have something to do with the school."

Jackie O frowned.

"Do you think Emma might have been the target? Isn't she with the Hayden Commission? I read that they broke a big case a few months back about a contractor with state social services engaged in human trafficking. Maybe this was payback of some kind?"

That didn't fit the facts as Alibi knew them, but he didn't want to discourage Jackie O from thinking outside the box. "It's good to look at every angle," he said. "But Emma wouldn't have been the lead on that case. She was an assistant investigator then, that would have been her predecessor."

Carlos spoke up. "Emma dated Tommy—when was that two, three months ago?"

Alibi nodded. It had been common knowledge around the department. Tommy had brought Emma to a couple of after work events, where she'd attracted plenty of attention. She'd projected a professional air in her trim pastel suits, but she and Tommy had never been out of reach of one another, where she could brush his hand or he could lean in for a soft word.

"I only rode with him for about a month and he wasn't much of a talker," Carlos continued. "But even though I knew they'd broken up it seemed like she was on his mind because he brought her up a few times. Maybe they stayed friends? I'm thinking he might have disclosed to her that he was still looking for Quan's killer. Or if not that, she might be able to recall any odd behavior of his. Places he went that were unexpected. She might know things that could help us to lock down his having used Samson as an informant."

"Good," Alibi said, drawing a new line from Emma's name to Tommy's. He'd already connected her to Kate and Luke.

Privately, he wasn't surprised Tommy hadn't shared much that was personal with Carlos. Though he and Tommy had confided in each other about a lot of things when they were partners, he doubted Tommy could have gotten a word in edgewise very often with Carlos.

Alibi moved on to Luke.

"How about Luke Doyle? What are the main things we know about him related to these investigations?"

Jackie O spoke first. "Luke's bike was at the scene of his mother's shooting. It was unlocked, so it's a fair assumption he left it there in daylight, today rather than last night when it would have been at risk at the school's downtown location of being stolen. Also, like Samson, Luke worked for Marty at the bike shop, though Luke quit two weeks ago. And Luke was picked up with Samson for a possible hate crime, defacing the synagogue, though they said they were cleaning the wall." She paused. "That's already three, but I think most important is Luke gives us a possible starting point for Tommy and Samson. Maybe that night at the station when Tommy went to pick up Luke is when Tommy first met Samson." She paused for a beat, frowning. "Or could Luke have been Tommy's informant? And then Samson got involved, too, in a way that got him killed?"

Carlos responded. "Maybe. I mean that could fit. But while I hate to say this, isn't it also possible Luke was working at the bike shop because he was into the white supremacist stuff and either intentionally or unintentionally had a role in his mom's shooting? Do we know what kind of relationship they had? Teenagers sometimes lose it in the worst way."

Alibi knew Carlos was thinking of a case the year prior, when a teen had shot and killed both his parents. He'd said in his confession that it was because they'd put limits on his video game play, but then the abuse the teen had suffered at home had come out.

"We also still have the blackmail theory," Jackie O said. "With both Samson and Luke working at the bike shop, maybe one or both of them overheard something Marty said about illegal activity, and Marty found out Luke had told his mom, resulting in her being targeted."

Alibi looked at the board. Lots of good information there. Maybe too much. He felt they were getting further away rather than closer to the answer.

Tommy would definitely have called them out for chasing zebras.

"Let's go back to basics," he said. "We have the Gambler, Samuel Miller, telling us Samson was an informant, and a statement from Janie Kieu that supports Tommy having been at Samson's apartment. Carlos, anything yet on who, if anyone, Miller spoke with in the medical ward this morning? If that's how Miller got the information that led him to believe Samson was an informant, perhaps there's something there."

"Not yet. It would be quickest if I go to the jail and do it on site rather than waiting for them to get the information to us."

Alibi nodded, and Carlos began packing up his tablet to go. But Carlos stopped as he read something on his screen. His eyebrows shot up.

"I have a message from Marty Lightzer. I had left him my card. He says he wants to speak with me about something important related to Samson's death. He wants to meet tonight, eight o'clock at his house."

Alibi said, "Well, that's certainly interesting. Leave the jail records until tomorrow—no telling how long that might take. Ask Rachel to go with you to Lightzer's.

Though he appears to have an alibi for Samson's death, that shouldn't be a one-person interview."

Alibi knew Carlos would prefer Jackie O accompany him to the bike shop owner's home. He could see the two of them got on well. But Jackie O was short-term with the department and gang-focused. He didn't want to broach the subject with Carlos yet, but with Tommy's death, Carlos would need a new permanent partner sooner than they'd thought, and Rachel was a good cop who was due a promotion.

Nishad stuck his head in the office door.

"The hospital called for you. A Ms. Lawson told a nurse she had an emergency and had to leave. They wanted to know if they might release the room she'd been using."

An emergency? Another one?

Now what's happened?

Alibi didn't like it that Emma wasn't picking up her cell. He'd feel better if he knew where she was.

Also, he needed to speak with Luke about anything he might know about Samson's death, since they were friends and had worked together at the bike shop. He also wanted to know why his bike was left at the site of his mother's shooting.

He thought he might be able to accomplish both things if the hunch he had was correct. He turned to Jackie O.

"You'll know the questions to ask Luke Doyle about his working at Marty's and about Samson, to see if there are gang links relevant to these cases. But since he's a minor and Kate's unavailable, we'll want Emma present. Tommy told me she had some kind of legal standing with Luke." He pocketed his notebook and reached for his jacket. "Given that Emma's left the hospital, I've a good idea where they both might be."

Matchbook Lane

ALIBI HAD BEEN to Emma's place several times with Tommy and thought it would be easy to remember the route. He was concerned now that he might have been overconfident. He was about to look up her address, to enter it in the Camry's GPS, when he recognized a large red house on the corner of an approaching side street, the landmark he remembered.

They'd reached Matchbook Lane.

He had just parked at the curb in front of Emma's home, a small, cocoa-colored, mid-century bungalow, and braced himself for stepping out into the heat when the silence of the quiet cul-de-sac was broken by a powerful series of barks.

Emma's dog, Crash, appeared at her living room window.

When Alibi and Jackie O were both out of the car, Crash persisted, unabated, which Alibi knew meant Emma was not at home. Had she been there, she would have quieted her dog. Alibi remembered her being a stickler for not letting the barking continue if she could help it since she'd had multiple complaints from a neighbor.

"Over here," he said to Jackie O as he turned and strode across the street.

She joined him in front of what looked like a modest single-family home except for the two bright blue front doors. One had a small metal "A" at eye height, the other, a "B." Alibi stepped forward and knocked briskly several times on each door in turn. No answer.

The drapes were closed on both front windows. He and Jackie O went around the side where they found the blinds up on what was clearly a teenager's room. A poster of Muhammad Ali and one of the singer Phoebe Bridgers were visible on the far wall.

But it was when Alibi saw the tenor saxophone in a corner that he was sure it was Luke's. Emma and Tommy had both talked about the boy's talent on the horn.

A laptop sat open on the bed. While its contents might have been helpful in figuring out where Luke was, Alibi wasn't about to break into the duplex to get it. They headed back across the street.

Jackie O had her hand on the passenger door to the Camry when Alibi continued walking past the car. He climbed Emma's front steps, crouched, and removed the key from underneath the last step before moving on to the landing.

Jackie O caught up with him. "You're not going to use that, are you?" she asked.

Alibi figured his knowledge of where the key was hidden offered some defense against an unlawful entry charge. Plus, Nishad said Emma had an emergency, and she wasn't answering her phone or her door. It seemed appropriate to check on her safety.

Crash was now barking nonstop in a decidedly unfriendly manner. But Emma had brought the dog along with her and Tommy on numerous occasions, and Alibi had gotten on well with him.

Once Crash recognized his voice and his scent, they'd be fine.

Or at least Alibi hoped so.

He spoke loudly as he put the key in the door. "Good boy, Crash."

He could feel Jackie tense behind him.

He slid the door open slowly, keeping the side of his body against it, his weight in place, calmly continuing his soothing, one-sided conversation.

"Hey, Crash, hey boy, good boy."

The barking stopped, replaced by a whine and a loud thumping of Crash's tail on the floor as he moved back into a sit position, the equivalent of giving an all clear. Alibi opened the door the rest of the way and bent to scratch Crash behind the ears as he'd seen Emma and Tommy both do.

He heard Jackie O let out her breath. He wondered how long she'd been holding it.

With Crash settled, Alibi took in the front room, and a memory, or perhaps another ghostly resurrection, hit him hard.

In a shimmering grey light he saw Tommy sitting with Emma on the couch, his arm around her, her hand resting on his thigh.

She said something low, inaudible. Her eyes lit up, and the ghostly Tommy laughed.

"What is it?" Jackie asked.

"Nothing," Alibi said, though privately, he was concerned Tommy wasn't passing easily to the other side. He wondered what it would take to help his old friend and partner make his journey in peace.

Crash followed Alibi as he started up the hall, but Jackie O stayed where she was, her eyes on the dog.

"Stick with me. He's fine, really," Alibi said.

They passed a bathroom, then a small room that had been set up as Emma's home office, before reaching the master in the back.

"What are we looking for?" Jackie O asked.

Alibi didn't answer. He wasn't sure. But when he stepped inside Emma's bedroom, he felt a chill.

Though the room looked like something out of a 1960s fantasy, a snug and cozy space decorated in white and orange dominated by a double bed with a vintage frame, his eyes fixed on the bloodstained suit jacket neatly laid out on top of the bedspread. Alibi thought again of the vacant chair in his office among the spirits of the recently and violently departed. Had it signified there was one more ghostly guest yet to come? And why had Emma been with Tommy in the brief otherworldly vision he'd just experienced?

Where is she? Why hasn't she picked up?

He needed fresh air. He turned and retraced his steps without explanation, but when he was at the front door, he realized Jackie wasn't with him.

She called his name from the kitchen. He passed through the swinging door. She was staring at a small notepad on Emma's kitchen table. Crash sat quietly at her side. Immersed in whatever it was she had found, Jackie O seemed to have forgotten about the big dog.

Alibi stepped closer and could see the notepad was dense with writing. It appeared to contain two distinct messages, both handwritten by the same person.

Luke,

I've gone to LCC to find you.
If we miss each other there,
message me as soon as you see this.

Love,
Aunt Emma

Deb,

You at Beryl's (BLUE-GREEN) house?
I got Death by Violetall (OPPOSITE) Rejoinder (RESPOND) tix for us!! Don't tell Antiphon (RESPONSE IN A CHANT).
Serious don't. Concert is total surprise HAHA.
Would be like LCC (LINVILLE CREEK CAFE) x 5, right on! (?).
A 10 plus one(?) if they open with Ubiety (POSITION/STATE OF EXISTENCE) of Gendar (GENDER MISSPELLED?)

Jackie O took out her tablet, checked for service, and sat down in one of the kitchen chairs. Within a minute, she announced, "A search for LCC yields a few things. Linville Creek Café makes the most sense. It's about twenty-five miles from here."

Alibi was focused on the rest of what was on the paper.

"Who is Deb?" he wondered aloud.

Meanwhile, Crash's eyes traveled back and forth between Alibi and a Labrador-shaped cookie jar on the counter. Alibi understood and got him a treat, then considered the size of the big dog and took out three more before looking again at the note.

Evidently, Emma had located Luke in Linville and was on her way there.

Alibi knew that as Head of Major Crimes it wasn't really his role to run down individual leads. And if asked, he wouldn't have been able to explain the sense of urgency he had to find Emma and Luke. Mentioning an empty chair in the spirit world and a vision of Emma with a dead man wouldn't cut it. But it's not like he had anything else pressing to do, and the interviews with Emma and Luke had to happen sometime. He made up his mind and once they were outside, having replaced the key under the top step, he turned to Jackie O.

"When we get in the car, call ahead to the café. Provide descriptions of Emma and Luke to whoever answers. Let them know we're on our way to Linville and we want the woman and teen to wait for us."

THIRTY-NINE

On the Road

PHONE IN HAND, Jackie O said, "I can give a description of Luke from the photo I took at Marty's. What does Emma look like?"

Picturing Emma was easy enough for Alibi to do.

He stuck to the basics as he pulled the Camry away from the curb.

"Five foot five or six, slender. Dark hair that doesn't reach her shoulders, green eyes."

Before Jackie O could tap in the number for the café, Alibi's phone, which he'd placed in a holder on the dash, buzzed loudly.

The caller ID showed "The Mayor."

Jackie O raised her eyebrows.

Alibi shrugged, then answered using the car's built-in hands-free mechanism.

"Good afternoon, Mayor. I'm in the car with a colleague, Jackie Oliver. You're on speaker."

"Good afternoon to you both," the mayor said curtly before launching into what was clearly the purpose of her call. "Alibi, exactly when were you planning on telling me playing cards were found on that boy's body by the river this morning?"

Alibi had known details of the crime scene would leak at some point, but he hadn't anticipated they would get out this fast, although, of course, the mayor would be interested, and she would have her sources.

"We are at the beginning of this investigation," he said, "but one thing we know with certainty is those cards do not match specifics of the type found on the Gambler's victims."

"Then why were they there? Is this a copycat killer, another bigoted son of a bitch who is out to kill young people who are any color but white?"

A fast thinker and an even faster talker, Mayor Melissa Ruiz didn't bother choosing her words carefully the way most politicians did. It had gotten her into trouble at times, but since being a truth teller was at a premium in today's politics it had also gotten her reelected.

"We have considered that possibility, Mayor, but we believe this was a targeted hit on this young man, likely related to his uncovering something the killer didn't want known."

"I see. And do you have a suspect?"

Alibi thought about Marty Lightzer's size-eleven feet that didn't match the footprints at the murder scene, about Tommy's size thirteens that did, about Luke Doyle knowing Samson, and about Marty Lightzer's fear of the third roommate. "We are following several lines of inquiry—"

She cut him off. "No arrest imminent?"

Alibi said nothing, correctly assuming the question was rhetorical. Mayor Ruiz barely took a breath before continuing.

"Suppose you are wrong? Suppose this is the beginning of another string of executions of young people in our immigrant communities? If we have not warned them and they walk home alone in the dark tonight on an untraveled path, down an alley or along the river, and one of them is shot and killed, that is on us. That is on *you*. That is on *me*."

Alibi remained quiet.

He could see her point.

"I want this online and on the air as soon as possible," she said. "An hour ago would have been the right time. I don't want to start a panic, but I do want our young people to be forewarned so they can take precautions."

"We'll get something ready to release right away," Alibi said. "I know you understand we need to keep tightly held anything on the type of cards. But we should be able to prepare a statement that will generate caution, without including that information."

"Fine. I will leave the specifics to you," the mayor said. "Be on the steps of City Hall in thirty minutes for a press conference. I will see you then."

She rang off without giving him a chance to indicate whether he could make that work.

While thirty minutes wasn't much time, he figured he could get there if he stepped on the gas, so long as they didn't run into any roadwork or traffic problems.

Seeing Emma and interviewing Luke would have to wait.

He thought briefly about his wrinkled suit coat on the back seat and was happy he'd at least managed a shower and change of clothes that morning since the mayor was a believer that professional appearance inspired confidence.

Although he was more concerned with what exactly he was going to say.

Then he noticed Jackie O had taken out her tablet and was already in the process of drafting the press release he'd just promised the mayor.

FORTY

Linville Creek Café

DYLAN SPOKE SOFTLY.

"Emma, we're here."

She opened her eyes at the unfamiliar voice and with a start realized she'd fallen asleep in Dylan's car, her head resting against the passenger side window.

She sat upright and saw that in the absence of an available space, Dylan had double-parked in front of their destination, the Linville Creek Café.

She'd been here dozens of times with Luke over the years.

It was a small, one-story building painted a cheerful daffodil-yellow with a bright leaf-green door, colors evocative of spring. The broad front porch had tables for outdoor seating, all of which were full, despite the stubborn heat, with early diners just off work. The café was known for its fresh salads, homemade pies and pastries, and freshly squeezed, honey-sweetened lemonade.

"You go in," Dylan said. "I'll find a place to park and wait."

"This shouldn't take long," she said, and then realized that might not be true.

She wasn't only here to give Luke a ride. She had a difficult task in front of her. To tell him about his mother, if he didn't already know, and either way to comfort and reassure him. Maybe it would be better to have that conversation over lemonade and pie.

"I appreciate that," she said, opening the car door as she spoke, suddenly anxious to get inside. "But I think I'll get a ride service home with Luke."

"Suppose he's not here?" Dylan asked. "I'll stay a few minutes. If you don't come right out, I'll take off."

Dylan was beginning to feel hard to get rid of, but Emma didn't want to overthink it. She thanked him and got out.

Inside, the voices of customers rose and fell against the background strains of Willie Nelson crooning "Always on My Mind." Two couples waited their turn as a young woman with bright pink hair worked the register. She stood behind a glass counter filled with tempting pies bursting with peaches, apples, and blackberries beneath golden-brown crusts, and walnut bars, one of the café specialties.

To Emma's right were booths along a wall of windows that looked out on Linville's two-lane State Street. To her left, the main room held over a dozen tables and provided counter service for those willing to sit on stools.

She dodged wait staff carrying trays of treats, glasses of lemonade, and pots of coffee, as she did a walk-through to thoroughly check both sides for Luke. She had to do it twice because the first time she'd been looking for a young teen with shoulder-length, curly dark hair. The second time she adjusted her criteria, scanning for the Luke she'd encountered that morning: older-looking, with a shaved head.

Neither Luke was there.

But she wasn't ready to accept defeat.

Luke had texted her "LCC." Linville Creek Café—

it couldn't mean anything else. Why would he have done that if he wasn't going to be here? She stopped a waiter who was empty-handed, headed back toward the kitchen.

"I'm supposed to meet a young friend here. Tall. He has a shaved head."

"I don't recall seeing anyone like that," the waiter said, already in motion, walking away, though he called back over his shoulder, "but it's been really busy."

Emma wasn't done. She decided it was time to treat the problem with the seriousness it deserved. She was Luke's guardian. In that capacity, she was to protect him, *to guard him*, from pain and suffering as best she could. Today, that required finding him.

Now.

She wished she hadn't changed out of her suit. She could do with some sign of her authority. She stood straight and marched up to the cashier, bypassing the line.

"I'm looking for a young man, a teenager. Tall, nice-looking, shaved head."

The cashier shook her head and looked past her at the other people waiting.

"It's important," Emma said firmly. "I'd like to speak to the manager."

The cashier registered Emma's tone and called to a young woman who was clearing a nearby booth. "Chloe, would you get Lori? This lady needs to talk to her."

After what seemed like a long few minutes, Chloe reappeared alone. She looked like she was holding back tears.

"Mike burned his arm. It was oil from the fryer. Lori is getting a doctor or something."

"I'm sorry," Emma said. "I hope he's okay."

She was sorry Mike had gotten burned, but she was also sorry she was making no progress locating Luke.

She felt about out of ideas when she noticed there was no longer anyone in line for the cashier. She approached the counter and asked for a walnut bar and a lemonade to go, and also if she might borrow a pen and paper. While the cashier prepared her order, she scribbled a note to the manager.

That accomplished, she rummaged in her bag for her wallet, but as she moved her phone to look underneath it, the screen came to life, displaying a notification that she'd missed a text.

I understand you've left the hospital.

Please call me.

Alibi

Tucking the pastry bag in her satchel, with one hand holding the lemonade and the other her phone, she stepped out onto the café's front porch. She intended to call a ride service and then Alibi when she saw Dylan leaning against his Jeep, parked in a spot right in front that had opened up. She'd completely forgotten he'd said he'd wait for her, and in any case, it had been far more than a few minutes.

Still, it's probably for the best he's here, she thought.

It would be faster to go back with him rather than waiting for a ride service. And Luke must be at home, where else could he be? Although maybe that's why Alibi wanted to speak with her. Maybe he had an update on Kate. Perhaps Luke had heard the reports about the shooting at Rainbow Alley and had shown up at the hospital.

She waved to get Dylan's attention and held up her phone, indicating she had a call to make.

She didn't want to speak with Alibi while riding in Dylan's car.

Dylan was, after all, a stranger to her. She hadn't known him back in high school, not really, and she certainly didn't know him now.

FORTY-ONE

On the Road

ALIBI HAD JUST hung up with the mayor, when his phone rang again.

"Alibi? It's Emma."

It was only when he heard Emma's voice that he realized how truly worried he'd been about her having gone missing, even briefly.

There'd been too many deaths today. He supposed he was expecting another one around every corner.

"Thank you for getting back to me," he said, more formally than he felt. He was conscious of Jackie O beside him, able to hear.

"I'm sorry I didn't let you know I was leaving the hospital," Emma said. Her words sounded rushed. "I went to find Luke, Kate's son. I think you've met him? I wanted to tell him what had happened to her, before he found out some other way."

Alibi heard dishes clinking in the background, a low murmur of voices. She must still be at the café. But she hadn't indicated whether Luke was there or not.

As he braked at a stop sign, he thought about how best to frame the next thing he had to say.

"Yes, I remember Luke. In fact, I was hoping to speak with him and thought you might have his contact information. When I couldn't reach you, I went to your house, and when no one was home I used the porch key to go inside. I saw your note to Luke on the kitchen table."

There was an extended silence on the other end.

Jackie O frowned, undoubtedly wondering whether they were about to be busted for illegally entering someone's home.

But all Emma said when she finally spoke was, "Did Crash let you in?"

She sounded like she found that unlikely.

Alibi smiled at Jackie O.

To Emma, he said, "Yes, Crash was fine. Is Luke with you?"

"No. He wasn't where I thought he would be. I got a text from the hospital that there's been no change in Kate's condition so I'm headed home. I figure Luke must be on his way back, if he's not already there."

"That makes sense," Alibi said. "I texted you because I'd like to interview you about the specifics of your experience at Rainbow Alley today. I've got to be somewhere now for an hour or so. Maybe after that? Also, if you're able to share Luke's cell, I'd like to set up something similar with him."

"Luke doesn't have a working phone right now. That's why it hasn't been easy for me to locate him." A beat passed before she asked, "Why do you want to talk to him?"

Alibi thought he detected wariness in her voice, though maybe she was just tired. This was one more thing for her to deal with. He considered what to disclose.

"Luke's bike is at the school. We're wondering if it was left overnight or if he was also there today. He might have seen something out of the ordinary, maybe someone checking out the place before the incident happened."

He realized he was avoiding mentioning Kate's name. He recalled Emma, her hand gripping his in the hospital, how she'd collapsed to her knees.

"Luke was there this morning," Emma said. "He brought papers to the capitol for me to sign. We walked back together to Rainbow Alley. That was around eleven, maybe closer to noon. He told me he had band practice this afternoon. My guess is one of the kids picked him up. They're not all from around here, which is why Linville made some sense."

Alibi heard muted laughter, then a car passing.

"Listen, I've really got to go," Emma said. "I don't know about meeting later. Would tomorrow work?"

Alibi hesitated.

For some reason that he couldn't identify, he didn't want talking to Luke and Emma to be put off. He supposed he was letting the combined events of the day push him into overdrive.

But he had the press conference to get to, and he didn't know how long that would last. Later might be impractical for him, too. And Emma had an awful lot to cope with. Her best friend's fate was uncertain, and she had at least short-term responsibility for a teenage boy.

He reminded himself Samson was gone, Janie was gone, Quan was gone, and Tommy was gone. Nothing was going to change in twenty-four hours that could make a difference to any of them. There'd be no harm in giving Emma and Luke a bit of breathing space.

FORTY-TWO

The Blue House

LUKE LOOKED CAREFULLY around the small bedroom.

Maybe he'd find a previously undetected escape route.

No such luck. There was still only the single window with alarm sensors and the door leading to a house populated by armed men.

He experienced conflicting signals from his brain. One conveying overwhelming fatigue, the other, desperate agitation.

Lie down, give up... Go, go, act now.

Meanwhile, Vivian sat cross-legged on the bed, headphones on, smiling at a movie she'd undoubtedly seen a dozen times already. Observing her, Luke thought maybe he'd had it all wrong. Maybe rather than wanting to get older faster, he should have wished to become younger, to find some magic dust that could make him three years old again with the weight of the world on someone else's shoulders.

He'd told Vivian they would be going home soon, and she'd believed him.

He wanted to believe it too.

When he'd said it, he'd felt optimistic. After all, he'd succeeded in sending a message to Emma. It hadn't worried him that the text was in code. Emma hadn't missed an SAT word yet. And she must have understood he didn't want her to respond, because the Creep had Walter's phone and if she'd texted back, there definitely would have been trouble.

But doubt crept in when he remembered he hadn't been able to see the final message the Creep sent, and when he tried to picture whether he'd typed everything he'd memorized, he thought he might not have completed the last word. *Gendarme.* Meaning "police." It wasn't an SAT word. He'd learned it in French class. If that part of the message had been unclear, would Emma have understood the text was something more than a weird vocabulary test he'd decided to spring on her?

He tried to estimate how long it had been since the message was sent.

Fifteen minutes? Thirty? More?

He didn't have a watch or a phone.

Vivian laughed, then paused the movie and slid her headphones off one ear. "This is funny. Want to watch with me?" she asked, scooting over to make room for him.

Luke smiled. A movie invitation must mean he was definitely a good guy in her eyes. And a distraction, even one meant for a preschooler, was welcome right now. But when he stood to join her, he felt dizzy.

"Be there in a minute," he said as he headed toward the bathroom.

"Again?" she asked, rolling her eyes.

"I want to wash up." He hoped it would help clear his head. "I'll be right back."

But he'd no sooner gone inside, splashed cold water on his face and toweled it dry when he heard Vivian cry out, "Kelly!"

Luke was through the door in an instant.

The Creep was standing at the end of the bed. Vivian

had backed into the corner farthest from him, BeeBee clutched tightly against her chest.

"What are you doing?" Luke asked him.

The Creep didn't answer. He didn't take his eyes off Vivian.

Luke recognized something in the man's glazed expression, something he'd seen before, in a fifteen-year-old friend who was really into watching porn. He felt sick. He stepped forward and blocked the Creep's way, putting his body between the man and Vivian.

"She might need something," the Creep said to Luke. "Go in the kitchen, make her a sandwich."

"No," Luke said. "She brought snacks. She doesn't want anything else. She told me her stomach's upset."

Vivian looked at Luke, frowning. He thought she might be deciding whether lying was acceptable in this situation. He gave her a small reassuring nod.

The Creep bounced from foot to foot for what seemed like a long time, but seeing that Luke did not budge he finally left the room.

It occurred to Luke then that the only time he'd seen the Creep still was when he was staring at Vivian.

After he'd left, Vivian said, "I don't like him."

"I don't like him either," Luke said.

And in that moment he knew where he'd seen the man before.

Hanging around the bike shop.

He guessed the Creep didn't recognize him because he wasn't wearing his Marty's Bikes employee uniform, the red shirt. Then he realized it wasn't that. He'd had his long curls when he was working at the store. Aunt Emma hadn't even known it was him at first with his shaved head.

The Creep had been there a lot, riding up and down

the back alley. He'd also purchased a few things. The red bike rack Luke had seen in the garage when he pulled in the SUV had looked new, and that model was the bestseller at their shop.

He wondered if the Creep's having been at Marty's often meant something.

About the kidnapping.

About any of this.

But Walter had taken Vivian from Rainbow Alley, not from the bike shop.

Maybe the Creep was just seriously into bikes.

Luke sat down next to Vivian. She restarted the video, but she was no longer smiling.

He looked at the screen with her, but he wasn't watching.

He was wondering about Emma, about the text, and about time passing.

FORTY-THREE

On the Road

EMMA AND DYLAN had left Linville's small downtown behind and were driving through a residential neighborhood on their way to the freeway. She hoped Luke would be at the duplex with Crash when they got back to Matchbook Lane, though she was having trouble convincing herself it would happen.

Something was nagging at her. Something about Luke's text. She tried to put it out of her mind. She would see him soon.

She wished she'd thought to bring Dylan something to eat. She offered him half her walnut bar, which he graciously declined. She was enjoying its shortbread-like texture and the sharp flavor of fresh walnuts from nearby trees, when it suddenly came to her. What it was that she might have misunderstood in Luke's coded message.

She looked out the car window at each home they passed, and then abruptly said to Dylan, "Wait. Stop here." With what was left of the walnut bar in her hand, she was out of the car and onto the sidewalk before he'd put the Jeep's transmission into park.

She strode up a stone path lined with bright pink asters in full bloom to the door of a pale blue, two-story Victorian. When she rang the bell, a young woman answered, a toddler clinging to the back of her skirt.

Emma spoke with her briefly, then returned to the Jeep idling noisily at the curb.

"What did you say to her?" Dylan asked.

"That I'm looking for my friend's son, who said he was at band practice at a blue home in Linville."

"Is it your plan to check every blue house?"

Dylan didn't sound judgmental. More curious than anything else.

"Maybe he included 'Linville Creek Café' in the message to give us the general area, but 'beryl house' was the primary clue," Emma explained. "So I think it makes sense to at least try the streets right around the café. Anyway, blue isn't that common of a color for homes."

They stopped at a deep blue ranch-style house where no one answered, then at a cottage that was more green than blue where an elderly man seemed highly irritated by the random interruption in his day.

"No kids here," he said, as he slammed the door in Emma's face.

After three more failed attempts, she said to Dylan. "This might take longer than I thought. If you don't have time, it's no problem. I can walk the neighborhoods and get a ride service home."

"Look, there's one at the end of the block," Dylan said, pointing to a duplex in a deep royal blue. "Let's check it out." He added, "I'm happy to help."

After knocking on the doors of four more blue and bluish homes of various vintages and architectural styles without success, Emma felt discouraged.

Maybe this wasn't what Luke had meant.

Or maybe it was one of the houses where no one had answered, and he'd found a way home by now.

She checked her phone, no messages, and let out an

audible sigh. Wherever Luke was, the more time that passed the more likely it was that he'd heard about Kate on the news.

Dylan was watching her.

He slowed the car and said, "This kid means a lot to you."

It was a statement, not a question.

Emma felt tears stinging her eyes. Dylan eased to a stop along the curb in the next block. She looked out her window, but there was no blue house in sight.

"Let me see the text he sent," Dylan said, extending his hand for her phone.

She looked at him, a question in her eyes, but he gave no response.

She located Luke's message. Dylan read it quickly, then without comment made a U-turn and increased his speed. He retraced their route past the café and through Linville's shopping district until they were out the other side on a long, straight, two-lane road.

Emma could see he wasn't taking her home because he was heading away from the freeway.

"Where are we going?" she asked.

He didn't answer.

It made her nervous, but she figured he must be pursuing some new idea to find Luke, something he'd seen in the message. They passed an elementary school and adjacent playground, the swings and climbing structure empty and quiet. After that there was nothing but acres of trees and summer fields, yellowed from months without rain, until Dylan slowed and made a right on the first cross street Emma had seen in some time. She hadn't been expecting it, she didn't catch the street sign, if there'd been one.

It was poorly paved, a bumpy ride, though Dylan did

his best to avoid the largest ruts and sinkholes as he silently piloted the Jeep through rows of walnut trees. The only building they passed was a low, brown farmhouse in the distance, until the road curved, and a small, well-maintained home came into view. It was a soft blue with cream-colored trim.

Dylan parked opposite it.

Emma's mouth dropped open. "Whose house is this? How did you know it was here?"

Dylan didn't answer. He appeared to be studying the exterior of the home, maybe checking for movement behind the drapes, in the windows.

When he looked back at her, his expression was inscrutable.

"Wait here," he said curtly.

He got out of the Jeep, leaving the engine running and the air-conditioning on and crossed the road toward the blue house.

FORTY-FOUR

The Blue House

DYLAN HAD HOPED never to be here again. But when he'd
reread the message he'd had no doubt as to what Luke
had been trying to tell Emma. The only place that fit
the clues the teen had given was this cornflower-blue
house in the heart of the orchards, miles outside of town,
the headquarters for Gregg Corbel Properties. And that
had presented an opportunity Dylan could not ignore.

Of course, it would take more than this one thing. He
knew that. When he was elected senator, he would finally have the authority and power that attracted Emma.
But being the one to find Luke, to meet a desperate
need of hers now, could begin to shift her outdated
view of him.

He never liked coming here, but he told himself there
was no reason to worry this time. As he approached
the front door, he took a deep breath. His contract was
over, he'd gotten his money, and he'd thought through
how to handle things on the brief drive over. It was a
quarter past six. Dropping by at this hour wouldn't be
rude. The blue house was a place of business, after all.
And Dylan had his story ready.

He wouldn't ask about Luke, at least not at first.

He didn't want to put Gregg on the spot. He probably hired a lot of temporary employees to help him flip
houses and Dylan didn't know whether all of that was

done legally. Maybe the kid had lied about his age and was working without his mother's permission, under the table for less than minimum wage. Or maybe he really was here for band practice. The guys Dylan had seen at the blue house might jam in their downtime.

It was a small house. He'd take a look around, ask to use the bathroom. He'd be able to tell if one or more teenagers were there. If that failed, he might ask, though he doubted that would be necessary. It had been a while since Luke had sent the text. Whatever the reason for him having been here, he'd probably already gone home.

But as Dylan took the last few steps, he hoped the boy hadn't left yet. He'd win a lot of points with Emma if Luke was still there.

EMMA WATCHED DYLAN approach the tidy little blue house with its freshly painted cream trim. It didn't suit its surroundings. Who would build anything other than a farmhouse out here?

Perhaps it had started out in Kansas and was lifted by a tornado, whirling through the sky, until it dropped here, in the middle of a walnut orchard. So long as there wasn't a witch crushed beneath it whose sister was on the hunt for revenge, Emma guessed that was okay. Although some people just *really* liked their privacy. She supposed that's what this was about.

Either way, it was a bad idea for Dylan to go up to the house alone, even if he knew the people who lived there. If Luke was inside, she didn't want to embarrass him if he'd wanted to hide from his bandmates the fact he'd phoned her to come get him. And what if he'd already heard about Kate? She couldn't leave that inter-action to Dylan.

She reached for the key to turn off the Jeep and saw

only a flat button beside the steering wheel. Having driven the vintage Mustang for years, she was always a little surprised by keyless starters, despite their growing popularity. She pressed the button and the engine noise stopped. She searched briefly but couldn't find where Dylan had left the key fob, then decided she didn't have time, and besides who was going to steal a car out here?

She caught up with him on the stoop just as Dylan knocked on the front door.

When he turned and saw her, he snapped, "Get back in the car."

She was about to tell him she had every right to be with him each step of the way while they looked for Luke, when the door opened and a man stepped outside to join them, pulling the door closed behind him.

He was tall and fit-looking with short white hair.

"Dylan, hello," he said. "This is a surprise."

PART FOUR

FORTY-FIVE

The Blue House

THOUGH HE DIDN'T appear to Emma to be unfriendly, the man with the white hair didn't smile.

"Barry, I apologize for dropping in like this. I'd like to speak with Gregg," Dylan said.

Then he turned to Emma with a hard look, as though to forestall any contribution she might want to make to the conversation. "Why don't you go to the car? If Gregg's able to see me, this should only take a few minutes."

Emma didn't care what kind of look Dylan gave her. She was not going to be sent away to wait as though she were a child. She'd just opened her mouth to make that clear when she heard a grinding noise and the garage door opened. A large black SUV backed out at a startling speed down the short drive. When the small man driving took notice of the three of them, he slowed to a stop.

Barry signaled to him to roll down his window.

"Take it back inside."

"But the Chief told me to…" the SUV driver began. He seemed uncertain how to continue. "To…to dispose of, you know, the unexpected—"

"Inside," Barry repeated, and the driver backed up, returning the vehicle as directed into the garage.

Barry's phone pinged.

"Excuse me," he said before disappearing into the house, closing the door behind him.

Dylan spoke in a low tone to Emma. "I know what I'm doing. Go back to the car." When she didn't move, he spoke more gently. "Please, I'll find out if Luke is here. It won't take long."

The front door opened again. This time Barry did not join them outside.

"Gregg is able to see you, Dylan. Come on in."

He looked at Emma. "You too, ma'am."

"No," Dylan said. "She has some calls to make. She'll do that from the car."

Emma heard an edge of panic in Dylan's voice.

Maybe he hadn't grown up quite as much as she'd first thought, which she feared wasn't going to help set things right here.

She didn't want to get off on the wrong foot with this man, Barry, or whoever else might be inside. People could be funny about teenagers. Perhaps Luke and his bandmates had done something they shouldn't have. Broken a vase, spilled a drink on a valuable rug, who knows, and an apology from a parent, a reimbursement for the damage, was needed before they could leave. Getting Luke home quickly with the least drama, given what awaited him with his mom, was the most important thing.

It had to be about that, not about what made Dylan most comfortable.

She said to Barry, "Thank you," and stepped inside.

After a beat, she heard Dylan's footsteps behind her, and Barry closed the door.

SEQUESTERED IN HIS private space off the kitchen, Gregg had been projecting year-end profits for his business, an activity he found calming, when he heard a vehicle pull up across the street and then voices on the front step.

Within minutes, Barry had informed him via text that the unexpected visitors were Dylan Johnson and an unknown woman.

That had piqued Gregg's curiosity.

Why would Dylan come back? He'd received all his agreed-upon money.

Then it had occurred to Gregg that Dylan must have heard the news of Detective Tommy Noonan's death. He'd probably driven out here without forethought, a woman in tow, to obtain reassurance that his having unearthed the officer's name had not somehow led to this tragedy.

Gregg could provide that comfort to Dylan. He could ease the man's guilt. In fact, he was happy to. Because despite his unfortunate history with Quan Noonan's accidental death, he'd had no role in Tommy Noonan's sudden transition to the afterlife, and he certainly didn't want Dylan believing that he had.

And as he thought about it, a brief unscheduled business meeting, letting people into the house to see him as though it were any other work day could be prudent.

Gregg had estimated that the operation, as planned, yielded a less than one percent chance he would be identified by the authorities as being behind Vivian Lange's kidnapping. But that had been before the nanny was shot dead and Walter's cousin was drafted to act as the girl's caretaker and guard.

Bottom line, there'd been considerable unexpected noise in the system. Better to add a layer of normalcy to muffle it, to quiet things down.

And in the still highly improbable event circumstances deteriorated to the point that Gregg found he required an alibi, who better than Border Lake's Councilman Dylan Johnson, bound by his oath of office, to act as his character witness?

So he'd told Barry to first let Kelly know they had visitors and to caution him to keep the girl quiet. Though as it turned out, there'd been no need for that. Barry had reported that both the girl and Kelly were sleeping. It must have been her nap time, and Walter's cousin, with more excitement than he'd bargained for and nothing to do but wait, had also fallen asleep. With that settled, he'd asked Barry to bring Dylan directly back to his office. The woman could remain in the main room under Lee's watchful eye.

Gregg gestured to Dylan to sit in the chair opposite him. Barry remained standing in the open doorway to the kitchen, his posture erect.

"Thank you for seeing me," Dylan said, sitting down in the offered chair. "This should only take a minute." His tone was businesslike. "Could you clarify one condition of the agreement? How much time will I have to remove my mother's things after she passes away, before you take ownership of her home?"

Gregg was disappointed. They'd gone over those terms in the contract carefully before signing, and Dylan was not a stupid man. He obviously wasn't able to muster up the courage to ask about Tommy Noonan and was going to come at it obliquely.

He'd expected better of Dylan, who had never wasted his time before.

Still, keeping an elected official at any level happy was never a bad thing. There might be other matters with which Dylan could help him in the future.

FORTY-SIX

The Blue House

WHEN LUKE OPENED his eyes, he felt a small weight on his chest. He looked down to see Vivian, her head resting there, her arms wrapped tightly around BeeBee. He wondered how long he'd been asleep. Through the gap in the drapes, the tall line of hedges was only a silhouette in the soft light of dusk.

He thought of his mother.

Barry had said she'd made it to the hospital. That was something. She was getting care.

She was getting better.

She had to be.

He couldn't believe what had annoyed him most about her lately had been her overprotectiveness, the feeling she was always looking over his shoulder to know where he was and what he was doing. From these hours with Vivian and the responsibility he felt for her, for the first time he thought he understood his mother's seemingly outsized drive to protect him.

Walter's voice, low and raw, carried from the next room, breaking the silence.

"No. Oh my God. No."

He sounded shocked, even hysterical. With horror, Luke thought, *what if he's lucid, remembering what actually happened? Seeing his cousin, Kelly, die?*

He had to get to Walter before anyone else did.

"Vivian, it's time to wake up," he said.

She opened her eyes, stretched one arm and yawned.

Walter's voice grew louder. "No. Stop it. No."

Vivian abruptly sat up. She scooted back against Luke, away from the frightening voice.

"That's the man who was hurt," Luke told her. "It'll be all right. I'm going to check on him. C'mon."

He picked Vivian up and carried her into the bathroom, pulled a bath towel from the rack, and set her and BeeBee down on it on the floor.

"Wait here. Call me if you need me, okay?"

She rubbed her eyes and lay down, clearly still sleepy, perhaps hoping this was a bad dream. The air was cool in the tiled room. Luke pulled a second towel from the rack and used it as a blanket to cover her.

Leaving the bathroom door barely ajar, only a sliver of light coming through, he stepped into Walter's room.

He was relieved to see the door to the hallway was closed. He hoped that meant no one else had heard and would be coming to help.

Though Walter's position was unchanged, lying on the sofa with his head propped on a small pillow, he looked worse. His face was ashen. He opened his eyes and saw Luke standing there. When he spoke, his voice was hoarse.

"I told you to drive. To keep driving."

He lifted his hand as though it still held a gun and pointed it at Luke, but his arm soon wavered and fell to his side.

Luke felt sick. Walter was going to identify him as a captive, not a criminal. It was all going to end. But as Walter's breathing slowed and his eyes closed, Luke grasped at a new thought.

One that alarmed him, because he knew what he must do.

As long as he's alive, I'm in danger.

If he's alive, Vivian's in danger.

Luke moved slowly to Walter's side and eased the pillow from beneath his head. His arms shook as he held it inches from Walter's face and urged himself to act. But the room was suddenly awash in bright light. Luke squinted into it as he turned to see Vivian, who had pushed the bathroom door open wide.

"BeeBee doesn't like waiting in the bathroom," she said.

"Shh." Luke said. He set the pillow guiltily on the floor. "The hurt man is sleeping."

He took her hand, walked her back to the bed, and lifted her onto it. He needed her as far away as possible. He couldn't let her witness this.

"I'll be right back," he told her.

But when he returned to Walter's room and reached for the pillow, he could not make himself pick it up. He felt weak, as though he'd run a long way. He couldn't summon the utter desperation he'd experienced when he'd heard Walter's voice, when the man had pointed the imaginary gun.

Then his eyes fell on the pills he'd knocked over earlier and the half-glass of water on the table by the couch. He picked up the bottle and read the label. There were warnings up and down the back. The directions were one pill every eight hours. Luke didn't recognize the name, but it was clearly some type of heavy-duty painkiller. He shook two of the small white pills into his palm.

He recalled he'd seen a guy at the bike shop take two Oxy with some beers and get pretty looped. But he hadn't passed out. Luke shook out two more. Then, after a moment's hesitation, four more. He needed Walter to be knocked out for a long time.

He thought about when he'd given medication to Crash. That had been easy. All he'd had to do was hide it in cheese. Not an option here. He put the pills in the water glass, all of them, knelt next to Walter, put his hand beneath his head and gently lifted it. Walter's jaw hung slack, his mouth slightly agape. Luke tilted his head back, hoping that would open his throat. He poured the water and pills slowly into his mouth.

Walter stirred and opened his eyes, but he didn't appear to see Luke. He was focused on the glass, he gulped the contents down.

Too late, Luke realized Walter had taken it in too fast as he coughed and gagged and some of the water came back up. Not much, but Luke worried the pills might not have stayed down. He traced the wet spots on Walter's shirt with his fingers. It was gross, and something rose in Luke's throat. But he felt no pills.

Walter lay back, still again, his eyes closed. Luke waited a moment. Walter didn't move. Sitting up, talking, drinking, must have taken all the energy the man had.

How long before the pills take effect? Luke wondered. *Was it enough? Was it too much?*

He thought of his hands gripping the pillow and shuddered.

He really hoped the pills wouldn't kill him, that they'd only knock him out.

As he passed through the bathroom, Luke felt a bit better, he could breathe again.

Until he stepped into the bedroom and saw the door to the hall was wide open, and Vivian was gone.

FORTY-SEVEN

The Blue House

DYLAN HAD BEEN unable to come to the point.

They'd spoken for another five minutes and had gotten nowhere. He'd devolved into asking what Gregg considered random and intrusive questions regarding how many temporary workers Gregg had hired, his taste in music, and whether he or any of his staff played musical instruments.

Gregg leaned forward and fixed his eyes on Dylan.

He'd have to take charge. He didn't have all day, and putting this to rest would be good for both of them.

"Barry will review the contract language with you. But I wonder whether you heard the news about Detective Noonan's death."

Though surprised that Dylan looked confused, Gregg was still certain the policeman was the reason for the man's visit. He supposed Dylan was taken aback at his having raised the officer's name without being asked.

"Terrible," Gregg said. "To die so young, so suddenly, in an act of heroism. But given this tragic turn of events, I imagine you might be curious about why I asked you to obtain Officer Noonan's name this morning."

Dylan said nothing.

Getting half-truths right was the hardest so Gregg chose his next words carefully.

"I was considering a significant investment in a property, so one of my staff was meeting with the seller when Officer Noonan appeared at the man's office unexpectedly, saying he must speak with him. Though Detective Noonan identified himself as a police officer, he did not give his name. My employee happened to see his car through the window as he drove away and made note of the license plate." Gregg lowered his voice, intending to convey the seriousness of his concerns. "I couldn't risk becoming involved with someone who might have a criminal history or current difficulties with the law. But if I had the policeman's name, I might be able to determine his interest in the seller, enabling me to make a responsible decision regarding whether to move forward with the funds. Time was of the essence. I knew there was another prospective buyer, which is why I called you with some urgency."

Gregg sat back, expecting to see the tension go out of Dylan's face now that he had been informed of a legitimate reason for the request. But that didn't happen.

Because that was when they heard the scream. A high-pitched wail of terror from the next room.

Greg nodded at Barry, who, without delay, left to take care of whatever else had now gone wrong.

"Dylan, it's best if you and I wait here," Gregg began, but Dylan, after appearing momentarily stunned, shot out after Barry.

Gregg sighed. Making the world a better place was proving to be much harder than he'd anticipated.

THE GIRL SCREAMED, a high-pitched wail.

In the few minutes prior, it had seemed to Emma that everything had happened at once.

Dylan had been escorted by Barry into the kitchen, while she'd been told to wait with the driver from the SUV, as nervous an individual as she'd ever seen.

He'd shifted his weight from foot to foot and patted his front pocket as though there was something important in there that might run away if he didn't keep tabs on it.

She'd pictured a tiny lizard, scrabbling to get out.

Then the girl had suddenly appeared from the hallway behind him, freezing there until her eyes had found Emma's. Emma had only realized who she was when she launched herself across the room toward her, like she was in the pre-K Olympic Trials for the fifty-yard dash.

But as the child passed close by the SUV driver, he'd lunged forward and scooped her up.

That's when the girl had screamed.

Now, she'd found words.

"Put me down."

She was twisting and turning, kicking the man. He held on tight.

Emma heard footsteps coming at a run from behind her, but before she could turn to see who it was, what she saw in front of her caused her heart to contract and her weak knees to go soft.

Luke appeared from around the corner, just as the girl had done.

Emma opened her mouth to call out his name, but he gave one firm shake of his head, *no*, then turned his attention to the child struggling in the man's grasp.

There was a fury in Luke's eyes that Emma had never seen.

With barely contained rage, he said to the man, "Give her to me."

The girl's screams turned to sobs as she reached for Luke.

Then a voice Emma recognized came from behind her.

"Lee, give the child to Kelly."

Barry's tone made it clear he would tolerate no hesitation. Nonetheless, the man Barry had just called "Lee" appeared to Emma to be considering rebellion, as though he wanted nothing more than to hold fast to the girl and make a run for it. But after a beat, he grimaced and reluctantly handed her over to Luke.

To Luke. Who Barry had just referred to as "Kelly."

The girl noticeably calmed in Luke's arms, but when her eyes met Emma's again, Emma saw in them a desperate plea.

Without a glance back, Luke left the room, carrying her up the hall from which they'd both come. No one objected, though Lee tracked the girl's growing distance from him. Something in his single-minded gaze chilled Emma to the bone.

"Are you okay? When I heard that scream, I thought it was you."

Dylan had stepped up beside her.

He sounded and looked relieved, which disturbed Emma deeply. Though it made sense since he didn't know what she knew.

That the teen who'd just left was Luke, that the girl he was carrying was the governor's granddaughter, and that right now she and Dylan were standing in the company of kidnappers who with a high likelihood were also murderers.

FORTY-EIGHT

The Blue House

GREGG FROWNED. The number of unexpected complexities in the operation had definitely fallen outside the bell curve and was now at the far end of what had been statistically probable at the start. Still, what was happening in the other room, whatever had led to the girl's scream, was not his side of the business, and he had faith in Barry. He rose and moved to the last cabinet on the wall in his small office.

When he opened it, he took a moment to honor the powerful allure of the array of mind-altering substances on the top shelf. The scotch, the weed, the narcotics. To admire their seductive promise of escape, the respite they offered his ever-active brain. But with only a little effort, he looked away. Because in the end, an artificial high could bring only a short-lived peace, if that, and he had work to do.

He turned his attention to the middle shelf, on which sat two cell phones.

He had to admit, it had been a stroke of genius on his part when he'd started having Lee monitor Marty Lightzer.

Though Marty had extorted money from Gregg for not revealing what he'd witnessed years ago, Gregg could imagine him at the bike shop, sharing stories, some real, some imagined, of how he'd once been a part of the Gambler's inner circle. Perhaps even claiming credit, saying he had led the charge to teach a white police officer who was a traitor to his race a serious lesson. And once Marty had placed himself at the scene, at Tommy Noonan's apartment that night, how long would it be until someone leaked that information, and the press or the police uncovered what had really happened in that otherwise forgotten years-old cold case?

That it was Gregg who had pulled the trigger.

Gregg who had killed a cop's pregnant wife.

Though Marty had not yet, to Gregg's knowledge, intentionally shared anything about that night with anyone, the man's inability to control his temper (and the volume of his voice) would have had the same disastrous result, had Lee not been there. Staying close, riding up and back in the alley behind the shop had put Lee in position to witness the boy's reaction when Marty yelled into the phone, calling Gregg a murderer. Lee hadn't known exactly what that was about since Gregg had never confided in him. But he'd heard Marty say Gregg's name and make the accusation, and he knew the boy had too.

What happened next hadn't been ideal, far from it, but Lee had made the problem go away.

He'd even brought Gregg back the kid's phone.

Gregg picked it up now. It was a simple model, black, a little scratched, with some sticker on the back. He looked forward to learning everything the phone's memory contained. Perhaps the boy had recorded conversations in which Marty revealed his own role at Tommy Noonan's that night, breaking in and planting the drugs. That would be enough to back Marty off, and this blackmail nonsense could finally end.

But first, the business with the girl had to be completed.

For that, Gregg considered the second phone. The nanny's. The plan had been to obtain access to its functions directly from her, using the girl as leverage if need be.

That would have enabled Gregg's team to respond to incoming calls or texts that might raise suspicion in the sender if left unanswered. But the dead nanny wouldn't be providing access to her phone anytime soon, and Gregg's go-to IT guy, Walter, who had successfully hacked the nanny's online calendar and found out about the appointment at Rainbow Alley, was lying comatose on a couch.

Gregg hoped he would come out of it soon. It was amazing how important tech expertise was in everything these days.

But one thing at a time, he reminded himself, as his gaze moved to the reason he had opened the cabinet. On the bottom shelf sat a green ledger embossed in gold with "Gregg Corbel Properties," in external appearance identical to the other ledgers he had.

Slowly, with ceremony, he opened it to view the note tucked between its pages, protected in a plastic sleeve. As he gazed upon the simple lines written there, Gregg felt refreshed and renewed, infused with the same white light he experienced when he exorcised the demons of addiction.

Soon, none of the challenges along the way, not even the deaths, would matter. For maximum impact, Gregg had intended Governor Lange to receive the message tomorrow afternoon, just before the girl's mother returned. But realistically, with each thing that hadn't gone according to plan, the probabilities had shifted.

He needed to move up the timeline. They'd have to end it with the girl tonight.

FORTY-NINE

The Blue House

BARRY GUIDED LEE across the room, where he spoke to him in low tones. Lee shook his head in response, paced a few steps in one direction and then the other, then shook his head again. He was demonstrably upset, though whether it was over Vivian or something else, Emma couldn't tell. Dylan stood beside her, also watching the two men. There was a wariness in Dylan's eyes, but she was certain he was not experiencing anything close to the cold pit she had in her stomach, mostly a result of fear but made worse by her growing sense of guilt and remorse.

Emma had met Vivian and her mother, Cassandra, on several occasions related to her work at the commission, once at the governor's office, another time at a holiday event at the capitol. It was through that connection that Cassandra had selected Rainbow Alley, and it was because of it that Emma was supposed to have led the tour with them today.

If only I'd written it down.

If only I'd kept a list.

If only I hadn't gotten lost in my thoughts of Tommy and of my father.

True, Emma couldn't say exactly how her being at Rainbow Alley when the kidnappers arrived would have prevented the men from taking Vivian and Luke or from shooting Kate, but if it had been the three of them, Kate, Luke and her, instead of only two, surely they would have had a better chance.

I should have been there.

But as Lee and Barry continued their intense exchange, Emma knew there was no point in looking back, in closing the barn door after the horses had run out.

She needed to focus on the here and now.

A random memory came to her. Watching quarterback Tom Brady being interviewed after his fourth Super Bowl win. With a huge grin on his handsome face, his supermodel wife by his side, he'd said, "I'm never going to be fast, and no one's ever going to mistake me for being fast." Brady had said it like that shortcoming was a good thing because, forced to rely on skills other than speed, he'd become one of the winningest QBs of all time.

Maybe that applies here, Emma thought. Not the fact that she also wasn't fast. (She wasn't.) But that, like Brady, she should be able to rely on what she could do well.

She'd shot up in the ranks of investigators at the commission, leap-frogging over more senior staff, because she had the ability to fully analyze a complex problem and lay out the options quickly, without overthinking it, and without getting stuck in the planning or processing stage.

Most importantly, while she occasionally jumped in too soon, she never failed to act.

She needed to apply those skills here.

Luke appeared to be safe from harm, relatively speaking, at least for the moment. The men believed he was someone else, someone trusted enough that

Barry made Lee give Vivian up to him. As for her and Dylan, the chaos of the girl's appearance had been over so quickly Emma didn't think the men had noticed she recognized Vivian as being anything other than a random child.

Clearly, it was little Vivian Lange who was most at risk. If the plan was to exchange the child for a ransom, what would happen if they didn't get it? Or even if they did?

Emma asked herself what else she knew that mattered.

While she hadn't seen any weapons yet, these men or someone working for them had shot to kill at Rainbow Alley. So she had to assume some or all of them were armed.

The obvious outcome of her analysis was that her options to get them out of this mess were few. In fact, they narrowed to one. What she needed right now was the police to come and save them.

It was an easy answer, and she liked those best. But as she considered the circumstances of their plight a minute more, she knew what she needed were not just any police officers. She needed the kind who wouldn't rush in and get innocent people killed. The kind who would figure out a way to get them all home safely. What she needed was Alibi. She trusted him. He would know exactly what to do and, fortunately, she had his private cell number.

She leaned over to Dylan. "We should go now."

"I'm sorry we didn't find Luke," Dylan said. "I'm sure he got a ride home from wherever he was some other way. Why don't you check your messages to see whether he got home and found your note?"

Emma didn't answer. She took his hand in hers, and

started toward the front door. His face flushed bright red. She couldn't deal with whatever that was now. She gripped his hand harder and pulled him with her. They didn't get far. Emma felt a chill go up her spine when she heard Barry's one-word command.

"Stop."

As she released Dylan's hand so they could turn around, she expected to come face-to-face with the barrel of a gun. But instead, Barry, weaponless, calmly addressed Dylan.

"I'm sorry your meeting with Gregg was interrupted. Let me check to see whether he feels the discussion was complete." He turned to Lee. "As we discussed, Mr. Johnson is your responsibility. Be certain he is comfortable and well-looked after until I come back."

When Barry had left the room for the kitchen, Dylan looked at Emma and shrugged as though to say "nothing to be done but wait." He pointed to two armchairs that faced the back of the property and said, "Let's sit."

But Emma was not in a waiting mood, not usually, and certainly not now.

As Dylan sat down, she saw Lee fix his eyes on him, though they were the only part of Lee's body that was still. Observing the small man's symphony of disjointed movements, it occurred to her he might not have space in his head to monitor her at the same high level of vigilance he was demonstrating toward Dylan.

It was worth a try.

"I need to use the bathroom," she said politely, as though she were a dinner guest who needed to use the facilities while she waited for a delicious meal to be put on the table.

"Yeah, alright," Lee said, waving her away, not taking his eyes off Dylan.

But as she turned the corner where she'd seen Luke go with Vivian, Lee abruptly hurried after her. "That middle door," he said, pointing. "The john's in there. The other doors are private. Off limits."

Her heart pounding, Emma felt him watching her until she'd followed his directions into the bathroom, and closed the door behind her.

FIFTY

On the Road

WHEN THE MAYOR had called to say she needed to push the press conference back half an hour, Alibi had known exactly how he wanted to spend that time.

It would be cutting it close, but if there was any chance he could come up with something concrete to back up his theory that Samson's murder had not been a hate crime, he had to go for it.

If he could accomplish that, perhaps he could convince Mayor Ruiz to cancel the press conference altogether, or at the very least to refocus it on issues that would help them find the killer, rather than creating false leads and hysteria that used up department resources he didn't have to give.

He'd explained to Jackie O his reasoning for visiting the one place where he thought evidence might be found.

She'd been enthusiastic about the idea, and he was glad to have her along as they pulled in to the lot of the River Top Motel.

The Blue House

EMMA FOUND HERSELF in what her mother had called a "Jack and Jill" setup, a single bathroom sandwiched between two bedrooms, with a connecting door to each one. This bathroom also had a door to the hall, which she'd just come through.

What a nightmare it must be to use, she thought, *having to remember to lock all three doors so no one would walk in on you while you were naked or on the toilet.*

Though that type of privacy concern was the least of her worries right now.

The door to her right was closed, but the one on her left was ajar. She could see Luke sitting on the edge of the bed next to Vivian. The child's face was streaked with tears.

Emma stepped forward to draw attention to herself, her index finger pressed to her lips, cautioning them not to react out loud to her unannounced appearance.

When Luke saw her, he said something quietly to Vivian, then lifted a set of headphones off the bed and offered them to her. She refused, shaking her head hard as she picked up her stuffed bunny and wrapped her arms around it.

When Luke stood, her bottom lip trembled.

As he approached Emma, she could see the strain in Luke's face. When he was close enough, she reached out and touched his arm. That was all she allowed herself to do. If they hugged, one or both of them might begin weeping, and there was no time for that.

"Did you call the police?" he whispered. "Are they coming?"

Emma shook her head no.

She saw the panic in his eyes.

"It wasn't clear, I should have—"

"It's okay," she said, not letting him finish.

They had to think ahead, of what would come next.

Over Luke's shoulder, she saw Vivian watching them, calmer now, perhaps thinking because they were grown-ups they would sort this out. She was grateful that as the granddaughter of a governor, the child no doubt would have been raised with the necessity of being patient during important conversations between adults in her life.

Then Emma noticed the window. "Does that open?"

"I think so," Luke said, "but there's an alarm. I can see the sensors."

Emma thought for a moment.

"When I leave the house, they'll have to turn off the alarm to open the front door. As soon as they disarm it, I'll yell—"

This time he cut her off. He frowned and looked at her as though she didn't understand the dire nature of their situation. "You can't yell. They think I'm one of them. If you yell, it could make it worse."

"I understand that," Emma said, ready to explain what she'd just worked out. "I'll fake a fall, as though I tripped, and I'll yell, 'Ouch.' As soon as I do that, you open the window, get out with Vivian and shut it as quickly as you can behind you. With any luck, it'll be closed before they reengage the alarm."

Luke turned and looked out through the window. She could see him processing the absence of neighbors and the darkening sky. He needed the rest of the plan.

"Once you're out, run up the side of the house to the front. Don't hesitate. Run. The fact that it's getting darker will help you. I'll be in the blue Jeep right across the street. My friend may be driving, so don't be surprised if you see a man at the wheel. Just run as hard as you can and jump in."

Luke's eyes were wide, but he wasn't saying no to the plan. At least not yet.

"Hopefully, it will take them a while to figure out you're gone," she said. "Have they been coming back here much?"

Luke shook his head no, then added, "Only once." Something dark crossed his face, as though the memory of it was bad.

Emma kept talking. She still needed him to look ahead, not back. "Good. So it's unlikely you'll be found missing right away. Once we're in the car, my phone is there. We can call the police."

Luke covered his mouth with a hand.

She thought he might be trying to prevent himself from criticizing her, from saying it was a bad idea. She understood his impulse. The plan did have holes. In particular, there was the unpleasant possibility the men did not intend to let her and Dylan ever leave. But she'd thought of that and had a backup plan.

"If I see them turn off the alarm for any reason, maybe for one of them to go out, I'll fake a stumble and yell, 'Ouch.' So when you get to the front of the house and see the Jeep, if it's empty, you still run for it with Vivian as fast as you can. But this time get in the driver's seat—"

"I can't leave you here," Luke said. "You don't know these men, you don't know what they're capable of. My mom…" He broke off, unable to continue.

"Your mom is fine, she's at the hospital."

"Fine" was a significant stretch, but Emma knew Luke had to hear that to function right now.

"If either one of us can get out, we have to do that," she said firmly. "We have to phone for help."

He seemed to think about that before reluctantly nodding. Then he asked, " Do you have the key?"

"It's a keyless ignition," she said, glad he'd thought to ask. "Push the button next to the steering wheel. You don't need to have the key in your hand, the car will start when you push that button. The main thing is to get out of here as quickly as you can, and when you're a little distance away, call the police."

Just then they heard Lee yell.

It sounded like he was at the end of the hall, steps from the main room where Dylan was, maybe belatedly realizing he should monitor Emma too.

"What's taking so long?" he bellowed. "Hurry up in there."

Luke backed into his room.

"Coming," she called loudly, flushing the toilet for effect.

But as she started to leave, she wondered whether Luke had searched to see if anything in the bathroom might be used as a weapon, if only for self-defense. A razor, or who knows, maybe one of these men forgot about a gun they'd left in here when nature called.

She opened the medicine cabinet and the cabinet below the sink, and checked the countertop. A bottle of aspirin, a comb, a cordless toothbrush and toothpaste, some liquid hand soap. That was it. Nothing remotely helpful.

But after taking a step away, she realized what she might be able to use. She turned back and quickly examined the toothbrush. It was the right brand.

She pushed it down into her jeans pocket, but the shape was visible against her thigh. So she tried tucking it in her waistband on her hip. The snug fit kept it in place, and her T-shirt was plenty long enough to cover it. That would have to do. She was ready. Or as ready as she would ever be to implement what was admittedly a very risky plan.

Focusing on her breathing, calm and steady, she opened the door to the hall.

FIFTY-ONE

The Blue House

WHEN EMMA TURNED the corner into the main room, there was no one there.

Dylan must be completing his meeting with Gregg. No telling where Lee had gone.

Having unexpectedly been left alone, she considered whether it made sense to go back to get Luke and Vivian and let the siren wail while the three of them made a dash for the Jeep. She quickly dismissed the idea. It was a small house, and given the speed with which Barry had appeared when Vivian had screamed earlier, the odds of their being shot in the back as they ran, or at least recaptured, seemed far too high. Even if they did miraculously make it out somehow, it would mean abandoning Dylan.

She decided instead to use her unmonitored time to look for a phone. There must be one in the house, and she didn't like putting all her faith in making it to hers, stashed in her bag in Dylan's car.

She hastily surveyed the room. It was minimally furnished, no drawers or cluttered shelves where a cell phone might have been left out of sight. Then she recalled Lee's warning.

"The other doors are private. Off limits."

A private room seemed a good place to find a phone. She returned to the hall. Of the three doors on her right, the last one was where Luke and Vivian were being held. The one in the middle was to the bathroom. It was only the first door that she hadn't yet entered. There was also one door at the back of the hall on the left. It was partway open. She didn't remember it having been that way before, though perhaps she hadn't noticed. Still, she decided it was possible Lee or Barry, or both, were in there now. So she opted for door number one on her right, grasped the knob, and firmly eased it open.

The small room was in near darkness. She couldn't look for a phone without light, so she moved her hand along the wall, seeking a switch. But as she did so, her eyes began to adjust.

A man lay on the couch, a blanket pulled to his chest, his head turned away from her.

She quickly backed out and quietly closed the door, breathing hard. She took a moment to reassure herself the blanket must mean the man was sleeping, because who would tuck in a dead person? Still, it was a reminder she had no idea how many people were in the house. And in any case, she didn't know how soon she might be discovered sneaking about. As she hurried to the only place left to check, through the door on the left at the end of the hall, she decided her cover story if there was someone in there would be that she was looking for Dylan.

Fortunately, she found the large room unoccupied. It resembled a barracks, with two metal bunk beds providing four narrow sleeping spaces. There was a table, on which a deck of playing cards was spread out as though a game had been interrupted. On the far wall were two heavy metal footlockers, one open with clothing spilling out the top. She sincerely hoped the other one, closed, did not contain weapons. But what interested her most was a desk to the right of the door. Its surface was crowded and messy, host to a closed laptop, a printer, several manila file folders, pens, and random pieces of paper. She hurried over and opened the laptop. She was greeted by a password request, so she closed it. She listened hard for approaching footsteps and, hearing none, lifted a file to see if there might be a phone buried somewhere in the clutter. She stopped her search when she saw the name handwritten in pencil at the top.

Governor Paul Lange

She checked the label on another folder.

First Lady Donna Lange

And another.

Lieutenant Governor Aminah Ali-Rosenberg

Hands trembling, Emma opened each one in turn, having no idea what she might find.

They contained printouts of press coverage, not much, no more than ten pages per individual.

Paul Lange's was dominated by his investment scandal and the millions he'd made in pharmaceutical stocks before becoming governor. Donna Lange's focused on her having sounded the alarm when she'd mistakenly concluded her daughter and granddaughter were in mortal danger, leading to a SWAT team being called to her daughter's home. There was a related piece questioning the first lady's overall emotional stability. Finally, Aminah's featured two interviews with her about her Muslim faith.

Emma replaced the folders as best as she could in their original positions, then completed a rushed search of the rest of the desk, opening and closing drawers, until she'd determined there was no phone.

When she left the room, she fought against a feeling of being overwhelmed. There were too many pieces to this puzzle, and it was getting more rather than less complicated. Why was the resurfacing of the Governor's investment scandal, now at least a year old, of interest to these men? Then she realized there was probably information in there about his net worth, which could help them decide how much ransom to request. For the First Lady, they might have been looking at the dynamics of a SWAT response, to see what to expect if they were found to be holding Vivian here. The strangest of the three was the lieutenant governor's file. How could Aminah's religion relate to any of this?

As Emma passed Luke and Vivian's room, she heard his voice, then Vivian's. She desperately wanted to go inside, to take each of their hands in hers, click her heels three times and get them all the hell out of Oz. But she knew that now, more than ever, she had to keep moving.

She had to bring those two children to safety, not through fantasy, but in real time, battling real obstacles, doing whatever was necessary to get them there.

FIFTY-TWO

The River Top Motel

MORE OFTEN THAN not, Alibi found the answers he sought in a homicide investigation by engaging with minor players or events in the life of the deceased well away from the immediate time and place of the crime, painstaking work that had not yet begun in Samson Kieu's case. But with the mayor's press conference looming large in under thirty minutes, Alibi had decided to return to the basics. To Investigatory Practices 101. And seeking witnesses who might have information regarding who owned the size-nine trainers, prints of which had been found at the scene, felt about as basic as it could get. Because, absent some new shocking revelation, whoever had worn those shoes was the heavy favorite for having pulled the trigger on the gun that killed Samson.

But when Alibi pushed open the heavy glass door to the lobby of the River Top Motel, he was concerned he might have brought Jackie O along on a fool's errand. Stooped and thin beyond reason, almost skeletal in appearance, Jerome Potter stood only a few inches taller than the reception counter. He squinted in Alibi and Jackie O's general direction, apparently trying to make out their features, though they were less than ten feet from him.

Alibi's hopes that Potter, the motel's owner, might

have seen something important the night Samson Kieu was killed were dwindling fast.

"Good afternoon," Alibi said, approaching the man. "Mr. Potter?"

Jerome Potter nodded shakily.

Alibi produced his ID. "We spoke on the phone."

Potter nodded again as he moved slowly to seat himself in an elevated chair behind the counter. Not a stool really, but something that looked like it had come from a medical supply store. When he leaned back against it, the chair lowered with a hum to take his weight. Then he pushed a button on the armrest and it rose again.

While Mr. Potter did that, Alibi noticed Jackie O was checking out the view from the glassed-in lobby, gazing in the direction of the river.

He'd already looked.

He could have told her it was no good.

He hadn't been able to see beyond the front of the parking lot. The pathway and gentle incline up from the grove weren't visible.

"Why don't you tour the property?" he suggested to her. The River Top was one of those old-style, two-story motels built with open walkways around a pool in a fenced courtyard. "See if anything occurs to you."

Meanwhile, Jerome Potter seemed ready to be interviewed, so Alibi withdrew his blue notebook and a pencil from his jacket pocket.

"I understand you spoke briefly with an officer this morning. I appreciate your taking the time to also talk to me. I'd like to double-check a few things."

Potter's pale blue eyes watered. He blinked frequently as he nodded again.

If Alibi hadn't heard the man speak on the phone,

he might have been concerned he didn't have the capability to do so.

"What hours were you on duty at reception last night?"

Potter licked his lips and cleared his throat. Alibi had to lean in to hear him, but the tremor in his voice seemed less pronounced than it had on the phone.

"Same as always. I come on at ten pm and get off at two am. Every night." He paused and gave what might have been a mischievous smile. "You may not have noticed, but I'm an old man." He licked his lips again. "It suits me to go to bed early, six in the evening. With four hours of sleep I'm ready to go by ten."

"Every night? Seven days a week? Is there anyone with you at the front desk during that time?"

"No. We're here one at a time, except for overlap when we change shifts. Last night, Clarence was on when I started, and Gretchen came in a little before I left."

Despite his frequent blinking, licking of his lips, and round-shouldered posture, Potter seemed alert, and he focused on Alibi as though waiting for the next question. Given the almost empty parking lot and the fact that no one had come in since they'd arrived, Alibi supposed the man might welcome the company.

"When was Gretchen's shift?"

"One thirty in the morning to nine thirty in the morning." Potter smiled. "The young people do eight-hour shifts."

Alibi didn't think anyone had interviewed Gretchen. She would have been there within the window the coroner gave for Samson's death. He would get her contact information when he and Potter finished.

"How many guests did you have register during your shift?

"None."

"Did any existing guests come or go during that time?"

Alibi thought how helpful it would be if Samson's murderer had run through the lobby, gun in hand, his size-nine shoes leaving muddy prints.

"There's a gate in the back to the parking lot," Jerome said. "Guests usually arrive and leave through there. It's closer to the public walkway."

"I'd like to take a look at that," Alibi said, not certain what he hoped to find.

"Beverly will show you." Jerome reached for the phone. His hand was shaking. The receiver seemed too heavy for him to lift.

Just then, Jackie O appeared with a woman who looked to be in her eighties. She had short white hair and a lived-in face. Whatever had happened in those many decades of life, it seemed to have agreed with her. She was the picture of energy and good health.

"Alibi, this is Mrs. Potter," Jackie O said. "She has something to tell you."

'I was just calling you," Jerome said, smiling.

A look of affection passed between the couple. Alibi didn't want to rush things, but he and Jackie would have to leave in ten minutes, no more. He surreptitiously tapped his watch. Jackie O saw the motion and took the prompt.

"Mrs. Potter, would you please share with Inspector Morning Sun what you told me?"

"Yes, dear," Beverly Potter said brightly. "We have a cleaner, but there's a lot for her to get to. Thirty-eight rooms. Even those that are vacant need freshening up.

While I'm waiting for Jerome to come to bed, I often do a bit of vacuuming myself and straighten things up. I like to stay busy."

Alibi hoped this was going somewhere.

"And last night?" he asked. "Did you do some cleaning? Did anything unusual happen?"

"I was in one of the rooms on the river side. Room two-seventeen. I had just finished up and had turned the lights out when I realized the drapes weren't quite shut. I went to close them and saw a man running up the slope from the river, toward the direction of town."

Alibi tensed. He didn't want to invest hope in the information being what he needed and jinx it. "Do you recall the time?"

"A little before midnight. I always bring Jerome his tea at twelve fifteen, so I had looked to be sure I wouldn't keep him waiting."

That fits with time of death, Alibi thought.

"Could you see whether the man who was running had come out of the tall grove of eucalyptus at the bottom of the hill?"

Jackie O started to speak, but Alibi gave her a look that cautioned her to let the woman answer.

"I don't know," Mrs. Potter said. "He was quite a ways from the grove when I saw him, though I suppose he could have started there. What struck me was how fast he was running. He was a small man, slight, with short legs, but he could really go fast."

So definitely not Tommy. No one would say Tommy was a small man, Alibi thought. There'd been only one other set of footprints.

This has to be our killer.

And now Alibi had a physical description.

At least, the beginnings of one.

FIFTY-THREE

The Blue House

EMMA HAD JUST returned to the main room from her unsuccessful phone search when the door from the kitchen opened. Barry addressed her brusquely.

"Come with me."

It seemed she was finally being brought into one of Dylan's meetings with Gregg.

She tried to tell herself that was a good thing, a necessary step for the man in charge to clear her and for Dylan to be able to leave. But her body seemed to have a different idea than her mind. She had trouble commanding her feet to move toward Barry rather than turning on the spot and running away.

They passed through the kitchen quickly. She only had time to form the impression that it was a long and narrow room, everything modern and sparkling clean.

When they came to a door on the far right, Barry knocked. They entered what appeared to have been a breakfast nook or small dining room, now set up as an office. The man who must be Gregg sat at a desk chair behind a small table. Younger than Emma had expected, in his mid-thirties, perhaps forty but no more, he was of average height and build. His jet black hair flowed from a prominent widow's peak. His pale skin was unlined. He might have seemed unthreatening, even handsome, if not for the feverish glow in his eyes.

The surface of the table where he sat was clear except for a dark green ledger, several sharpened pencils, and a single photo in a frame, its back to her so she was unable to view the image.

Dylan was nowhere to be seen. Gregg inclined his head toward a vacant chair across from him. Barry stood in the doorway, intentionally or not blocking her exit. So she sat.

"Where's Dylan?" she asked.

Gregg didn't answer as he slid a manila folder toward her from beneath the ledger, identical to the ones she'd seen in the barracks-style bedroom. She felt an almost electric shock at the site of the words penciled at the top: "Rainbow Alley."

Like the others, it contained press printouts. But the headline on the top page of this file was all too familiar to her. It had run in the local news section of the *Sacramento Bee* when she and Kate first made their venture public, several months ago. *"State Investigator and Impassioned Educator Give New Life to Shuttered Preschool Across From the Capitol."* She recalled how they'd laughed at the headline, though "impassioned" was a good way to describe how Kate took on any project. The photo that accompanied the piece was of the back of the school, pre-remodel, with its faded sign, the gate to the parking lot not yet childproofed.

The sight of it brought back to Emma the image of Kate lying on the ground, motionless, blood trickling down her face.

Whatever this man wanted, she couldn't just sit here. She had to get the kids out *now*.

She started to stand, but Gregg raised a palm and motioned her to stop.

"Ms. Lawson, I understand there was a violent incident at your school today. What can you tell me about that?" Though his voice was soft and uninflected, his eyes remained alight, cold and intense.

Emma tried to push down her panic.

He knows my name. He has a file on my school.

Dylan and I came unannounced. Did they just print this out?

"Ms. Lawson?" Gregg prompted her.

She tried to focus, to analyze, to bring her strengths to bear on what felt like a disastrous, unsolvable problem.

What would be safe to say?

Certainly not the thoughts foremost in her mind. That *Kelly was really Luke or that she knew full well the girl Gregg and his men were holding captive was the governor's granddaughter.*

"I understand this is upsetting," Gregg said. "The media has not released the names of the individuals who were shot. Have you been told? Do you know how the woman is doing?"

Emma's mind instantly cleared. Gregg had a file on Rainbow Alley to plan the kidnapping, not to be ready when she showed up today. And he was asking about the victims of the shooting because he wanted to know whether there was a surviving witness.

Though again, she hesitated.

Would it make Vivian and Luke safer if she said Kate was alert and could speak? Or perhaps had already spoken? Or should she say Kate's injury was so great she had not gained consciousness and was not expected to survive, so she could be no threat to him in the future?

Since she had no way of knowing what he wanted to hear, she decided less was better.

"I don't know," she said.

He nodded, though whether he believed her or not she couldn't tell.

He took the folder from her, closed it and leaned forward.

"In the interview, you indicated you worked with the lieutenant governor. Do you think Dr. Ali-Rosenberg would make a good governor?

Emma frowned. She thought of the file on Aminah in the back room of the house, of its laser-like focus on her religion, her Muslim faith.

Was there something she should say now to keep Aminah safe? She felt lost.

"I understand she's abstemious," Gregg said.

Abstemious? What?

Emma knew the word meant someone who "abstains." But did it always mean abstaining from vices, say, from alcohol and drugs? Or from sex? Or could it be from anything? From French fries, from carrot cake? She wished it had been an SAT word of the day.

"What do you think?" he asked. "Would she make a better governor than Paul Lange?"

Saying "I don't know" a second time seemed risky, as the manic glow in the man's eyes hadn't diminished. But as Emma tried to work out what might have motivated him to ask so she would know how to respond, a tremendous bang shook the small room.

Emma immediately recognized it as gunfire. Two more blasts followed, and from the magnitude of the sounds she knew the weapon had not been fired up the street or even in the yard.

She felt as though she was back at Shoot The Lights Out, the indoor shooting range, because inside this house, someone had just pulled a trigger three times.

FIFTY-FOUR

The Blue House

LUKE HEARD GUNSHOTS in real life for the first time earlier that day at Rainbow Alley.

It had just happened again, although these shots had been much, much louder.

Vivian had heard them too, even with her headphones on. She'd grabbed BeeBee and scrambled across the bed onto Luke's lap.

He held her, her eyes tightly closed, her face pressed to his chest, as though if she couldn't see what was coming it couldn't get her.

Luke considered what the gunfire might mean.

He flat out refused to believe Emma had been shot. He would have sensed it, he told himself, or she would have called out. Maybe Lee and Barry, who didn't seem to get along, had had an argument that had resulted in their firing their weapons at each other. Or someone new had appeared at the house, who had posed a threat.

He decided what he should focus on was whether the gunshots changed anything for their escape plan.

He was ready to take Vivian out the window as soon as Emma yelled, "Ouch!" He'd pulled aside the drapes to fully clear the way, and located the latch to unlock and push open the slider. He'd even explained to Vivian what they would be doing, including the details, reasoning if there was going to be any challenge from her, he had to address it ahead of time.

The only protest she'd made was when he'd told her they would leave her backpack behind to make it easier to run fast.

She'd explained when she was going with her mom or Shelby somewhere that BeeBee could get lost, BeeBee didn't mind being zipped into her pack. Just for those times. Luke had agreed that was a good idea. He hadn't thought about the risk of BeeBee being dropped as he ran full out to the car carrying Vivian. So they had packed the backpack with only BeeBee and the handkerchief-sized blanket inside (for BeeBee's comfort).

Finally, the bag was left unzipped a sliver at the top so Vivian could whisper to BeeBee to keep him calm.

Luke thought again of how great it would be if he were bionic or had superpowers. If he were somehow more than human, if he could fight with the strength of Jason Bourne or climb and leap with the agility of Spiderman. But he couldn't.

Vivian had only him.

He resolved to wait ten minutes for Emma's signal. If it did not come, if anything prevented her from sending it, he would have to think of another plan.

He had no way to tell time, so he began counting in his head as he'd done when he was a kid. Adding the words "one thousand" to each number so it would take a full second to say it.

He began, "One thousand and one..."

AT THE SOUND of gunfire, Greg and Barry had exchanged a wordless look.

Then Barry had left the room.

When he returned, Gregg asked, " Everything all right?"

"More or less," Barry said.

Gregg rose and the two men went out of the office, leaving the door open. They walked through the kitchen to the far side and began a conversation out of range for Emma to hear.

She looked around the small room. The men seemed unconcerned with her for the moment, so she stood and feigned a stretch, putting her hands on her lower back, before going to the only window and peeking through a gap in the drapes. There were the same small white alarm sensors there that she'd seen in Luke's room.

Next, she considered the line of cabinets on the wall behind Gregg's table. After checking to see that Gregg and Barry were still absorbed in their conversation, she backed up to the cabinet farthest from the kitchen door and with an arm behind her back eased it open an inch. She moved her hand blindly inside and felt around. There was a large flat book on the bottom shelf, and on the shelf above that was...

A cell phone.

Her heart raced.

If it's charged, if it works...

But before she could decide whether to take the risk of sliding it into her back pocket, Gregg and Barry had split up, Barry leaving for the main room and Gregg walking back toward her.

She quickly pressed the cabinet door closed and took a step away. She picked up the framed photo on Gregg's table, as though that had been her reason for standing up. It was of a thin young woman in her late teens or early twenties, with blonde hair and a brilliant smile.

"She's lovely," Emma said to Gregg, who had

stopped at the entrance to the room and was watching her closely.

He nodded and said nothing.

"Is she a relative?" Emma ventured, trying to find some way to connect.

"My wife," Gregg said. He took the photo from her hand and set it carefully back on the table. "Was," he said. "She was my wife."

It was unsettling to Emma, how calm, how emotionless he seemed. Although on the plus side, he seemed too calm for the topic of discussion with Barry to have been a murder by gunshot a few feet away. She hoped that was true. Perhaps the sounds had been Lee blowing off steam, firing his gun into the air out of frustration and anger. He seemed capable of it.

Gregg interrupted her thoughts. "Barry will show you out now."

WHEN EMMA REENTERED the main room with Barry there was no one else there. At least no one standing. She scanned the floor from corner to corner. No dead bodies either.

Barry said, "Come over here" as he moved toward a small table with a desk chair, to her left. It was similar to the one Gregg had in his office. But instead of a framed photo on top of this table, on a white hand towel there was a handgun, a 38 revolver of the type she'd used at the range.

"Pick it up," Barry said to her.

She looked at him, confused, even as she felt a tiny glimmer of hope. Did he intend to help her escape? Was this military-seeming man an undercover officer for the police, part of the governor's security team, or an FBI agent there to foil the kidnapping plan?

Barry repeated his command.

"Pick it up."

She did so and, recalling her firearm lessons at the range, with trembling hands checked the cylinder.

Barry stood patiently at her side. Which she soon realized he could afford to do, because he'd known all along what she'd just discovered. It was unloaded and clearly would not be her ticket out. She set the gun back down.

She was curious about what would come next, when, appalled, she suddenly could think of only one reason for his having made her handle the weapon. As she was about to lunge to wipe the gun clean, without a word Barry briskly crossed the room toward the door from the house to the garage. He punched a series of numbers onto the white pad next to the door. There were several beeps as the flashing red light went off and a green one came on.

He turned to Emma.

"This way, please."

She took one step and collapsed to the floor.

But not to her knees.

She sat halfway up, reached for her ankle, and yelled, *"Ouch! Ouch!"*

FIFTY-FIVE

The Blue House

EMMA GRIMACED IN what she hoped looked like pain.

Barry crouched next to her.

"This one?" he asked, gesturing to her left ankle.

She nodded.

He gently unlaced and slipped off her left sneaker, then her right one. He left her socks on. She wondered if he'd removed both her shoes to compare possible swelling, but if he was skeptical of her performance it didn't show in his face.

"Are you able to stand?"

"I don't know," she responded, keeping her voice low and weak. "Maybe."

She needed the injury to seem real, but she didn't want to overplay her hand. He put an arm around her waist and easily raised her to standing, her left side pressed against his as he bore nearly all her weight. Keeping her upright, he moved toward the open door to the garage.

She had to buy Luke and Vivian time.

She made it as difficult as she could for him to make progress, feigning pain and weakness, but after a beat, Barry simply picked her up and, like a groom would carry a bride walked with her in his arms across the threshold into the garage.

Lee was waiting there, leaning against the black SUV she'd seen him driving earlier.

"Open the door." Barry said.

Lee was heading around the vehicle toward the other side when Barry said, " No. The driver's door." When Lee had reversed course and had it open, Barry set Emma down gently on the seat behind the wheel. "It's automatic. No clutch," he said. "You should have no difficulty operating the vehicle with your right foot."

Emma had only begun to consider why he wanted her to drive and where she would be going when Barry strode back through the door into the house, not closing it behind him.

Then she noticed a keypad on this side of the door. Its light was also green.

How long has the alarm been off? she wondered. Three minutes? Four?

Certainly, enough time for Luke and Vivian to get out of the room. They must be running toward Dylan's Jeep now. Toward her phone.

Toward safety.

But as she inhaled deeply, relieved, ready to consider next steps, two things happened at once. Barry returned carrying the hand towel that had been on the table. From the shape of it, the gun was wrapped inside. He tossed it through the open car window behind her onto the back seat. While he did that, Lee got into the front passenger seat, now holding a gun of his own. He rested it on his leg, though it bounced up and down in his hand.

Emma felt stricken by the stark reality that she was about to be taken somewhere against her will, held at gunpoint. She lowered her head, bit down on her lip and forced herself not to scream. With Luke heading to the Jeep or already there, she couldn't do anything that might cause him to think he had to turn back to rescue her.

Barry told her to put on her seat belt, then turned to Lee. "Do it all. Don't miss a step."

"Sure. I got it. First thing when we get there—"

Barry cut him off. "Don't talk until it's done."

Lee nodded, "Yes, that's why—"

Barry made a zipping motion with his hand across his lips.

Lee nodded and this time, with what clearly took effort, said nothing.

Barry turned back to Emma. "The key is there, in the cupholder. Lee will give you directions."

He stepped back and a moment later she heard the whine of the automatic garage door opener. Seeing no alternative, as the heavy door lifted she turned her head to check for clearance and slowly backed out.

In the soft light of the setting sun, Dylan's sky-blue Jeep was easily visible, still parked in the shadows beside a row of walnut trees. She couldn't make out whether anyone was in it. But she steadied herself. It had been enough time, she knew it had.

It would have been smart for Luke not to drive away yet, not once he'd heard the voices in the garage and saw the door opening. He and Vivian must have their heads down or be crouched behind the Jeep, ready to move when the coast is clear.

"Get going," Lee said. "That way."

He pointed to her left, away from Dylan's Jeep and away from town.

As she made the turn, Lee began to hum, evidently unable to bear the quiet, though it appeared he was trying to stick with the command he'd been given not to speak. She shivered as he tapped the gun against his leg in rhythm to the music in his head, his eyes fixed on the road that would take them to a destination only he knew.

FIFTY-SIX

The Capitol

As ALIBI MADE his way through the scrum of reporters at the bottom of the steps to City Hall, he was grateful the mayor had been true to her word.

In the few private moments he'd had with her before the media arrived, he'd told her a witness had come forward with a physical description of a man who'd fled the scene of Samson Kieu's murder. His team was following up now. He shared his concerns any hysteria around Samson's killing resulting from characterizing it as the start of another hate crime spree could only complicate the nuts and bolts of that police investigation.

The mayor had responded that until they had more to support his theory this was a targeted crime unrelated to the Gambler's orchestrated execution of young immigrants, the need to warn the community remained. But she had committed to being clear with the press and the public that the extra precautions they were asking people to take were being requested in an abundance of caution, and that they did not believe there was cause for undue alarm.

Her Honor had said exactly that in her opening remarks. Still, the press had quickly figured out there must be significant missing pieces in the briefing she and Alibi were giving them. A teen living in marginal circumstances shot by the river was, sadly, not typically big news, and Alibi's refusal to confirm or deny any link to the Gambler's crimes—instead, providing answers like "We are pursuing all leads... This is an active investigation... I'm not able to say..."—had done nothing to allay the reporters' suspicions there was more to the story. But when things had turned accusatory and, to Alibi's mind, way off track, with one cable TV host calling out, "Do you think you have the wrong man in prison for the Gambler's earlier crimes?" the mayor had returned to the podium.

"Let's give the department some breathing room," she'd said. "It's been less than twenty-four hours. When Detective Morning Sun has concrete information to share, you will be the first to know. After me, of course." That last phrase had ratcheted the tension down a bit. There'd been mild laughter in the room. "We are out here early on this case because we want to make sure the community is aware and takes appropriate precautions. Until we have a clear understanding of what happened and why, we urge everyone to avoid walking alone after dark in isolated areas. That's always a good practice to follow, but we would like everyone, especially our community's precious young people of color, to take special care now."

After that, while the questions continued to fly fast and furious, the press had leap-frogged from the case under discussion to stalled negotiations with the teachers union and the perceived high price of tickets at the new downtown basketball arena.

Alibi made eye contact with Jackie O.

She was waiting for him on the sidewalk, away from the action.

He'd hoped she might learn something about how to handle the media by attending the press conference, but each time he'd looked in her direction she'd had her head down, absorbed in her tablet. He hadn't suspected her of idly browsing the Web. He'd assumed she was catching up on work, but it had still annoyed him.

His feelings changed when he saw the expression on her face now.

It was obvious that her time spent in cyberspace during the conference had yielded information she was excited to share.

"I've got something," she began as soon as he reached her, but he held up a finger for her to wait and walked her to the end of the block, well out of the reporters' hearing.

"I've got the name of the third roommate who lived with Samuel Miller and Marty Lightzer in college. It's Gregg Corbel."

Alibi's head was filled with the details about Samson's case that he'd reviewed for the press briefing. The third roommate wasn't one of them. He tried to think back to why he believed it might have been important.

"I did a search, and he has some kind of high-end mortgage business," Jackie O continued. "By appointment only, no advertising. The only listed address Corbel has is a post office box."

Alibi hadn't been planning to immediately go out and find the guy, so he wasn't sure why Jackie O was pursuing this line of reasoning.

"It's in Linville," she said. "At the post office in Linville. So we can assume his business is located there, too."

That did seem a notable coincidence since Luke Doyle was thought to have gone to Linville. On the other hand, Luke hadn't been found there.

"But that's not my main finding," Jackie O said, reverting to the language of academics he'd heard her use before. "The thing about Corbel is interesting, but his relationship with Marty Lightzer and the Gambler, other than sharing housing, is unknown and it's kind of old news. With Linville on my mind, I went back to the text Luke Doyle sent."

She pulled out her tablet and was scrolling and tapping as Alibi yawned.

The day was definitely catching up to him. He wanted to get home, listen to a little Van Morrison, and pour a glass of wine. He hoped Jackie O would get to the point soon.

"Look. Here," she said, moving so he could see her screen. She'd pulled up the image she'd taken of the notepad in Emma's house. "Where it says, 'You at Beryl's house?' and then at the bottom, the numbers and what looks like a percentage?"

Alibi gave in, and read it, paying close attention to the phrases Jackie O had just referenced.

Deb,

You at Beryl's (BLUE-GREEN) house?
I got Death by Violetall (OPPOSITE) Rejoinder (RESPOND) tix for us!! Don't tell Antiphon (RESPONSE IN A CHANT).
Serious don't. Concert is total surprise HAHA.
Would be like LCC (LINVILLE CREEK CAFE) x 5, right on! (?).
A 10 plus one(?) if they open with Ubiety (POSITION/STATE OF EXISTENCE) of Gendar (GENDER MISSPELLED?)

He couldn't see what she was getting at.

"It was the numbers that got my attention," she said.

"Emma thought 'LCC' in this message told her where Luke was. But I couldn't imagine whoever wrote this would include the numbers unless they had a reason. I played around with a map of Linville, starting at the Linville Creek Café. I tried quite a few things."

That could explain her paying no attention during the nearly hour-long press conference, Alibi thought.

"If 'five times, right on' means go five miles from LCC and then turn right, there is one long road away from the café and five miles out there is a single right turn. I used Google Street View and when I made that turn virtually, I was able to see two residences, one a large farmhouse, the other a house with two small structures in the back. I cross-checked with online public sales records to get the addresses. Right now, it's a private drive, gravel and dirt through walnut and almond orchards. But that acreage, all of it, was recently sold to a developer who plans to pave the road and build upscale homes. A model is already under construction. The developer has registered the planned complex as "Green Zebra Lane."

Alibi was incredulous.

Green Zebra Lane? Are we seriously looking for zebras now? And green ones? Is this Tommy's idea of a cosmic prank from the hereafter?

Jackie O was on a roll. She kept going. "The existing farm and house don't have street numbers, but the land they are on has plot numbers. Remember the 'ten plus one" in the message? Here's the kicker. The text mentions 'Beryl's house.' 'Beryl' means 'blue-green,' and plot eleven on what will be Green Zebra Lane is a blue house."

She abruptly stopped talking.

She looked hesitant, even embarrassed, her jubilant manner of a moment ago gone.

Alibi had seen her do this before, second-guessing her conclusion, concerned she'd gotten something wrong or she'd gone too far.

"It fits," he reassured her. "It all fits." But he didn't know what to make of it. "Suppose you have found the place from which Luke or someone with Luke sent Emma a coded message? We don't know why. This is a young teenager we're talking about. The message refers to concert tickets."

She looked deflated.

He needed to resolve this in a way that respected her hard work, but allowed him to go home.

"Let me see if Emma is at her house with Luke. Maybe we can get a quick answer as to what that message was about."

There were four rings before Emma's phone went to voicemail. It didn't seem to be shut off, but she wasn't picking up. He sent her a text asking her to call him.

"She and Luke are probably at the hospital," he told Jackie O. "Possibly even with Kate, if she's awake now."

He considered what to do next. But nothing, other than going home, came to him.

Since shortly after dawn, when he'd received the call about Tommy's death, it had been one thing after another.

First, the trip to the river, the scene of Samson's murder. Then the jail, to interview the Gambler, next the hospital, where he may have been the last person to speak with Janie Kieu before she died. Then finding Emma with the fallen Kate at the preschool, going with them back to the hospital, afterwards to meet with

Jerome Porter and his wife at the motel. And finally, negotiating with the mayor and facing down the press.

It was no wonder he couldn't think straight any more.

Jackie O watched him, waiting for direction.

"This is amazing investigative work," he told her. "Nothing short of brilliant. And I agree with you, Luke may well have been or could still be at the address you've identified. But he's a minor, and it will be necessary for us to have a responsible adult in his life present if we're going to interview him. The minute I hear back from Emma, we'll make those arrangements. And if she hasn't found him yet, I'll let her know what you've discovered about where Luke likely is, at this blue house on Zebra Lane, undoubtedly hanging out with his friends, getting into some minor teenage trouble that he shouldn't be. That will put her mind at ease."

Jackie O nodded, though she still looked a bit let down.

"Great work," he said again, mustering the last of his energy to repeat it with conviction. "I promise, we'll pick this up where you left off, first thing tomorrow morning."

FIFTY-SEVEN

On the Road

AFTER LEAVING JACKIE O in front of City Hall, Alibi had been feeling Tommy's presence more strongly than ever and with it an unexpected craving for the crispy deep-fried chicken in a Worcestershire-based sauce Tommy had ordered the night they'd gone to the Hawaiian restaurant. The young woman who took his phone order at Delicious Island Fare told him his chicken katsu would be ready in thirty minutes. He hoped his stomach would forgive him.

Meanwhile, Emma had not returned his texts or calls. He'd phoned the hospital. She wasn't there. While it seemed unlikely Kate's shooting had been motivated by some kind of grudge against Rainbow Alley, the fact that Emma was again nowhere to be found weighed on him. After a moment's thought, he decided it wasn't too far out of his way to swing by Matchbook Lane on his way to the restaurant.

Emma's home and Kate and Luke's duplex were both dark. Crash's head appeared briefly in the window, but since Alibi didn't stop the car, the big dog didn't bark.

He didn't think there was anything else he could do but let it go for now, and he expected he'd hear from her soon. Ten minutes later, with his dinner bagged on the front seat of the Camry and the sweet smell of the katsu sauce filling the car, he was en route home when his phone rang.

Carlos's torrent of words left Alibi no space to say hello.

"I'm at Marty Lightzer's, out front now. Rachel's inside with Marty and his wife. Marty wants to make a deal. He says he was there when Quan was shot, that he was a witness. He says if we give him immunity for his role in the break-in that night, he'll give us Quan's killer. He also says Samuel Miller ordered the drugs planted at Tommy's, not the murder, but the drugs and—"

Alibi cut in. "Carlos, slow down." He needed some context for what was happening. "Why does Marty want to give us this information now? After four years?"

"Samson," Carlos said. "Marty says he was on the phone with Quan's murderer last night and it got kind of heated. Marty was loud and said some things about the killing. He thinks he called the man by his name. Right afterward he saw Samson leaving from the back alley. Marty says he didn't think anything of it then, but after he learned Samson had been killed, he figured Quan's murderer did it to keep the kid quiet. Marty is terrified he'll be next. Or at least his wife is terrified, and she's convinced him to ask for this deal. Anyway, he says he'll tell us if we give him immunity and protection until we arrest Quan's killer."

Alibi pulled the Camry over to the side of the road. He didn't trust himself to keep driving as he tried to process this information. He had suspected Samson's death and Quan's could be linked, but not in such a direct fashion. He needed to be sure he understood Carlos correctly.

"Marty says he can tell us who Quan's murderer is

and will also provide firsthand knowledge of Samuel Miller's involvement?"

"Yes," Carlos said. "But he wants protection until the killer is in custody, and he wants a deal before he'll give up the name."

"Alright," Alibi said. "Call HQ for an officer to park in front of Lightzer's home 24/7, visible to anyone driving by. Don't leave until they arrive. I'll see if I can reach the DA tonight about a deal. If I can't, I assume the mayor can."

"Got it," Carlos said.

Two more things occurred to Alibi.

"How does Marty think the killer, on the phone with him at the time, could have learned Samson overheard Marty say his name?

"No idea," Carlos said, "but he's convinced that's what happened."

"Okay," Alibi said, though he was concerned about that gap in Marty's story. "Does Marty have any idea how any of this, Samson's death or Quan's murder, might link to the shooting at Rainbow Alley today?"

"Oh, right," Carlos said. "I forgot about that. It didn't seem as important as the other stuff. But Marty's wife, her name's Jill, said one of the things that got her so upset was when it was on the news that the mother of another kid who worked for Marty had also been shot. Jill had been at the shop when Kate had come in a couple times to get Luke, and recognized Kate's photo in the reports. Anyway, she figured Samson told Luke the killer's identity and Luke told his mother, so they were both on the killer's hit list. It seems kind of far-fetched, but that's what she said."

Alibi wasn't as ready as Carlos to dismiss Jill Lightzer's theory. If she was right, Luke could be in danger, maybe Emma too. And they'd both gone quiet for too long. Once he was certain Carlos had everything straight for the next steps to lock down Marty's statement, he pulled sharply away from the curb and made a U-turn.

He didn't need to check his notes to recall exactly what Jackie O had told him, that Luke's coded message provided directions to a blue house at 11 Green Zebra Lane in Linville. Late Friday night traffic might be a problem, but he thought he could get there in forty-five minutes or so.

When he saw the entrance to the freeway ahead, he signaled and made the turn, then turned up the music from one of his favorite personal playlists piped through the Camry's speakers, an eclectic mix of international bands with a little country thrown in.

For once, chasing zebras might be the right thing to do.

FIFTY-EIGHT

The Construction Site

As EMMA GUIDED the SUV along the narrow gravel road through rows of walnut and almond trees on either side, she became hyperaware of the fading light, of the deepening blue of the sky. The evening would soon give way to night, and she experienced the cold realization it might be her last, since surely the purpose of this trip was that she never return. But as she felt herself drifting toward despair, she forced herself to think clearly, to evaluate her options, no matter how bleak. She needed to focus on something other than her fear of the darkness closing in.

There had to be some aspect of her situation that she could influence, if not control.

Really, all she had to do was stall. Luke would have called the police by now. He must have. Even now, there could be officers running silently through the trees toward her, one a trained sniper with night vision goggles who would put a bullet through Lee's head. That last thought made her feel guilty when Lee, evidently unable to endure the silence any longer, finally spoke.

"I want to be helpful. I take no pleasure in hurting people." His words tumbled over one another, as though they couldn't wait to burst forth from his lengthy silence. "But having a gun at the ready is a good idea. Being prepared, you know?"

Emma considered volunteering her belief that having a gun at the ready rarely led to anything good, but decided instead to be positive, to try to build some kind of rapport.

"You're right. Being prepared is a good idea," she said, in as calm a tone as she could manage. "But I suppose you can't be prepared for everything. Sometimes things go wrong—"

"I helped the Chief," Lee interrupted. "That's why he gave me a promotion." He hesitated, looking sideways at her. "I can't give you the details. But believe me, it was a promotion. But it fell through. Not my fault. I was given another assignment, but then that went wrong too."

He gripped the gun more tightly. She could hear bitterness in his voice. Then, without warning, he called out, "Stop driving. Stop the car. We're here."

He sounded worried she was going to sail right past whatever their destination was. She would have liked to, but his gun was an effective deterrent.

Here? Where?

At first, all she could see were more trees.

They were deeper in the orchard, but it was still just an orchard, rows and rows of trees, seemingly identical to those they'd driven past, mile after mile, to get here. Then she saw a building, a structure of some kind, straight ahead. It was two stories high, maybe a barn, thirty to forty yards in the distance, off to the right.

"Open the back hatch of the vehicle," Lee said. "There's a button. To your left."

To buy herself time to think, she made a show of being unable to locate it, then finally pressed it and heard the hatch pop open.

"Get out on my side," he said.

The SUV didn't have a bench seat. She'd have to lift her hips up to clear the center console. She'd just begun the awkward process when he said, "Wait. Turn off the car and give me the keys."

She sat back down and shut the lights off, then the engine.

He barked at her. "Lights on. Engine off and lights on. It'll be dark soon. I don't want to stumble around out here."

She switched the headlights on manually, put the keys in his outstretched hand, then managed to get out of the vehicle on his side, as directed.

She remained standing by the front passenger door as he walked slowly backward, his gun pointed at her, until he was even with the rear bumper of the SUV.

"Come closer," he said. "Come on."

As much as she wanted to slow things down, he definitely wanted her to hurry.

Some of her inability to move quickly was genuine, since Barry had removed her shoes back at the house. The loose gravel drive was uneven, at places sharp and painful through her thin summer socks.

She took three steps. Then two more.

"Kneel," he said.

She tried to think, but nothing came to her.

She was out of moves.

She knelt, bent her head and closed her eyes, and asked forgiveness for every wrong she'd ever done to others in her thirty-two years of life.

Each thoughtless word, every callous mistake.

It seemed the only thing to do.

But then there was the sound, not of a trigger being pulled, but of Lee's footsteps on the gravel, moving away. She opened her eyes. He'd disappeared.

She heard him behind the SUV, first a grunt, then he said, loudly, "Ow, my back."

That was followed by a heavy thump on the ground.

She'd hadn't had time to gather her thoughts when he reappeared, squeezed past her, and opened the back passenger door. He removed the gun that had been wrapped in the hand towel and jogged around the back of the SUV, now with a gun in each hand.

He returned seconds later, having left the second gun behind.

Emma was still kneeling.

Pointing the other gun at her head, he said, "Stand up."

She wasn't sure she'd heard him correctly.

"Stand," he repeated.

Emma was terrified, exhausted, and now vaguely annoyed Lee couldn't decide in which position he wanted to kill her. Still, his indecision had to be good. At least, he hadn't shot her yet. Perhaps she could still find a way out. Disguised in the movement of getting to her feet, she could launch herself at him before he could get off a shot. Or maybe she should take off running in a zig-zag pattern into the gloom, away from the car's lights, so he couldn't see her.

Her mind racing, she placed a hand on the ground for balance and pushed herself to standing.

But before she was able to execute any of her half-baked plans, Lee walked right up to her until the barrel of the gun nearly touched her chest.

"Turn around," he said, quietly. "Walk straight. Keep going until I tell you to stop."

She turned as she was told, and again saw the barn-like structure in the distance. Was that their destination? If so, it might take ten minutes or more to walk there, and every minute, every second mattered since help had to be on its way.

She clung to the idea that if Luke had been hiding in the Jeep as she'd driven the SUV away, he'd know exactly the direction in which she'd gone, and her bottom line was still simple. Buy time for her rescuers to get there.

And she knew how to do it.

Lee was a talker, she just needed to get him going. As she took one small step, then another, moving as slowly as she could, she asked him, "What was all that noise back there?"

No response. There was only the sound of his boots on the gravel close behind her.

Come on, Lee, she thought. *You know you want to say something.*

She took another two small steps, remembering now to limp, to favor her ankle, hoping he hadn't noticed it was an injury that seemed to come and go.

"You sounded like you got hurt," she said. "Are you okay?"

The footsteps behind her slowed.

"It seems like you get the most difficult jobs." She spoke to the empty air in front of her, hoping to tap into one of the many grievances Lee seemed to have. "That doesn't seem fair."

The night went quiet.

The footsteps behind her had stopped.

"It wasn't fair. I should have gotten to drive the van," he said.

Long seconds passed.

Emma was aware of his breathing, he was so close. The gun must be only inches from her back.

"Turn around," he told her.

She didn't want to.

"Turn," he said again.

When she did, she saw his expression had softened.

"No one listens when I say things ought to be fair," he muttered.

Then he nodded, apparently to himself, and waved with the gun for her to walk back in the direction they'd come.

Toward the waiting SUV.

For a moment, Emma thought he was going to take her back to the blue house, or even set her free. She felt as though she might collapse with gratitude, that she might be overtaken by pure joy.

Then Lee said, "It may be difficult, but this is better. This way you can say goodbye. That seems only fair."

FIFTY-NINE

The Construction Site

DYLAN LAY ON his back on the ground behind the SUV, his left arm across his chest, his eyes closed. Emma moved slowly toward him. When she knelt at his side, he gave no indication he'd heard her approach. Behind her, Lee was saying something, but she paid no attention. He didn't sound angry, he was just letting his mouth run again.

She took Dylan's hand.

It wasn't cold. She felt his forehead, if anything he seemed feverish.

She touched his shirt. It was damp with blood all down his right side. The source was a wound high up, almost under his arm. He also had a hole in his pants leg below the knee. She gently touched there, felt more blood, and he groaned.

Dylan was alive. Bleeding, maybe badly, but definitely alive.

Then she saw the gun that had her fingerprints on it, no longer wrapped in a towel, a few feet from where he lay. It was out of reach. She'd just angled toward it when suddenly Lee was there. He grabbed one of her arms and yanked her up and away from Dylan.

"Enough," he said. "You got to see him. Let's go. Let's get this over with."

He took his phone from his pocket and turned on

the flashlight function, using it to brightly illuminate where he stepped as he pushed her in front of him, his gun in his other hand.

He walked fast. When she slowed, he pressed his weapon into the small of her back. She had no choice but to match his pace.

"Where are we going?" she asked, running the same play she had before, trying to keep him talking.

This time, Lee gave no response. They walked in silence until they'd passed out of the line of trees into the clearing where the structure stood. Up close, she could see it had been a barn once, but was undergoing a significant remodel to have new life as a home, maybe a mansion from the looks of things. There were stacks of high-end lumber, slabs of black marble with golden veins, and several sets of custom French doors that hadn't yet been put in.

Lee steered her toward the back of the building where a temporary staircase with metal risers led to the second floor. She looked up and saw a balcony had been put in place, but there was no railing around it yet.

When they got to the base of the stairs, she stopped.

Emma definitely did not want to be twenty feet off the ground. She thought of Tommy falling through the air, crashing onto the concrete below.

The packed dirt she was standing on would be only slightly more forgiving.

"Go," Lee said, poking her in the back again with the barrel of the gun.

She took the first step on the riser, then another, as slowly as she could.

For what it was worth, which didn't feel like much, she understood now why she and Dylan had been taken here.

They would have been seen together today by someone, a neighbor perhaps, leaving her home, then outside the café, driving around. Now, out in the heart of the orchard, if nothing was done, Dylan appeared likely to bleed to death from a gunshot wound. The weapon, with her prints on it, lay at his side. Her body would be found where she'd "thrown herself" from the balcony, the final act in a lover's quarrel that had turned violent and deadly.

She took two more steps, then three, then five. They were halfway up the stairs, time was running out. Still, one advantage she had was she knew now that Lee wasn't going to shoot her.

He could push her once they got to the top, or even from where they were on the stairs now if she refused to climb any farther—they were high enough. But the murder-suicide story would be much harder to sell if she'd been shot dead with a different gun.

She felt for the toothbrush tucked neatly in the waistband of her jeans. It hadn't been uncomfortable, she'd gotten used to it there, and she'd been so sure help was on its way that she didn't think it would come to this.

But no one else could save her now.

She would need to be very close to Lee, almost on top of him, and she couldn't hesitate. Hesitation would cost her her life.

One hand on the metal handrail to the stairs, she used the other to try to push the head free from the base of the toothbrush. It wouldn't budge. It would take both her hands, she'd have to grip the base tightly with one and pull with the other. She feigned a stumble (she thought she was getting pretty good at that), fell onto one knee, leaned forward, yanked the head off and let it drop to the dirt below. That exposed the short, sharp metal rod that fed up the neck of the brush head when in use.

She yelped, though not quite her trademark "ouch."

Then she held her position, half-kneeling, and waited.

Lee was one step below her, his arm outstretched with the gun in his hand.

"C'mon. Let's go," he said.

"It hurts," she moaned. "My ankle."

It was so hard to stay still, her adrenaline was flowing, and her fear it wouldn't work made her want to do it now. But only when he'd closed the gap between them and she could feel him right behind her, did she tense her muscles, ready.

When he bent forward and reached for her, whether to help her up or throw her off the side, she whirled around and buried the sharp exposed hilt of the toothbrush in his right eye.

His scream was unlike anything she'd ever heard.

He staggered upright. His hands flew to his face, his gun dropped through a gap in the risers, his phone clanged as it bounced down the stairs. His foot slipped and he fell backward, his arms windmilling as he rolled, still screaming, over and down, and over and down, like some otherworldly mutant tumbleweed, until he landed with a thud in a crumpled, twisted heap at the bottom of the stairs, quiet at last.

SIXTY

The Construction Site

HAVING WITNESSED WHAT it looked like to fall the length of the metal staircase, Emma gripped the railing tightly and placed her stockinged feet carefully in the center of each riser as she made her way down.

Lee had made no movement and no sound since he landed.

As she got closer, the jagged edge of a bone was visible through a tear in his jeans. Fortunately, his head was turned away from her. She did not want to see what, if anything was left of his eye where she'd speared it with the metal toothbrush rod.

When she reached the bottom step, she charted a wide path around him and resolved not to look back.

Having stuck to that plan, and now far enough away to dismiss her irrational fear that he would rise like an injured zombie, she focused on reaching Dylan as quickly as she could. She had to get him to a doctor. She tried to think whether Linville was large enough to have a hospital, or if she should find a twenty-four-hour urgent care facility. Would that be good enough? Then she realized the route she would drive out of the orchard would take her past the blue house. She hadn't heard sirens—the police must have made a silent approach—but there would be someone official there by now who could take Dylan to a hospital right away, so she needn't worry about speeding along unfamiliar streets in the dark to rush him to care. She was reassured by her plan until she recalled Lee saying, *"Lights on. Engine off. Give me the keys."*

She stopped, furious with herself for not thinking of the car key sooner.

As she turned around and jogged back toward him, she was at least comforted by the fact that Lee no longer had his gun. He'd dropped it before he fell.

Even if he was conscious, she figured she could take an unarmed man with a compound fracture in his leg and no depth perception since he was absent one working eye.

When she got close, she approached from the side that gave her a view of only the back of his head. Even so, he was a gruesome site. In addition to his broken leg, his right arm was bent at a very painful angle.

She thought she could see him breathing, though it was hard to tell as it had continued to get darker.

The sky was a deep gray, no longer a hint of blue, and the waning moon wasn't much help.

She knelt beside him, as far back as she could and still reach what appeared to be the raised outline of the SUV key deep in one of his front pants pockets. Holding her breath, she slipped her hand inside until it met with resistance. But it wasn't a key. It felt like the edge of several folded papers or maybe a business card. When she pulled, she found she was holding a playing card. The Queen of Hearts. For one crazy moment, she thought Lee must be the Gambler, the white supremacist gang leader responsible for multiple execution-style killings of young people of color, who had left playing cards behind on his victim's bodies. But that couldn't be right.

They'd arrested that guy with what the media had reported was an airtight case. He was in jail awaiting trial.

Maybe Lee kept the queen as a lucky card. That seemed like something he would do.

She reached into his pocket again, further, and this time came up with two more cards that were stuck together.

A ten of diamonds and a three of hearts.

For a total face value of twenty-three.

There was something really not right about this.

Had Lee intended to commit a copycat crime, to confuse the authorities by leaving the same signature cards on her body? She couldn't think about that now. Not with the rate at which Dylan must be losing blood. She tucked the cards in her back pocket. She would tell Alibi about them later.

With the cards gone, she was able to reach the key and slide it out. But as she turned away and started to stand she was pulled off balance, hard, as her ankle was yanked backward. She strained to get away, but Lee's grip was viselike. She screamed and kicked out, connecting with muscle and bone, with what she thought must be his rib cage. Perhaps a rib or two of his had already broken, as he yelled in pain and released her leg.

She scrambled away from him on her hands and knees in the dirt, her only thought to put as much distance between them as possible. Although once she was out of reach, she realized while Lee did still have one functioning arm and hand, with which he'd just grabbed her, he was in no position to run her down. She slowed to catch her breath, then stopped altogether when she saw the gun. It was on the ground about six feet away, camouflaged in the gloom, nearly the same color as the earth. She retrieved it, then stood and managed a hobbled jog through the clearing, since now her ankle really did hurt.

A moment later, she heard Lee sobbing.

In a weak and pitiful tone he called after her.

"Help me. Please, don't leave me. Help me."

Emma kept going. Faster, as fast as she could. Only when she was out of the open space, surrounded again by rows of trees where she felt hidden, where she felt something close to safe, only then did she say softly, "I'll send someone for you."

She didn't look back. She knew she hadn't been loud enough for him to hear.

SIXTY-ONE

The Blue House

GREGG GLANCED AT his watch. It was late to eat dinner, but one thing after another had gotten in the way.

From his office, he could hear the familiar sound of Barry in the kitchen, the water running, the rhythmic thump, thump of the knife on the chopping board. He guessed it would be Barry's mother's chili recipe tonight.

Barry cooked like Gregg reconciled the numbers for his business, as a way to center himself.

As he entered today's final revenue calculations in the ledger, he reflected it was too bad about Councilman Dylan Johnson and Emma Lawson. They'd been in the wrong place at the wrong time. It could happen to anyone. He, of all people, knew that.

When their bodies were discovered, their families would learn a lover's quarrel had escalated beyond repair, and in the heat of the moment, Emma had shot Dylan.

No more tragic than what had actually happened, but loose ends had to be tied up, resetting the scale to zero.

Kelly's job performance had also been an unexpected variable today, though it had accrued positively for the operation.

Kelly's parents had died when he was ten, and he'd gone to live with nearby family, his cousin, Walter, and

Walter's mom, a single parent, making Walter the closest thing to a father Kelly had, despite there only being a ten-year age difference between the two men.

When Gregg had needed another man for the job, Walter had explained that his cousin was as loyal as they come.

Of course, the original plan had been that Kelly would not be read in on anything meaningful. His participation was to have been limited to dropping Walter off at the school before the girl showed on the scene. But then the twenty-year-old's role had necessarily grown when Vivian's nanny had been killed and Walter seriously injured.

Kelly had handled it well. Most importantly, it turned out he had a way with little kids.

Barry had told Gregg how much the girl trusted Kelly, which was the reason Gregg had concluded Kelly would be the one to finish this with her. It would mean the least drama and the highest chance of success. He'd go speak with him now, and when Lee got back they'd sort the rest of it out, and despite the considerable unexpected bumps, the operation would be a success.

Gregg could feel it.

It had to be.

For Giselle, and for all the innocents like her who had lost their lives to deadly legal drug pushers.

At the thought of the mega-million-dollar pharmaceutical companies and their political enablers who had been responsible for his only having had one precious night with his wife before finding her dead of an overdose in their new marriage bed, Gregg felt the old, red-hot anger growing inside him, crowding out reason and burning away rational thought.

With effort, he shut it down.

He couldn't lose his self-control. He had work to do.

When he passed through the kitchen, Barry was crumbling ground beef into a frying pan. Gregg paused to sample the sauce. It was good. Everything Barry made was good.

When he reached the small bedroom in the back, he knocked, then quickly spoke, not wanting Kelly to open the door just yet.

"Kelly, come out. Only you. Tell the girl to stay."

He heard no movement. Nothing. He wondered if they'd fallen asleep again, as they'd done when Barry went to check on them before he let Dylan and Emma in the house.

Gregg didn't like thinking about that, when things had really gone sideways, when the girl had awakened and run into the room.

He knocked again, then eased the door open and peered around it, only a sliver of his face visible. He was certain it wouldn't be enough for a three-year-old to later identify him.

From what he could see, the room was empty. He called out. "Kelly." Still nothing. He opened the door all the way. There was no one in the small room. He stepped inside and checked the bathroom. No one there either. He passed through and opened the door on the other side. Walter lay on the couch. Kelly and the girl weren't with him.

When Gregg returned to the bedroom, he noticed the drape on the only window had been opened, pulled all the way to one side. His heart beat faster.

If that's what happened, if the alarm had failed...

He focused on calming himself.

He had this. There would be an answer. There would be a solution.

He just had to play the odds.

When he looked down to gather his thoughts, he saw that the small plastic wastebasket beneath the desk contained a balled-up paper. Barry was obsessive about details, he wouldn't have left it there when preparing the room before the kid arrived.

He retrieved the crumpled ball and smoothed it on top of the desk.

It was a page from a child's coloring book, nearly covered in writing that had to have been done by an adult, despite it being in blue crayon.

Much of it had been crossed out, but in the jumble he saw a word that made the rage he had successfully fought back rise tenfold within him.

Emma.

He pounded hard once on the desk with his fist, then again, and let out something close to a growl as he put the facts together.

Kelly knew Emma. Dylan coming here with her hadn't been a random visit or even an attempt to find out about the policeman. Somehow, Kelly had gotten a message to her, and she'd come to find him.

The first thing that flashed through Gregg's mind was he was glad that Emma was dead. He hoped she had suffered when it happened.

As to Kelly, he'd think about how best to handle him later, and what his treachery meant for Walter.

Right now, he had to find the girl and bring her back, with Kelly or without him.

Everything depended on the girl.

And he knew exactly where she had to be.

SIXTY-TWO

The Blue House

LUKE HAD BEGUN to worry. He'd counted to "one thousand four hundred and twenty," which meant seven minutes had passed. Then Emma yelled, "Ouch! Ouch!" and Vivian climbed onto his back like they'd practiced, piggyback, her arms wrapped around his neck and her legs around his waist, her backpack on with the straps nice and snug. BeeBee inside. Luke had squeezed the window latch, and it slid open without a sound. He'd ducked his head and told Vivian to do the same, climbed out, then slid it shut again.

Perfect.

Unfortunately, that was the last thing that had been perfect.

Luke had run up the side of the house with Vivian on his back, as planned, only to come face-to-face with a ten-foot-high smooth wooden gate, held in place with a heavy bolt, beneath which was a metal weatherproof box.

Luke had opened the box to find a keypad, and a light flashing red.

There'd be no escape that way.

He'd been able to hear voices nearby. He thought they were coming from inside the garage. *Hard to make out, but it had sounded like Barry and the Creep.*

He hadn't heard Emma say anything since she'd yelled, "Ouch."

Maybe they'd let her leave.

Which meant she must be in the Jeep now, driving away and calling the police.

She'd said, "If one of us can get away, we have to do it. That's how we can get help."

Okay, good, he thought. *A different plan, but this will work.*

He just needed to find a safe place for him and Vivian to wait.

They couldn't go back into their room, the window had undoubtedly been armed again and would go off if he opened it.

He crouched down and moved along the side of the house toward the back of the property.

"Where are we going?" Vivian asked in a loud stage whisper.

"Shhh. I'll tell you when we get there."

Not that he knew where "there" would be.

He put Vivian down next to him and holding her hand squeezed through the dense line of hedges to see if they might be able to get out through there. But he wasn't surprised to find that the ten-foot wooden gate up front connected to a ten-foot-high fence that extended as far as he could see. He figured it enclosed the entire property.

He fought back a wave of discouragement, reminding himself help was on its way, Emma would have called the police. But what if before help got here the men discovered he and Vivian weren't in the small room where they'd been kept captive? Wouldn't their first order of business be to search the property? It wouldn't do to be out in the open like this.

He peered around the back corner of the house.

There were two shed-type buildings in the yard. Maybe one could be locked from the inside to buy them a little time if a search was underway.

He picked Vivian up and circled around until he was behind the shed farthest from the house. It was also the biggest one, the size of a large garage. But he discovered to his dismay it also had a keypad inside a metal box, its red light flashing, just like the gate. There would be no getting in. So he moved to the smaller shed and almost couldn't believe his luck when he found it was unlocked. He quietly eased the door open. It was pitch-black inside.

"I don't want to go in there," Vivian said firmly.

"It's okay," he told her. He wished he could see her face, let her see his as he spoke. But it was too dark, and their eyes would have to adjust. "It's like hide and seek. We'll stay in here until Emma comes to get us."

He carried her in, turned around and felt for a latch, but unfortunately no lock on the outside translated into no lock on the inside either. He stood still until he found he could begin to make out shapes. Slivers of reflected light from the back of the house came through tiny gaps in the slat roof, so it wasn't as dark as it had first seemed.

When he looked around, he could make out garden stuff. A large wheelbarrow, rakes and a pitchfork, bags of fertilizer. Luke hadn't seen flowers or vegetables on the property. Then he realized someone had to take care of all those hedges.

He set Vivian down next to him and said, "I have to move a few things around in here to make us more comfortable."

She didn't protest, but slipped an arm around his leg, staying close against him.

"Here, help me," he told her as he rolled the wheelbarrow until it was flush with the door. "You hold this steady. Don't let it tip." As he'd hoped, she released his leg and grasped the edge where he'd shown her, giving him freedom of movement. He hoisted heavy bags of fertilizer and transferred them into the wheelbarrow until it was full.

It wouldn't stop anyone trying to get in, but it should slow them down. Vivian looked at the setup thoughtfully, then turned and located her backpack. She unzipped it and took out BeeBee.

Luke picked up the pitchfork and sat down with his back against the opposite wall, where he could see the door. He called Vivian to bring BeeBee over. She came at a run, dragging the backpack, and sat shoulder-to-shoulder with him, BeeBee on her lap.

Luke took stock of their situation. The weighted wheelbarrow against the door, the pitchfork at his side, and Vivian within reach, where he could get between her and anyone who came in. If he had to defend them, he decided he'd done what he could.

But he was so very tired.

He was frightened too, he couldn't help it. He was having a hard time believing things would really turn out okay.

Then his thoughts went to Emma, who he knew would kick ass and take no prisoners if required to get them out. And he thought about his mother, all she had done for him, and how awfully he'd treated her lately, just because he could. He'd never known his father or grandfather, there'd been no stepdad in his life. For as long as he could remember, he'd only had his mom and his Aunt Emma to rely on, to protect him.

He took a deep breath and willed himself to keep it together for a little longer, to be as strong as the two women who had taught him to be a man.

SIXTY-THREE

The Blue House

BARRY WAS CHOPPING the last of the vegetables for salad to accompany the southwestern chili bubbling on the stove when he heard the low rumble of a large vehicle approaching. No doubt it was Lee returning since there was next to no traffic on this private road.

When he'd rinsed the knife and cutting board and turned the water off, he listened for the sound of the alarm beeping as it disengaged, for the door opening as Lee came in. It remained quiet. Too quiet. Lee made noise wherever he went.

Barry crossed to the front window and moved the drape so he could see outside. The SUV was parked across the street, almost nose-to-nose with Dylan Johnson's Jeep.

Idiot.

What was Lee thinking?

Barry dried his hands and went into the living room. The alarm was engaged. He entered the code and stepped out onto the front stoop. He couldn't see inside the vehicle from where he stood. It was too dark.

Why had Lee turned the engine off?

"Lee? Put it in the garage. What are you doing?"

On the Road

MOVING DYLAN FROM the ground behind the SUV into
the backseat had been challenging. He was conscious
but couldn't put any weight on his injured leg, and was
bleeding so profusely from his right side that Emma
didn't want him to exert himself even if he could.

The relatively easy part had been dragging him to the
open passenger door and maneuvering him to sit with
his back and shoulders resting against the edge of the
seat. Then she'd climbed in on the other side, crawled
across the seat, threaded her arms beneath his arms and
as though she were doing a bicep curl, had heaved him
up a little bit at a time.

His cries of pain had been almost too much to bear.

Once they got going, she'd found her way back to the
main road without incident. She figured they were now
about a mile from the blue house. As she got closer, she
narrowed her eyes and tried to see ahead as far as she
could, hoping to spot the shape of a police car and other
emergency vehicles in the growing darkness. She wondered why there were no flashing red and blue lights.
When she closed the gap, her heart sank, as there was
only one vehicle parked across from the blue house.
Dylan's Jeep. And as far as she could tell, it was unoccupied.

At the last minute she cut the lights on the SUV,
killed the engine, and coasted to a stop nose-to-nose
with the Jeep. She wished she'd thought of the stealth
approach sooner.

Where were Luke and Vivian? She'd feigned the injury to her ankle, Barry had carried her to the car, he'd
gone back to get the gun with her prints on it. During
all of that, the alarm had remained disengaged.

But suppose Vivian had resisted when the time actually came to leave?

Or perhaps they'd made it to the Jeep, but Luke had been unable to start it. Maybe there was a trick to the keyless car so that once it had been off for a while, he had to do something special to get it going again.

But if that had been the case, wouldn't he have used her phone to call 911? And if he had, shouldn't the police be here by now?

Dylan let out a groan.

His color was worse and a much larger area on his shirt was soaked with blood.

She had to get him to the hospital.

She got out, and was about to quietly close the door when she remembered Lee's gun. She retrieved it from the front passenger seat. With the gun in hand, she scooted along the side of Lee's SUV and kept going until she was at the passenger-side door of Dylan's Jeep. She opened it and reached for her khaki bag under the front seat, where she'd left it.

It wasn't there. She looked in the back storage area of the Jeep.

No bag.

Would Luke have taken it with him if he couldn't start the car and had to hike to the main road with Vivian? It was heavy, it served as her traveling office. He already had to carry a little girl.

Wouldn't he have removed the phone and left the bag? None of it made sense, and she had to make sure the kids had gotten out, that they were free. The best plan she could come up with was to sneak along the side of the house and look through their window.

If they were still there, they could crawl out now even if the alarm sounded. Because she had the gun.

True, she was a pretty bad shot. But she had gotten good enough to sometimes hit the target at the range, and more times than that to get close. If nothing else, she could use it to bluff while the three of them ran to the SUV and drove away.

She moved to the back of the Jeep and, bending low, gun at her side, was about to sprint across the street, when she thought she saw the curtain to the kitchen twitch, move an inch, then fall back into place. She froze. Nothing else happened.

Nerves, she decided.

But just in case someone had been at the window, she ran, bent at the waist, across the street, straight through a row of tall privacy hedges that shielded the side of the house from view, at which point she nearly collided with a solid barrier.

A tall, dark, wood gate.

She skidded to a halt.

She was in the process of hastily searching for how to open it, and had just discovered it had a metal keypad where a latch should have been, its red light flashing, when a voice she recognized broke the silence of the night.

"Lee? Put it in the garage. What are you doing?"

Holding her breath, Emma peered through the protection of the dense hedges.

Barry stood at the top of the front steps, the door open behind him, his white hair shimmering like a halo, backlit by the light from the interior of the house.

When he received no response from Lee, he hustled down the steps.

He was halfway across the street when Emma decided she could not let him reach the vehicle and find

Dylan on the backseat, because if Barry had a weapon, he might kill Dylan on the spot.

Without hesitation, she moved forward to the edge of the hedges, lifted her arm and took aim to wound, not to kill. Just his leg, just to stop him in his tracks. The bullet left the chamber with a deafening crack. Her shoulder jerked back at the recoil.

Barry turned and looked in her direction, then took a few steps toward her.

Not limping. Not hit. Very much unharmed.

She pulled the trigger again.

And missed.

And again.

And missed.

He kept coming. Was he not afraid of being gunned down? Or had he correctly determined she was as likely to hit a star overhead as she was to fire a bullet that would make contact with him?

Still, she had no other play.

She steadied her hand and fired again.

This time, Barry went down hard.

Too hard.

She had a bad feeling it hadn't been one of his legs that she'd hit. But that couldn't be her priority right now.

She considered her odds.

Only Gregg was left, and maybe the guy who was sleeping or unconscious on the sofa. If either of them had heard the gunshots, the sooner she moved, the less time he (or they) would have to react, to prepare, to stop her from getting to Luke and Vivian.

As adrenaline coursed through her, her arm outstretched, her gun at the ready, Emma ran up the steps and inside.

SIXTY-FOUR

The Blue House

EMMA WAS TWO feet into the main room when she heard the front door slam closed behind her. She had no time to think before Gregg launched himself at her, wrenched the gun away, and aimed it with a steady hand dead center at her chest. She realized, too late, that he must have been hiding behind the open door.

His dark eyes shone, and his pale skin bore bright pink blotches. He looked furious, but his voice was even. He seemed entirely too comfortable with the gun.

"Let's go in my office and sort this out," he said.

Emma couldn't move.

Not because she was frightened. In fact, it occurred to her she wasn't as scared as she should be. No, she was incredulous and starting to get really mad. She couldn't believe she'd escaped one man with a gun, used it to shoot a second man, only to involuntarily surrender that same gun to someone else who now had it pointed at her.

"I'm not a violent person. But I don't have time for this. Come with me. You know the way." Gregg gestured toward the kitchen.

Not a violent person?

As she walked in front of him to his office in the back, Emma flashed on the deaths and near-deaths that had occurred *today* as a result of his schemes.

The painter at Rainbow Alley.

Kate.

The guy comatose on the couch in the next room.

Barry and Lee. (Yes, they were his fault too.)

Dylan.

And those were only the ones she knew of.

When they reached his office, he gestured for her to sit as he moved to the far cabinet on the wall, the one where she'd found the cell phone. He returned with a green ledger and sat down opposite her.

"I think an exchange of information is in order," he said.

He paused and looked at the framed photo of his wife, then fixed his gaze on Emma.

"You first. Who did you shoot?"

She had not expected that question, and she wasn't sure whether she should answer it truthfully.

"You left with Lee and came back without him but with his gun," Gregg said, "so I'm going to assume you shot him. Is he dead?"

Emma didn't know the answer to that.

"I heard gunshots close by, likely in front of the house. Barry isn't anywhere to be seen. Did you shoot him too? Is he alive?"

Emma still didn't answer.

Gregg sighed. "Okay. I'll go first. We've got to get through this."

The glimpse of rage she'd seen when he'd grabbed the gun from her was no longer evident. He appeared to be conducting this like some kind of contract negotiation.

"I'm not a violent person," he repeated. "I've only shot someone once in my life. It was a case of mistaken identity." He saw her eyes go to the gun in his hand. "Which is not to say I don't know how to use a weapon." He quieted and looked past her, his eyes unfocused, as though seeing a scene in which she did not play a part. "I thought the woman's husband was coming through the door," he said. He looked again at the photo on his desk. "That night changed everything for me. The universe extracted its due, and a year later my wife was dead."

He seemed to Emma to be rambling. She couldn't make sense of what he was saying.

Her thoughts returned to Luke and Vivian, who, as far as she could tell, hadn't made it to the Jeep. Were they still in the small bedroom?

She was happy to let Gregg keep talking, to nod occasionally, while she figured out what to do.

She thought again of the phone in the cabinet behind him.

"So though my debt is paid, a one-for-one trade, I am in the process of giving back in the asset column in exponentially greater amounts. I need your help to do that."

Wait, what?

He'd recaptured Emma's attention.

He thinks I'll help him?

"You know Kelly. I don't know in what capacity, but you do. And when he decided he didn't want his new role in our operation, he found a way to get a message to you."

Emma's heart sped up.

How could he possibly know that?

She clasped her hands in her lap to keep them from shaking.

"The thing is, he's out there." Gregg gestured toward the back of the property. "And he can't leave. I keep large sums of cash for business transactions back there, so I can't have people coming and going without a record. Each employee has a personal code to use to open the gates." He paused. He seemed to be thinking about what to say next. "He's got the girl with him, who I have no doubt you also know, based on Barry's description of her reaction when she saw you." He pointed a finger at Emma. "I need the girl here now. There are two fenced acres back there, and it's dark out. It will be much easier if Kelly brings her in on his own."

Emma said nothing.

"I promise you no harm will come to Vivian Lange. All you need to do is call out to Kelly, tell him that everything's under control, and it's safe for him to come back with the child."

"But it's not," Emma said. She couldn't help herself.

Even if Gregg wasn't planning on harming Vivian, if he still needed her for a ransom or whatever this was about, Luke would be dead the moment he was in range.

And she would be next.

This delusional and dangerous man simply couldn't let either of them go, not with what they'd seen.

Gregg said nothing for a long moment.

He studied her face. Emma didn't know what he hoped to find there. She tried to keep her fear from showing, her expression neutral, a blank slate where he could see what he needed to see.

Then he opened the ledger he'd retrieved from the cabinet and took out a single sheet of paper inside a plastic sleeve.

He turned it so she could read it.

It was a typed note, so brief that it took up less than a quarter of the page:

One, two buckle my shoe.
Your little girl's life depends on you.
Resign today or sow what you dread,
Next time I take her, she'll wind up dead.

It made no sense to Emma.

Your little girl?

Was the note to Cassandra Lange? What would Gregg want Cassandra to resign from?

Then she understood.

She met Gregg's eyes, unable to hide her disbelief. He was being a fool, and she called him on it.

"What makes you think Governor Lange will resign? People in power don't give in to these kinds of threats. They can't."

But as soon as the words were out of her mouth, she realized her terrible mistake. It was essential that Gregg continue to believe that giving Vivian back would work. Otherwise, why take the risk involved in returning her?

She thought of the file on Donna Lange she'd seen in the back room, the information about the time the first lady had called in a SWAT team on a false alarm. Collecting those articles hadn't been preparation to fight off a rescue attempt. It was support for Gregg's belief that Donna Lange's hypervigilance where the safety of her daughter and granddaughter were concerned would cause her to urge her husband to comply with his demand that the governor resign.

"You know what?" Emma said. "You're right. The governor would undoubtedly consult the First Lady about the deal you have proposed. I'm certain she would be on your side and would insist her husband resign if that is what it takes to keep Vivian safe."

Gregg nodded. He seemed pleased that she was finally catching up. When she saw his reaction, Emma figured it was worth staying on that theme. If Luke and Vivian had gotten out of the room, and it sounded like Gregg had checked, even if they'd only made it as far as the back of the property, keeping Gregg talking kept him from them.

It was all she had, until she could think of something more.

"Donna Lange is quite concerned for her granddaughter's safety," she said. "I believe she will be key in getting the governor to do the right thing."

Then she remembered Gregg asking her about Aminah, about whether the LG would make a good governor. "When he does resign, it is your desire that Lieutenant Governor Ali-Rosenberg become governor?"

"Yes," Gregg said, as though selecting the head of the executive branch of the state of California to govern thirty-five million people was his right. "I believe Dr. Ali-Rosenberg would make an excellent governor." For the first time, he smiled. "I've known people who hold the false belief that a person's goodness is determined by their ethnicity or perhaps by the religion they practice." He returned the sealed note to the ledger and closed the cover. "In reality, it's much more basic than that. Random, thoughtless behavior and greed together enable the evil in each of us, while selflessness and abstinence support goodness. The lieutenant governor understands this. She practices it, neither drinking nor using other substances. She has built a life of public service on self-discipline."

He's a nutcase, Emma thought. But at least now she knew what kind of crazy she was dealing with. Or at least she thought she did, until the next thing he said.

"Dr. Ali-Rosenberg has a history of supporting policies to assist those who have been harmed by corporate greed. I am certain she would not hesitate to tax pharmaceutical manufacturers to support treatment for the addiction that their most lethal drugs cause. That would save untold numbers of lives, which on its own would make her a far superior governor to Mr. Lange."

Emma felt light-headed, she had trouble believing she'd heard him correctly. Did this lunatic just tie his kidnapping a three-year-old girl to the bill Senator Ted Hutchins had introduced on opioids? But before she had time to review what Gregg had just said, to see where she must have gotten it wrong, he stood up.

"So now you know. The girl will not be harmed. But we're running out of time. All this random noise, gunfire, and people missing makes it harder to get her back safely."

He gestured with the gun for Emma to walk ahead of him.

They moved quickly back through the kitchen, until they stood at the sliding glass door in the main room that looked out on the dark lot beyond.

SIXTY-FIVE

The Blue House

STANDING AT THE open sliding glass door, Emma was not about to call Luke to bring Vivian back in. It was out of the question. But Gregg seemed to think they were on track, because he continued to give her directions.

"I'll be right here," he said, the gun still pointed at her. "You step out and call Kelly. You'll have to be pretty loud. They may be at the edge of the property."

Emma looked at him with more pity than defiance. The guy really had no clue what made people tick. She shook her head no.

Gregg appeared surprised.

Then he looked as though he were assessing her level of conviction, considering whether this was her last word on the subject. Finally, he sighed unhappily and stepped forward. He put one arm around her waist to pull her tightly to his side, and with the other hand pressed the gun hard against her temple. He dragged her outside and called into the darkness.

"Kelly, I need you to come back right now or I'm going to shoot this woman, Ms. Lawson, who I believe you know."

Emma couldn't breathe, she couldn't think. The gun was cold and hard against her skin, and Gregg's hand hurt her where he clasped her waist. He was stronger than she'd expected.

"Bring back the girl, Kelly, and she won't be harmed," Gregg called out. "But I need you to do it right now or Ms. Lawson will die. And I'll find you anyway."

To Emma's horror, she heard footsteps.

A moment later, Luke appeared from the shadows on the far side of a small blue shed about twenty feet from them.

Gregg removed the gun from Emma's head and pointed it at Luke, though he kept his hold on Emma's waist.

"Where's the girl?" Gregg asked him.

Emma thought she could hear a hint of panic in Gregg's voice. Maybe he was worried Luke had found a way to get Vivian out of the yard, though Emma couldn't think how. "The only way this ends without someone getting hurt is if the girl comes to me," Greg said, louder this time.

There was the sound of a door creaking, then opening, followed by a shuffling noise in the loose dirt as Vivian appeared from inside the shed. She was wearing a child-sized backpack, and her small hands were covering her eyes.

When he saw her, Luke's face contorted with despair. He looked devastated.

But Emma had no time for an emotional reaction.

Because having gotten what he wanted and with Vivian in sight, she saw Greg's arm stiffen as he took aim at Luke. Then she realized that in that moment, Gregg might have forgotten about her.

After all, she was just a woman terrified out of her mind, what threat could she be?

She decided he was about to find out.

She threw her elbow as hard as she could at his chest, knocking him off balance as he pulled the trigger, a shot pinging off the side of the shed. Then she tackled him. As they both tumbled and fell, a second shot narrowly missed Luke, just to his left and low, into the dirt. But though Emma had had the advantage of surprise, Gregg was stronger, and he shoved her off him, the gun still in his hand.

Luke yelled at Vivian.

Emma could hear him, "Lie down, don't look, don't look, don't look."

Luke was still yelling when he pulled something long and sharp from his back waistband. In the moonlight, Emma could see it glinting in his hand.

He rushed at Gregg, who had just sat up and raised the gun again. *He has some kind of garden shears,* Emma thought, as Luke dived and plunged them deep into Gregg's chest before Gregg could get off another shot.

Blood spurted violently while Greg's heart continued to pump until his eyes rolled back in his head, his body seized up, and he was silent and still.

Luke looked at Emma, who felt dazed, but she managed a small nod.

When he saw that Emma was all right, he ran to Vivian, who was lying facedown as he'd told her, her small hands still covering her eyes. He lifted her gently onto his lap, cradling her head against his chest. "Good girl, good BeeBee," he whispered softly. "It's okay now, but don't look. Don't look yet."

He held her that way, close and protected, past Emma and into the house.

SIXTY-SIX

The Blue House

EMMA LOOKED OVER at Gregg, his lifeless eyes, his blood-
ied shirt.

She noticed he'd finally released his grip on the gun.

For a man who had considered himself nonviolent,
he'd certainly made a number of recent exceptions to
that rule.

Luke was just inside the sliding glass door, still holding Vivian, speaking softly to her.

Emma thought of the unnamed man she'd seen lying
on the couch. Had he gotten up? Was he lurking somewhere? Could there be others, reinforcements, who had
arrived while she was off with Lee?

She crawled slowly over to retrieve the gun, then
pushed herself with effort to stand and hobbled the few
steps inside. Her left foot hurt, and when she looked
down there was blood soaking through the end of her
sock. She was leaving bloody footprints. She must have
stepped on something sharp in the gravel. She ignored
the pain and gently took Luke by the arm.

"Come with me," she said as she steered him, still
carrying Vivian, into the kitchen.

He looked at the weapon she held by her side. He
seemed neither alarmed nor comforted by it. He appeared numb. She kept a hand on him until they were
in Gregg's office.

"Sit here," she said, leading him to the sofa against the wall.

She wished she had time to get him some water. Was that what you were supposed to do for shock? She had no idea. In any case, that would have to come later. She had to call an ambulance for Dylan. Right now, before she did anything else. And maybe one for Lee out in the orchard. And also Barry. And she needed the police to come.

She and Luke had to stop doing this alone.

She put the gun on the table, opened the end cabinet, and took out both cell phones that were inside. She set them next to the gun so she could see them in the light.

She picked up the one that looked newer. No charge. Its battery was dead.

The second phone immediately powered up, but its home screen was locked. As she was trying to determine whether she could access an emergency function that didn't require a password, she felt Luke looking at her.

"Where did you get that?" he asked, staring at the phone in her hand.

"Here. In that cabinet," she said. "I knew it was there. I couldn't get to it earlier."

"Give it to me," he said, reaching out his hand.

"Luke, I have to call for an ambulance. Dylan is—"

"Please, give it to me." Luke stood. "See that?" he said, pointing to a small black sticker with gray letters on the back of the phone. It said "The Hold Steady."

"That's a band," Luke said. "That's my friend's phone."

Emma wondered if he was not thinking straight. Because of the garden shears. And Gregg. But she handed him the phone.

"It's Samson's," he said. "We worked together." He tapped the screen and unlocked it. "He let me use his phone since mine died. He gave me the password."

"Luke, right now what we need most is an ambulance. Dylan is badly injured out in the car. We also need the police. We need Alibi to come." Then she realized she didn't know Alibi's cell number by heart. It was in her phone in her bag, location still unknown. So she added, "Any police. Call nine-one-one."

But Luke still seemed to be trying to figure out why he was holding Samson's phone. He was scrolling through its content, maybe seeking a clue in the messages. He looked up at Emma.

"Do you think this means Samson is here? Maybe he's hiding somewhere? He said he was helping someone. He had money lately, he never had any before. He was always insisting on paying for food for us, and he bought me new reeds for my sax." Luke suddenly looked stricken. "You don't think he could have been working for these guys, do you?

Emma didn't know why Luke's friend's phone was here or why he had money or who he might have been working for. But she knew one thing for certain. They had to keep moving. They weren't home yet, they weren't safe, and Dylan could be bleeding to death. She glanced at Vivian, who was cradling a small stuffed bunny and talking to it.

Emma picked up the gun and said to Luke, "Come with me, bring Vivian. I need to check on Dylan."

Luke lifted Vivian, who clutched her bunny tightly but did not protest. Emma kept her hand lightly on Luke's arm to keep him moving into the kitchen, where she paused to pull open several drawers until she found some clean dish towels. She hoped she could use them to stem Dylan's bleeding until the ambulance arrived. She desperately hoped he still needed that care.

She guided Luke into the front room.

She took the phone gently from his hand, punched in 911, and returned it to him.

"Luke, listen. We're almost through this. You've been amazing. Tell them we need help. Stay on the line. If they can't get the location off the cell, describe where we are."

When she saw understanding in his eyes and heard him respond to the emergency operator, she crossed to the front window and pushed aside the drapes. There were no streetlights, and the darkness was near complete. Still, she was able to make out the rough outlines of things. The SUV, the jeep, and the trees.

But she felt a gut punch when the one shape she'd gone to the window to confirm was there was gone. Barry was no longer where he'd fallen in the street. And in the next moment, she saw someone crouched, moving along the side of the SUV, where Dylan lay inside, helpless, if he was still alive.

She shouted at Luke, "Stay back, get down," as she ran to the front door.

She threw it open, took a wide shooter's stance with both hands on the gun and yelled "Stop!" just as the figure across the street whirled and raised a gun and pointed it at her.

It wasn't Barry.

She could see, as he straightened up in the light from the open front door, his dark hair, his familiar face.

"Alibi?" she said, incredulous.

"Emma?" he asked, lowering his gun.

She turned back to Luke and Vivian.

"It's okay. It's Alibi," she said. "The police are here."

SATURDAY

SIXTY-SEVEN

The Hospital

IT WOULD BE another unpleasantly hot day in Sacramento. But to Emma, the weather outside Sutter Memorial Hospital seemed a world away. Despite the long-sleeved hoodie a medical assistant had lent her, she shivered in the centrally cooled air as she stood in the doorway to Kate's room, leaning against the frame.

Though bone-tired and hurting in too many places to count, seeing Kate and Luke together she thought she might be as happy as she'd ever been.

Luke sat on a chair beside his mother's narrow bed. There were deep shadows beneath his eyes. He looked worse than Emma felt.

"You sure you're alright?" Kate asked him.

"Yes," he said, "I am."

His voice was clear and firm.

When Kate shook her head, as though that couldn't be true, he reached out and took her hand in his.

Emma wouldn't have wished the last twenty-four hours on any of them, but there was no disputing the distance Luke had sought from his mother had lost its appeal for him.

She stepped out into the hall. She knew neither Kate nor Luke minded her being there, but she wanted to give them more time on their own since Kate wouldn't be coming home right away. She had a long way to go, and rehab was definitely part of that journey, but according to the doctor, there were no signs that there would be long-term or permanent deficits.

When she'd gotten that news, Emma had wondered whether her brief venture into prayer on Kate's behalf might have been a factor. She was certain science and modern medicine had been essential, along with the compassion and expertise of the many people who'd cared for Kate. She'd kept a running list of doctors, nurses, techs, other hospital staff, paramedics, and emergency workers, to whom she would be sending heartfelt thank-you notes soon.

Dylan was also doing well, all things considered. When she'd seen him last, he was being prepped for surgery on his leg. He'd seemed a bit embarrassed when he'd explained to her that when held at gunpoint by Lee in the garage, he'd lunged at the weapon-wielding little man, slipped and fallen and Lee had shot him in anger on the spot. Still, he'd smiled broadly when he'd pointed out that she'd fared so much better against the same adversary. If there were superhero tryouts anytime soon she should definitely go first. Emma liked this new Dylan. He was no longer the frightened, awkward boy she'd known in high school, but also not the take charge "I'll Fix It Man" who had shown up at her door earlier today uninvited. He seemed to her like he might be finding his way to somewhere in the middle.

Barry had a shattered elbow where the only one of her bullets that had even come close had hit him, the pain of it causing him to temporarily black out. The doctors said he would need surgery but should be feeling better soon and well enough to be processed and transferred to his new home in the county jail where he would await trial. The man on the sofa had suffered a bad stomach wound at the shoot-out at Rainbow Alley. He was showing signs of infection and had had his stomach pumped for a drug overdose last night. Lee was the worst off. Emma had followed through and sent the paramedics to get him, but he was in bad shape. His supervising physician had said he'd definitely lose that eye, and he had a broken leg, broken arm, a skull fracture, and a concussion. It was unclear whether he'd make it. Despite all he'd done to her and to those she loved, Emma felt bad about that. She was not "an eye for an eye" person, either literally or figuratively. She hoped he would pull through to face justice and that it would be both fair and forgiving, so long as she never had to be in his presence again.

All in all, yesterday's events at the blue house were keeping the hospital very busy.

But for the first time in twenty-four hours, Emma was not immediately needed for anything she could think of.

Her sister's flight had landed, and by now she must be at Matchbook Lane, getting to know Crash.

Jasmine had been a dog person practically from birth, so though Crash was a far cry in size and appearance from Reggie and Jasmine's mini Berniedoodle, Emma expected he and Jasmine would be fast friends by the time she got home.

She decided to go there now to change and to get cleaned up. Mostly, she wanted to put her hand on her sister's growing baby bump. New life, growing life, would be good to be around after what they'd all just been through.

When Vivian had arrived at the hospital last night, she hadn't been willing to let anyone but Luke carry her, and she'd called out when he was only steps away. But when her grandpa and grandma arrived, the governor and the first lady, she had willingly gone to them, and there'd seemed to be enough hugs and tears exchanged to last a lifetime.

In her sleep-deprived state, Emma found herself mulling over the interchangeability (though she wondered if that was actually a word) of family for friends, and friends for family. There were those who had a mother, a father, or grandparents to comfort them. Others found love in a sibling, a friend, a child of their own, or someone else's child. And of course, there was romantic love.

"Emma?"

She looked up to see Alibi walking toward her down the hall. He was a tall man, long-legged. He closed the gap between them quickly, though he stopped several feet away.

"Are you feeling up to talking for a few minutes?" he asked.

SIXTY-EIGHT

The Hospital

ONCE THEY WERE out of the elevator, it was slow-going down the long hall to the hospital cafeteria on the fourth floor. The bottom of Emma's foot, though cleaned and bandaged, had been badly cut. Still, she was happy to be back in her sneakers, which the crime team had returned to her late last night, along with her satchel and cell phone. She didn't think she would ever wear only socks again, not even in her house.

They settled at a table by a window that ran the length of the wall, Emma with an herbal tea and a chocolate chip muffin and Alibi with a large black coffee.

The view of Sacramento's clear, cloudless sky was beautiful, though Emma wished it were any color but blue. *That damn blue house.*

Wearing only socks, the color blue.

She wondered if those things and others she hadn't thought of yet would ever detach themselves from the trauma of last night.

When Alibi sat down, he looked at her thoughtfully. "There are a few things I'd like to ask you about. If it gets to be too much, let me know and we can do it later, another day. When you're ready."

Emma nodded. She blew on her tea to cool it.

"I saw you speaking with Luke earlier," she said. "With Kate, in her room. Was that helpful?"

"Yes. Very much so," Alibi said. After a beat, he added, "What he did yesterday was really something. Start to finish. Maintaining a false identity and caring for a three-year-old under conditions where the smallest wrong move could have been disastrous."

She noticed Alibi didn't include Luke having saved all their lives by killing their captor.

He withdrew a small blue notebook and a pencil from his jacket.

"Do you mind if I take a few notes?"

She nodded again, though she found the presence of the notebook unsettling, the idea that this conversation would have a written record, that what she said couldn't be taken back.

Alibi cleared his throat, then took a sip of his coffee.

"I guess it's easiest to start with the riverside murder, the shooting of Samson Kieu, Thursday night. Once you located Samson's phone at Gregg Corbel's house and Luke was able to unlock it, the pieces of that investigation came together quickly."

He scanned a page in his notepad. Emma felt relieved when she realized it wasn't only there for him to record what she said. In it, he had notes he was referencing.

"We've been able to take a preliminary look at the phone's contents. Samson was monitoring the bike store owner, Marty Lightzer, his employer, surreptitiously taping Lightzer's conversations when he could and making notes on his phone when he couldn't. Also based on Samson's call and message log, he was in close communication with Tommy for the last two months. That lines up with the evening Luke and Samson were picked up by the police, which we believe is when Tommy first met Samson."

Emma remembered that night, Tommy saying the

boys had just been at the wrong place at the wrong time. But beyond that connection, she didn't know if it was her exhaustion or if Alibi hadn't filled in some of the pieces yet, but she was having trouble following what he was saying.

"So Samson was reporting to Tommy about the bike shop owner, the guy I see in all the ads? Is he involved in something criminal?"

Alibi hesitated.

"It's not so much what Marty Lightzer *is* involved in, but what he *was* involved in." He looked again at his notes. "In college, Marty Lightzer and Gregg Corbel were friends with Samuel Miller, the accused killer referred to in the media as the Gambler. They roomed together. Miller was already deep into white supremacist beliefs at that time. When Tommy received press attention for a commendation, there were public photos of him and Quan. Miller fixated on their mixed-race marriage. He wanted to make Tommy suffer, to make an example of him somehow. He worked out a scheme to leave drugs at Tommy's house, which Gregg and Marty were to carry out."

"Gregg? Do you mean the Gregg who…" Emma trailed off.

She couldn't think of a way to characterize in a few words who and what the Gregg she'd confronted last night had been. She thought of his rage when he jumped from behind the door and pointed the gun at her, and of him firing off shots, desperate to kill Luke even as he fell. But she also thought of the pain he felt over his wife's death, of the hope he'd expressed when he talked of Aminah becoming governor, where he believed she would enact a massive opioid treatment program and save so many lives.

Then she remembered what Gregg had told her, when he was trying to convince her he wasn't a violent man so she would help him to get Luke to bring Vivian back into the house.

I've only shot someone once...an accidental death...a case of mistaken identity... I thought the woman's husband was coming through the door.

"Gregg killed Quan?" Emma asked. She felt herself trembling, her hand shook. She set her cup down as tea splashed onto the tabletop. "Gregg thought Quan was Tommy? Why? How could he make that mistake?"

Alibi stared at her. He put down his pencil. "How did you know that?"

Emma's throat felt dry. She tried to pick up her cup, but her hand was still shaking.

Alibi stood up, clearly alarmed. "Stay here, I'm going to get a doctor. I don't want to take this any further until someone's looked at you."

Emma couldn't understand why he was so freaked out. It's not like she was having a seizure. Her hand shook, that was all. She was exhausted, hadn't eaten, and had just found out that she had talked to Quan's killer, the man who Tommy had sought to bring to justice for so many years.

"Alibi," she said, "Please, sit down. I'm okay, really. I've been up all night. It's been a lot. But I'm okay. Here, I'll eat this muffin." She took a small bite of the chocolate chip muffin, as though it were medicine. After swallowing it, she managed a small smile. "I'm fine, really. We can talk a bit more if there's something you need, and then I should probably go home and get some sleep."

He sat down but didn't say anything. He continued to watch her, concerned.

Emma realized she had a question.

"How did you find out Gregg killed Quan? Was that information on Samson's phone?"

"Yes. Well, sort of. There was a brief recording Samson had made of Marty yelling, I'm paraphrasing here, but something like, 'Gregg, if you hadn't murdered her, you wouldn't have this problem. So don't blame me. I deserve something for being quiet."

Emma thought that through.

"So Marty killed Samson for that recording? Because it would show he hadn't revealed to the police who killed Quan or that he was present as a witness, which would have made him an accessory or an accomplice to the murder?"

"That's what we thought at first," Alibi said. "But when Marty learned Samson had been murdered, he remembered having yelled at Gregg. He figured Samson must have overheard him saying it. Marty knows he's loud when he gets upset." Alibi checked his notes again. "Marty figured somehow Gregg found out Samson knew he was a murderer, and Gregg killed the kid. Or had him killed. Marty was afraid Gregg would kill him next. Marty's wife was even more worried and convinced Marty to ask us for a deal, that if he identified Quan's killer, he would get immunity for having been there when it happened."

"Wait," Emma said. She needed him to slow down. "So Gregg killed Samson or had him killed? How did he know Samson overheard Marty?"

"We haven't been able to firmly make that link yet, the one from Gregg to Samson. In fact, we don't know who killed Samson. But from the information I just got from Luke, I think we're on the right track. We have a prime suspect."

"Luke?" Emma frowned, feeling protective. "What does Luke have to do with any of this?"

"Luke told me he'd seen one of Gregg's men at the bike shop, several times. This was before Luke got his new look, the shaved head, so I gather the guy didn't recognize him. We think this 'Mr. X' must have been at the shop Thursday night in a position to see Samson taping Marty, or maybe he just saw Samson leaving, acting strange or running off. If our Mr. X already suspected Samson of behaving oddly, being on his phone at weird times, maybe even thought he was eavesdropping on Marty, he might have followed Samson Thursday night. And one thing led to another until Mr. X shot Samson and took his phone."

"Mr. X?" Emma asked. "Do you mean Lee?"

Alibi looked at her like she was from another planet. "How could you possibly know that?"

She stood and winced, then shifted her weight off her injured foot. It was only then that she realized what a state she was in. She'd fallen, been shoved, and crawled around in the dirt. She'd washed her hands and her face, and they'd given her the borrowed hoodie, but her jeans were filthy. She ignored that as best she could as she extracted the three playing cards from her back pocket.

"They're kind of bent, and probably sweaty and dirty. I found them in Lee's front pocket when I was looking for the car keys. He was always patting that pocket, like he had a good luck charm or something in there." She extended them to Alibi. "The total value matches the Gambler's. Twenty-three. I don't know if that matters.

Alibi smiled. "Yes, it matters." But he didn't take the cards from her.

He asked her to set them on a napkin. He got up from the table, and in a minute had returned with a clean plastic food storage bag. He put the cards, still wrapped in the napkin, into the bag without touching them, and tucked it in the back of his notebook.

"Just one more thing. How would you describe Lee physically?"

She thought for a moment. "Agitated, always in motion. I guess that's his manner. Physically? Dark hair, slight and small, not as tall as me. Maybe five foot three or four?"

"With the playing cards and that description," Alibi said, "which matches someone seen fleeing the scene, I think we can say with near certainty that Lee killed Samson."

Over Alibi's shoulder, through the expanse of the hospital window, a single fluffy white cloud appeared in what had been the endless blue of the sky.

Emma didn't want to talk any more. Right now, she couldn't see the appeal of solving crimes.

Alibi seemed to read her thoughts. "I'll get you a bag for that muffin," he said. "It's time for you to go home. You've more than done your part."

SIXTY-NINE

Matchbook Lane

AFTER A LONG shower, Emma had put on her robe and while streaming an episode of *The Good Place* had fallen into a restless sleep on the couch, Crash at her feet.

She was startled when her phone rang. She fumbled to pick it up.

"Emma? I'm sorry, did I wake you?" Aminah asked.

Emma checked the time. She'd been asleep for four hours.

"No. It's fine. How are you?"

"How are you is the important question," Aminah replied. "I've been briefed regarding your role in foiling a plot to have me installed as governor. Thank you for that. I'd like to up my invitation for tea to also include cake. Probably chocolate."

"That would be great," Emma said. She smiled. Something to look forward to.

"I heard on the news that your codirector at the school, Kate Doyle, is recovering."

After a beat, Emma said, "Yes. I suggested postponing the school's opening, but Kate wouldn't hear of it, not with so many parents relying on us for childcare."

After everything that had happened, it felt surreal to Emma that more than a hundred children would soon be streaming into the center under the Rainbow Alley sign, which never had gotten freshly painted. Though that didn't seem as important as it once had.

"Zach and I would like to be put on Rainbow Alley's waiting list." Aminah said. There was a pause before she added. "First in line for a space. Three years from now."

Emma could hear the joy in the lieutenant governor's voice. "A new Ali-Rosenberg on the way?" she asked. "Congratulations."

"Due in January. Are you volunteering to babysit?"

"I don't know that I'd be much good with a newborn," Emma said, "but I have a young friend who I expect would be wonderful."

She pictured Luke holding Vivian, comforting her. But at the thought of him, she realized she'd slept through the time she was supposed to pick him up.

He was going to stay with her until Kate was out of the hospital.

After a hurried goodbye to Aminah, as Emma dressed quickly in clean jeans and a fresh T-shirt, she realized how much she was looking forward to seeing Luke, and to having him here.

She wondered if she might even rethink that "no kids of her own" thing one day, if she could convince herself they would turn out something like Luke. Or like Vivian. She recalled the courage each of them had shown, even the little one, as they'd faced danger to save each other.

After giving Crash several treats and a promise his new best friend, Jasmine, who was picking up takeout for dinner, would be back soon, she went out to her Mustang and started it up.

The sun was low in the sky and the light of the day was fading. She thought of Tommy and hoped that somehow he might know that his search for justice was finally over.

As she backed down the driveway, she realized she hadn't checked her work messages.

She never took weekends completely off. If she had, she doubted she would have been named the commission's youngest lead investigator. She braked so she could tap the passcode into her phone to see if there were calls she might handle as she drove to the hospital. But she stopped mid-entry.

If she'd ever needed a sign life was short and work might not be the only way to fill it, yesterday had been a billboard to that effect, framed in flashing neon lights.

As she was putting her phone away, it rang. No caller ID—she thought it might be Luke from a hospital line. He hadn't been home to get his birthday iPhone yet, which she suspected Kate, under the circumstances, would let him have before his actual "sweet sixteen" tomorrow.

She picked up.

"Emma, I hope I'm not bothering you. I've a statement for you to sign," Alibi said. "Would Monday work?"

"I can't get away Monday," she said, thinking of the school's opening, that she and Luke would have to handle it, greet the parents and support the teachers, with Kate still in care. "How about tomorrow morning? We can meet here. If you promise not to point a gun at me. And to bring your own coffee. I've only got tea."

"Tomorrow's good," Alibi said.

Emma smiled. She pulled the Mustang out onto the street and lowered the car's top. As she gathered speed, she felt an unexpected evening breeze gently lift her hair.

* * * * *

ACKNOWLEDGMENTS

HAVING FALLEN ASLEEP at night and awakened in the morning these past weeks thinking of little else than what I wanted to say here, in the end I concluded I can't do typical acknowledgments. I don't mean exactly that, since no heartfelt acknowledgment is "typical"; each is important and unique. What I mean is I have to do this some other way. I'll do my best to make a long story short.

I did not feel safe in my home as a child. I'm not alone in that, but the many of us who share a challenging beginning have found different ways to live with it that range from healthy to dysfunctional, often some combination of the two. For me, when someone is kind to me now, caring or supportive, I don't want to thank them. I feel like once I do, it closes the loop and the act of kindness fades. I can't hold on to it. But if I keep my feelings of gratitude to myself, unspoken, it feels like the kindness I received is still alive. It warms me, it strengthens me, it literally makes me smile.

Bottom line: acknowledgments are hard for me.

And here I sit, faced with a deadline (today) to put into words on paper, all at once, my "thank-yous" to those who have helped this book happen.

I thought about not doing it at all. A blank page. I'm sure few (no one?) would notice. But that seemed impossible too, selfish, and flat out wrong.

So here's where I am with it: I do want to thank here,

in fairly traditional fashion, the professionals who were nothing less than exceptional on ALL THAT FALL's path to publication: agent Abby Saul of The Lark Group, editor Terri Bischoff and the entire Crooked Lane Books team, including Madeline Rathle and Melissa Rechter, owner/publicist Dana Kaye and the Kaye Publicity crew, including Julia Borcherts and Hailey Dezort, cover designer Michael Rehder, and independent developmental editors Eileen Rendahl and Trey Geisman. Each one of them is whip-smart, and their extraordinary skills and experience were critical to making this book a reality. They also each treated me with care and respect. As I write this, these are crazy times with a worldwide pandemic, a major US election, and a long overdue (and hopefully sustained) reckoning on issues of justice and race. Taking time to listen, to really listen, in professional relationships is not at all a given amidst the noise, and I am grateful that they did.

As to friends, family, colleagues, librarians and independent booksellers, conference organizers and volunteers, fellow authors and readers, whose acts of kindness are the reason I am able to "put pen to paper" with joy, and who are collectively the reason I'm still here, I've thought of something else. I want to thank each of you in turn with a personal acknowledgment, perhaps a photo, something I remember you did or said, in a new section on my website where I can keep those things with me, not quite inside me, but close, not closed between the covers of this book. I don't know exactly what it will look like since I haven't done it yet, but it should be up by the time this is published.

There's one other thing related to this book (and all my writing) that I want to explain. Because of my own experiences you will not witness in any of my stories violence or unspeakable crimes against children. They may have hard histories, be frightened in real time, there might be suspense and times where we worry for them. Fictional adults, even beloved ones, may die. (These are, after, all thrillers and mysteries.) But every child you come to know will be safe.

Kris Calvin
October 2020